Tor Books by Ben Bova

TO
FEAR
THE
LIGHT

Ben Bova and A. J. Austin

TOR

A TOM DOHERTY ASSOCIATES BOOK   NEW YORK

TO FEAR THE LIGHT

This book is printed on acid-free paper.

A Tor Book
Published by Tom Doherty Associates, Inc.
175 Fifth Avenue
New York, N.Y. 10010

Tor® is a registered trademark of Tom Doherty Associates, Inc.

Library of Congress Cataloging-in-Publication Data

Bova, Ben, 1932–
    To fear the light / Ben Bova and A. J. Austin.
        p.   cm.
    Sequel to: To save the sun.
    "A Tom Doherty Associates book."
    ISBN 0–312–85449–8 (hardcover)
    I. Austin, A. J.   II. Title.
PS3552.084T58   1994
813'.54—dc20   94-28971
                                                                      CIP

First edition: December 1994

Printed in the United States of America

0 9 8 7 6 5 4 3 2 1

PART ONE

HISTORY

And if thou wilt, remember;
and if thou wilt, forget.

—Christina Rossetti

ONE
History

The Civilian Transport Service passenger jumper *L. H. Sylvan* was in trouble.

All her life-support systems were intact and working properly. The tachyon dish that enabled near-instantaneous communication with any point in the Hundred Worlds was functioning as it should, as was the slower conventional broadcast transmitter. Artificial gravity was on and normal *g* was in force everywhere on the ship except in certain areas of the cargo holds.

That, too, was normal CTS procedure.

Electrical systems, computer and file retrieval banks, communications—even the entertainment and personal library facilities—were performing properly.

The flight crew knew where they were, and where they were going: The *Sylvan* was still on course at a velocity of point-seven-five *c*—a standard cruise speed for a passenger ship of its class—on a heading that would take them to Gate 87, the entrance to the transit wormhole nearest 40 Eridani system, where they had departed a bit more than two weeks earlier.

All but a handful of the 1,350 passengers aboard the jumper had elected to sleep through the three-week-long ride to Gate 87, and the cryosleep containers in which they silently, dreamlessly rode were all on-line and functioning flawlessly. The row upon row of steady green dots on the brightly glowing display behind Captain Partane gave testimony to that. The relatively few passengers not in cryo were either enjoying themselves in the *Sylvan*'s lounges and recreational facilities, or were relaxing in their plush staterooms.

The captain paced before the holographic image at the head of the meeting room and recited the systems and their conditions as each graph, chart, report, summary and readout in the holographic display changed at his verbal order.

But even as the senior officer's demeanor remained steady during his description of system after system that was functioning as it should, Drew Hattan knew, felt, somehow sensed deep inside him, that the *L. H. Sylvan* was a ship in trouble.

"It doesn't fit," Captain Partane was saying in summation. He had stopped pacing and stood once more before a display that Drew had already seen a dozen times since this briefing began. Having made up his mind that there was nothing displayed there that could help them or improve their immediate situation, he found himself paying less attention to the captain. Instead, he watched the reactions of those around him as they listened to what was being said.

"However," Partane went on, "it clearly shows there's a breakdown somewhere in the Structural Integrity Shield." He waved an arm again in frustration at the blinking red warning sensor in the display. "I don't think I have to tell you what that could mean in a worst-case scenario." He didn't. Everyone in the room knew that without the SIS operating properly, the structural stresses and radiation heat load caused by near-light speed on a ship this size would rip it to pieces in a matter of moments. Dead in space, the *Sylvan* might remain intact, but at the rate they were going there wasn't a chance they could slow the ship down in time. For that matter, if the SIS *was* damaged, the simple act of braking the ship to a stop might be fatal in itself.

There were twenty others besides Drew in the briefing room below the bridge deck, all seated around a long meeting table littered with empty cups, notepads, computer data sticks and remnants of hastily consumed snacks. The coffee urn in the center of the table had long ago been drained, but no one had bothered to order more. Drew listened halfheartedly to the address, and noted that each time the captain moved or paced or pointed to the display, all eyes in the room followed the man in a way that told the young chief steward that most of them, too, felt the ship had a serious problem. Everyone here, however, was a professional at what he or she did and had spent too many years in the CTS to even hint aloud at the growing panic they each were struggling to deny.

When he looked around at his companions at the table, Drew's eyes locked briefly with those of Vera Conté, one of the few crew members actually under his supervision. She allowed the slight curl of a smile to appear at the corners of her lips and, as her face softened at his glance, she gave a darting look ceilingward and an almost imperceptible shake of her head. She, too, must have felt that Partane was doing his best to put a good face on a bad situation. That, and the fact that she was no more fooled by the captain's oratory than was he. Or anyone else in the room, for that matter.

Because of their respective seats at the table, Vera's position allowed her to be a good deal more facially expressive to him than he was to her, and he had to be satisfied with a slight nod and a quick clearing of his throat as a signal to her that he understood. He allowed himself one last moment to gaze longingly at her before returning his attention to the captain.

"Look, it's probably nothing," the officer went on, sitting wearily at the far end of the meeting table. He leaned back in the cushioned seat, slowly rubbing his eyes and face with his hands, and Drew noted for the first time just how exhausted the man was. He obviously hadn't slept since the potential problem with the SIS had been discovered, more than thirty hours earlier. He hadn't shaved, either, and Drew could hear the faint scratching sound the palms of his hands made as they passed haltingly over his cheeks.

"It's most likely nothing at all," Partane continued finally, his voice hoarse from speaking. He reached for the cup before him, sipped at what was left in it, and furrowed his brow at the bitter taste of the chilled remnants. "But I've decided to take a number of steps. Since we can find nothing on our own . . ." He paused and regarded Flight Systems Engineer John Rentil, seated at his immediate right at the head of the table. The man frowned in resignation and shook his head, wordlessly confirming everything that had just been said. "Since there's nothing we can do here, I've decided to network the *Sylvan*'s diagnostic and engineering systems to the techs back on Copenhaver with the dish. Johnny and I have been in contact with them for the last several hours and this is their recommendation."

A hand raised, then another, but Partane waved them off.

"Please, I know what you're thinking. I don't like cutting off our real-time communications any better than the rest of you do right now, but those techs have got to have at least some semblance of a hands-on look at the systems. I've already sent everything we have back to Copenhaver over the dish, with a set of duplicate transmissions to the people at Gate Eighty-seven." He paused again, and took a moment to scan the faces of everyone seated at the table. When the captain's eyes fell on him in turn, Drew saw behind them just how uncertain he was about what was happening. He finished his visual sweep around the table, then nodded to Co-Captain Edward Milliron, who stood and addressed them.

"Uh . . . the people at Eighty-seven are sending someone out to meet us; it's the, uh . . ." He glanced at the handheld display in his left hand, while he wiped sweat from his forehead with the back of his right. ". . . the *Glisten,* but they won't be here for another forty-five hours," he said. He wiped absently at his forehead again. The temperature in the room was quite comfortable, but Milliron was sweating profusely anyway, as he always did. Drew had served with Milliron before, both on the *Sylvan* and on a smaller jumper a few years earlier as an apprentice steward. The man was an extremely competent co-captain, the CTS equivalent of an Imperial first officer, but he was openly nervous and uneasy about his lack of the skills for public speaking and management that were required for a situation like this. It was probably that very lack of confidence, Drew thought, that had kept the man out of Imperial service. "When they arrive, they'll match velocity with us and lend any assistance they can, including a cruise-speed shuttling of engineering personnel and equipment from them to us; that way, we won't have to drop velocity and put any more strain on the SIS than we have to." He smiled weakly at them, the attempt aimed at putting them—or perhaps himself—at ease.

"Until such time as we rendezvous with them, velocity and all ship's systems will remain at current status unless otherwise cleared through Captain Partane." Milliron sat, relieved that his part in the briefing was over.

"Thanks, Ned," Partane said simply, then lowered his head. "There's one other thing." He rubbed his hands together on the tabletop and sighed, then faced them all once more. His voice had taken a new and, for him, unusual tone. Drew regarded the man as he continued, and decided that what he was relating to them now was with a mixture of apology and desperation. He looked to Milliron, and saw the same uneasiness reflected in his features. Drew looked quickly around him, and noted that most everyone else in the room, only moments before numb at what seemed an endless repetition of reports, had raised their own eyes in anticipation of what the captain might say next.

"We've been in communication with a Sarpan ship." He paused, allowing the new information to sink in. The room, already quiet but for the steady, ever-present hum common to the *Sylvan,* grew even more hushed. "They are only a few hours away at their present speed and are already on an intercept course. Their captain, uh . . ." He stumbled with the pronunciation of the name, trying to read the handheld Milliron had just slid across the tabletop to him. He shook his head feebly, giving up on what he saw in the display. "Anyway, the ship is called the—thank goodness it's a single syllable at least—the *Hinsth.*"

There was nervous laughter around him at the slur against the aliens, and Drew noted the tension had lifted slightly from some of his companions. Vera, however, sat ramrod straight in her chair, her face unreadable.

"They're a full scientific research and exploration vessel. Their authorization checks out with no problem. They're out of Eighty-seven, five months ago, with license to do a complete diagnostic and evaluation survey of the fourth planet in Forty Eridani system. They've been in constant contact with Copenhaver and have followed all required protocol."

"Has their shipboard armament been verified?" asked Conté.

"Excuse me?" Partane turned to her, obviously not anxious to begin a confrontation with her. No one really liked the Sarpan, but it was well understood by anyone who knew Vera at all that she possessed nothing but pure hatred for the aliens. "It's a research vessel. That's been confirmed."

"Have you scanned for armament?"

Partane took a deep breath and let it out in frustration. "The *Hinsth* is a legitimate survey vessel," he repeated. "It's been cleared by Imperial investigators and given the go-ahead—months ago, mind you—to do an extensive survey of number four here. All of their outgoing communications have been monitored." He took another deep breath, forcing down the frustration he felt at his ship's situation and his rising anger at her reaction to the news that an alien ship was in proximity. "Look, the *Hinsth* is clean. Don't you think I've had it checked out?"

Vera stared at him, silent for several moments. All attention was on her.

"Is it armed?" she asked again, slowly and deliberately. Each word seemed a sentence in itself as her eyes bore unblinking into his.

"Goddamn it, yes!" He pounded a fist on the tabletop, inadvertently catching the corner of Milliron's handheld and sending it flipping end-over-end to the floor. "Yes, it's armed! All Sarpan ships carry armament of some kind, but what the hell do you expect me to do?" He stopped short and leaned back in his seat, composing himself as best he could. He rubbed his face again and took several deep breaths, the exhaustion he must have felt fighting with his frustration at the situation in which he found himself.

"Vera, I'm sorry. But what the hell else can I do? I've got a red light on perhaps the single most important system on board, and an offer of help that'll be here—*here,* mind you! Not over some damned tachyon link!—two days sooner than anyone else can bring it! You tell me: What would *you* do?"

She sat, her face resolute, and Drew thought he saw the skin of her face quiver as it tightened over her jaw. Was she literally gritting her teeth? He almost expected her to lash out at the captain as strongly as the officer had with her, but an incongruous look of calm spread slowly, steadily over her features.

"You do anything, *anything,*" she said intensely, "except trust the fucking frogs." Her eyes continued glaring at him, her hands folded rigidly before her on the table. The gesture was meant, Drew could tell, to indicate a sense of calmness; but he could see a slight twitching in her fingers and knew she was exerting every bit of control she could to hide her feelings. Was she sorry for what she'd just said? He couldn't tell. Maybe later, when they could find a moment alone, he'd ask. Or, depending on how she felt about the rendezvous with the aliens a few hours from now, maybe not.

Captain Partane opened his mouth to reprimand her for the remark, then apparently thought better of it. "Cancel display," he said instead, and the holographic projection behind him disappeared. "That's the extent of my report." He stood, indicating that the briefing was over. There was some light, nervous chatter as the rest of them began to rise uneasily from the table and filed out one by one, anxious to get out of the room and go about their duties. Drew waited for several others to walk past before leaving the table to join Vera on her way to the door.

"Chief Steward, would you stay for a moment to discuss the passengers, please?"

She turned to him briefly as she exited, her face still unfathomable. He smiled weakly at her, shrugging his shoulders in resignation that he couldn't accompany her. At last, just before passing through the doorframe, she allowed a tiny smile and nodded: a signal that told him she'd wait for him outside.

Partane and Milliron were still speaking quietly to each other when he returned his attention to the head of the table. He remained standing, waiting patiently until the captain finished with Milliron. He noted that Milliron had retrieved his handheld from the floor and, with his arms folded as he listened to the captain, was tapping the edge of the casing absently against the elbow of his other arm. The two spoke only a few minutes longer before the other man left and the captain addressed Drew from the opposite side of the room.

"I've just told Ned to order all passengers not in cryo to return to their staterooms for the duration of our meeting with the aliens' ship. I anticipate your staff will be getting requests for explanations from them just about any time now." He paused and walked around the big table to stand before him. Partane was not a tall man, but somehow, with the weight of the last day and a half pressing on him, the captain seemed smaller still.

"Drew, most of the passengers would probably be more curious about the Sarpan ship than frightened by it, but I'd just as soon play it safe and keep it quiet. I think it'll go smoother if they don't even know it's there, all right?"

He nodded, and pulled his own handheld from his shirt pocket. "Do we know what orientation their ship'll have at rendezvous?"

"On their present heading they'll come up from behind and under us."

He tapped a few commands into the tiny unit, muttering softly to himself, then said aloud, "System."

It took only a split second for the room system to recognize his voice code and open the appropriate data paths for his area of the *Sylvan*'s computer net. "Yes, Mr. Hattan?" it said in a friendly, but bland, voice.

"Please take external monitors nine through fifteen off line."

There was a confirming chirp from the room system, then, "Ready."

"That's all for now." Again, a high-pitched chirp from the system as it reset. He slipped the handheld back into his shirt pocket and regarded the captain once more. "That'll keep the stateroom holoscreens from being able to orient on the Sarpan ship's approach angle. Let me know if their approach changes and I can feed in new values."

"Thanks, Drew." Partane walked with him the few steps it took to reach the door, but before they came within the pickup range of the opening mechanism he hesitated. "I know you've done this kind of thing before, so I'm sure you'll be able to handle any questions they may have. But I have some other serious concerns."

"I don't think there'll be a problem with the passengers. If anyone asks about the holoscreen blackouts for those angles, I can explain it away easily enough as a temporary—"

Partane held up a hand apologetically to cut him off. "I know, I know; but it's not you I'm worried about, Drew. It's Conté." Partane sighed heavily and stared briefly at the ceiling. "They're only offering to help us out a little bit here, and why shouldn't we let them? They've been cleared by every Imperial higher-up we were able to reach before linking the dish back to the techs at Copenhaver. Hell, the SIS was derived from their shield technology in the first place, so why shouldn't we let them have a look at it? They may be our best shot at figuring out what the problem is." He paused again. "If there really *is* anything wrong with it."

"What does Vera have to do with it?"

Partane looked at him and sighed heavily again. His breath was sour after too much coffee and too little sleep. "Look, nobody's comfortable with them when they're around, including me. But I'll be damned if I can understand this . . . this hatred she has for them. I *can't* have her talking to the passengers."

Drew nodded. He knew Vera intimately, knew only too well her feelings for the aliens. Partane was right. "I'll take care of it."

"Good." He took a step closer to the door and it slid obediently aside for them.

Vera Conté was outside, leaning on the opposite wall of the corridor. Her face beamed the moment her eyes met his, but the smile disappeared as soon as she saw the two men together. She crossed her arms before her, then moved wordlessly several paces down the hallway and leaned once more against the corridor wall, waiting. She didn't look their way.

"Anyway," Partane said, taking his hand in a firm grasp. "If you run into anything you can't handle, refer them directly to Ned. I'll be on the bridge if you need me." He turned away and walked briskly in the other direction toward the lift that would take him to the upper portion of the command deck of the jumper.

"That was nice," he said sarcastically once the captain had disappeared down the corridor. He tried to make himself sound angry as he confronted her, and remained standing just outside the briefing-room door. "What're you trying to do, get yourself busted out of the CTS?"

"He won't do anything about it," she snapped back defiantly, turning away from him and staring at the opposite wall, refusing to look at him directly. "He's on edge, everyone is. He'll dismiss it as a bad overreaction on my part."

"Yeah, you'd better hope so."

She said nothing for a moment, then suddenly seemed to let loose with what had been boiling up inside her since Partane had mentioned the aliens. "I can't believe he's going to allow one of those . . . those *things* on board!" she went on, and as she spoke Drew saw that this outburst made it possible for the genuine rage she felt at the captain's decision to begin to drain from her. He realized this was just what she needed to vent her feelings, and listened in silence as she paced the narrow width of the corridor, listing what seemed an endless string of complaints with the just-concluded briefing.

Where before he had actually tried to be angry with her, he now felt himself soften as he watched her. She wore the same steward's uniform as he, but the light blue shirt and matching shorts looked strikingly attractive on her, despite their unisex design, and he suspected she had altered them herself to give them a more alluring fit. Her pacing slowed, and each time she reversed direction he admired the way she turned. He found himself paying less attention to what she was saying than to the athletic curves of her body and the way her dark hair tumbled over her shoulders at every sharp movement she made. He wondered idly if the captain knew about the two of them, or was even suspicious. A few of the other stewards were in on the secret, and he thought Rentil might have some idea, but if the captain suspected anything he'd never even hinted at—

"Helloooo . . .? Anybody in there?" She was smiling at him now, all traces of anger spent. "Did we numb out there for a moment? Maybe I *was* ranting a little bit, but to shut me off entirely! Really!"

He felt his face flush as he realized she had stopped pacing and was now standing before him, staring, hands on her hips. He started chuckling in embarrassment and noted how good the sound of his own laughter made him feel. Vera allowed his embarrassment to continue as she coyly raised a hand to her lips, trying—without much success—to hide her own amusement.

The sound of her laughter—the first hint of humor he'd heard aboard the *Sylvan* in hours—felt good to his ears. If she was frightened by the SIS problem, she didn't show it. Then again, maybe her mind was just so occupied by the approaching alien ship . . .

He glanced around and, afraid that they might be spotted, said, "Come on, let's get off the command deck." He took her by the hand and led her to the lift at the end of the corridor.

There was another steward already on the lift, so Drew hit one of the passenger-level buttons at random. The man's name was Ternez and he knew that Drew and Vera were "involved." Vera didn't know he'd told the other man, of course, and Ternez made no overt comment as to the two of them being together at a time when each should have been doing separate chores in different parts of the ship. The man teased Drew incessantly about his ongoing affair with her, but with the SIS problem hanging over the ship like a dark cloud he probably didn't even notice they weren't where they should be.

The three of them chatted as they rode. Ternez told them that, just as the captain had predicted, there had been a number of inquiries regarding Milliron's order for passengers to return to their staterooms, but they hadn't posed any problems that couldn't be handled without his direct attention.

"That's good," Drew offered. "Has anyone asked to talk to Partane?"

Ternez shook his head. "No, none at all. I think Ned made it all sound fairly routine. Most of the walkers are new to jump travel and probably assume it's all normal procedure." He stopped and eyed the readout panel absently. "So, where are you two headed?"

"Partane wants me to be sure the walkers are all right in case they have any questions, but it sounds like everything's fine. Listen, could you handle any last-minute stuff that comes up with them? You can page me if you need me."

"Sure. No problem."

The lift stopped on five and he got out, and after the doors had closed Drew touched one of the buttons on the control panel. The lighted button indicating the deck he'd originally selected went dark, and he punched in a new destination. Vera noted his actions, but said nothing.

The lift opened after a few moments onto one of the stateroom decks and the two of them stepped out into the dim corridor. This level was filled with staterooms, and on a shorter flight would have been occupied, the halls filled with passengers eager to utilize the ship's many recreational and entertainment facilities. But on a longer jump like the one to 87 and then, through it, to Gate 21 at Barnard's, most of the passengers where in the cryo-tanks and had no need for the frills of the luxury cabins that made up this level.

He looked quickly down one way, then the other, and, satisfied the corridors were empty, reached out and pulled her to him. As he kissed her, she let her hands hang limply at her sides for several seconds in mock annoyance of his maneuvering her into a secluded area, then slowly put her arms around his neck and returned the kiss.

"You really make me crazy when you do things like that back in the briefing room," he said softly when their lips parted. "You know that, don't you?"

"Uh-huh."

He held her at arm's length and looked into her eyes. "Sometimes I don't know why I put up with you."

"Because you love me," she whispered, taking one of his hands in both of hers. "The same reason I put up with you."

He released her reluctantly. "Listen, Partane doesn't want you to interact with any of the walkers. He's afraid you'll say something that might panic them."

She pulled away suddenly. "Well, he can go to hell if he thinks I'm—"

"Wait a minute! Wait! It's all right. Just listen to me for a minute, would you?" He reached out for her again, putting his hands firmly on her shoulders and pulling her closer. "He asked me," he said, his voice becoming soft and suggestive, "to personally see to it that you didn't talk to them."

"Oh, is that so?" She softened instantly, and allowed him to pull her closer still. As he held her, he could feel whatever traces of anger left within her melt away. "And just how do you intend to do that?"

He leaned close and kissed her briefly, then took her by the hand, leading her to the nearest of the stateroom doors lining the opposite wall. Without a word he pressed his thumb on the entrance plate mounted in the doorframe. The system recognized the chief steward's print immediately, and the door slid aside to admit them.

The room was cold and dark. This level and the staterooms it contained had not been needed for this jump, so most systems—including heat and lighting—had been set to standby levels. The door slid closed behind them and he faced her, pressing her back to the wall. Again, they embraced tightly and he kissed her passionately.

"System," he said, pulling momentarily away. Vera continued to kiss his cheek and moved her lips slowly down his neck.

A high-pitched chirp. "Ready."

"Bring room temperature to normal; set lighting at fifty percent."

"Cancel!" Vera smiled at him, then said softly, "Bring room temperature to normal, but set lighting to twenty percent." Again, the confirming chirp. "I like it darker," she whispered into his ear.

"Then darker it is." He kissed her again, and moved the palms of his hands from her shoulders, slowly guiding them down the front of her shirt. Her breasts were soft but firm, and through the thin fabric of the shirt he could tell she was wearing nothing underneath. He slid his right hand inside the open collar of the shirt, softly caressing one of her breasts.

She smiled again and wordlessly unfastened the buttons one at a time, then pulled the shirttail out of her shorts and slipped it off her shoulders, letting it drop to the floor.

He used both hands now, rubbing them slowly up to her shoulders, massaging her neck, and back down the front of her again. The room had not yet reached normal temperature, and her nipples were hard and erect beneath his fingertips in the chilly air.

"I like when you touch me," she whispered, and took one of his hands in hers and kissed it, then pressed it to her chest again.

His heart pounded as he kissed her neck, and he felt himself wanting her more than ever. Without looking around, he tried to remember the layout of the stateroom, wondering where the bed was so as not to appear too clumsy as he maneuvered her in that direction. He leaned down, running the tip of his tongue down the center of her chest. Vera's breath came in short gasps as he did. It had been a long time since they had last made love, much too long, and it felt so good, being with her like this.

So why did he feel a mysterious queasiness come over him that he couldn't quite place? The unexplained feeling went away as suddenly as it had appeared and he put it out of his mind. He started to kiss her, but the feeling came back almost immediately, and with no more warning than it had the first time.

He straightened cautiously, his stomach turning. He looked at her and noticed that her breasts seemed to rise slightly, and that her hair was becoming fuller. When his eyes met hers, he saw an expression that was half confusion, half panic.

"Drew, I don't think I feel very—*oh!*"

And instantly, they were falling. The room seemed normal. There was no sound that hadn't been there a moment earlier. There had been no indication that anything was wrong, but they were unexpectedly without gravity.

The sudden involuntary movements each had made when the gravity field died now sent them tumbling, with both of them scrambling to grab on to anything close enough that offered solid support. Vera managed to snag hold of the doorframe leading into the stateroom lavatory and, gripping the frame as tightly as possible, twisted herself around to find him.

Drew had not been so lucky, and floated through the center of the room several armlengths away from any solid object. He made a futile, almost comical effort to "swim" to the ceiling fixture, but his frantic gyrations served only to keep him tumbling wildly. He had never spent much time in zero *g,* and the constant falling sensation was making him sicker. As he spun, he caught sight of Vera dangling from the doorframe. She was clearly terrified by what was happening, and he forced himself to calm down.

His arm brushed something, the edge of a wall, and as his feet swung around he managed to push away toward the opposite side of the stateroom, the effort sending him thudding much more forcefully than he'd intended into a low table mounted firmly to the wall. He caught the edges in both hands as he slammed into it and stopped himself at the same instant he heard a grisly *pop!* from his left shoulder. He cried out as an intense wave of pain shot through him.

"Drew!"

He gripped the table, holding himself down flat on the top as best he could with his good arm, and tried to ignore the pain in his shoulder. "I'm all right," he said, forcing his rapid breathing to slow. "I think I dislocated something when I hit. It hurts like hell, but I'm all right."

She started to say something, but he cut her off. "Hold on. Stay put and don't say anything for a minute." He surveyed the room, trying to figure out just what was going on.

The edges of the bed covering seemed to float, and Vera's shirt drifted between them. Hanging tightly with one hand, she snagged it with the other and pulled it to her, but made no attempt to put it back on. There were a few other small objects tumbling through the air that he couldn't make out in the dim light, but otherwise everything else seemed, like the table to which he clung, to be securely fastened to either floor, wall or ceiling. There was a small closet about halfway between the stateroom entrance and the doorframe where Vera floated, its outline glowing steadily in the dim light. The thumblatch blinked an ominous red, but he doubted that, from her awkward angle, she could see the first confirmation he'd been able to find that something was dreadfully wrong.

"Drew, what happened?"

"I don't know. System!"

There was the familiar faint chirp of the system acknowledging his query, but nothing further.

"System!" Vera tried. Again, a confirming chirp but no access. "System! System!"

"Listen, we have to get back up to the command deck; or at least to a working comm terminal. I . . . I'm going to need a hand."

She nodded and tucked her shirt into the waistband of her shorts, then oriented herself carefully in his direction and pushed gently off the doorframe to sail gracefully across the room. That she had spent more time in the zero-g recreation area than he had was immediately obvious as she landed smoothly at the edge of the table. Her long hair, a floating mass of brown without g, tumbled forward around her face as she stopped and cursed softly under her breath. Satisfied she was steady for the moment, she carefully pressed her fingers through the tangled mess and drew it behind her, then deftly tied it into a knot that left a short ponytail bobbing at the back of her head. Holding on with one hand, she helped him wrap his legs around the edge of the table and coaxed him into a sitting position.

"This may hurt," she said in warning, then took his dislocated arm and placed his hand against his chest. He winced, and sweat beaded on his face as she worked to tie her shirt around him to keep his arm firmly in place against his chest. "How's that? Can you move?"

"Yeah, if I don't pass out," he joked weakly, realizing as he heard the words that there was a good deal more truth in them than he would have liked to admit. "Let's go."

"All right. Follow my lead, but don't thrash around. Let me guide you over." He should have felt embarrassed at being carried along like an invalid or, worse, like a small child needing constant attention on a family outing. But the manner in which Vera viewed the situation in her matter-of-fact way told him she was just doing what needed to be done at the moment. There was no judging on her part. It was one of the things he liked best about her.

They made it to the stateroom's entrance door, stopping smoothly, if abruptly, against the smooth plastic surface. She reached for the opening plate.

"Hold it," he warned, stopping her. "Not yet." Using his free hand, he thumbed the closet switch and felt a momentary panic as the door hesitated, then opened to reveal its contents. A red emergency light had come on inside; it was the interior light that had caused the outline to be so easily visible in the darkened room. There were four life vests inside, and Drew could see that the status plate over the left breast of each garment blinked red in unison with the light on the closet door.

"You're right," Vera said, following his lead. As he steadied himself with one hand on the edge of the closet, she fished out one of the bulky vests and slipped it on. The status plate changed from red to green when she pressed it closed down the front, indicating that the garment's internal life-support unit was on automatic standby. Once it was sealed, the light continued to blink in time with the light on the door.

Good, he thought. *At least the emergency systems are on-line and working.*

She grabbed one of the other vests and gingerly helped him into it, then pressed the front closed with his injured arm tucked securely inside. Once it was sealed, his status indicator blinked green in unison with hers.

"Let's get out of here." Vera slapped the opening plate with the palm of her hand and the door slid aside to reveal a hallway that looked, at first glance, as if nothing had happened. A red warning light blinked over each stateroom door, but otherwise the overhead lighting was normal; no warning klaxon sounded.

However, any hope that the gravity failure was limited to the staterooms vanished when they carefully peeked out and saw that a series of handholds—rigid plastic loops that looked like nothing so much as pieces from a child's ring-toss game—had emerged automatically from their recesses in the previously smooth walls on each side of the corridor. Each handhold glowed softly, with a pulse of brightness moving along the row of loops as they extended down the hallway, and Drew noted that the pulses led away from the lift. A quick glance at the panel next to the lift doors showed it to be dark and lifeless, save the ever-present blinking red light: With artificial gravity shut down, the lift system was inoperative. The pulses, designed to direct confused passengers caught out of their staterooms during an emergency, would undoubtedly lead to the nearest control station on this level.

"That way," he said, indicating aft. "There'll be a personnel comm terminal at the station I should be able to access."

They moved into the corridor in the direction of the pulses, Vera towing him along with one hand while grabbing an occasional handhold with the other to keep them propelled in the right direction. There was a bend in the corridor a few meters ahead of them, and they could hear the excited voices of several people, indicating that a comm terminal was located in the next corridor.

"Brace yourself," Vera said, deftly swinging around to stop them feet-first on the wall where the corridor changed direction. There was a moment of pain when she braked against the wall, but once again he was quietly grateful for her zero-*g* experience. "Are you all right?" She was breathing heavily now, he noticed, and he realized it wasn't from the exertion of getting them both this far—she was frightened. She had responded to the emergency so automatically that she had not taken time to be afraid; but now that the adrenaline was fading, fright was beginning to well up inside her.

"Yeah, I'm fine," he said, hooking his good arm into a loop next to hers, allowing Vera to steady herself with both hands on separate loops. He forced himself to smile. "Everything's going to be fine. Look, we made it to the terminal." Pushing his thoughts away from his own rising concerns, he indicated the comm just a short distance down the corridor.

There were three people there. One of them, the one actually using the terminal, he immediately recognized as Ronatti, an apprentice steward who had signed on aboard the *Sylvan* when they left Copenhaver. Ronatti was holding, white-knuckled, on to a handhold loop while he talked animatedly into the terminal. The other two were obviously passengers, and from their disheveled attire he assumed they had sneaked onto the deserted level for much the same purpose Vera and he had. Neither wore life vests, and both were terrified and whimpering as they clung to each other, and constantly pleaded with the steward to tell them what was happening, even though he was doing his best to ignore them.

"Ronatti! What the hell is going on?"

"Hold on," he barked into the comm when he saw the two of them at the bend in the corridor. "Drew's here now." Still anchored firmly to the loop, he turned to them and called down the corridor, "Drew! This level's sealed, but I've got Captain Partane right here. All gravity is off and the SIS—"

A horrendous wrenching sound exploded suddenly all around him, and he watched in terror as the entire corridor began to come apart.

A huge rent appeared in both ceiling and floor about halfway between them and the terminal, and as the panels separated, the rest of the corridor actually fell away, exposing the midsection between this level and the one above.

He felt his ears pop at the same time the wall to which he clung jerked suddenly backward. Another tear appeared in the wall between the two of them as the panels pulled apart, and as he felt himself being snapped in one direction he saw that Vera, still clinging to her loops, was being tugged in the other.

"Drew!"

The tear completed itself around the circumference of the corridor, and the two sections pulled completely apart amid a jumble of jagged metal and plastic thrusting itself through what had been—only a few moments earlier—solid walls and floors. And as the corridor disintegrated around them, he felt a sudden hurricane of swirling wind and debris.

The abrupt loss of pressure sent the life vest into active mode, and a skin-shield snapped into place translucently around him. He heard a tiny voice from the wafer speaker in the lapel of the vest. "Emergency mode one enabled," it repeated at regular intervals. There was a soft hiss from the vest fabric itself, and he felt the pain in his ears ease as the pressure returned to normal.

Dizzy and disoriented, it took him a second to recognize that he was floating free, and he stared stupidly at the detached loop that remained uselessly on his arm. The corridor was still in convulsions as he tried to locate Vera, but the grinding debris and panel sections moved against each other in strange silence now with the lack of an atmosphere to carry the sound to him. A large section of metal paneling sandwiched him against another, but the skin-shield generated by the vest held firm and kept the jagged pieces away from him until he could wriggle free again. Once clear of the mess, he called out to her, but knew she couldn't hear him even if she was all right.

The hurricane receded and the motion of the debris that had once been luxury passenger staterooms subsided. Had he not known where he was, he would not have been able to recognize it. But the important thing was that whatever had happened was over, and he had a moment to think.

Internal pressure was gone on this level, he knew, but the fact that the life vest was only in emergency mode one indicated that the *Sylvan*'s hull must still be intact. He might yet find Vera, and if her life vest was functioning she should have been able to avoid injury just as he had.

"Vera!"

He picked his way gingerly through the mess using his good

arm and both legs, the frictionless skin-shield allowing him to slip deftly through the weightless chunks of metal and plastic. He found only one body, that of a man he recognized as one of the new engineers. He wore a life vest, but had apparently been killed before it had activated. There was an ugly purple bruise on the man's temple that extended up under his hairline, but other than that he appeared uninjured. Drew wondered how many others would have had time to don vests, and how effective they might have been. He made his way slowly, and once or twice he felt a shuddering in the debris or a disconcerting press of a large chunk against some part of his body as the damage settled itself, but he ignored it as he tried to determine which direction her portion of the corridor had shifted.

The skin-suit suddenly cast a soft glow and he felt a rapid, sharp stinging feeling in his chest just behind the status plate of the life vest. He tilted his head in confusion at the sensation; it felt like the bite of some tiny insect that might have crawled down the front of his shirt.

"Emergency mode two enabled," came the tiny voice from the vest, and the numbness now spreading through his body told him a stasis drug was being injected into his system. He sighed heavily as the drug began taking effect, and knew beyond doubt that the ship's computer must have sent the signal to the vest that the hull had breached. He heard the beeping of the vest's locator, which had also just become active. That, along with the soft glow the shield now emitted, were designed to make him easier to find by rescuers, but he paid little attention to it just now.

Everything started drifting apart, and he tried to watch the slow-motion ballet of the *Sylvan* breaking up around him. Somehow, although he knew the vest was maintaining his temperature, his first view of empty space made him feel colder as he dumbly watched the destruction complete itself. The pieces and chunks of the ship were spreading farther apart, and as the distance between himself and what was left of the corridor increased, he was able to see things better and recognize whole sections and subsystems of the ship.

There was an entire wall, tumbling serenely to his left. He looked closely and concentrated on something attached to it: Were those the two passengers he'd seen a few minutes earlier? Their arms still looped into the handholds, their bodies waved in a lifeless dance as the section rotated. A table, still attached to its own section of flooring, spun close. A mass of linens from some suddenly decompressed storage locker floated away from him, the sheets and blankets coming untangled from each other, giving the impression of an impossibly huge flower blossoming. He smiled stupidly at the beauty of it and waited for the stasis drug to put him to sleep.

Everywhere, there were bodies. Some had been badly mangled in the breakup, others looked deceptively uninjured. Some were in uniforms, but many more wore civilian attire. None of them wore vests.

And then, tumbling slowly a dozen meters away, another body. Vera's body.

She was dead, the lower half of her body cut cleanly away. Her skin-shield was intact and Drew could see the blood that had pooled within after it activated, probably mere seconds too late to save her.

He turned his head away in slow motion at the sight, wishing he could turn his own vest off, and even pawed clumsily at his chest for a moment in a useless attempt to reach the status plate.

The motion set him rotating slowly, and as his body turned he saw that he was floating away from the *Sylvan*. Through blurred eyes he saw that the entire rear third of the ship was gone, destroyed by explosive decompression. What was left of it was dark, lifeless. There were no other skin-shields to be seen.

His rotation brought him around again and he could see that the debris was spreading out rapidly. Vera's body was gone, drifting mercifully away to become lost in the jumble of grisly flotsam. After a moment of trying to locate her body through increasingly sleepy eyes, he forgot what it was he was looking for. His eyes grew heavier still and he felt his breathing become more shallow, and he knew that he was almost in stasis.

And as his rotation brought him around to face in the direction of the *Sylvan* one last time, he saw the huge wasp shape of the Sarpan ship outlined hazily against the backdrop of stars. *What was it called?* he asked himself through a stasis-clouded mind. *Hin-something. Something funny.*

His last conscious thought was of the Sarpan craft as it turned deftly away from the dead ship and disappeared.

". . . and it is just as I have told you before, my friends. But this time the loss of life is overwhelming, and not only because of the high number of casualties, but because of the profound innocence of the passengers. No, please—don't misunderstand me. I don't mean to insinuate that the many Imperial or military personnel who have died at the aliens' hands over the years are somehow less innocent

than the passengers and CTS personnel aboard the H. L. Sylvan. *No one knows better than I that those in service to the Empire of the Hundred Worlds have families—husbands and wives, children and parents. I meant only that those in Imperial service know the risks inherent in service, that's all. But those unsuspecting passengers, most of whom rode in cryosleep blissfully unaware of the danger presented to them, were attempting only to exercise one of their most basic rights—the right to travel from one human world to another.*

"The sad thing is that this is already being called 'an accident.'

"An accident.

"Of course, Imperial authorities are citing the lack of evidence that this was a hostile attack. They show records indicating the Sylvan's *Structural Integrity Shielding had displayed problems long before their rendezvous with the Sarpan ship. But think a moment: Do you know what the SIS is? Let me tell you. It is a variation on shield technology that acts as a reinforcing superstructure for large spacecraft. Just as the strength and rigidity of a shield can stop weapons fire or keep an atmosphere intact, it can also be designed to mesh with the actual structure of a spaceship, allowing construction of much larger, faster ships—with far less materials and energy cost—than ever before.*

"And do you know where the technology for this type of shield utilization came from? Yes, that's right. It came from the aliens. At best, who can say that their designs are not flawed? At worst, who can say that they have no ulterior motives? In either case, I am saddened to offer you proof once again that relying on anyone other than our human brothers and sisters has led to the death of innocents. That is what comes from dealing with the aliens.

"The same aliens your Emperor wishes to embrace as friends . . ."

PART TWO

A SILENT PASSING

One of the greatest pains
to human nature
is the pain of a new idea.

—Walter Bagehot

TWO
Awakenings and Arrivals

L ike the *H. L. Sylvan* twenty years earlier, the Empire was dead.

It did not die a valiant death, going down to defeat in a decisive battle either from within or without. Likewise, no cataclysm occurred to strain the fabric of what the vast Empire of the Hundred Worlds had become. Rather, the Empire suffered the most meaningless of deaths: It had become unnecessary. It had been, for want of a better description, forgotten.

The Empire was not entirely gone, of course. The Imperial government still sanctioned research in numerous areas and still aided exploration efforts for the newest frontier Worlds whenever asked for assistance. The Imperial treasury still existed, but years of funding the project to save Earth's Sun had depleted it severely. Not that it mattered: The rapidly expanding human civilization that had been the heart of the Empire had grown increasingly self-sufficient and needed little from the parent body.

Even the Imperial Court still remained, located on Earth's Moon, but its purpose had long ago been relegated to only the most ceremonial of duties.

Eric, son of Javas, was now Emperor; but he no longer spent much time on the Moon. There were instances when his presence at the Court made it necessary to return to Armelin City, but a mere holographic appearance sufficed as often as not. However, on those increasingly rare occasions when he felt his actual presence mattered, he would not hesitate to travel via wormhole to even the most remote regions of the Worlds in the hope that he might reach out to a people once bound by a common thread. From time to time it seemed his words meant something to those he addressed, and sometimes he felt that maybe, just maybe, he'd managed to rekindle a spark in the imaginations of those to whom he spoke. However, as the years passed, those occasions became depressingly infrequent.

Finally, weary of the false sense of importance and formality attached to both his title and family name—and feeling no small degree of shame at having been powerless to stop the rapidly changing course of history—he stayed mostly in the family home located in the Kentucky hills on Old Earth.

Old Earth, he would think bitterly whenever the phrase was uttered. *There is very little "old" about it!*

The Emperor was right. In the two hundred years that had passed since the wormhole method of space travel had been inadvertently discovered during a crucial test of the project to rekindle Earth's dying Sun, the planet itself had been reborn. While the Imperial Court no longer remained the central focus of the Worlds, Earth—and the entire Sol system for that matter— had become the technologically centralized hub of an ever-expanding Imperial civilization.

The technological revitalization that had come about as a result of the Sun project—as his grandfather Nicholas and, later, his own father had predicted—was, in fact, at the very heart of the project's success. The rush to develop new science to support the project branched almost geometrically in dozens of areas: communications, medicine, physics, construction techniques, genetics—even philosophy and religion.

Emperor Nicholas and Javas after him had been revered as the men who had begun the renaissance. Eric, too, had been praised for his efforts by a people grown increasingly out of touch with their history. His own mother, the scientist who had developed the theory that would breathe new life into the dying star that was the Sun, had been most honored. Even as she lay suspended in the cryosleep tank before him, awaiting the day for the final phase of the project that was her lifelong dream, she had become a virtual legend.

Do you know that your name is looked upon with near-religious fervor on some of the outlying Worlds? he asked wordlessly, kneeling at the side of the receptacle where she lay. He leaned close to the tank's thin plastiglass cover, his breath momentarily fogging the shiny surface. He straightened, then, and added silently, *I wonder, Mother, how you'll react to the changes that have come to pass as a result of your efforts.*

Eric often reflected on the irony of the events of the last several centuries: The project to save the Sun, itself designed to revitalize a stagnant Empire and reunite the individual Worlds to a common goal, had instead become the main cause of its death.

Wormhole spaceflight had made it possible for near-instantaneous travel to almost any point in the Empire. Instead of voyages lasting years, even decades—huge segments of time during which starship crew and passengers achieved little—ships arrived in the blink of an eye, ready to colonize and develop new Worlds or to bring new technology to existing ones. Instead of taking years for information developed on one planet to disseminate throughout the Empire, it became immediately available to all. Free of the restraints imposed by time and a centralized government, existing well-developed worlds soon began their own colonizing efforts, quickly forming new alliances and new partnerships. There had even been instances where mini-empires, consisting of five or six planets ruled by a single tyrannical leader, had arisen as the unbridled expansion continued. Many of these totalitarian systems were crushed by the weakening Empire, but after a time even these were permitted to go unchecked in the knowledge that those who preferred better could easily emigrate elsewhere. In these instances the Empire was there to assist, and eventually the tyrants found themselves with no one to rule.

And if the speed of planetary development was unprecedented, so, too, was the speed with which new cultures and customs were born. New ideologies, new social orders, new terminology sprang up more quickly than could be accounted for. In some cases, the people of one World—while still sharing a common language and heritage—seemed as alien from those on another as did the residents of different continents on Earth in the days before long-distance ocean voyages were possible.

These were young Worlds, their fledgling societies as self-centered as they were self-aware. Concerned with their own development, and with the progress of their own colonial efforts, they had no need of an all-encompassing Imperial bond.

And even less need for me.

As there was no longer a necessity for a common thread, the Empire quietly, slowly died.

The Emperor took one last look at his mother, peacefully unaware of all the history that had passed her by during her time in the tank, and turned away. The cryosleep chamber door slid aside at his approach, revealing a sterile antechamber where two cryotechs awaited.

"Sire?" asked one, bowing slightly.

The Emperor stopped and looked back into the room momentarily, then proceeded from the antechamber.

"Move Dr. Montgarde to the recovery room in preparation for tomorrow." He paused, accessing the estate computer system with the integrator woven into the very molecules of his brain. It took less than a second to find the right files, select the proper command sequence, and route the coded instructions to the recovery facility.

"I've just installed the room environment for her awakening. See to it that no other programming is substituted."

On the opposite side of Earth, a dark-skinned man looked wistfully out over the deep blue waters of the Timor Sea. It was hot, and the sea breeze carried with it the mixed pleasure of heat and humidity that he had missed so. He gazed around him, the air bright and clear, and he caught the sound of a boat horn, faint and wistful on the wind. He looked to the north in the direction from which the sound had come, and although he could see as far as Cape Londonderry, there was no boat to be seen. But that, in itself, wasn't unusual; the sea here could carry sounds for many kilometers.

Billy Woorunmarra waded into the warm surf. He was out of shape, although he hated to admit it, and the water splashing up around his aching calves invigorated him after his bicycle ride from Kalumburu. On an impulse he stripped, tossing his balled-up trousers back up on the sand near where he'd already left his shirt and shoes. The pants unfurled in the breeze, however, and fell far short, landing just at the edge of the undulating surf. He didn't care at all.

Ignoring his pants as they rolled over and over in the water sweeping up the sand, he turned and dove into an incoming wave. He felt the warm salt water rush over him as he dove down, then back up into the sunshine again. Putting all else out of his mind, he swam for the better part of an hour, stopping only when he noticed that the Sun had begun to dip low on the horizon. Standing now in waist-deep water, he closed his eyes and tilted his head back, drinking in the scents, sounds of the Timor: the sea spray in his nostrils, the salt water on his tongue, the screech of gulls, the sand washing between his toes. And above all else, the warmth of the Sun on bare, wet skin.

There was little of this in Kalumburu. The burgeoning economic center, once a tiny Aboriginal settlement, had blossomed in his time off-planet, and after only a short visit there he had been anxious to get away from it. He saddened as he remembered the excitement with which the mayor had greeted him on his arrival to Earth. The mayor was Aborigine, just as he was, and could trace his ancestry back to the same area of the outback where he himself had grown up—but all that had changed. The mayor of Kalumburu was an Aborigine only physically, much as the town remained Aborigine in name only. The man's Song Lines were gone, severing him from his people, his past, as completely as a knife separates the skin from a fresh-killed roo. He had arrived nearly a week earlier, but Billy was beginning to think there was little of what his people had been anywhere in the Kimberley region. The thought so disturbed him that he gave little consideration to how his deputy governor was making do during his absence back on Darson, a frontier world nearly ten light-years distant.

For the moment, Billy's thoughts were on his homeworld, and on what it had become. Perhaps a walkabout was what he needed. He could follow the track from Kalumburu down to the Great Sandy, to his birthplace, then back again. Surely by doing that he could reconnect the Song Lines to these people's origins. Surely. But he realized the effort would be futile. Besides, a proper walkabout would take many months to complete, and he would miss the last phase of the project.

The project.

He had been present at a turning point in Adela de Montgarde's efforts to gain support for her dream and had played a major role in her life then; he'd promised her that he would be here for her proudest moment, had even looked forward to it. According to the communiqué from Eric, she would be awakened tomorrow from her long slumber. It had been so long, and he admitted inwardly how much he had longed over the years to see her again. But so much had changed here!

It has been much too long, he thought as he let his eyes scan the horizon. *I am grateful that this, at least, has remained the same.* He made out Long Reef and, a short distance to the south, the Bonaparte Archipelago, just as he'd remembered them; he wondered idly which of the islands he'd visited as a boy nearly three centuries earlier. A solitary gull screeched loudly overhead, and he followed its flight as it sailed across the face of the Sun, red and bloated as it neared the watery horizon to the west. Behind him a horn grated, spoiling the moment.

He turned to see a small motorcade arriving a bit farther up the shoreline, pulling to a stop near where he'd left the bicycle in the sand. Despite his best efforts, several Kalumburu town officials, in their indefatigable efforts to fete him as a returning son, had found him. Beyond them he caught sight of the towers of the once-sleepy town, their plastiglass panels glinting brightly in the setting sun, and shook his head at the unwelcome reminder of what his people had become. The horn sounded again and the mayor stepped out onto the soft sand, waving for him to return to the vehicle. Billy waded to the edge of the surf and retrieved his trousers, still washing up and down in the waves. As he stood there, the mayor finally reached him, and Billy took a moment's pleasure from the shocked look on the man's face when he suddenly realized he was naked.

"Governor Woorunmarra!" the man sputtered over the wind and surf. "It's time for the banquet!" He snapped his fingers, and one of his companions sprinted to the car to bring fresh clothing. Another had gotten the bicycle and was now stowing it in the back of one of the vehicles.

"Tell me, Mayor Moora," Billy said. "When's the last time you had a corroboree? Or even been to one?"

"What?" The mayor tilted his head, genuinely puzzled by the question.

Angered, Billy asked, "Hell, when's the last time you swam in this sea?"

"What are you talkin' about?"

He was about to challenge him further, but turned instead to the Sun, the distended, scarlet disk just now kissing the water.

"This is all your making," he whispered, and wished once more that he'd never made a promise to return here.

"It's not a big flower at all, is it?" asked the wizened old man. His bony, blue-veined hands shook as he lifted the fragile crimson bloom to his nose and inhaled deeply. "It is not even particularly beautiful. And yet, the magnificent beauty carried by its fragrance alone is so overpowering that I feel I may fall into it and be lost forever."

You're a part of me, part of my life, she thought, trying

desperately to bring the man's identity up from the depths of a memory gone fuzzy with time. *I should know you.*

"Of course you do, Adela, my love," he answered, as if she'd spoken aloud. She opened her mouth to ask how he'd been able to hear her thoughts, but no sound came out and she felt the panic of helplessness wash over her.

The old man laughed softly, the kindly sound immediately easing her fears, and handed the flower to her. When she took it from him, it was no longer a flower, but a tiny sparrow with delicate feathers the color of freshly fallen snow. The songbird regarded her from the cupped palms of her hands, then tilted its head back and sang. She closed her eyes and listened to the lovely music, and felt herself smile. How long had it been since she'd smiled?

"The song is no longer mine," he said. "I give it to you freely, Adela my love. It's yours forever now. Forget me, and fly with it."

She opened her eyes at the words, but the old man was gone, which was as it should be. She looked at the tiny bird in her cupped hands and raised it to the breeze. The sparrow took wing and flew high above her, into branches of trees that had not been there before. As if to admit the bird to the sky, the breeze parted the uppermost boughs as the bird flew up and up and up. She strained to follow it, but the Sun broke suddenly from behind a fleecy white cloud, the unexpected brightness bringing tears to her eyes. Her vision blurred, she lost sight of the sparrow when it cleared the treetops.

"No!" she cried out, attempting to shield her eyes from the brilliance.

Dr. Adela de Montgarde had experienced cryosleep many times; enough times to know—now that the edges of consciousness returned slowly to her—that she had been dreaming. There was a coolness on her cheek as a gentle, sweet-smelling breeze played across her features. Her eyes still tightly closed, she reached a trembling hand to her cheek and brushed tears away. That part of the dream, at least, had been real.

She had gone to sleep two hundred years earlier at Woodsgate, the Emperor's family estate on Earth, surrounded by a serene holographic forest her beloved Javas had ordered made for her. She had loved it so, and he had promised that when she awoke, the forest would be there. She lay there for several long minutes, afraid to open her eyes; afraid that the promise of a man made all those years ago would not be kept. Surely, after all this time there had been more important things for him to remember. But the sounds! As she listened, she became aware that the very air around her was alive with the calling of birds, and—each time the breeze softly swept over her—of rustling leaves.

Finally, her mind almost fully conscious, she opened her eyes and stared at the brightness above her. Fresh tears formed at the corners of eyelids unused for so many years. What she managed to see was a blur of greens, moving and swaying dizzily before her. She blinked, her eyelids seeming to move in the same slow motion as the undulating mass of greens and blues, and her vision became clearer. There were trees here, and a patch of blue sky dotted with the most beautiful white clouds she could remember seeing. And, just as in the dream, a sudden shaft of sunlight fell upon her. But this time, the tears that came to her eyes were tears of happiness.

Thank you, Javas, she thought, and felt a smile come to her lips again.

There was another sound, that of voices in quiet conversation. Turning her head, she saw that there were three people here; a middle-aged man stood a few meters away, his back to her as he spoke to two very young men. The pair wore identical featureless smocks that had a medical look about them. Occasionally he would nod at what they were saying, but he himself said very little. It was obvious they were talking about her, and although she could hear most of what they said, they used a number of words and phrases that were meaningless to her. What was a "corpser"? A "pullback"? What did they mean when they nodded in her direction and used the phrase "slow timer"?

Adela shook her head to clear it, causing a sudden rustling of sheets that attracted their attention. The man turned and, smiling broadly, approached her. "Hello, Mother," he said, then bent and kissed her softly on the cheek.

It was Eric, she realized. He was older now, his hair—once the same dark brown shade as her own—mostly gray, his face lined with the passing of years and the weight of his office. It startled her to see her own son looking nearly twice her apparent age; he appeared, in fact, the same age Javas had been when she went to sleep. Assuming he'd followed Imperial custom and had stopped taking rejuvenation the day he became Emperor, then judging from his appearance he must have ruled the Imperial Court for nearly fifty years.

The thought cut itself off abruptly as another realization suddenly struck her: Her beloved Javas must now be a half-century dead.

THREE
Transmission

(PAUSE)

"*My name is Drew Hatton. I, uh . . . I mean . . .*"

"*It's all right, Drew. Take your time. Take all the time you need.*"

"*My name is Drew Hatton, and I'd like to thank Lord Jephthah for the opportunity to talk to you today. At one time I served as chief steward aboard the passenger jumper* H. L. Sylvan. *You may have heard of her. Twenty years ago we were heading to Gate, uh, Gate Eighty-seven I think it was, after departing the colony world Copenhaver at Forty Eridani. We had developed a problem with the SIS—uh, that's the Structural Integrity Shielding. That's what reinforces and holds the big jumpers and starships together when we make the wormhole jumps. Without it, the ships would have to be a lot smaller and heavier with all the metal reinforcing. Anyway, we got a red light on the SIS, but we couldn't figure out what the problem was. All our diagnostics showed it was all right. Even the Copenhaver techs said it was fine. We got an offer of help from a Sarpan ship that had clearance in the Eridani system and we accepted, even though some of the crew objected. Everything was fine until just before they rendezvoused with us, and then everything started happening at once. Our internal gravity went off suddenly, and a few minutes later the SIS disengaged.*"

"*Drew, was there any indication that the alien ship had anything directly to do with the SIS failure?*"

"*I don't know! I mean, we never found out; it all happened too fast. All I know is that we only had a red light until they showed up, and then . . . one minute I was with . . . another crew member and the next minute the whole ship was breaking up around us. I saw her pulled away right in front of me, and the next time I saw her she was dead . . . they were all dead!*"

"*I'm sorry, Drew, but I don't quite understand. You mean that everyone died, except you? How did you survive?*"

"*What . . .? Oh, the life vest saved me. Vera and I had time to put one on. They're computer-controlled to make an air shield around you automatically in the event of a hull breach. But there was only a minute or two's warning, and Vera . . . she was killed*

*just seconds before the vest activated. I remember I was floating in
open space, chunks and pieces of the ship all around me when she
. . . floated . . . I'm sorry, but I . . ."*

"It's all right, Drew. Thank you."

(PAUSE)

*"My friends, I don't need to tell you how dangerous our encoun-
ters with the Sarpan nonhumans have been over the years. And I
don't need to remind you that the dangers—and deaths—have increased since we enlisted their help with the noble project to save
Earth's Sun. Now, as we near the project's end, still more nonhuman ships approach Sol system. Even now, more of them make
themselves at home near worlds where humans live. And think of
this: Because of the aliens' short life spans, human systems are the
only homes that some of them have ever known!*

*"It grows worse by the day. You are not aware of this, but even
now preparations are being made to awaken an alien that lies side
by side with humans at the sunstation on Mercury in Sol system. An
alien that worked with our human scientists years ago, at the beginning stages of the project, somehow convinced project scientists to
keep it secretly in cryosleep until the time came to bring the project
to its conclusion. Imagine! A nonhuman that, when it awakes, will
share two centuries of human knowledge with its waiting, eager
colleagues. Is this what you desire for humanity?*

*"Make yourselves heard, my friends. Stop this madness before it
is too late. . . ."*

FOUR
Tsing 479

Gareth Anmoore's stomach lurched, and he fought with
every bit of strength he possessed to keep from vomit-
ing. He concentrated on the ceiling above his jump
couch, carefully attempting to distinguish one tiny bump from
another in the decoratively textured pseudoplaster that made his
personal quarters look as much like a normal room as the design-
ers felt necessary for a mere exploration ship. But the tiny bumps
kept *moving* in the dim light, making him dizzier still as he fur-

rowed his brow. Past experience made him keep concentrating, however: to close his eyes would send him plummeting into a deep well of vertigo guaranteed to set his stomach heaving, despite the antinauseants he'd taken before the jump began.

He—and every conscious crew member aboard the exploration vessel *Paloma Blanco* who had ever experienced jump travel— had eaten nothing in the twelve hours it had taken to deorbit and enter the wormhole. Fasting didn't really help to keep a jumper from getting sick, however; it merely reduced the amount of material. His stomach lurched again and, not for the first time, he wished he could ride the jump out in the tank like the majority of the crew.

But he was captain and, like all other essential personnel, protocol and practicality demanded he stay awake through everything that made up the dizzying ride: The unrelenting sensation of the twelve-hour spiraling fall into the hole, for which Imperial scientists had been unable to compensate with even the latest artificial-gravity technology. The moment of stretching during the jump itself that seemed to last forever, when the body felt as if it were being pulled in two directions at once. The "snap": that instant upon reentering normal space when a jump ship would shoot out the other side of the wormhole very near c. The sudden deceleration caused by the jump ship's energy bleeders as their forward momentum was slowed before the ship could shake itself apart.

Gareth almost wished for a full stomach, so he could just do it and get it over with, rather than be forced to endure the punishment his body was going through now. . . .

"Jump complete." The soft computer voice startled him, but as the lighting returned to normal levels, he felt himself begin to feel better. "All systems on standby, Captain, awaiting your orders."

Gareth took several deep breaths and, gritting his teeth, sat up slowly—and waited. He sat on the edge of the couch and closed his eyes, trying to ignore the warm sensation spreading from the base of his left wrist. He felt calmer, more relaxed within a few seconds. Opening his eyes, he blinked several times, then peeled the tiny adhesive jump patch from his arm. The drugs it had contained now dispensed into his system, he rolled it between his fingertips until it disintegrated.

His head clear and the stomach ache now all but gone, he was on his feet immediately.

"System!"

There was a confirming chirp from the cabin's integrated com-

puter the moment it recognized Gareth's voice pattern, and it
instantly channeled him directly to the ship's post-jump program.
A holographic display came to life over his work desk, the readings showing that all ship systems were normal.

"Are all emergency re-jump sequences in place and locked in?"
he asked, wanting to reassure himself that the *Paloma Blanca*
could immediately turn about and re-jump at the first sign of
danger. The question was unnecessary, however, as the post-
jump program would already have brought them about if anything was wrong.

"Yes, sir."

"Please give me location stats. Visual."

The holographic display altered immediately, and showed that
they had come out of the wormhole exactly as planned. Unlike
most jumps, the energy bleeders had decreased momentum only
as much as was needed to avoid damage to the ship. To maximize
travel time, their exit was aimed in such a way as to take advantage of the snap speed to get them to their destination faster than
they would have been able on the ship's power alone. Tsing 479,
the closest of the three star systems they were to investigate at this
wormhole, was still more than a month's travel time from the exit
point. At their current rate of speed—near maximum for a survey
vessel of this class—they should reach the system in just over five
weeks.

Good, he thought. *Very good.* He took another hour to look
over the readouts, studying the computer records brought back
by the original probes and comparing them to the readings now
being gathered by the larger, more sophisticated scanning array
on the exploration vessel. According to what they were receiving,
the Tsing system looked even more promising than they had
initially thought, based on the probe data. The decision to aim
for Tsing had been a good one.

Time to get everyone up. Gareth ordered the system to begin the
wake-up sequence for everyone who rode out the jump in the
tanks; then, after taking care of the last bit of post-jump business,
he placed a personal call.

"Good afternoon, Hannah," he piped cheerily when the image
coalesced in front of him. "You're looking especially lovely
today." The woman who gazed back at him looked ill, almost
literally green; but then, Gareth expected no less. Hannah Cee
had served with him sixteen years, and the two of them had
successfully undertaken dozens of exploratory missions together,
but at no time had he ever known her to ride out a jump in

cryosleep. As captain he could order her to, of course, and each time he saw her following a jump he thought of doing just that. But she would sooner resign a job she dearly loved than become a corpser, even for the short amount of time a jump took.

"Go to hell." The words came out in a single croak, the effort visibly painful, and she clamped here eyes tightly.

"Hannah, the least you could do is use a jump patch. I hate to see you get so sick each time."

She opened her eyes and glared up at him again. The expression on her face was so pitiful that it would almost—if he didn't know from personal experience just how sick she really was feeling—look funny.

"Anyway," he went on, "I've looked over the preliminary scans we've been getting back, and I've got some news that should make you feel at least a little bit better. It appears Tsing is a good deal more promising than we originally thought. There are eleven planets in the system, three more than the probe showed. Two of them are Earthlike, and one of them—number four—even has atmosphere and temperature range that'll support almost immediate colonization."

Hannah's face brightened, but her head still bobbed woozily. "Water?" she managed. "River systems?"

"We're still a little too far out, but our snap speed from the wormhole is pretty high, so we should be close enough to get hydrographic data in less than a week. There appear to be at least two moons, so there should be plenty of tidal action if there is any appreciable amount of water. I've already routed everything we've gotten so far to your ID, and I've coded the files for constant updating." He stood up and pulled his jacket off the back of the chair, slipping it on as he added, "I'm heading to the mess. Care to join me?"

She gave him a look of pure hatred before ordering the connection broken at her end.

FIVE
Threats and Regrets

I have no power anymore," Eric said, gazing out over the serene valley. "No true power."

"I find that hard to believe."

"Believe it, Mother. Believe it." He rose from where he'd been sitting at her side and walked a short distance down the limestone outcropping. "I am still a leader, and there are many who follow me, but . . ." A glint of light reflecting off the surface of the river below them had caught his eye, and he regarded it silently.

She remembered the many times Javas had looked out over the same valley and attempted to set aside for a short time the weight of his office. During the eight years she had spent on Luna and here at Woodsgate before going into cryosleep, she and Javas often walked the grounds of the Imperial estate. Sometimes it was she who tried to forget that she would lose him during her many years in cryosleep. More often, though, the occasions they spent alone here were devoted to enjoying the time they shared, and not what they were trying to escape.

Behind them, several meters up the steep slope down which they had climbed to reach the outcropping, one of the horses snorted and pawed the ground impatiently. She turned to check the magnificent animal, a gift from her son, to make certain that everything was all right, but it had already returned to its grazing. Beyond the horses lay the estate itself, she knew, but it was out of sight owing to the steepness of the slope. For all appearances, the two of them could be alone in the wilderness somewhere, imagining themselves far from civilization—not to mention scientific and Imperial matters. She and Javas used to do the same thing, then. The rare quiet moments were welcome; but always, they were forced to return to the realities of their lives.

The Woodsgate grounds were considerably larger than they had been two centuries before. Back then—except for the final weeks before she went to sleep—the Emperor of the Hundred Worlds could afford little time here, and there was little need for more room. But since Eric was in residence much more frequently now, the diameter of the security shielding had been expanded by more than two kilometers, and now included much of the Kentucky backwoods surrounding the estate, not to mention a significant portion of the hillside itself.

She leaned back on her elbows, nearly reclining on the bare rock, and enjoyed the heat of the Sun as it played across her face. The sunlight was not "pure," of course—the invisible shielding above them filtered out all harmful UV radiation—but somehow it still felt "real" to her. Since awaking several hours earlier she couldn't get Eric to agree to accompany her outside soon enough to bask in the sunshine, filtered or not.

"I can still command," he went on finally. "On my word a fleet of ships will go wherever I send them, will do whatever I tell them to do. No commander would refuse my order. I can still . . ."

He hesitated, turning to face her. In his eyes she could see the emotions fighting within him, threatening to tear him apart. He turned away again and she sat up, waiting silently for him to continue.

"I still hold an Emperor's power of life and death." He spun about to face her once more, his hands balled into fists as he spoke. "Mother, I could command a starship to obliterate a planet if I thought it was the right thing to do. I wouldn't even have to justify my reasons for doing it. But there are so many more than 'a Hundred Worlds' that make up this Empire now that even the name no longer fits, and it is not possible to control them all any longer."

"Don't control them, then," she said simply. "You told me a few moments ago that there were those who follow you. If you are still a leader, then you must lead your followers, not 'control' them."

Eric sighed. "A long time has passed, Mother, and the Empire has changed. You've seen this new future for only a few hours; there is so very much of which you are still unaware."

"I know," she admitted guiltily, "and I've probably been babbling on about something I know absolutely nothing about. I should have gone right to the files you had prepared for me as soon as I woke up, but I'm just not ready for them yet. They're not going anywhere. In all honesty, I just wanted to put it off for a while; have some time as myself before becoming 'Dr. Montgarde' again. I just wanted to spend some time here with you."

Eric smiled, and when he did it occurred to Adela that it was the first time he had done so in the last two hours. "I'm glad for it," he said simply, "as it gives me time to be myself again, too. And it has become increasingly important of late to remember who I am."

He looked out over the valley again and sighed heavily. Or could it have been the wind that swept gently through the permeable shielding? He seemed nervous, anxious about something more than his words revealed.

"Mother, I am no failure. I know that. What has happened to the Empire is a perfectly logical result of the technological avalanche that has overtaken it. The people of the Hundred Worlds have responded the only way they could—they have grown. On the one hand I am frightened by what I see and feel helpless to stop it. On the other, I sometimes wonder if I even have the right to do so. There is much that is good about the direction the Empire has taken: New discoveries are made almost daily, sickness and suffering have all but disappeared on even the most remote of the frontier worlds, self-sufficiency exists for even the newest colony worlds, science has advanced further than ever before."

He looked absently to the side for a moment, his head tilted slightly, in a way that reminded her so much of Javas that her heart quickened at the unexpected resemblance. Adela had seen the mannerism before, and realized that Eric was either accessing his integrator, or he was receiving a private page. He concentrated a few seconds more on the unseen speaker, then crossed to her and extended a hand to help her to her feet with no indication as to the contents of the communication.

"Throughout the Hundred Worlds," he continued, indicating that they should begin the steep climb back to the horses, "the people seem, for the most part, happy with the turn of events. But there is also a disappointing trend. Just as the Worlds have become open to discovery, they have become closed to new thought." He chuckled briefly at the puzzled look she shot him, but his serious tone quickly returned. "I know, I know; it seems such a contradiction—"

"Hello!"

The voice came from above, but from this vantage point the curve of the slope prevented her from seeing the speaker. From here, even the horses were no longer visible. Eric put a hand to her shoulder, and the two of them paused midway up the slope.

"I'm sorry. I'll have to leave it at that for now, Mother, but trust me for just a few hours longer." He let a warm smile spread across his face, then pointed to the top of the hill. "Right now, though, I believe there's a friend of yours here to see you."

Adela followed Eric's gaze.

"Billy!"

He was heavier now, his shoulders even broader than she'd remembered, but as he easily clambered down the hillside she could see that despite his wider frame there wasn't a bit of fat on him. His hair had grayed, looking for all the world like a salt-and-pepper lion's mane, and bounced wildly as he effortlessly trotted down the steep slope. His face, too, had aged, although his dark, round features still radiated the unlimited youthful energy she had come to associate with him. Above all else, the wide, toothy grin told her that this was truly the same friend she'd left behind all those many years ago.

He lifted her off the ground in a smooth motion when he reached her, swinging her around in a tight hug. Had anyone but Billy tried such a thing on a slope as steep and uneven as this she might have been frightened, but he had the surefootedness of a mountain goat and the thought of the two—or three—of them tumbling down the incline never occurred to her.

"Ah, lady, it's so bloody good to see you again!" he barked happily in a voice that still carried with it his thick outback accent, even after all this time. He planted her feet firmly back on the slope, then held her at arm's length. "Have you had a good nap?"

"I'm fine," she said, grinning back at him. "It's good to see you, too, Billy. Or should I call you 'Governor Woorunmarra.' "

"Awww, you went and told her, and ruined the surprise." He regarded Eric with mock disappointment, then extended his hand. "Hello, old friend."

"Welcome home, Billy." It was obvious to Adela that even though the two had not even been on the same planet for years, their friendship had remained strong as ever.

"I wish I could say I was happy to be home," he said, his voice now serious. There was genuine sadness in his eyes. "But the word 'home' just don't seem to fit much anymore. There's too much changed since I left for Darson."

Clearly, Billy was happy to see her again, but Adela could tell just how unhappy he was to be back on Earth. Only a few moments earlier, when Eric had been describing the great changes to both Earth and the Empire, it had been easy to disconnect those changes from her own efforts; but right now, looking into the downcast eyes of her best friend, she felt a personal involvement for the first time. *What have I done to disappoint you so?* she wondered. *What has so intimately changed for you here that even a visit could cause you such pain?*

As if he'd read her thoughts, his demeanor changed suddenly to a lighter tone as he said to Eric, "Well, no worries now that she's back. Maybe with her help the two of you can start to fixin' some of the things that have gone wrong, ay?"

Eric sighed again, but this time the air was still and there was no mistaking the sound for the wind.

The main house was not far from the outcropping, and Eric had ridden back ahead of them, allowing Adela and Billy some time to themselves. Eric had been somewhat apprehensive, at first, knowing that many of the details of all the changes to which he had alluded could easily be taken out of context without a full accounting of everything that had occurred. But it was clear the two men trusted each other. They took their time as they crossed the grassy estate grounds, the wide expanse of bluegrass broken only occasionally by karst outcroppings. They were both on foot, with Adela leading the remaining horse.

"Don't be silly," Billy was saying. "Of course I don't hold you personally responsible for what my people have allowed themselves to become. How could I?"

"There is, apparently, a lot I don't yet know; but it's abundantly obvious that the project to save the Sun—my project, my idea—is responsible for many of the changes that have taken place." She shook her head in resignation at the way things were, and regretted again that she had not made the attempt to bring herself up to date the moment she awoke. "I'll see everything for myself soon enough. I'm leaving in a few days to review a number of project sites, and that should give me an opportunity to observe what's happened."

Billy regarded her silently for several long moments, a look of concern plain on his features. It was obvious that he and Eric had already discussed this, and had come to some agreement that he would say little until her son had told her himself.

"You may not like what you find," was all he said. "There's some things out there that aren't very pleasant."

"I know." Adela nodded, smiling weakly in acceptance. "Eric tried to talk to me about them, hinted with more than a little worry at some of the things that have come to pass, but I wouldn't let him go into them yet. I was being selfish. I'm going to make up for that."

Billy arched a bushy eyebrow at her. "Have you accessed any files since awakin'?" His voice was hesitant, and the look on his face indicated that he already regretted the question.

"No," she replied, looking sheepishly to the ground. "I've been putting that off, too."

"I see." He dug into a pocket and pulled out a data stick, handing it to her. "When you're ready to start reading history, be sure to look at this."

Adela stared at it nervously, rolling it lightly between her fingertips. She wanted to ask what was on it, but didn't. Billy would not have given it to her if its contents were unimportant. "All right, I will," was all she said as she slipped the stick into a blouse pocket.

"You said a moment ago that you felt selfish," Billy said, changing the subject. "I've been wondering ever since I returned if *I'm* bein' selfish. I have my memories of the way things were, and somehow feel that it's the way things should always be. But if my own people have gone beyond all of it, if they have no more use for the old tales . . ."

She took his hand in hers, squeezing gently as they walked. "Maybe both our lives have been displaced in time," she said. "Yours by distance and a duty to the people of your new world; mine by some overwhelming dream that has literally stolen the years away from me."

They crested the top of a shallow rise, beyond which lay the main house. The horse snorted behind her, impatient to return to its stall and the meal of fresh hay and oats it knew would be waiting. She slipped the bridle and bit from its head and, patting it gently twice on the flank, allowed the well-trained animal to return to the stable on its own.

"I've chosen the life I've led," she went on, slinging the bridle and reins over one shoulder. "And despite what you and Eric may think, there's really very little I can do to change what the Empire has become. He's right: The manner in which the Hundred Worlds has evolved is completely natural and expected. I'm surprised it wasn't anticipated. But Billy . . ." She turned to him, studying the sadness that had remained in his eyes since he first spoke of the changes in his people. "There is no reason why you couldn't be a factor in helping your people to remember the old ways. Surely there are those among the Arunta who remember and honor the legends?"

"There are some," he admitted, shrugging. "But they're very few, and very old. I'm afraid they're looked upon as feeble old men hangin' on to the ancient habits and customs. The Dreamtime is still within them, but I'm afraid it'll be forgotten once they're gone. The younger leaders are all too caught up with what's happened to bring them prosperity, more than they are to what the old ones think important."

They had reached the front steps to the estate, and Adela paused, taking a seat halfway up the ornate stairway. A face appeared momentarily at the curtains covering the tall, narrow windows on either side of the massive oaken doors. Adela recognized the round-faced man as Fleming, the house Master, and although he had respected her privacy by not running excitedly to greet them at their approach, she knew that even now he would be hurrying to inform Eric that she and Billy had returned.

She set the bit and bridle beside her and continued, "But you have enjoyed the benefits of technology, and have shared in the same prosperity. You've been an officer in the Imperial fleet, even serving as my son's first officer aboard the flagship he commanded before becoming Emperor. You traveled twenty light-years to help me put down a rebellion on Pallatin at the beginning of this project. When Eric ascended, you turned back to the stars, settling on a frontier world and guiding its people to a new life there. You've done all these things, and you still hold tightly to your heritage. Your Song Lines are still strong within you; I feel it, Billy." She paused. "So what's different? Why can you grow and evolve with the Empire and still be a part of your past, while it seems the Arunta have not?"

"I dunno, really," he said, shrugging in genuine puzzlement. "Maybe it's because I never took the old ways so seriously that they became the guiding force in my life. Yeah, sure, the old ways were always important to me. They not only brought me closer to those I loved, but always gave me something to hang on to whenever I was in a new situation. They're legends, I know, like the tales of the Sky Heroes; but the messages and lessons they taught were always worthy ones. They've always been something familiar."

"The 'Sky Heroes,'" Adela mused. "You told me once that we were the Sky Heroes, come to save the Sun and preserve the Dreamtime. Do you remember?"

"Yeah." He chuckled nervously, guiltily. "Some of the older ones even thought I had risen to join them. Well, I've returned a hero, all right—but they're lookin' at me more like I'm some kind of 'commercial success.'" He nearly spat the words.

Adela reached out and placed her hand on his shoulder. He felt firm and solid beneath the thin fabric of his shirt. Despite the inevitable aging that occurs even with regular rejuvenation, the single touch told her that he was still strong and vibrant.

"Then do something about it," she said simply.

SIX
Running Away

Adela sank tiredly back into her chair, leaning her head on the cushioned backrest as she rubbed at her burning eyes.

"System, cancel display," she said, her voice croaking from the lateness of the hour. The image on the holoframe—in mid-playback of a lengthy report on the feeder star that would be used to "refuel" Earth's Sun—froze briefly and faded out, leaving a soft blue glow within the frame. The gentle radiance played over the dark wood and leather furnishings of the old study Eric had given her to review the numerous files he'd amassed for her.

"Would you like the current file restarted from the beginning?" The voice of the room system, usually soft and unobtrusive, seemed jarring and annoying after so many hours.

"No."

The system on standby, Adela enjoyed the relaxing stillness. She tucked her legs up underneath her in the warm embrace of the leather-clad wing chair and, with her eyes closed, listened to the ever-present tiny sounds the centuries-old estate made in the loneliest part of the night as she let her thoughts wander.

The Empire had changed even more than Eric had let on. The technological advances, exploration of new worlds, the extending of humanity to the farthest reaches of the stars—no wonder Eric felt that the "Empire of the Hundred Worlds" was an outdated concept.

Her project to save Earth's Sun, meanwhile, had proceeded apace, seemingly unaffected by the changes in the Empire other than the greater efficiency with which it progressed courtesy of the many technological breakthroughs. Indeed, when the final phase went into effect several months hence, the chances of a successful conclusion to her lifework would have increased a hundredfold.

But the changes!

She sat forward again and took the data stick Billy had given her from her blouse, then crossed wearily to the terminal on the antique cherry desk, slipping it into the input slot.

"System."

"Ma'am?" came the reply, followed by a confirming chirp that the system was ready.

"Please display contents of the data stick in this terminal."

The shade of blue changed subtlely, and an identifying logo appeared in the center of the holoframe. *Comm Number: 247729-AE32. Source: Mark-89. Subject: Jephthah Address.*

"So, this is Jephthah," Adela said softly, unaware she was speaking aloud. The name had appeared several times in the files she had already seen.

"File is ready for playback, Ma'am."

"Proceed."

The image faded in, revealing a neatly dressed man seated casually in what appeared to be an office or study. There was a terminal on the desk, as well as other work-related and personal items, but nothing that identified where this recording had been made.

Jephthah was—visually, at least—about Eric's apparent age, but from what she had learned from the earlier files she had viewed, there was little hard intelligence available on his actual birth date. The gently creased skin of his face was tanned, his dark hair sun-streaked. He had high cheekbones and an angular jaw that radiated an aura of strength and determination even as he smiled benignly into the pickup lens. His hands, well-muscled and somewhat weatherworn, were clasped on the desktop before him.

"I won't take up much of your time," he began in a voice that was tempered, even, and deep-throated in a way that simultaneously commanded both trust and attention. Knowing little else about him save the vague references in the other files, Adela felt drawn to him as he spoke, felt herself wanting to hear what he had to say.

"The danger I told you about last time," he continued, "the threat that had been made on the frontier world Vondurmoran, has been dealt with." The image cross-faded to a small city silhouetted against a deep orange sky, then zoomed in to one of the main structures in the center of the picture. "This is the Menke Laboratory, the main scientific center of the growing colony at Vondurmoran. As many of you already know, there has been a great deal of dispute here of late, culminating in a request for Imperial mediators to come to the planet in person, not via tachyon link, to settle a number of Sarpan claims to exploration rights of a number of uninhabitable planets in the Vondur system. However, the situation was resolved before the mediators arrived."

At that, the image changed again, this time displaying a tight shot of a crowd of two or three hundred people milling about the steps leading to the entrance to the facility. Natural sound at a low level played beneath the scene, and, judging from the voices she could hear and the movements of some of the individuals at the edge of the assemblage, the crowd was not a happy one. There were a number of Imperial soldiers lining the steps, keeping the crowd back on either side.

The high glass doors of the facility opened and four Imperial guards emerged, followed by a handful of people whose clothing indicated they were local government officials. Accompanying them were five shorter figures who moved clumsily, clad in bulky E-suits: Sarpan representatives. Their bubble helmets glistening in the orange sunlight, the five huddled close together, staying as far back from the crowd as they could. The moment they came into view the level of anger in the mob escalated, and Adela could even hear individual threats and shouts of anger from them as the guards struggled to keep them back.

Suddenly, one of the E-suited figures—apparently hit by something hurled from the crowd—jerked backward, falling to the steps hard enough to crack open his helmet. The downed alien clawed frantically at his fellows and, as the crowd pushed through the guards on either side of the steps, was lifted and carried by the soldiers and others who had exited the building with them. The scene degenerated into chaos then, and the last thing Adela saw as the image faded back to Jephthah was the ineffectually small group of humans struggling to get the aliens back into the safety of the research facility.

"The people of Vondurmoran have chosen their own direction," he said simply, still seated at the desk with hands clasped before him. "Before Imperial intervention arrived—indeed, without even the *need* for Imperial intervention—the people of Vondurmoran have asserted their influence over the outsiders to the Vondur system. Within hours of the event you have just seen, every Sarpan ship at Vondur departed." Jephthah leaned back in his chair and gazed sincerely from the image. Just the hint of a smile appeared on his face.

"Take a lesson from those at Vondurmoran. There is no need for you, for any of us, to accept a nonhuman threat in our lives."

The holoframe image disappeared, and was replaced with the

identifying logo again. The date of this recording showed it to be about six weeks old.

Adela sat in stunned silence and stared at the holoframe, her eyes unblinking as it returned to its plain blue standby mode.

A throat cleared behind her, the deep timbre telling her that Eric had come into the room sometime during the playback.

"System," he said delicately. "Cancel playback."

She felt a hand on her shoulder, and knew without looking that her son was standing beside the chair.

"Were they all killed?" Adela was shocked to hear the trembling in her voice.

"None of the Sarpan you just saw, as far as we know, died in the riot. The one attacked was returned to his ship in a state of shock. However, the chief administrator of the Menke Lab was killed, as was one of the Imperial guards." Eric paused, kneeling at the side of the chair, and Adela could see that he had obviously been sleeping. His hair was mussed, and he wore only a loose-fitting robe drawn over his nightclothes. His feet were bare.

"How much must the people of Vondurmoran hate the Sarpan?" she asked rhetorically. "How did this happen?"

Taking the chair next to hers, Eric sighed heavily and rubbed at his face, and she could hear the scratching sound his hand made against his unshaved skin.

"It's not just Vondurmoran, Mother. Anti-Sarpan sentiment, although not as vehement as that you just saw, is everywhere. And this man is responsible."

"But how!"

He pursed his lips and shook his head almost imperceptibly. "He's recognized the need for unity in the Empire, and he seeks unification through fear and hatred. He's played on the natural distrust that has always existed for the aliens, feeding it at every opportunity, using anything—or anyone—he can to make the sentiment against them grow."

"What are you talking about?" she demanded. "What do you mean, 'anyone'?"

Eric looked at Adela, his eyes meeting hers for the first time since he had entered the study.

"He's getting people to hate you, too."

What Eric told her had hurt, deeply and nearly to the depths of her soul. He had made no attempt to soften what he had to tell her, but the love behind his words made the disconcerting picture he presented seem somehow easier to take.

But once she saw for herself . . .

Adela tried to contact Billy numerous times in the busy weeks that followed, but with little success, to tell him that she now understood what it was he had left unsaid that day they had walked across the estate grounds. She spoke to him only once, shortly after he'd left Woodsgate, and he told her that he was resigning his governorship of Darson to devote himself to his people. She also found out that he was making plans to take a "walkabout." She had read of the Aboriginal tradition, and Billy had tried once before, years earlier, to explain the deeply personal significance it held for the Aborigine, but she still had trouble grasping just how important it was to her friend. In her brief talk with him, however, two things became clear.

First, the experience would somehow serve as a cleansing for him, removing the burden of guilt from his shoulders. It didn't matter that nothing that had come to pass for his people had been his doing, directly or indirectly. He still felt that part of the blame was his for "allowing" his people to lose their way and their traditions. Billy felt it so strongly, in fact, that there was little she had been able to do to convince him otherwise.

"Don't you see?" he had asked. "I came back feelin' that this is something I could've prevented. I know now that's not true. But I'm still an outsider, even though no one here thinks of me that way; *I* think of me that way. It's a necessary step for my own personal growth. Not to do it would be to deny who I am, and who I can be. It will allow me to . . . become 'me' again." He was so excited by his upcoming journey and the effect he anticipated it would have on him that she found herself feeling differently about her own voyage. Perhaps her own trip to survey the work of the project—and, in the process, rediscover a world she barely recognized—was her own "walkabout." For this valuable insight into herself, she was grateful to her friend.

The second was more important: Billy looked happy again. Every reminder of the disturbing discussion they'd had at Woodsgate had disappeared, and in its place was a peaceful, untroubled man who stood taller and prouder than just a few weeks earlier. He still carried whatever blame he'd placed on himself for the direction his people had taken, but he seemed to have his life in perspective again. It was this very trait that had endeared the man to her so many years earlier on Pallatin, the rebellious frontier world, and had given her strength to complete the difficult mission. As the time had come near for her to enter cryosleep, she had remembered Billy's ability to place himself and

his world and surroundings into perspective, and had gone to
sleep less troubled than she might have otherwise. To see that
Billy had regained his greatest strength told her that he would be
fine.

And, just perhaps, if she could learn from his example, so
would she reacquaint herself with humanity and learn to adjust
to this new Empire. As she traveled, she kept trying to reach him,
but each time she was told that he had not yet returned, and that
contacting him in the outback was impossible. Each time she
inquired as to when he would return she was always told cheerfully and matter-of-factly that no one ever knows when a walkabout ends.

Billy had tried to reach her once, at her research facility on
Luna about a month after her awakening, but had missed her,
literally, by only a few minutes. Further attempts to contact him
failed, more often than not because of the hectic itinerary Adela
had imposed upon herself.

Eric had agreed with her decision to see this new Empire for
herself, but made her promise to limit her trip to two months, and
she agreed to return to Woodsgate immediately afterward.

The trip was evenly divided between "sightseeing" and official
stops to check the progress of the project. As was her nature,
however, with every research facility she toured, with every completed segment of the project she observed and approved, Adela
grew excited again about the project, unintentionally allowing
her initial concerns for the changes that had taken place—and the
resentment toward the Sarpan—to fade into the background.

But the reminders were always there.

Of the four sunstations on Mercury, the facility located in Chao
Meng-fu crater at the south pole was the largest and most complex on the small planet. Unlike the stations built in craters
spaced equidistant around the equator at Al-Jahiz, Theophanes
and Robertson, the Chao Meng-fu sunstation was a completely
self-sustaining research station with a full lab and monitoring
equipment, real-time communication links to Earth-Luna as well
as the orbital platforms nearing completion around the Sun, even
a local heavy-launch facility. The station enjoyed a permanent
population of twenty people, evenly divided between Academy
scientists and Imperial military personnel, but had extensive ac-
commodations that could host three times that number comfortably. As always, Adela doubted the need for a military presence,
but Dr. Rice, Mercury director-in-residence, was quick to point

out that despite their military uniforms and training, the soldiers served more in a technical capacity than a military one.

"I'm afraid we never came up with anything more exotic than 'Main Control,' " Rice was saying as he led her through the facility. Each turn he made, through every hallway and corridor they walked, was with a practiced ease that required barely a glance at the well-marked directional signs and arrows located every few dozen meters. Adela was grateful for the signs: If she somehow became separated from Rice, she wouldn't make a fool of herself finding her way back to the personnel dome.

"This whole place is like a labyrinth, with nine separate buildings and domes," he went on, "all connected by ground-level corridors; one room is pretty much like another here, except for size and function. All but Main Control, that is. It functions as the heart of the sunstation. . . . Well, actually it's the heart of the entire project. From here we control the three monitor stations on the equator, as well as all activities in solar orbit." They rounded yet another corner and Rice paused in front of a doorway, momentarily studying the terminal screen next to it. "That'll become even more important when the time comes to actually start it all up."

"I don't know," she replied. " 'Main Control' seems to fit nicely. That's what its function seems to be, after all."

Rice shrugged with a hint of embarrassment and reached for the opening plate. "When I designed the station fifty years ago, I had in mind to honor you by naming the facility after you. But once the station was built and I assumed authority here ten years ago, I, uh, just got busy doing things. 'Main Control' was what stuck."

"I *am* honored, Temple," Adela said warmly. "Putting the project first is much more important than naming things; it's what I would have done."

Rice chuckled. "Thanks. Oh—and speaking of names, we haven't gone in much for formality around here. Call me 'Tem.' It's a nickname I got used to about a hundred years ago. No one's called me Temple since—well, since I can remember."

It was good to see Templeton Rice again. The astrophysicist had been present at the initial test of the wormhole feeder system that was at the very heart of the project to save Earth's Sun, and Adela had worked very closely with him for several years before going into cryosleep. Like everyone else she encountered from her past, he looked older. But Rice had been quite young when she knew him before—when she met him following the test, he had been in cryosleep only twice: once on the way to the test site eight light-years from Earth-Luna, and again on the way back. Adela shook her head in frustration at trying to sort out apparent ages from chronological age, and promised herself for the hundredth time since her awakening to try to stop mentally tallying the passage of time in people's lives.

"Here we are."

They entered a small chamber, obviously an anteroom to Main Control. The tiny room appeared to be used mainly as a lounge area. There were soft chairs here, a video entertainment unit, and two small tables surrounded by stools. A galley kitchen had been set up on a low countertop in one corner, and the smell of fresh coffee filled the room. The rich aroma was delightful, but the lure of seeing Main Control was stronger.

Even as they walked through the doorway, Adela could see that Main Control was a beehive of activity, most of it centered around an equipment console that had been turned over on the floor to her right. Several people—some in lab coats, others in clothing with a distinct military aspect to it—had gathered around the unit; one had even crawled halfway into the open bottom and was cursing softly as he fidgeted with something on the inside. But once she was in the room her eyes were immediately drawn to the panorama at her left, and what she saw there made her immediately forget what was happening at the console.

Occupying the entire far wall, and arcing halfway up the ceiling nearly over her head, was a curved holoframe that displayed perhaps the most awesome vista of space Adela had ever seen. In the center hung the Sun, bold and beautiful, the image dampened to naked-eye brightness. A low range of hills on the horizon cast long, somber shadows and gave the image the appearance that she was standing—alone and unprotected—on the Mercurian surface. She knew better, of course: located a mere two degrees' latitude from the planet's south pole, the sunstation was too low below the rim of Chao Meng-fu to ever see anything but perpetual shadow. This image was obviously being taken from atop the tower located on the south pole itself.

She knew instinctively that this was a genuine, real-time image taken from above the shielding, even though what she was looking at now had obviously been enhanced. Numerous captions and notations seemingly floated in space at various points, and bright yellow circles gave the location of the orbitals, too small to be seen at this magnification.

But it was the roiling surface of the Sun that called out to her, as if trying to draw her into the very heart of Earth's daystar. It almost seemed that she could see the ever-burning flames of the star itself, moving gracefully in the same light-giving dance it had performed for countless millennia. Waving in incongruous silence, the wisps of flame seemed to call out to her, beckoning for her to come dance with them for all eternity.

This is what I am here for, she thought, and suddenly realized that she had been holding her breath as she stared openmouthed at the magnificent display of omnipotent power. She let her breath out slowly, deliberately, and tried to imagine this star as a living being. And as she did, she felt an incredible sadness flow over her to think that this mighty presence would—without human intervention—die.

I am not going to let you die, she said silently, purposefully, and felt a smile come to her lips. *I am going to save you.*

"It's something when you see it like this for the first time, isn't it?"

The new voice pulled her back, too quickly, from her reverie. Turning, she found a tall, balding man standing before her, Rice at his side. She recognized the grinning man as one of the lab-coated men she'd seen at the equipment console when she first entered Main Control.

"This is Dr. Sander Boscawen," Rice said by way of introduction. "As my feeder insertion specialist, he's in charge of the solar orbitals. That's his console they were fussing with a few moments ago." He nodded toward the other side of the room, where Adela now could see that the console had been righted. Five people stood near it, their attention focused in her direction.

"New configurations," he said in an annoyed tone as he grasped her hand and shook it vigorously. "They're always reconfiguring the thing. Wish they'd just leave it alone."

Adela got the impression that the scientist was truly irritated by whatever work was being performed on the console, but as he spoke all traces of aggravation melted quickly away. "Dr. Montgarde, it is such a pleasure to meet you! I've followed your work all my life. It was your original theories on the project to save Earth's Sun, in fact, that first drew me to astrophysics. If you have a few moments, Doctor, I'd like to show you what we've been able to do with the . . ." Boscawen's voice trailed off, his excited mood changing from sheer delight to embarrassed disappointment as he looked to his console. "Uh . . . maybe later when we have the reconfiguration done."

"It's all right," Adela assured him. "I'll be here for several days. I've been going over all the additional work that's been done on my original data, and must admit I'm impressed with what you've been able to do here, 'reconfigurations' aside."

Rice laughed. "It's a constant battle between us and the solar orbitals. Every time they take new header readings for the feeder insertion, we reconfigure the console manually. It's easier than rechipping."

"Rechipping?" Adela asked.

"Sorry, it's a slang term for reprogramming console memory."

Adela let her breath out in frustration. "Sometimes, Temple, er, Tem, I think I've awakened into an entirely new language. Hardly a day goes by that I don't feel I'm being left unintentionally out of one conversation or another. So what's this 'rechipping'? Is it a problem that I could be working on?"

"Oh, no; nothing like that. We can do it easily enough, and do so from time to time as a matter of regular maintenance with all the new data we're constantly getting from Luna. But on a busy day like today the orbitals might take a dozen or more header readings and request a new configuration every time. It's not exactly prescribed procedure, but we've found it's easier to have some extra bodies on duty, flip it over and just to do it manually." Rice lowered his voice to a near whisper, then added, "And *that's* where having the military around comes in handy."

One of the others had moved away from the console and joined their discussion. The woman was tall, almost statuesque, with a figure that was hard to disguise even in the all-purpose lab coats nearly everyone here wore.

"What else would we need the Imperial guards for?" she asked jokingly as she approached, extending her hand. Like Boscawen, she almost literally beamed as she spoke. When the woman shook Adela's hand, she seemed barely able to contain her excitement. Adela felt a twinge of self-consciousness at the unabashed admiration she'd received, at least from the scientific community, nearly everywhere she went.

"Hi. I'm Juliette Le Châtelier," the woman went on, "Tem's subdirector. Call me Julie. It's so good to finally get to meet you."

"And you," Adela replied, finally managing to pry her hand loose from the admiring scientist's. "I've been studying your work here ever since I came—what's the accepted expression now?—'out of the tank'? I'm very impressed with what you've all accomplished here." She paused in thought a moment, then asked, "I'm trying to place your accent. And your name—I think I once knew a Le Châtelier family a long time ago."

"You honor me, Doctor." Le Châtelier grinned, and nodded delightedly. "I'm from Gris. It was my family you knew."

Adela's mouth dropped. "You . . . you're from home?" Le Châtelier's head bobbed. "I've called up every file I could find on home, but you're the first Grisian I've encountered since waking up. *Gris me manque beaucoup! Quelles nouvelles de patrie?*"

"*Tout il fait beau patrie soi. Gris il* . . . ah, I'm sorry . . . *Je regrette d'avoir à dire que, Français* . . ." Le Châtelier shook her head and spoke once more in English. "I'm afraid we don't speak French on Gris much anymore. My grandmother taught me years ago; I'm surprised I even remembered how to say that much. . . ."

"It's all right," Adela said, raising a hand to stop her. "I understand completely. If there's anything I've learned in the last month it's that tachyon communications and wormhole travel have a tendency to homogenize things, especially languages. I'm sorry if I embarrassed you, but please, I'm dying to learn more about home than what's in the recordings I've viewed." The two began chattering ecstatically—Adela asking question after question, Le Châtelier telling Adela of how her homeworld had grown from the harsh mining planet of her birth to the thriving world it was now.

"Maybe you two would like the rest of us to leave," Rice asked facetiously after several minutes. "We could all come back later . . .?"

"I'm sorry, Tem," Adela replied. "You're right, we'll save it for later. Please, show me around."

Rice did just that, describing and demonstrating each system and subsystem in Main Control, much to Adela's delight. Although her team had brought her completely up to speed on every step that had been achieved over the last two centuries on the project to save Earth's Sun, this was her first chance to have some literal hands-on contact with one of the most important aspects of the actual hardware that would get the job done. Her satisfaction regarding the implementation of her work turned sour, however, as they neared the end of Rice's impromptu guided tour of Main Control.

The three Imperial guards who had been helping Boscawen reconfigure the troublesome console earlier had not left and had, instead, remained quietly to one side of the room. "This is Lieutenant Jerzy Koll," Rice said, introducing one of them, a tall, muscular young man who looked barely old enough to be in the Imperial service. The man was partially out of uniform, reflecting the casual atmosphere of the station, and wore only a tank-top undershirt. "He's in charge of the military detachment assigned to Chao Meng-fu."

"It's good to meet you." Adela had begun to offer her hand, but reconsidered when the young man abruptly drew himself to attention, hands riveted at his side, and nodded curtly. The other two stood straighter as well, although they seemed considerably less respectful in their manner than Lieutenant Koll had been. It was clear that the relationship between the military and the eager scientists here was a strained one at best.

"Ma'am" was all the man offered. His eyes didn't meet hers. The others, too, merely stared across the room.

There was a sudden, awkward silence that lasted several moments. Even the other scientists who had, until now, been actively chattering among themselves, discussing what the esteemed Dr. Montgarde had said about their work, turned and watched what was happening. There was something more going on here, Adela knew, than simple discomfort between the military and scientific arms of the Empire. In fact, she almost got the feeling that more than a few people in the room had expected this.

"I think that'll be all for now, Jerzy," Rice said uncomfortably, but with authority. "The orbitals have pretty much finished up for today, I think. And we can put off any further reconfigurations on the console until tomorrow. You and your men are dismissed."

The soldier hesitated for a moment, then reached for the shirt he'd tossed casually over the back of a chair. Slinging it over his shoulder, he nodded weakly at Rice, and left. The other two followed wordlessly.

Julie Le Châtelier yawned audibly and stretched her arms as far in front of her as she could. Adela heard a tiny cracking sound that must have been her elbows.

"Well, I've had it for tonight," she said good-naturedly. "You two can talk all night if you want to, but I'm turning in."

Adela and Rice wished her good night, and she left Main Control. As she left, Adela thought she heard another stifled yawn from the anteroom before the door slid shut.

The room was empty now but for the two of them, the lights had been dimmed and the holographic image of the Sun—also at a subdued level of brightness—was the only illumination. No other light was needed. There was another disconcerting moment of silence, similar to the one earlier in the day when she had first met the Imperial guards; but this time, the silence was one between friends, the kind where neither knew what to say first.

"Do they hate her, too?" Adela finally offered, her voice tinged with bitterness. "The soldiers? And how about the others working with you here, the ones who wouldn't even be here today to meet me? What did they do, hide out in their rooms to avoid being around all of us? Or was it just *me* they were avoiding?"

Rice shook his head. "No, they don't hate her. But they distrust her, just as they distrust me or anyone else who looks to the aliens as anything but a threat to humanity." He stared away for several quiet moments, his eyes on the beautiful solar vista lighting the room. After a minute, he turned from the Sun and looked dejectedly to the floor.

"Things are happening here that are not good, Adela," he said in a disappointed, if not fearful, voice. "Relationships are strained and there've been a few confrontations. As you saw earlier, some people aren't even talking to each other except when necessary, and our efficiency is beginning to suffer as a result. Even simple tasks—ordinary, everyday things like . . . like rechipping the consoles are becoming difficult. If I don't do something to correct this situation soon, I'm afraid our productivity will be compromised to the point where the project itself may be affected." He paused, looking quickly at her. "I'm sorry. I don't mean to indicate there's any real danger to our work here, but I'm concerned that the completion date might need to be pushed back if we can't put these differences aside."

"I see. What are you thinking of doing?"

Rice let his breath out in a long, slow puff. "I'm thinking of reassigning some of the more resentful research personnel to Luna or to one of the other facilities, and bringing in some fresh faces. The Imperial guards, too. Oh, I suppose Koll's all right, even though he's a bit on the moody side."

"Moody's a good word for him." Adela chuckled.

"Yeah," Rice said, returning her smile. "I suppose so. Anyway, I'm concerned that if I don't break up the mix of personalities here soon, somebody's going to snap."

"More of Jephthah's legacy, I suppose." Adela shook her head at the thought of this mysterious man whose sole purpose seemed to be to spread fear. "I see his handiwork everywhere. I wonder if I'm to blame for that as well?"

He sighed heavily, the sound echoing plaintively in the empty room. "Look, they don't hate you. Not really. It's just that . . ." His voice trailed off.

"It's just that they blame me for every bad thing that's ever happened between humans and Sarpan, that's all."

Rice shrugged in resignation. "Yeah. I guess so." He stood, stretched. "If it's any consolation, they don't feel all that much better about me. I'm the one responsible for bringing an alien corpser to the sunstation, after all."

Adela sat straighter in her chair. "Oidar? He's here?"

"We were transported here together. I came out of the tank as soon as I arrived; his tank has been in our makeshift cryosleep chamber for nearly a decade. I'm sorry, I thought you knew."

"No, I didn't. Nor did I know the full extent to which this insane xenophobia has swept across humanity. There was always a sense of fear toward the Sarpan—I know, I remember it from the very beginning of this project. And since I awoke I've gotten a sense that it's worsened, but is it really so pervasive that it's begun to disrupt everyone's lives?"

Rice didn't say anything for a moment, but instead leaned back in his chair, folding his arms behind his head, and watched the silently roiling surface of the sun in the holoframe.

"You've heard of Lord Jephthah, I know, but has anyone told you of the extent to which his paranoia has spread throughout the Hundred Worlds?"

Adela remained silent, waiting for Rice to answer his own question. He sighed deeply, as if dreading what he was about to say.

"Adela, Emperor Eric has been a wonderful leader. Carrying on where Javas left off, he has brought generations of peace and prosperity to the Hundred Worlds. But there is one thing he could not achieve, any more than his father before him. He could not get the member worlds to trust one another. With travel between worlds lasting many years, it was natural to become suspicious of a 'neighbor' whose habits, customs, traditions—even slang and clothing styles—could change drastically between visits. Your son couldn't conquer this.

"But with instant communication and wormhole travel, the Empire became suddenly smaller; its people became closer and more intimate."

"Eric should have seen it, should have acted on it."

"No!" Rice's voice came out louder than he must have wanted, for he quickly lowered his tone. "No," he repeated, "he should not have. And it's to his credit, really, that he did not."

"I'm not sure I understand."

"Your son has the best interests of his people at heart at all times, that's why he has made himself available to travel to the farthest reaches of the Empire to help the member worlds. But it took someone with selfish interests to see the opportunity a more closely knit humanity represented. Eric is not a selfish leader." Rice shook his head sadly at the irony. "Jephthah, on the other hand, saw the opportunity afforded by a humanity suddenly presented with a common heritage, and united the paranoid among them to a common cause: an unreasoned, blind hatred for the Sarpan."

"But they have never meant harm to us!"

"I know that; most everyone does, in fact. But when you consider that humanity has spread so far beyond a mere hundred worlds, even a small percentage of humanity allied to just a single cause makes for powerful numbers, especially when they're vocal."

Adela considered a moment, then: "If I thought that only a small segment of society followed this man, I wouldn't be so concerned; but just who *does* follow him?" Adela stood and paced tensely, the image of the Sun casting jerky shadows across the room. "I see that a third of your staff doesn't even want to meet me; several others managed to find 'something else to do' when I came in here just to avoid alienating those who do hate me. The Imperial guards stationed here act as though I'm diseased."

"I can't make excuses for how they feel about you," he admitted.

Adela stopped, and turned to face him. His features glowed an eerie yellow-orange in the light from the holoframe. "And if that's what they think of *me* after all these years of this Jephthah's stupid propaganda," she asked softly, "what will Oidar find when he wakes up?"

SEVEN
Jephthah

Adela was not looking forward to the next few hours, yet she knew the threats facing her son had to be discussed. Eric—and Billy, before he returned to Kalumburu—had been totally open with her about everything that had passed during her two centuries of slumber. Eric had answered her every question, obtained whatever information she requested, and had even gone so far as to put no fewer than a score of Imperial aides at her disposal, their sole duty to bring her as completely up to date as possible.

There were two things, however, that Eric appeared reluctant to discuss as fully as Adela would have wished. No—"reluctant" wasn't the right word, but it seemed to her that he was holding back something. Holding back for fear of—what? Hurting her? Or hurting himself?

One was the subject they would discuss this afternoon: Jephthah, the only truly organized opposition leader to many of Eric's goals. The other was personal, much more personal. . . .

"The drawing room is right this way, Dr. Montgarde."

Fleming, his round bulk jiggling as he waddled animatedly down the cavernous hallway, was genuinely delighted to have a visitor to fawn over, especially one so highly regarded as the Emperor's mother. He conversed over his shoulder, seemingly paying little attention to where he was walking, and each word carried with it an excited tone that threatened to break into a giggle whenever he spoke—which, Adela had quickly come to realize, was often.

"Please watch your step. These carpets are very old—been in the family for centuries, really—and each is commissioned by a House of the Masters of Woodsgate. Here, do you see?" He stopped for a moment, actually holding still for the first time in what seemed days, and indicated the enormous carpet beneath his feet. "This is from House McLaren, the Master who taught your son. And over here . . ." He waddled hurriedly to a side hallway, standing aside so she might better view the carpet there. ". . . is the gift of Montlaven, Master to Javas. The carpet from my own House, of course, will not be completed until I have ended my service to the Emperor."

Adela followed him as he resumed moving down the long hallway, nodding politely whenever Master Fleming turned to point out with pride some other House feature—about which he knew absolutely everything.

"Tell me about my grandchildren," she said abruptly during one of the rare moments he actually paused for breath. "As their Master, you were nearly a surrogate parent to them."

Fleming halted in his tracks, the skin of his puffy cheeks quivering at the sudden stop. As he faced her, he did not seem surprised at the question, but rather appeared unsure as to exactly what it was Adela wanted to know. Then, too, he might have been self-conscious about what to say; maybe he just didn't like talking about himself, and thought he was being asked to account for his teaching methods. He clasped his hands behind him and resumed walking—at a more measured pace, this time—down the hallway. "I, ah, understood that the Emperor had given you a good deal of information about his children. I'm not certain what more I can . . ."

"I'm sorry," she said quickly, sparing him further embarrassment. "I didn't mean to put you on the spot. You're right, of course; I've seen numerous recordings of their early years." She smiled warmly at him, then added, "You have a nice touch for capturing just the right moments and expressions, by the way."

"Well . . ." A tentative hint of a grin returned, and his initial show of discomfort at the subject eased somewhat. "I wasn't responsible for *all* the recordings, of course. There are other members of the staff who can take credit for many of them. Ah, here we are."

They arrived at the drawing room, but Eric was not yet there. As Fleming busied himself with the draperies, allowing the late-afternoon sunshine to come streaming into the room, Adela went to the center window on the side of the room opposite the door and gazed out over the grounds. Eric was there, talking to two members of the House staff. Stable personnel, judging from their attire. He looked around and saw her there, then glanced at the timepiece on his wrist. He waved to indicate he was on his way, then turned to quickly wrap up his business with the others.

He seems so comfortable in his role, she reflected. *And it's no mystery why he still has so many who follow him.* There were many subtle mannerisms he had that made those with whom he had to deal feel more at ease. She liked the way he wore a timepiece, for example, even though his integrator could give him the precise time more quickly than he could even raise his arm to look. There was an air about him that was much less officious than Javas, and certainly less so than Emperor Nicholas. She remembered how Javas' casual style had grated on some of his advisors and much of the Imperial Court. A smile came to her lips as she thought of Bomeer, the stuffy, by-the-book Academician who was, at one time, the greatest critic of her project. Bomeer had fought her at every turn in those early days, and was quick to point out the project's every weakness. But once Bomeer had finally accepted the validity of her ideas, it was Javas' ruling style that truly won him over.

From what she had managed to learn in these last weeks about the Empire of the Hundred Worlds, she was more convinced than ever that Eric's rule—characterized by the strength of his convictions and the one-to-one honesty he had certainly acquired from Javas—was stronger than it would have been if he had attempted to rule with the inflexibility that was common when the Imperial Court had first been moved to Luna.

A throat cleared behind her, pulling her out of her musings.

"I'm sure the Emperor will be along directly, Doctor. Is there anything I can do for you in the meantime?"

Adela crossed to the nearest seating group and sat in a chair facing the fireplace. No fire had burned there in some time, she could tell: There wasn't a speck of dust or ash on the cast-iron log rack, and the acrid but pleasantly comforting scent of smoke common to fireplaces simply wasn't there. The fireplace was also a holoframe, she noticed, and she assumed that the only glow that had emanated from it in recent months had been a cold, emotionless holographic projection. Somehow, it saddened her; and she made a promise to herself that she would ask one of the House staff to build a fire there the next cool evening.

"Sit with me a moment, Master Fleming." He hesitated, and started to protest. "No, please; it's all right." She waited until he sat, barely resting his considerable bulk on the very edge of the plush leather-covered chair two places down from her own. "Tell me about my grandchildren. The recorded journals are very complete, and told me everything I'd want to know about their childhoods and their lives today. Please believe me when I say that you've done an outstanding job in their upbringing, and have every right to take pride in who and what they've become." She waved a hand in the direction of the hallway, and added tenderly, "The carpet from House Fleming will occupy a place of honor in Woodsgate." She leaned forward, resting her elbows on her knees. "Eric talks lovingly of his children—what father wouldn't? But there's something missing, I can sense it whenever he speaks to me of them. Tell me what isn't in the journals."

He hesitated once more and seemed to wrestle with himself over just what to do. Looking deeply into his troubled eyes, she confirmed that she had been right—there was something else. Further, it was plain that whatever it was concerned him tremendously. He took a deep breath and let it out slowly, noisily, and seemed to come to a decision. Fleming sat back in the chair, allowing himself to be completely at ease in her presence for the first time since she had met him weeks earlier, just after awaking from cryosleep.

"Your grandchildren are the Emperor's greatest joy, and he takes great pride in the fact that all three are successful in their chosen endeavors. Lewis has turned into a fine, strong leader in his own right. As commander in chief of the Imperial military forces, he has the respect of every man and woman in the fleet. Eric is especially pleased that Brendan, meanwhile, has followed in your footsteps." Fleming chuckled. "I understand that Academician Bomeer himself, shortly before his death, recommended that Brendan head the Imperial Academy of Sciences. With your grandson as its driving force, I'm sure you wouldn't recognize the Academy as the same obstinate body you knew at the beginning of your project."

"I know," Adela agreed. "I've made looking over his work among my top priorities since I awoke, and you're right, the Academy has returned to its long-lost origins. I doubt that it will ever find itself stagnating again. I'm so looking forward to meeting Brendan and comparing notes on the project."

"Ah, but it is Cathay who is his favorite. She has been his best ally in reaching out to the emerging worlds of the Empire, and in many ways has been his greatest asset in keeping the Worlds from falling into anarchy. However, I personally think it is her resemblance to you, dear Lady, that touches his heart so." Fleming smiled at the thought, but behind his eyes lay something else.

"They are his greatest joy," he repeated. "But they are also, in a way, his greatest disappointment." His face saddened then, and Adela could see that the man shared her son's regret in a way that she—who had never raised a child—could never know. "For

none of them wishes to follow in his place." Fleming was about
to go on, but became suddenly aware that no more needed to be
said.

Adela nodded, understanding now Eric's double regret at what
had become of the Empire. Not only was he powerless to stop its
evolution, but he undoubtedly realized that his efforts at promot-
ing the importance of an Imperial philosophy to the Hundred
Worlds was destined to be futile. Even his children—who, in their
chosen endeavors, supported and protected the citizens of the
Empire—no longer believed in a royal succession.

From the hallway came the sound of a heavy door closing far
down the corridor, followed by approaching boot steps. Fleming
was immediately on his feet.

"Master Fleming," Adela said sincerely, extending her hand,
"thank you for your candor. I feel I've learned more about my
son and his world in these last few minutes than in all the traveling I've done or all the hundreds of recordings I've viewed these
past weeks."

The Master returned her smile warmly, and Adela knew that
a silent bond of trust had just been forged between them.

The fireplace was gone, masked by the holoframe, and with it had
disappeared the coziness that had made the sitting room feel
warm and inviting despite the lack of burning logs. Nothing but
the Imperial crest was displayed in the frame now, and Adela
wished Eric would give a silent integrator command to wipe it
out, too.

"How can you say he's not a threat?" she demanded, unsure if
the feelings rising within her were rooted more in anger, or in
fear. "After only a few weeks of exposure to him and this, this
. . . *hatred* he's spewing, even I can feel the danger he presents."

Eric turned slowly in the chair, and when he spoke, his words
carried with them an accusation that his tone did not. "Are you
sure, Mother, that you're not thinking of the implied threat Jephthah presents to your project?"

Adela stopped short, and found herself unable to protest his
obvious, if blunt, point. Instead, she leaned back heavily in the
chair and waited for him to go on.

Eric rose. "I'm sorry, Mother," he said, staring out the window. The sky was darkening, the red glow of the just-set Sun still
hanging over the hills to the west. "I know how you feel about the
project, but believe me when I tell you that there is very little that
could interfere with its conclusion. In spite of what the Empire

has become, there is no one who doubts now that the center of humanity is located here, on Earth. Ironically, his rantings about the sanctity of the human race have strengthened support for saving the Sun. After all, if humanity is to reign supreme, how can the birthworld of humanity *not* be saved?"

"Jephthah." She said the name like a curse. "It's an old Hebrew name that means 'the opposer.' I researched it."

"I know what it means, and it fits him. He opposes everything that has to do with an alliance with the Sarpan, but he seems genuinely disinterested in what has led to our friendship with them."

"What's left of our friendship, you mean."

Eric's lips drew into a tight line. "Point taken."

"In any event, if your private intelligence is correct—and it seems to back up everything that's been on the public nets—then he is amassing a tremendous following, with more accepting his rantings as truth every time he speaks."

Eric was about to reply, but turned instead to the holoframe a few seconds before it came to life. A young woman in uniform— one of the few trappings of formal protocol Adela had seen in Eric's presence since she awoke—nodded politely from the frame. A designation in a lower corner of the image indicated that the report was coming from the Imperial communication center on Luna.

"Sire, we've been receiving a countdown for several minutes now. The transmission from Mark-89 should begin in thirty seconds."

Eric nodded a silent thanks and the screen blanked. The Imperial crest was gone.

" 'Mark-89,' " Adela said in soft resignation. "You don't even know where he is, Eric. If he's so harmless, why does he need to hide himself?"

Mark-89 was the designation given to the direction from which Jephthah's transmissions always seemed to originate. Years of tracing the signal, however, had turned up little more than a complex system of relays. Whenever Imperial forces disabled one link in an attempt to follow it to its origin, the transmissions always rerouted to another. But each time, the apparent direction was the same: the direction of the Sarpan Realm. That little touch of irony—that Jephthah would purposely go to such lengths to call attention to the aliens in such a manner—unnerved Adela the most. It made it seem that he considered what he was doing to be some convoluted game.

As the image in the holoframe coalesced, Adela saw that the transmission was coming from an idyllic outdoor setting on a green world that could have been any one of many score of Imperial planets, Earth included. There were several trees dotting the landscape, but identifying the common species would give no more clue to where this was coming from than did the direction of the relayed transmission itself. A wooden fence came into view as the image panned to the side, then centered on the man himself, and as it did Adela was struck with the same thought she'd had the first time she saw a recording of one of his earlier talks. He looked and acted so untroubled, so completely at ease as he greeted his listeners with a smile and a silent nod.

Jephthah wore his trademark suit, neatly tailored in a style normally better matched to a social gathering; but his attire somehow didn't seem out of place as he leaned casually against a fence, his arm resting on one of the posts. The casual pose belied both his athleticism and actual size, but having seen him in the recordings of earlier transmissions, she knew he stood quite tall.

An excited giggling from somewhere outside the picture caught his attention, and as the image panned back and swept to his right, she saw that a group of children played happily on a climbing set just on the other side of the fence. There were maybe ten of them, their ages ranging from toddler to preteen, and whether they played breathlessly on the equipment or impatiently watched and waited their turn it was clear they were having the time of their lives. Jephthah chuckled happily at the playing children, then turned and looked out of the holographic screen.

"I love my children," he began simply in his deep, measured voice. "Just as I know you love yours. Even in an age when our own lifetimes can span centuries, we look to our children not only as a source of love and happiness for ourselves, but as the best hope for the future.

"But what kind of world will your children grow up on? Will it be a human world, with a common ancestry and biology; or will it be a world where the threat of outsiders will constantly hang over them?" He moved away from the frolicking children and walked slowly along the fence, his hands in his pockets as he spoke easily, giving the impression that he was merely talking to a neighbor about the mundane changes in the weather.

"I know what you're thinking," he said, glancing to the pickup lens with an almost apologetic look. He stopped and, with an ominous tone, said, " 'Here comes another lecture on the dangers of the evil Sarpan.' " He resumed strolling casually along the fence, waving a hand momentarily at the lens as if to dismiss the thought before returning it to his pocket. "Well, I'd be less than honest with you if I said I didn't think of them as a threat. And, by now, you know my reasons. But this time I'd like to talk to you about why I feel that now is an even more dangerous time for us than ever before. For our children." He stopped and turned to look meaningfully out from the image. "I would also like to make a personal appeal to someone who is with us for the first time, someone you all know even though many of you may not even have been born when she first began her great work. Her name, Adela de Montgarde, is heralded on many of the Worlds, and deservedly so."

Adela stiffened in her chair.

"Friends, we are approaching a time when the end of a very large, important project draws near. I'm sure you know I'm speaking of saving Earth's Sun, and saving the birthplace of all humanity. It is to you, Dr. Montgarde, that we all owe a debt of gratitude, for without your vision, humanity would surely have become something less than it was intended. Without your dream, the means to accomplish this formidable task would never have been discovered. Without your strength, your drive to succeed, we might surely be looking at a future where the children of a stagnated, lethargic humanity were overcome by stronger, opportunistic forces from outside the human worlds." The image slowly began to zoom in, centering on Jephthah's face. His features looked almost embarrassed, almost contrite. When he spoke, his voice was subtly different, with an edge to his words that hadn't been there before.

"However, while you have slept, a great many things have occurred that you could never have anticipated; changes have come about that I'm sure you never, ever desired. In your efforts to serve—and save—humanity itself, you were forced to make certain concessions regarding the aliens. Concessions that I'm sure were distasteful to you personally, but were nonetheless necessary to achieve a successful culmination for your lifelong dream.

"More than two hundred years ago you envisioned a plan to save Earth's Sun that was so ambitious, so difficult, that it required technology not possessed by humankind. I'm certain you would have done anything, anything to avoid relying on nonhuman technology to accomplish the worthiest of human goals, but I also know that your options were, sadly, limited. And so the Empire of the Hundred Worlds entered into an uneasy, but unavoidable, partnership with the Sarpan Realm. Then, after proving your theories, you went into cryosleep, unaware of how that partnership would be bastardized while you slept, and how we would allow gratitude to an alien servant to blind us to the true peril they represent."

Adela did not know when it had happened, but she suddenly noticed now that his voice—powerful and commanding no matter how he talked—had grown gradually more intense as he spoke, his mannerisms sharper, his choice of words more precise. The ease with which he had affected the change was uncanny, and it was evident that he was well practiced at working an audience.

"Look what has happened!"

He did not shout the words, but they were filled with so much passion that she felt her attention being drawn to him almost against her will.

"Look what your legacy has become," he went on, shaking his head. "Did you ever imagine that your dream would become a nightmare?"

Until now, Adela had been watching him with as much open-mindedness as she could spare, paying more attention to this first "live" talk more from a critical standpoint than any other. After all, his message was simple xenophobic preaching she had heard many times before and, as such, rarely changed. Having viewed and studied the many recordings Eric had ordered assembled for her she was well aware of how he manipulated his followers. She had even had the chance to observe, firsthand on Mercury and elsewhere, the reactions and sentiments of those who accepted his way of thinking. What she was not prepared for, however, was the emotional stirrings battling within herself now.

"You are honored, Dr. Montgarde, for delivering humanity from a most certain genetic extinction, but I fear that you will ultimately be remembered for *surrendering* humanity to inevitable slaughter by outsiders." He paused. "I'm sure you know by now that your dream led to an unwise alliance that has been directly responsible for the deaths of many humans since our two species crossed paths, the most blatant example being the slaughter of more than a thousand innocent human souls aboard the CTS jump ship *Sylvan* twenty years ago—"

"No!"

"—and I hope you realize the scope of the danger you created, when you sought only to help us all. I hope, too, that you realize what you must now do to correct this unforeseeable, unfortunate mistake."

Adela felt a sharp pain in her hands, and was startled to discover that she had unknowingly risen to her feet, her hands balled into tight fists at her sides. She lifted her shaking hands and stared at the bleeding cuts where her fingernails had dug into the soft flesh of her palms.

"This, then, is my appeal to you. . . ." He had walked back along the fence to where the playset was, but there were no children there now. Had there ever been any children there, or were they merely projections used as tools to reach into the hearts of those listening? As he continued, he extended his hand to her, his fingers curling in a display of desperation. "Redeem yourself, Dr. Montgarde, before it is too late.

"You are honored, you know that, and you have truly earned the honor you receive. There are billions who will accept what you would say to them now. Tell them to reject the Sarpan. Let them know it was a grave error to ever trust them. Once the Sun is linked to the feeder star that will sustain it, tell them we no longer need anything from the aliens. Tell them that with the birthplace of humanity safe for all time they must grow strong, and force the nonhumans back to the Realm before we join those from the *Sylvan,* as well as the countless others over the years."

He paused again, then, in the soft, deep voice, said, "The Empire of the Hundred Worlds is nearly gone, Dr. Montgarde. Its decline began the day the Empire embraced your dream as its own. What you see around you today is the result of your dream, but as much as I'm sure it saddens you, you can redeem yourself. Join your dream with mine, and the 'Hundred Worlds' will not be missed; because in its place will be born a new empire, with a newer, more fitting name. No longer will we be known by our numbers—a concept too long out of date anyway.

"With your help we can for all time be known by who we are: the 'Human Worlds.' "

The pickup lens pulled back slowly, and Jephthah leaned against the fence post once more in almost the exact same position as at the beginning of the transmission. He gazed solemnly around him at the peaceful countryside and the playset, the empty swings moving gently in the breeze. The picture faded to blue.

The room was quiet, the silence so complete that the faint creaking of centuries-old floorboards could be heard from the hallway.

Adela, still on her feet, stared dumbly at the empty blue screen, somehow expecting more. She knew that Imperial communication techs on Luna would already be attempting to trace the source of the signal, and that Eric expected no further visual communication on the screen. Indeed, any orders or requests Eric had for Luna regarding the just-ended transmission would have been sent through the integrator. But for some unknown reasons she expected more to come from the screen and waited wordlessly for—what? An apology? Absolution that everything that had happened was somehow, after all, not her doing? A tiny part of her mind even toyed with the thought that this had all been some horrible cryosleep-induced nightmare. Adela knew better.

"Mother, I—"

"No!" Adela snapped at her son. "No! I don't want to be responsible for this!"

Eric rose to his feet, but Adela jerked her arm away as he touched it softly. "Don't listen to him," he said. "He's desperate, because he knows that most people have enough common sense not to fall for his brand of rhetoric. He knows better than to think you'd actually support him, but he's hoping that his appeal— carefully wording it the way he did to indicate the ridiculous notion that you never wanted to turn to the Sarpan in the first place—might convince those who are sympathetic to him, but still undecided."

"No!" She turned on him sharply, her hands clenched into taut fists in front of her, and screamed, "Don't you see it, Eric?" Tears welled up in her eyes, blurring her vision, but she made no effort to wipe them away. "Don't you see?" she said again, collapsing into the chair. Her voice was a hoarse whisper this time. She shook her head and sobbed openly. "Don't . . . don't you see?"

Eric knelt at the chair's side and took her hand. She allowed him to touch her this time, but left her hand limp in his. He waited for her to continue.

"He's right about . . . one thing." A movement at the door caught her eye, and Adela turned to see Fleming standing silently in the doorway, his hands clasped behind him in his familiar pose. Had he heard her outcry, or had Eric summoned him, she wondered, but decided it didn't matter; she was glad he was here. She wiped the back of a hand across her eyes, then took a deep breath, then another, and another, until certain she could speak clearly again.

"He's right when he says this is all the result of what I once considered to be my dream." Adela took Eric's hand in hers and managed a weak, if sad, smile. "Thank you for telling me that what he said wasn't true, but I know now that it is."

"Mother, no. It's not."

"Shhhhh." She put a finger to his lips, silencing him. "It's all right. After everything I've seen these past weeks, after what Billy told me before returning to Australia, I think I already knew. I just regret that it took the likes of *him* to make me realize the truth." She stood and ran a hand through her long hair to straighten it, and buttoned the cuffs and collar of her blouse. Turning to Fleming, she said, "Master, could you please get my things ready? I'll be leaving Woodsgate in the morning."

Eric was immediately on his feet. "Where are you going, Mother? I need time to arrange proper—"

"It was a mistake to sleep. It was simple vanity to want to be around to 'throw the switch.'

"My work here is finished, and I'm leaving," she said simply. "I'm going home to Gris." She walked to the door, and allowed Fleming to lead her from the room.

PART THREE

THE GATHERING DARKNESS

A man who is afraid
will do anything.

—Jawaharlal Nehru

EIGHT
Mercury

hump!

"Come on, Rice! Open the gods-damned door right now!"

Whump!

Templeton Rice glared at the door; for a moment he'd almost thought he saw it shudder when they hit it that time. But the door was heavy, much too heavy for them to even shake it in its servo tracks, much less break it down. Besides, in the anteroom's dim lighting there was little chance that something as subtle as a shaking door could be seen by any but the sharpest eyes. He glanced around the small room and tried to decide just how much he really wanted the lighting back on, or if he even needed it in here. If so, he realized that he'd have to carefully reroute the connection to avoid negating the lockout he'd hastily programmed into the door circuitry. He decided not to decide for now. In the meantime, the light coming from Main Control would have to do.

The pounding finally stopped, and in the sudden quiet all that remained was his own labored breathing and something else, a tiny sound he couldn't quite place. He tried to calm himself and, forcing his breath to come in regular intervals, leaned closer to the door. There it was, a scratching sound from the other side of the wall at a spot slightly to one side of the doorframe, about a meter down from the ceiling. In frustration and anger at their incessant attempts to get in, he kicked at the door almost as loudly as when the table they had been using as a makeshift battering ram had slammed into it.

"Leave me alone!" he shouted. "I've disabled the circuits at the primary control panel, so there's no way you can reroute from that access hatch on your side. You might as well not even bother." He listened again, but the scratching sound continued unabated as they continued their attempts to hot-wire the door circuit from the other side.

"Idiots!" he spat, more to himself than to his adversaries. There were six of them trying to get in, and the thought that they had all once been his friends—or at least trusted associates— filled him with disgust. Now they were little more than animals controlled more by their own bloodlust than their intellect.

He turned his back on the door and leaned heavily, wearily against it before allowing himself to slide down the smooth surface into a sitting position on the floor. He let his eyes travel around the room until they came upon Boscawen's body lying in the doorway opposite him. The man lay on his back, his left arm twisted grotesquely beneath him, his head turned as if to stare accusingly at him. There was a single wound just above his left eye, but the bleeding had stopped long enough ago that the blood had turned dark against the man's cheek, as well as in the surprisingly small pool that had collected where his head touched the floor.

Bloodlust. The word was perfect.

"Listen, Tem . . ." It was a new voice this time, one of the Imperial guards the others had been holding in the cafeteria. "They brought me up here; asked me to talk to you."

"Go away, Jerzy."

"They only want the frog, Tem. Let them have it, and they've promised to let us all go."

Rice paused, considered their promise of safety for the hundredth time, then said, "You know they're lying. The longer this door is locked, the longer I stay alive."

"Come on, Tem . . ."

He felt uneasy, and wondered what they would do with the guards. In spite of himself, he found that he actually liked the big marine. For a military type, the man had proven himself remarkably literate about the scientific research and preparations they had been conducting at the sunstation. Was the man still tied? Or were they simply holding a gun to his head as they had Boscawen's? He looked back to the body in the doorway, and felt guilt wash over him at how many had already died because of his resistance. "Jerzy, are you all right? How about the rest of your team?"

"We're all fine, Tem," came the reply. "They've got us sealed in Three-A. Since there's only the one door to cover, they've removed all our leg braces. They're treating us well; we're all right."

Rice was relieved to hear by the tone of the man's voice that what he was saying was the truth. But then, why should they kill the soldiers? As long as they were unarmed and contained they weren't a threat to them or anyone else. And if it came to it, they just might need hostages when help arrived. If help arrived. *Does anyone on Luna even know what's happened here yet?* he wondered. He stopped to think a moment: *How long has it been since I spoke to anyone at the Academy? Two days? Three?* He sighed unhappily. He had gone weeks at a time without finding a need to talk to anyone there and, assuming that the gang outside the door was feeding false reports back home, it might be a very long time before anyone became suspicious about anything being amiss at a sunstation that was all-too-frequently ignored anyway. Maybe now that Dr. Montgarde was active with the project, there would be sooner contact.

Rice closed his eyes and tipped his head back exhaustedly against the door. He let his hands fall limply at his sides—but still maintained a tight grip on the needle gun that was his only weapon. He wished again that he had some metal flechettes that could be electrically charged instead of the chemically filled glass ones. The momentary darkness and the quiet—save for the uninterrupted scratching at the control hatch outside—felt positively wonderful, and he actually permitted himself to enjoy the temporary peace.

"Tem? You still there?" He ignored Jerzy's question, and had no intention of answering; he didn't even open his eyes. There was a soft knocking, then, "Templeton?"

On the other side of the door Rice could hear voices softly, hurriedly discussing something, but he couldn't make out what they were saying. The scratching sound had finally stopped.

A faint, steady beeping from Main Control startled him and he sat forward abruptly, blinking his eyes at the stream of light from the opposite doorway. His mouth was dry, his joints stiff, and he realized that he must have dozed off. He rubbed at his face with his hands, balling his fists into tired, burning eyes, then suddenly panicked over the missing needle gun. His heart racing, he searched the floor on all fours, finding it easily enough where it had fallen from his lap and had been inadvertently knocked behind him against the door as he slept. He thumbed the test button on the side and checked the readout. He must not have slept long, he reasoned, setting the power switch on standby; it still held nearly a full charge. The microflechettes were another matter, however. Although the gun still had enough narcozine for a full magazine of projectiles, the readout showed only five flechettes left. Even if he was a crack marksman instead of an astrophysicist, he couldn't hope to get all six of his tormentors.

Maybe he'd get lucky and could overpower one of them and get a real gun. Maybe the Imperial soldiers locked up down in 3-A could take charge of the situation. Or maybe help would get here before he needed to use it at all. Then again, maybe he'd only need the use of one flechette, fully charged with narcozine—on himself.

He leaned an ear against the door and listened carefully. Nothing. There wasn't even any light coming beneath the door from the hallway. He rose slowly, relieving the pressure on his aching knees, and slipped the gun into one of the pockets of his lab coat as he headed for Main Control. Rice stepped almost casually over Boscawen's lifeless body, not allowing himself to think about how accustomed he'd already become to seeing it lying there. He couldn't afford the luxury of feeling grief for his friend and coworker. Maybe later, if he was very, very lucky; but not just now.

There was another body here, that of Julie Le Châtelier, but she had been the first to die when things had started going crazy, and her death had been treated with more respect. He and Boscawen had moved her body to one side of the room and wrapped it as best they could in lab coats. The bundle itself was featureless—unrecognizable as a human body—and, but for a large dark stain where her chest would be, Rice would not have been able to distinguish head from foot. He spared only a moment's thought for her, wondering briefly what her face looked like. His brow furrowed deeply, and he somehow felt worse about not being able to remember the face of someone who had once been his lover than he did about the fact that she had been lying on the floor, dead, for at least twelve hours now.

The steady beeping that had awakened him several minutes earlier had continued unnoticed throughout his reverie, but finally drew his attention back to the task at hand even though his eyes remained fixed on the wrapped bundle.

"System," he said softly, and was surprised at the halting scratchiness he heard in his voice. He turned abruptly away from

Julie's body, his eyes clenched tightly. "System," he said again, a bit louder this time.

There were several chirping sounds from the room system as the computer links searched the emergency coding he and Boscawen had recently installed. "System ready, Tem," it finally responded once it had verified his identity. The voice and speaking patterns were Julie's. She had reprogrammed the system with her own voice as a joke more than a year earlier, but no one had gotten around to changing it back. Everyone had grown accustomed to it over the months, but now Rice regretted not having ordered it changed.

"Bring lights to full." The room brightened considerably, and a quick glance into the anteroom showed that it wouldn't be necessary to repair the lighting there. "Has any contact been made yet with the outside?"

"I'm sorry, but those circuits are no longer available, and it's been impossible to shunt into any of the other communication lines. I've created a priority subroutine, however, and have dedicated it to the task of rerouting as many combinations as possible."

Good work, Rice thought, smiling, almost as though it were Julie herself who had come up with the idea. He caught himself, burying the painful notion deep inside him, and added silently, *Think, think, think! I can't let any of this get to me. Not yet. I've got too much to do!* "Are the circuits for incoming transmissions still accessible?"

"Yes."

"Have any transmissions been received?"

"No."

"Is it possible that transmissions have been received through equipment elsewhere in the sunstation, but have been intercepted without your being able to detect them?"

A pause, a tiny electronic chirp as she—it—checked, then, "No. Only the regular station support links are operating."

Although the operation of the sunstation was autonomous, a two-way support link with the Imperial computer net on Luna functioned around the clock. The link constantly supplied updated software, information, even news and entertainment programming directly into the station system. Ironically, it was this very link to Luna—which was apparently working normally—that undoubtedly kept Imperial officials in the dark about the mutiny underway at the station. Since the communications chan-

nels were the only thing that could give away the current situation
here, and those were being carefully controlled by the group on
the other side of the door, there was no hope of calling for help.

Actually, there *was* one other way to contact the outside. Rice
looked around the room, considering yet again the alternative of
sabotaging some vital system in Main Control. The break in the
information stream on the real-time links would certainly arouse
someone's curiosity. But every system now operating here was
vital to the project, and could set things back an undetermined
amount of months, even years; worse, shutting something down
could pose a danger to personnel aboard the orbitals. Rice wasn't
quite desperate enough yet to risk that course of action. Besides,
he realized gloomily, any inquiry from the outside might be intercepted and explained away by the mutineers.

"Thank you," Rice said, and heard the despair in his own
voice. "In the meantime, keep trying to shunt into one of the
communication links."

Chirp. "All right, Tem. Anything else for now?"

"Yeah." There was another doorway, this one directly opposite the one he'd used to enter Main Control. He touched the
opening plate in the wall next to the doorframe, nodding in
satisfaction when nothing happened. "Please unlock the access
hallway from Main Control to building five."

"Ready."

There was no sound, no click or buzz or anything that might
indicate that the circuitry preventing the door from opening had
changed in any way. His voice patterns already verified, there
hadn't even been a pause. Rice touched the opening plate again,
and this time the door slid obediently aside to reveal a cold, dimly
lit hallway about twenty meters long. The narrow corridor, one
of several located throughout the facility, led to building five, the
support section of the sunstation. Supplies, storage, cryosleep
chamber, vehicle repair and other infrequently used services were
housed here, and support systems were purposely kept either at
low levels or on standby.

As Rice entered the hallway, he shivered in the chilly air but
didn't bother to have the system reset the levels—he wouldn't be
here that long. But for a lighting strip running the length of the
ceiling, and communications terminals set into the wall at either
end, the hallway was featureless and lent a frigidity somehow
more keenly felt than the temperature of the air itself. Rice approached the opposite doorway and looked at the small screen on
the terminal. On it was the floor plan of building five, showing

every room, corridor and facility it contained. The portions of building five located on the side farthest from his current location—the garage and vehicle-repair facility, equipment storage, even-numbered emergency evac pods, and associated corridors—glowed red. Those areas were accessible from the engineering building connected by a similar hallway on the other side, and the mutineers had managed to breach them. They had not, however, gotten as far as Rice had feared. His lockouts of the door circuitry still mostly intact, all other areas in five—including cryosleep—were outlined in a soft yellow light.

"Please update display of building-five security; indicate all current activity." The floor plan remained as before, but one area—the corridor doorway that connected vehicle repair with one of the temporary cargo holds—blinked rapidly. Rice allowed himself a chuckle when he saw it, knowing they would have little luck with that door above all the others: Even if they were successful in breaking the circuitry, they'd find the door immobilized in a decidedly low-tech fashion. He'd merely taken a motorized lifter from the facility, drove it into the hallway and, after ordering the circuitry changed, reversed the lifter and rammed it into the door itself from his side. They would have an easier time cutting through a wall.

Satisfied that most of five was, and would remain, secure, he traced a route on the floor plan with a fingertip, watching as a soft dotted line appeared along the way. "Open access to indicated areas, please, and activate all terminals along the indicated route. Leave all others mute. Reseal each access doorway on my voice as I pass through."

"Ready."

Rice touched the opening plate on the wall, and the thick door slid noiselessly aside. He moved quickly, touching the plate on the opposite side with a barked "Secure this!" as he did. He walked to the first side corridor and turned, pressing the plate at the door he found there, going through, and vocally resecuring the lock just as he had done before. There were directional signs and arrows on the walls of every corridor in building five, intended for station personnel who rarely visited this section, but Rice ignored them as he strode purposefully along the path he had traced on the screen until arriving at his destination.

The door had been crudely stenciled with the words CRYO-SLEEP—TANKS AND RECOVERY in black lettering that appeared slightly angled and off-center. Rice had often wondered whether the construction tech responsible for the sloppy paint job had been in a hurry to complete his task, or simply hadn't cared how the finished job would look in what was intended to be little more than a warehouse. The door slid aside at Rice's touch, and he entered.

After resealing the entrance, he immediately noticed the sound of his own labored breathing in the quiet room and realized that he must have run the entire distance from the main control room. Leaning his back against the secured door, he took a moment to catch his breath and inspect the spartan room, checking for any signs of entry.

The room bore little resemblance to most cryosleep facilities; there were no comfortable beds, there was no superfluous furniture, and there was nothing that lent the welcoming feeling of warmth so important to most people coming out of hibernation. There were, in fact, only two pieces of furniture—a divided cabinet he knew contained basic clothing and supplies on one side and a small refrigerator on the other; and a simple chair. The room was exactly as it appeared: just another featureless multipurpose compartment, like so many at the sunstation and similar installations, that had been adapted for other use.

There were a dozen nearly identical medical terminals evenly spaced on the far wall. Below each were the necessary jacks and dangling life-support connectors for cryosleep tanks, but there were only two tanks in the room. One of them—dark, and obviously not in use for some time, judging from the thin coating of dust on the once-polished plastiglass cover—was the tank in which Rice himself had arrived at the station nearly ten years earlier. The room's single chair had been placed next to the other. The panel on the wall above was different from the others, and sported additional readouts not featured on the rest. It glowed in a multicolored display of biomedical readouts that Rice studied briefly, nodding when he saw that everything was normal in the tank below.

Rice approached the tank wearily and leaned against the plastiglass covering, letting out a long, exhausted sigh as an icy chill seemed to creep into the palms of his hands from the transparent cryotank cover.

Oidar seemed to be all right; at least, he looked the same as he had the last time he'd checked. When a human went into the tank, it was difficult to tell from appearance alone whether the person was in a decades-long period of deep hibernation, or merely taking a nap. Skin tone, hair, coloring—everything looked normal. But the Sarpan had never attempted to extend their short life spans beyond their normal ten or twelve years, even during long space voyages. The Sarpan Empire, unlike the Hundred Worlds, had been forged over generations. A Sarpan citizen—whether scientist or general, colonist or historian—embarking on a journey to a new world knew that only a descendant could carry on his work upon arrival. Oidar had been the first of his race to attempt cryosleep.

Looking at the alien now, frowning deeply at the dry, leathery skin that made his friend look more like a mummy than a living being, Rice was forced to carefully examine the readouts to assure himself yet again that the wake-up procedure was still going correctly. He compared what he saw in the readouts to his wristwatch, then tapped the watch's face to set the countdown timer. A human could be brought out of cryosleep in a matter of hours, but the alien's delicate physiology required a days-long process that was more experiment than anything else. There was no guarantee, for that matter, that it would even work. He glanced at his watch again; in a little under fourteen hours, he'd find out.

Maybe it would be better if I didn't do it, he thought morosely. *Maybe you and I and everyone else would all be better off.* The readouts blurred softly as he stared, and he rubbed at his eyes and face, trying to force away the fatigue he felt. The palms of his hands felt cold against his cheeks.

"I'm sorry, friend," he said to the silent, corpselike alien. "I hope we're doing the right thing."

He allowed one last look at Oidar, then crossed to the cabinet and examined the contents, verifying that everything was as he and Boscawen had left it. The refrigerator was still stocked with everything he'd need when Oidar awoke, dehydrated and thirsty after his long sleep. There was also food and several packets of ordinary fruit drink, and he tore one open, sipping absently of the beverage as he checked the supply side of the cabinet.

The top shelf was lined with four-liter jugs of water, and a quick inspection showed that the seal on each was still green, the water untampered with. The tiny electric water pump and sprayer were there, along with a number of Oidar's personal items. Specialized clothing—a sterile wet suit and bubble helmet for Oidar to wear when he awoke—remained tightly sealed in plastic on the bottom shelf. It would be especially important now since the section containing the cabin reserved for the alien was under control of the others and no longer accessible. Without that cabin, and the Sarpan-normal environment it would maintain, the wet suit was all that would keep Oidar alive until they could get help from Luna.

Rice hefted two of the jugs down and set them near the tank, then retrieved the pump and sprayer. It took a few minutes to hook the pump to one of the jugs and test the sprayer mechanism, but Rice was glad he did. The water was too cold for Oidar, and he set the pump control to bring the water up to the proper temperature and carefully coiled the sprayer around the top of the jug. It wasn't until then that he realized that he, too, was cold.

"System, reset room environmental levels to normal." There was a soft chirp in way of response, and Rice felt the slightest movement in the air.

In the hour that followed, Rice removed the rest of the water jugs and anything else he thought he'd need from the cabinet and stacked it against the wall near the tank.

That's it, he thought, and, realizing there was nothing left for him to do now except wait, he felt the tiredness he'd been fighting for so long pour over him. Yawning deeply, he decided there was no reason why he shouldn't give in to the feeling—in not too many hours, he reasoned, he would need all the strength he could get.

There were shrink-wrapped sandwiches and fruit bars in the refrigerator, and Rice took one of each, washing both down with another packet of juice. Suddenly ravenous, he finished the food in only a few bites and wasted little time in helping himself to more.

His thirst quenched and hunger gone, Rice was pleased to notice that he now felt almost comfortably tired instead of exhausted. He accessed the comm terminal by the door and requested an updated security check for building five. He noted his watch and the biomedical readouts again and, reassured that there was no danger for the present, settled himself as comfortably as he could on the floor near the cryotank. The room was warm now, and he removed his coat. Placing the needle gun within easy reach, he balled the coat into a pillow and curled up on the floor with his back against the tank.

There was a gentle humming sensation that he could feel through his shirt and that relaxed him almost involuntarily, and he allowed his mind to drift for the first time since the shooting began.

Nine more hours, Oidar. Hang on for just nine more hours.

Sleep overtook him before he could reflect on just what he was going to do after that.

NINE
Airborne

The hike had been both long and hard, and Gareth Anmoore was grateful for the pleasant weather. The early-
morning sky was a deep blue above the trees, and the rays
of the warm sun were tempered by a dry, cool wind that came up
from the south and wafted through the forest. They were nearing
the end of a long uphill climb and had stopped in a small clearing
for a short break before reaching the top. There was plenty of
time to rest before peering out over the river valley that he already knew, from the many orbital scans and recordings from the
previous scouting missions, would be there.

Staring up through a break in the trees, he could make out the
largest of the planet's two moons directly overhead. The natural
satellites had merely been designated in the official log as moon
one and moon two, although the name "Big One," as it had been
dubbed by a crew member, seemed to have stuck and was in
general use now by almost everyone. The smaller moon, "Little
Two," would not be visible until well after nightfall. Big One was
close, the features on its barren surface easily visible, even in the
light of day.

He stretched tired muscles and leaned against the thickness of
a large deciduous tree with deep crimson-and-green triangular
leaves. He couldn't see too far through the trees as he looked
back down the long, gentle uphill grade they'd just climbed, but
his legs and back told him they had come a long way. Gareth
took great pride in how well he kept in shape, and was never a
stranger to the ship's exercise and recreation area, but even he
had been winded by the strenuous workout he'd received today.
He took another swallow of chilled water from his canteen, letting the cool liquid slide slowly down his throat, and regarded the
others in the party.

There were ten of them, not including himself, and he noted
with pleasure that nearly all of them were still out of breath from
the brisk pace that Hannah had set through the thick woods. All
but one of them were younger than he—truly younger, not the
visage of youth gained by rejuvenation or cryo—and he smiled
with an inward satisfaction that he was in better condition than

they. The oldest member of the party was the xenoguide, Hannah Cee, and she had not been fatigued in the least by the exertion. While the rest refreshed themselves with cold water and fresh fruit or snack bars from their packs, she had impatiently continued to the crest of the rise and peered carefully over before coming back to rejoin the group, where she dug wordlessly into her own pack, searching for something.

"Well, Hannah?" he asked. "How's it look?"

She said nothing; she didn't even acknowledge his question. Instead, she retrieved what she wanted: a cylindrical roll of hard candy. She peeled back the wrapper and, not offering to share, popped one of the brightly colored confections into her mouth. She sucked on the treat for several seconds, the only sound she made was the gentle clicking of the candy against her teeth as she rolled it about her mouth with her tongue, and looked around the clearing—left, right, above their heads—as if trying to locate something high up in the trees.

It had taken Gareth Anmoore a long time to get used to her, nearly all the sixteen years they had served together. One of the men in the group, a young anthropologist who had signed on for this survey at their last stop, had overheard the captain's question and raised his head curiously in Hannah's direction, then looked to him, puzzled why his captain would tolerate such a thing. Gareth smiled again, deciding that the young man had mistakenly thought the xenoguide was either hard of hearing or was ignoring the captain altogether, and the man clearly wondered why the question had not been repeated. Gareth caught his eye and nodded in the direction of the rest of the party, dismissing him, and watched as he joined his companions.

No. Hannah had heard him all right. When she had an answer with which she was satisfied, she would speak, but not before. There was a time when the habit had irritated him, but once he'd learned that anything the woman said was worth listening to, he found that it was always prudent to allow her as much time as she needed. There was no need to repeat the question.

She turned her attention to him finally and approached, nodding, and bit loudly into the candy. He could hear the candy crunching as she chewed it into small bits. As she stopped before him, he caught the scent of strawberry for just the briefest of moments before the fruity aroma was lost on the steady breeze sifting through the trees.

"They do not know," she said in her heavy frontier-world accent, "that we are here." She nodded again and regarded him directly, and lifted her eyebrows in a silent question that told him she was waiting for his decision to continue up the hill. Her eyes twinkled in anticipation, and with her brow lifted he could see the wrinkles at the corners of her eyes. The pale lines stood out sharply against her deeply tanned skin, and he knew she had spent many long hours in the sun without the protective goggles that were regulation for surface work. He had no plans to mention the violation to her.

Regulations—and common sense—had dictated that they set the landing shuttle down in a remote area of the forest and hike in to the valley. The shuttle had been left in a glen about five kilometers west of the river valley, holographically shielded to minimize detection. The electronic camouflage was so effective that the two crewmen left behind to guard the lander should have little cause to move the craft to keep their presence secret.

Gareth checked the group and noted that they appeared rested, and had had sufficient time to replace canteens and packs.

"All right," he said at last. "Let's get set up." He reshouldered his own pack and nodded to Hannah, who led them the short distance to the top of the hill. The others were already setting up monitoring equipment when he reached the top. Most of them had been here at the observation site before and concentrated on their own tasks, paying scant attention to anything else. The seeming nonchalance of the survey party made what he saw upon clearing the top of the hill all the more fantastic.

"My God," he whispered when he viewed the sight that lay below. "It's even more fabulous than the aerial scans suggested." The recordings had not done the visage justice, he realized as he studied the intricacies of the native village. No, "village" was far too inappropriate a word, one better suited to more primitive dwellings. What he gazed at now was a town.

Hannah turned, and for a moment allowed just the hint of a smile to appear at one of the corners of her mouth.

You knew what my reaction would be to this, didn't you? he asked silently, appreciating the woman's skill at being able to surprise him. He let his gaze sweep the peaceful settlement in the valley several kilometers below them and, when he looked again at Hannah, found himself staring at her back.

Her work done, for the moment, she had moved away from the group and had found a quiet spot on the trunk of a fallen tree to rest and take food and drink from her pack. Although she sat and ate casually on the tree trunk, Gareth knew that she continued to keep a close watch on their surroundings. The place where they now stood overlooking the town had been carefully selected: The terrain was difficult and unsuited to regular transportation routes. With so much wilderness available on the planet, and with game so abundant in areas of the forest considerably easier to traverse than this remote spot, it was unlikely that even the most diligent of hunters would come this way. Still, she kept a watchful eye for any sign that they might be discovered. Gareth trusted her completely and turned to the others, who had by now completed the setup of the observation equipment.

Just as well that you're not looking at me now, Hannah, he mused as he watched the survey party busy themselves at their duties, *because you've always been able to read me like a book.* His initial reaction of wonder at seeing the beautiful town below had subsided to an acceptance of the realities of what they were doing here. As much as he wanted to allow himself to enjoy the excitement he felt at the discovery of this new race, he instead concentrated on the main reason for his accompanying the survey party: his personal assessment, as commanding officer of the mission, of the technological development of the natives. Later, perhaps, the two could share a private moment of giddy joy at the wonderful discovery they had made here; but, for now, they had other duties to perform.

A pair of cameras had been set up on tripods and two men were already recording separate areas of the town. Another was scanning through the structures with a handheld camera, his eye pressed close to the telescopic viewfinder, recording buildings and individual objects of interest at random as he came across them. He wore a lightweight headset and spoke frequently into it.

There was a flatscreen tablet on one of the small, folding stands they had set up, and Gareth picked it up. It was linked to the handheld camera and he watched the image as the crewman surveyed the town. Most of what he saw as the camera panned first left, then right—occasionally holding and zooming in on one feature or another—resembled most of the recordings he had been viewing for the last week. Even though the close-up views on the flatscreen were incredibly detailed, he still found himself preferring to look at the valley itself.

"Have you found them yet, Jonato?" Gareth asked, not taking his eyes from the quiet town.

"No, sir. Not yet," Jonato answered, sweeping the camera steadily over the settlement. "Hold on, sir, and I'll check with the other party." He spoke softly into the headset for a few seconds, then turned. "They've reached their observation point on the other side and are set up, but there are a lot of heat sources down there—ovens, open fires, boilers—and they're having a hard time pinning them down. Shouldn't take them too much longer, though."

"Fine. Let me know when they have something."

The young cameraman nodded and went back to his work. Gareth was pleased with the time and effort they had all put into this since the discovery of the natives was made. He had felt some trepidation about this at the beginning, a fear that Jephthah and his message of hatred of the Sarpan might spread to their work here. He need not have been concerned. He had chosen his crew well; these were men and women of science, their excitement over this incredible find holding infinitely more power over their emotions than the ravings of some hatemonger.

"Captain?" Hannah called from her perch on the downed tree. They were old, close friends; but she never addressed him by his first name in front of his crew, in spite of the fact that nearly every person on the survey ship who had served with him before was on a first-name basis.

He crossed to the tree and sat beside her. "Is everything all right?"

She looked at him, not understanding his concern for a moment, then shook her head quickly in apology. "No, no; I am sorry. Everything is fine. But I wonder: We are almost done with the first phase of our observation here. It is almost time that we made a report. What will you say?"

He furrowed his brow and sighed deeply at the question. "I haven't exactly made up my mind, Hannah, and that's the honest truth. A lot depends on what we find out down here today. But look at what we've already been able to document about them." He held the flatscreen out to her to emphasize his point, but she refused it with a frown and a wave of her hand.

"I do not need pictures. I did not use them on my homeworld, and they do not help me here to know what my own senses tell me." She stood, pointed to the valley. "Do you truly need more pictures to tell you that you have found a civilized people here?"

He chuckled softly and set the flatscreen gingerly on the tree trunk. The tablet rocked slightly on the rounded bulk, but did not fall.

"No, I don't." He rose and stood at her side, following her gaze over the valley.

The town was quiet, and from here—without the benefit of the close-up view offered by the flatscreen display—it was impossible to see any of the natives going about their business. There were sailboats visible in the river, and a larger craft, also sail-powered, appeared to be moored at one of the several docks dotting the shoreline. As the big boat drifted in its mooring, he caught sight of a smaller craft, sailless, in the slip next to it, and the dark smoke pouring from a high stack amidships told him it was steam-powered. Smoke curled from dozens of chimneys in the town in long streamers that disappeared on the wind. The buildings seemed to be well designed and constructed from a variety of materials, but even at this distance the unmistakable ruddy red color of bricks was dominant. There was occasional movement, but it nearly always disappeared among the buildings or among the boats moored along the waterfront before he could orient his eyes on just what it was.

He'd already seen the natives, of course, on the recordings. He had already received report after report from the anthropologists. Their lifestyles, what they ate, and how they carried out commerce—all had been covered by them. Chemical and spectrographic analysis of the air and water told him what they manufactured, what they burned, what they ate and what they threw out as garbage. In short, he felt that he knew them as well as one would know the foreign neighbors who might live in the apartment next to yours without really ever meeting or talking with them.

And that, sadly, he would probably never do. For the *Paloma Blanca* was a planetary survey vessel that had discovered intelligent life only by accident. And once his report was filed, he would most likely be ordered off-planet until ships carrying a team geared for more intensive study of his find could be sent.

"Sir!"

Jonato's call sliced through his thoughts, and he reached behind him almost automatically for the flatscreen, nearly knocking it off the tree trunk as he did. He glanced at it expectantly, but saw nothing that wasn't there before.

"Have you got it?"

"We think so. Second team has pinned down a heat source that looks about right approximately four kilometers from here, in the woods north of the town." The handheld camera dangling in his right hand, Jonato gestured with his free arm to a spot farther up the river valley. "There."

Gareth strained his eyes in the indicated direction but saw nothing out of the ordinary, then returned his attention to the flatscreen. "Where the hell is it?"

"Sorry, sir, but I don't have the right angle from here for visual yet; but second team assures me it's there behind that series of hills."

His own headset had been hanging loosely around his neck and he fumbled it over his ear, barking into the collar pickup, "Control, Anmoore here. I'm using flatscreen . . ." He turned the tablet over in his hand, frantically looking for an identification number, but Jonato, overhearing, broke into the communications link.

"Control, put your feed to Captain Anmoore on tablet nine, priority link."

"Thanks," he said quickly to the young cameraman, then: "Control, feed me the signals from the handhelds from both teams combined with your overhead. Three-part image, please."

The flatscreen immediately divided into three separate windowed images. One of them, the signal from Jonato's handheld, blurred unsteadily as the man reoriented his camera on the location of the heat source. The image from the second team was steady, but it offered no more clue as to what was there than had Jonato's a few moments earlier—whatever it was, was located in a slight depression and was effectively shielded from view on both sides of the valley, despite their higher elevation. The third image, however, was being sent by an observation shuttle hovering above the town at too high an altitude to be seen, and it showed the same oval object they'd detected a few days earlier from orbit. A mixture of brown and green, the object blended almost perfectly with the ground below it and had remained undetected throughout most of their surface scans as long as it was immobile. In fact, only by watching the slight change in coloration as it moved could one even see it at all.

But now, as it had when first detected, it seemed to move slowly, with no indication as to purpose or design. The orbital recordings they had were limited and inconclusive regarding what it was, registering only its size, color and density, and the fact that it was a mobile heat source of some kind. Unlike the steam-powered boats, whose purpose and nature were self-evident, this object had been a mystery to them and was the main reason for his presence today.

The object had been moving north, with the wind, but according to its orientation on the flatscreen it was slowly rotating to a heading that took it in a more westerly direction. *Could these be controlled?* he wondered.

There was a slight buzz in his ear, then, *"Captain Anmoore?"*

"Go ahead."

"We've got a second heat source, sir, that's originated near the first."

He stared hard at the flatscreen, trying to find it. The first object was centered in its window, and nothing else appeared to be moving. The other two images showed only the wooded hills that maddeningly hid the objects from view. Gareth tapped the overhead view with a fingertip, outlining the window in which it appeared and opening a menu. He tapped the latter hurriedly, canceling the two useless views and expanding the overhead image to fill the entire flatscreen.

There! In the upper right corner was another of the green-brown oval shapes. This one, too, first started moving to the north, but was now swinging around to fall in behind its companion, which appeared to have slowed down to allow the second object to catch up. There was no question is his mind now that these were controlled objects.

He was aware that there was an increased chattering of voices all around him, but he was so involved with the image on the flatscreen that he paid little heed to what anyone was saying. It was Hannah's hand on his shoulder that finally made him look up to see what had caused the sudden commotion.

One of the objects was just now clearing the top of the hills, and as he compared it with what he saw on the flatscreen he realized that from its position it must be the second of the pair. Farther behind the first, it was not only rising faster but appeared to be gaining speed. He watched it in silence for several moments, and was startled when the other hove boldly above the line of hills. It too had gained speed and was closer than he had originally imagined, giving him a better look. The green-brown coloration apparently was limited only to the upper portion of the things and gradually diffused into a lighter color, leading him to believe that the darker coloring was intended only to make them harder to see from the air. There were markings of some kind on the sides, slightly below what would be the widest point, but he couldn't quite make out what they were.

It occurred to him suddenly that now that the objects were clear of the hills, the cameras could give him a closer view, and he returned his attention to the flatscreen. Calling up the menu, he brought back the other two windows and gasped loudly enough that Hannah turned to him and, against her nature, stood closer to afford herself a better look at the screen. She, too, stared openmouthed at what she saw.

"Airships." Her voice was an awed whisper.

They were identical. Long and cylindrical, they tapered to a rounded point on both front and back. There seemed to be lines or ribbing in the material that covered them, running lengthwise. An open basket of a woven material was suspended below each of the fliers, attached to the main cylinders by thin spars that were either constructed from some rigid material or flexible lines stretched taut. The baskets, like the cylinders above them, were roughly oval in shape and must have been quite roomy, as the four natives inside them seemed to have more room to move around than might have been expected. But Gareth had to remind himself that the flatscreen view was not to his own perspective, that the natives were smaller than human normal by many centimeters.

They were basically humanoid in appearance, more so even than the Sarpan, and early observation indicated that they were as mammalian as humans themselves. Even in the flatscreen view Gareth could make out the wide-spaced, expressive eyes; the tiny ears set well back on the sides of their heads; the small, bridgeless noses. The rich, tawny coloring of the light fur on their faces and exposed forearms indicated that all but one were males in early adulthood. The fourth, who seemed to be in charge, was an older male with fur of silver-brown. As he watched, he saw that the older one was showing the others various techniques of handling the clumsy craft. With a nod, one of the younger fliers took the control lines as the others stood back, causing Gareth to wonder if they were watching a training flight. The four wore clothing of a woven fabric that was very similar in both coloration and style, and it occurred to Gareth that they had a uniform look about them, perhaps indicating that the airship's function was military or law-enforcement in nature. He made a mental note to compare his thoughts with Hannah and the others later.

In the flatscreen view the markings were clear. A bold red stripe, tapered at the front and broadening gradually as it approached the rear, ran the length of each cylinder just below the widest portion. There were darker markings that could have been lettering or numbers on the thickest part of the red stripe at the very tail. As the two airships swung farther to the southwest, the view from the second-team camera showed a full side view, and as he studied the image more closely he noticed what looked like vanes standing out above and below the craft, giving it a general fishlike shape.

"Hannah, they're incredible," he breathed, his eyes fixed on the flatscreen.

"Shhhhhhh. Listen."

He looked up and, seeing that she was looking away from them and not at the screen, followed her gaze. While there was little danger of their being spotted from above under the cover of the trees lining the edge of the ridge on which they stood, he became immediately concerned that the two airships were heading in their general direction. He was about to say something to the others when he heard it: a dull, thrumming sound.

"Everyone keep still," he admonished. "Keep the cameras on them as best you can, but don't take any chance that you'll be seen. Understood? Stay here under the trees."

The thrumming grew louder as they watched, and in a few moments the two airships passed as close to them as they would come. Gareth watched as they floated majestically by, still a half kilometer away. They rose steadily in altitude and crossed behind their position, disappearing, and headed out over the woods. The sound lingered a full minute; then quiet returned to the forest. There was some restless murmuring among the others in the party, but that, too, died away as Gareth spoke into the collar pickup.

"Ah, second team, can you still see them from your position?"

"No, sir." The voice was shaking, uncertain. *"They've disappeared over your location."*

"Pack it in, then. Control, we're heading back, too. Keep recording from above." He pulled the headset off and let it hang around his neck. "Let's go."

The equipment was quickly dismantled and repacked, and the party started into the woods the way it had come. As before, Gareth brought up the rear and kept an eye out for Hannah, who stayed behind after them to make certain no evidence of humans remained that might be found by the natives. Satisfied by her inspections, she trotted silently up behind him a few minutes later.

They had walked in silence for a long time when finally she touched his jacket sleeve and whispered, "Gareth, I must speak with you."

He slowed his pace and allowed the distance between them and the others to lengthen a bit. The terrain was fairly easy here, the path wider, and the two could walk side by side, although whether she had timed it this way or not he could only guess.

"I think I know what you're going to ask," he offered when the others had hiked just out of earshot. He transferred his pack to his left shoulder and faced her as he walked. "You want to ask again what my report will say."

She smiled at how well he had read her intentions, but remained quiet.

"Very well." He sighed deeply. "I will tell them we've found a growing civilization here. That they are intelligent. They have commerce. Their transportation has developed to a degree we had not expected when we found them a week ago. They have steam power produced by gas-fired boilers. They forge and use metals. And they have a highly developed technology."

There was a sudden rustling in the leaves to one side of the trail and a small animal, startled at their passing, ran noisily to the nearest tree, where it climbed quickly to safety. Gareth watched the animal as it disappeared into the branches above them.

Still staring above him at the blue sky appearing through the boughs, he sighed again, softly this time.

"And they have a highly developed technology," he repeated worriedly. "And they can fly."

"Lord Jephthah will not like that," she responded. "He will use this discovery to further his campaign of hatred."

He stopped.

"Yeah, I know."

TEN
Rihana

Overtly, Rihana Valtane's ship was little more than a yacht-class vessel, albeit an enormous one—the kind possessed only by the very rich. It could, in fact, easily be identified by anyone interested enough or curious enough to check an official ship registry as one of several such vessels belonging to House Valtane.

Externally, the ship resembled—by design—the many others belonging to her House. This vessel, however, was her personal yacht, its simple and utilitarian exterior belying the luxurious appointments to be found inside.

Rihana stood before a huge circular expanse of ray-shielded plastiglass that made up nearly one entire wall of her plush office, staring at the vessel approaching from aft. The viewpoint was genuine—a true window, not a holographic port—and gave a normal view of space whenever the opaque security shield was off. The window was surrounded by a holoframe, and she could have ordered an enhanced view of the nearing ship, but she preferred, for now, a natural view. At its present distance and bearing she could not quite make out the markings on the craft now closing on hers, although Poser had already informed her that it was the *Chodha.* As she watched, the small craft disappeared below the bulk of her yacht on its heading to the aft docking bay in the lower level.

She continued to stare out the viewport, even after the shuttle had passed out of sight, although she no longer looked at the magnificent panorama of space spread before her. Her eyes, focused now on her own reflection in the plastiglass, weren't even aware of the stars.

Rihana stared instead at a woman she almost refused to acknowledge as being herself. By any standards, anywhere in the Hundred Worlds, she would be regarded as a beautiful woman. Her hair, long and full as it tumbled over one shoulder, still glowed a fiery copper. The priceless sapphire clip pulling her hair back on one side perfectly matched her deeply penetrating eyes. She had taken care of herself physically, and her body—alluring, clad in a clinging gown of the finest silk—retained a figure that could yet turn many an appreciative head. Her face still displayed the classic features that more than a few men had admired.

I should be grateful, she thought, turning her own image first one way then the other in the mirrorlike glass. *There are countless women for whom this reflection would be a dream come true.* To one side of her own reflection she could see her personal aide, Poser, standing silently at the door. The small man stood with a slouching, inattentive posture, and even in the limited image of the reflection she could see that every hair on his head was slicked back in place in the only concession the man was ever likely to make to popular fashion. She smiled, imagining that the man was watching her, desiring her, although she promptly found the thought of her faithful servant of many years longing for her—in any way other than a source of extremely well paid employment—personally repugnant.

But the years that had passed in her life were reflected here now as well. She had enjoyed many rejuvenations over the centuries, but the treatments were becoming less effective no matter how much money she spent on them. She was still beautiful, but to her the reflection began to carry with it a word she dreaded: "matronly."

I wonder what the famous Adela de Montgarde looks like now? Rihana smiled distastefully, knowing that the Montgarde woman—enjoying the luxury of cryosleep these last two centuries—most likely looked no different than she had at their last meeting on Luna. Damn her! Unlike rejuvenation, with its limited ability to temporarily turn back time, cryosleep could truly cheat it.

Adela de Montgarde had managed to cheat it, and in so doing had managed to cheat Rihana Valtane of something more precious than the years themselves.

"Poser!" she demanded, turning away from the reflection so abruptly that the hapless man—until now paying little attention to her at all—nearly jumped. "Opaque this viewport!"

A disingenuous, subservient smile spread across Poser's mousy face and he tilted his head slightly, causing Rihana to laugh inwardly. All the image lacked was a set of curiously twitching whiskers to make the comparison to a rodent complete. The window's holoframe circuitry jumped to life, obediently hiding the outside view and replacing it with an enhanced image of a painting, a computer-perfect holographic copy of one of the many original artworks in House Valtane's collection of antiquities. The work Poser had selected was da Vinci's *Lady with an Ermine,* one of her favorites, and he had picked it no doubt in the hope that it might calm her.

"Has the shuttle been berthed yet?" Rihana didn't condescend to glance in his direction as she took one of the large leatherbound chairs in a seating group placed to one side of the office, away from the ornate desk that lent the only air of business to the plush, comfortable room.

Had Rihana bothered to look his way, she might have noticed a nearly imperceptible faraway look fall over the man's eyes as his integrator checked the yacht's computer logs. "Yes, Mistress. The *Chodha* has docked and has been berthed. I've taken the liberty of having one of the docking personnel direct Mr. Rapson to the guest level. Let me see . . ." He paused, his plastic smile not wavering. "Yes, he is on his way there even now. I'll have refreshments sent—"

"Don't bother." She turned to glare at him accusingly. "I want to meet with him immediately, in this room. He can refresh himself later, on his own time." She rose and approached the desk, leaning against it and crossing her arms as she regarded him. His smile faded as her eyes bored into him. The look on his face pleased her, and she was glad the man still held a healthy awe for her power and position, even after several hundred years. "In the future, Poser," she offered with mock casualness, "please do not take it upon yourself to do anything—*anything,* do you hear me?—on your own initiative as it regards our dear Mr. Rapson." She smiled almost sweetly, showing that she, too, was at least as adept at ingenuousness as he. "Do I make myself clear, Poser?"

He began a sputtering response, but she waved it away, effectively dismissing him, and returned to the seating group. She remained on her feet, however, as she added, "When you have word that he's on his way, I want you to go meet him yourself and accompany him here."

Poser nodded curtly, and almost immediately turned for the door.

"Oh, Poser . . .?" The man stopped in his tracks. "How do I look?"

He hesitated a moment, his beady eyes narrowing imperceptibly as he warily tried to determine what game, if any, she might be playing now. Apparently deciding the question was genuine, he relaxed somewhat and accepted the query at face value.

"You look as attractive as always, Mistress." He nodded again, then said, "If you'll permit me, I'll fetch Mr. Rapson."

Only a few minutes passed before there was a soft knock at the door. Rihana took more than a small amount of pleasure in the thought that Poser must have dragged their visitor, kicking and screaming, at a full gallop down the yacht's corridors to have arrived back at her office suite so quickly. The efficiency pleased her and she made a mental note to scold the man more frequently.

"It's good to see you again," Rihana said sweetly to her guest when he entered. "May I offer you some refreshment?"

Rapson was a young man, or at least looked it. Either he was truly very young—in which case, Rihana mused each time she saw him, he should be easy to manipulate—or he had had only a few rejuvenations. Tall, with deeply tanned skin, he gave the image of a rugged outdoorsman. His suit was immaculately tailored, and yet it failed to entirely hide the strength in his well-muscled frame. His dark hair was cropped short and brushed back in a style currently fashionable on Earth. He accepted her offered hand, bowing his head respectfully.

"No, thank you," he replied in a deep, measured voice. There was more than a hint of sarcasm behind his words. "I'd much rather learn what it is that you're so anxious to see me about that just couldn't wait until I'd had a chance to change and freshen up after my trip."

"Good. I was hoping you'd feel that way. Poser, that will be all for now. Will you see to it that a guest suite is prepared for Mr. Rapson? I'm sure he must be exhausted from his journey."

The aide nodded and, a look of relief spreading involuntarily across his features, scurried hastily from the room.

"Let's do without any more of the phony pleasantries, shall we?" she said bluntly once they were alone. "We were not supposed to meet until next week. What is so important you took the risk of coming all the way out here now?"

"It's so good to see you, too." He ran a fingertip gently across her cheek, and fondled one of the sapphire earrings she wore. Cupping his strong hands behind her neck, he pulled her to him as he leaned down and kissed her.

It had been many weeks since she had last been with him, and Rihana felt an unbidden longing stir within her, but she forced the feeling aside. For someone so accustomed to manipulating others, she was not about to let him control her in this way. At least, not until whatever business they had was concluded and she was ready to "allow" him to manipulate her at her leisure. Reluctantly, she pushed him away at arm's length.

"I thought you didn't want any refreshment," she said, hoping that her mocking tone would hide her desire. "System!" She paced to the far wall, reaching it just as a darkly burnished oaken panel slid aside to reveal a small but well-stocked bar. She tumbled several ice cubes into a glass and poured herself a drink, then took a seat behind the desk. "If you've changed your mind," she said, gesturing with the glass toward the bar, "help yourself to something other than me. Now, I'll ask again: What's so important that you could not stick to the very schedule that *you* set up?"

Rapson said nothing as he went to the bar and selected a bottle of wine, then uncorked it. "Other refreshments we'll save for later, then." He poured two glasses and, taking both in one hand, the bottle in the other, he sat in the single chair facing the desk. "Get rid of that," he said, placing the bottle and one of the glasses in front of him as he handed the other glass to her. "It's too early in the day for anything but a good wine." She thought for a moment, then set her original drink aside and accepted the offered glass. Rapson smiled, genuinely this time, and took a long sip from his own glass.

"This is the reason I requested meeting you out here, instead of waiting for your arrival next week." He reached into his jacket and pulled out a data stick, tossing it on the desk. The stick rolled on the desktop until finally slowing and coming to rest in front of her on the pocket clip at one end. "You can examine the contents if you want, but suffice it to say that things have started happening at the sunstation on Mercury a bit sooner than I'd expected."

"What—?" She had raised the glass to drink but paused now, the glass mere centimeters from her lips. "What's happening there, and just how does it affect us?"

"It's all right, I think. It alters the timetable somewhat, but shouldn't really force us to change any plans." Rapson settled back in his chair and poured himself a second glass of wine. If he was disturbed by the turn of events, he didn't show it. Or perhaps he had already had enough time to digest this worrisome bit of information and adjust to the changes it would dictate. "Some of the personnel there who are sympathetic to our, ah, 'needs'—one of the Academy scientists and, I think, a couple of the Imperial guards—got a little out of hand and started something they couldn't finish, although I'm not sure why. Adela de Montgarde was there until a few weeks ago, however; maybe it was her presence at the station that set things off. In any event, once things turned sour Rice apparently decided to wake the alien up sooner than we expected."

"I see." Rihana reflected on the news. "It makes sense, I suppose. If he had any thoughts of getting out of there after it all started, he and anyone loyal to him stood a better chance if the thing was moving around under its own power than if it was still lying frozen in a cryosleep tank. Still . . ." Taking her glass with her, she rose from the desk and walked slowly, deliberately around the room as she spoke. "What kind of help does he have?"

Rapson smiled. "That's the good part. Boscawen and Le Châtelier are dead; and the one or two Imperial guards Koll wasn't able to control are under lock and key. Rice has recircuited security and barricaded an entire section of the sunstation, but he's effectively on his own and cut off from them. Or, at least he thinks he is. Under my direction, Koll's essentially let him do pretty much what he wants, which is to hide out in his little secure area and take care of the alien."

"Good." Rihana nodded, smiling. "This works out better, actually. This way Rice is doing a lot of the work for us. All we have to do is wait. You said he'd already started waking the alien up; how much longer before the thing is up and around?"

Rapson slid the sleeve of his expensive suit coat up a few centimeters and looked at the gold timepiece on his wrist. "Tomorrow morning."

She thought a few moments, sipping delicately at the wine. As always, Rapson had picked a perfect vintage.

Rihana reached into her hair and removed the jeweled clip, tossing it casually on the desk as she shook out her hair.

"In that case, then," she said, turning demurely to him and extending her wineglass, "I suppose that leaves us more than enough time for refreshment."

ELEVEN
Outback

The water was silent; utterly quiet and deliciously warm. Their hike from Ellenbrae had been long, the primitive Aboriginal track hot and dusty. Trudging through the lengthy gorge to reach this pool, Adela hadn't been sure her tired feet could carry her farther, but the aching fatigue she'd felt in her legs and calves only an hour earlier was but memory now, soothed by her swim. She was alive again, and relished the way the tepid water slid past her naked skin as she glided gracefully, weightlessly upward.

As she swam slowly up to the air, Adela opened her eyes and saw the brightness rippling on the mirrorlike surface of the pool. The Sun itself was too low on the horizon now to be seen from their vantage point deep within the notch, but the rock faces were very light in color and easily reflected the remaining daylight, as well as its life-giving warmth, well down into the placid water.

A flash of silver caught her eye: a school of fish, startled at the unexpected intrusion into their private, quiet world. She stopped all movement, allowing herself to float casually upward, and watched the little animals as they turned in unison, sending another sudden flash in her direction before they wriggled out of sight.

She broke the surface and inhaled deeply, enjoying the heated, friendly scent of the Australian outback as it mixed with the water splashing at her shoulders. Closing her eyes, she ran both hands up across her face, then back over the top of her head, smoothing down her long hair. Another deep breath, then another; the air proved to be nearly as invigorating as the swim had been.

She floated there a moment, orienting herself. She had come up "backward," facing the rocky crag that formed one side of the bowl-like notch containing the hidden pool. The entire area reminded her of a deep, narrow crater on the moon, but unlike the desolate surface of Luna, this "crater" was alive with greenery, its sides lined with every manner of shrub and tree native to northwestern Australia. Even the very water glowed a translucent emerald. Treading to keep herself afloat, she rotated to face Billy, calling out, "You never told me it was this beautiful!" Her excited voice echoed back at her from the steep sides of their enclosed paradise.

In contrast to the far side of the notch, which was a vertical, enclosing rock face accessible only by climbing precariously down from above, Billy had set up their camp on a sandy, crescent-shaped beach measuring some twenty meters at its widest point. Behind and to one side of their camp, a narrow, featureless gorge led back the way they had entered, to the somewhat more even terrain of the outback itself. The beach tapered as it encircled the pool to only a few meters at each end of the crescent before disappearing beneath the water; another ten meters, and the sand might have completely enclosed the pool instead of presenting a sheer rock face at this single spot on the far side.

"Glad you like it," he replied, walking to the water's edge. As he always did when outdoors, he had discarded most of his clothes, and now wore only a tattered pair of cutoff denim pants. "Now you know why I like comin' back here so much."

"I love it, too!" Delighting in the echo, Adela tilted her head back, cupping her hands over her mouth while treading with her feet. "Helloooooooo!" She laughed out loud, feeling relaxed and happy for the first time in weeks. As the echo died away, Adela waved and dove one last time into the welcoming depths of the pool before swimming back to the beach.

"You're lookin' a bit waterlogged," Billy said, smiling, as she walked waist-deep toward the shore, then turned back to tend the small fire he'd built. "I've about got the water hot enough if you're ready for some *kapati.*"

She retrieved her clothes and dressed unhurriedly, feeling little false modesty about covering herself after her swim. With anyone else she might have been uneasy, or at least a bit self-conscious about stripping to bathe in the sunshine, but around Billy everything seemed—what? More relaxed? More easygoing? There was a tranquillity about the Aborigine—and about this special, secret place that he was willing to share with her—that somehow transcended stuffy rules and protocol. Here with him, in this place, she could be herself.

No worries, she said to herself, remembering the phrase he liked to use whenever he thought that everything was all right, that all would be for the best.

There had been a dramatic change in her friend since she had last seen him, back at the Imperial estate in Kentucky. Physically, although he remained stockier and more broad-shouldered than when they had first met, he had slimmed down a great deal since his return to Earth. "I got too soft, in too many ways," he'd told her, "like some jackeroo on the dole." He vowed never again to lose sight of what he had always believed to be important. The many weeks of his walkabout had returned him to a physical condition he'd not enjoyed since assuming the governorship of Darson. Even the simple act of reaching over to the fire sent muscles rippling beneath the dark skin of his back and shoulders.

He had changed emotionally as well. Working with his people, he was sure of himself again. As it turned out, there were many among the Arunta who shared his concerns for the changes taking place among his people. Billy had been able to rally them, not to a "cause," but rather to a reaffirmation of their Song Lines. The more people he spoke to in Kalumburu, the more he came to realize that the old ways were not dead at all, but merely sleeping. And he was helping to wake them up.

No worries, she thought again. A warm smile came to her lips. *It's a good phrase.*

Buttoning her blouse, she picked up her boots and socks and crossed barefooted to the camp, dropping them unceremoniously next to their rolled swags. There were some rocks here near the fire, and she sat cross-legged in front of one, using the big stone as a backrest.

"Thank you, Billy, for bringing me here."

"I've not shared it with many others," he said, handing her a tin cup of steaming, freshly brewed tea. The battered cup looked ancient, and was in nearly as bad shape as the matching tin pot—the "billy," as he had referred to it—that he used to boil the water. "A coupla me mates knew of it, years ago. And I brought Eric here once. Way back before he was Emperor. I think he liked it here as much as you do. . . ." He glanced skyward briefly, gauging how much daylight was left, then regarded her as he sat on one of the rocks and sipped at the hot liquid in his own cup. "When'd you say you're leavin' again? Before you go, you should talk'm into comin' back here with me. I think it'd do him good."

Adela nodded wordlessly, considering the suggestion. "I've arranged passage to Gris and will be leaving in about three weeks." Eric had offered Imperial transportation, of course, but she had refused it, preferring to run away on her own. "But I do plan to see him before I go."

There was an uncomfortable silence that lasted several seconds. In the quiet moment, the gathering twilight and growing night sounds seemed to weigh heavily on both of them.

"I promise I'll talk to him about it. Before I leave."

"Hungry?" Billy asked, changing the subject. He reached for the worn canvas rucksack he had brought and rummaged around inside.

"Starving." She hadn't thought about food at all in the last hour, but the mention of it now set her stomach to growling and she reached for her own backpack, a more modern carryall constructed of brightly colored synthetic fabric. "What have you brought?"

Billy produced a variety of foil-wrapped packages as well as several pieces of fresh fruit sealed in a cool-sack. "If you want," he said, smiling, "I'll catch us a fish and cook it right here."

"No, that's all right." Adela wasn't entirely certain if he was even serious or not: The smile on his face indicated that however reacquainted he may have become with the outback since his return, he still looked a bit doubtful about remembering the necessary hunting skills. "I'm so hungry, I don't think I can wait that long," she said, opting for discretion, and tore open one of the pouches. Between what the two of them had brought, their appetites were more than adequately taken care of.

An hour later, they each lay back next to the fire, staring at the star-filled sky above them. Adela had unrolled her swag, and was surprised at how comfortable the simple sleeproll could be on the packed sand underneath. Billy, meanwhile, lay on the bare ground, hands clasped behind his head, leaving his own swag untouched. She wondered why he'd even brought it along.

The fire was still hot, the heaped coals glowing a dull red-orange, but the flames had died down. Their camp now in near-darkness, the stars visible beyond the rim of the notch glimmered in the night sky like white-hot diamonds.

"I don't think I'm ever goin' back there," Billy was saying. "There's not much more I can do there anyway. Eric gave me the governorship, asked me to have a go at helping turn it into a civilized world. Well, I done that."

Adela smiled at her friend's show of modesty. She propped herself up on an elbow and looked at him across the fire, but was barely able to make out his prone figure in the ruddy light. "From what I've been able to learn, you did considerably more than that. You took a failing colony and made it thrive. Eric told me that were it not for you, Darson would most likely have been abandoned."

"I doubt that." He shrugged, the gesture more felt in his words than seen in the weak illumination cast by the glowing coals. "Anyway, I did what I could and it looks like she'll be sweet up there without any more help from me." Billy got abruptly to his feet and walked a few meters away from the camp, then returned with several pieces of dry driftwood, which he dropped next to the fire.

"I hated you, ya know," he went on as he squatted to stir the embers and add the pieces of wood one at a time. He remained in a squatting position, curling one strong arm around his knees and absently poking the embers while he spoke. "I saw what'd become of my people—the whole bloody Earth!—and I blamed you for all of it."

The fire glowed brightly now, and in the light Adela could see how important this confession was to him. Obviously, this time they shared alone together before she returned to Gris was as meaningful to him as it was to her.

"But you savin' the Sun was no more responsible for changin' the world than my leavin' was for changin' my people. I was a bloody hoon to think it was."

"You were not a fool," she said sensitively. "In truth, I've done my own share of self-blaming, too. I let Jephthah get to me. I knew, somewhere deep down inside me, that nothing he said was true, but I used what he said to punish myself for something that I knew was . . . Well, I know better now." She paused, swallowing audibly as she formed her thoughts. "And I'll tell you something else: When I decided to go back to Gris, I was just running away. I didn't admit it to myself then, but I just wanted to run away from everything that had to do with the decisions that are a part of my past. Decisions I had made." She sat up into a cross-legged position and regarded her old friend across the dancing flames. Billy met her eyes silently and wrapped both arms around his knees, waiting for her to go on.

"But you know what, Billy? My situation and yours are more similar than you might think. You did everything you wanted to do on Darson, accomplished what you wanted to accomplish. But knowing that your work was done is what allowed you to come back to Earth, it's what allows you to work so hard now for your people." There was a sudden high-pitched cry, that of some night bird, and Adela waited, listening, as it faded in the distance. "Let me ask you something: When you left Darson, did you leave anything behind?"

"I . . . No, nothing. I was finished there."

"You didn't want to stick around, watch what became of your handiwork? Become a part of it yourself?"

Billy's eyes narrowed, a look of puzzlement spreading across his face. "Adela . . . I don't know what you're gettin' at."

She nodded, a new realization coming to her for the first time, and sighed deeply, sadly. "I did," she said finally, her voice a whisper. "Everything was done on the project when I decided to go into cryosleep; to become a—what do they call it? A 'slow timer'?" She snorted distastefully at the word. "There was no need for me to stay involved, Billy. I wanted to be there when my project was completed, work with it through the centuries. I didn't even realize that I had equated this thing with myself—I *was* the project, and felt that the project was nothing without me. I was selfish and self-centered." She paused, exhaling heavily. The fire was dying again, the shadows deepening around them once more. Neither said anything for several long minutes as they listened to the ever-present insects singing their night songs.

"Billy, when you left Earth for Darson, did you leave anyone behind?" she asked finally.

The Aborigine shook his head in understanding. "Nah. I had someone once, before leaving Earth. But she and I had different goals and parted long before I met you. I had a lot of good mates on Darson, and even fell in love once, but it ended decades ago."

"Do you think about them?"

Billy hesitated at the question, then said, "I s'pose so, now and again."

"I've fallen in love only once," she said. "And I gave him up just so I could keep myself involved in something that no longer

truly needed me." She chuckled somberly at the newfound awareness. "I thought I had to keep myself as young as I could, so I
could see everything about this project through not only to its
completion, but for centuries afterward. I let that blind me to just
how important Javas was to me, and how unimportant I had
become to this project. It seduced me, Billy, away from what I'd
really wanted all along: to be with a man who loved me above all
else. I could have had that." She pointed to him. "Look at you,
Billy. Other than short periods of cryosleep before wormhole
travel was perfected, you've not slept your whole life away. Medical rejuvenation still has its limitations, I know, but I could have
stayed with Javas and *still* have been here right now, working on
this thing if I'd wanted to."

The driftwood in the fire shifted noisily and the glow increased,
bathing them both in unexpected brightness.

"But no," she said, turning away shamefully from the gentle
radiance. "I wanted more assurance than that. And I traded
Javas for it. I'm the fool, Billy."

Her friend started to say something, but she paid little attention as she lay back on her swag and turned away from the fire.
Billy, sensing her need for solitude, said nothing more and he,
too, settled in for the night.

Adela lay thinking for a few minutes longer, listening to the
crackling of the dying fire, the chittering of the insects and the
occasional night animal. Before long, however, she fell into a
troubled, restless slumber.

TWELVE
Back in the Game

It was still dark, but only barely, when she opened her eyes at
the sound of some incongruously loud and annoying night
bird. Overhead, the stars twinkled in a sky that was just now
beginning to show the first hint of gray with the approaching
dawn. The chirping cry was muffled and seemed, once she
managed to blink a bit more of the sleep away, to be coming from
the other side of what was left of the fire, now reduced to a pile

of smoking, dull orange embers that peeked out from beneath a blanket of gray-white ashes.

She sat up, shedding the thin blanket she must have pulled over herself during the night, and in the growing light found Billy digging into his canvas rucksack.

"Billy, what is it?" She was wide awake now.

"Nothin'. Just me bloody . . . Ah, here." He pulled out a chirping communication handset—a "handlink," as it was customarily called, due to the way it was linked into the cislunar satellite communication network. She had several of her own and had, in fact, brought one in her pack. She had purposely turned her handlink off, however; Billy's, evidently, had been left on the normal standby setting. He unfolded the unit into an open position, abruptly silencing the incessant chirping, and pressed it to his face.

"Yah?" He waited several moments, then, "Sure."

Seeing that he was obviously waiting for a connection to be put through, Adela asked, "What's going on?" She was surprised at the hint of irritation in her own voice, and wondered why Billy's carrying a handlink should annoy her so. Maybe it was the contradiction with his lifestyle the piece of high technology represented that was so jarring. Or maybe it was the passing thought that because of her presence here in this untamed environment, he felt he needed to remain in touch with civilization out of some personal obligation to look out for her, take care of her. As the first rays of sunshine crept over the notch walls and illuminated the tiny paradise, she quickly discarded both ideas. In truth, it was the intrusion into a private moment of her life that the demanding handlink represented, and nothing that Billy had done in carrying it. Noting that his own expression had changed from one of annoyance to concern, she instantly regretted her tone of voice and asked again, more delicately this time, "What's going on? Is everything all right?"

"It's Eric," he answered, apparently unaware of any unintended slight on her part. "They're putting him through now."

"What's your setting?" She scrambled for the pack that had served as a makeshift pillow the previous night and hastily found her own handlink where it had settled near the bottom. Flicking the power switch, she snapped it open, deftly touching in the setting as Billy read off the sequence of numbers, and put it to her ear just as the connection went through.

"Billy?" There was an urgency to Eric's voice she had never heard before.

"Yes, I'm here," Billy said, nearly all traces of his informal, outback speaking patterns gone. Clearly, he had not been expecting a call from the Emperor—or anyone else, for that matter—and took this turn of events seriously. "Adela's here, too."

"Good, you're still together. When they told me her handlink was off-line, I thought . . . Anyway, I need to see you both. Immediately."

"Eric, what's wrong?" she demanded.

Even in the tiny speaker of the handlink, she heard him exhale heavily. "It'll be better if I wait until I see you."

"All right," Billy cut in. Even as he spoke he gathered odds and ends of their belongings and started tossing them into the open packs. "As soon as we break the connection I'll call Ellenbrae and arrange to get a hopper out here to pick us up."

"Don't bother. I'll be waiting for you at the opening of the gorge, in the flat area to your left as you come out. Leave your things. I've already got someone coming in to collect them for you; you'll probably pass them on your way out."

"You're *here?*" Adela asked. "Eric, can't you at least give us a hint of what's going on?"

"Not on a handlink, Mother. I'm sorry, but it may not be safe. See you both soon. Good-bye." The connection immediately went dead.

"Crimey," Billy said under his breath as he folded his handlink, slipping the thin unit into a back pocket of his shorts. "Now, why would he worry about sayin' something over an Imperial communications link? With the security scramblin' built into the Imperial nets, no bloody way anyone could possibly listen in."

Adela pulled on her hiking boots and hastily yanked the laces tight. "I don't know," she said, on her feet and already heading for the gorge leading away from the now-forgotten bit of paradise. "Let's go find out."

They heard the approaching team Eric had sent before they saw them. There were ten of them, all jogging double-time in precise military formation in their direction. All were armed. When they reached them, the group stopped only long enough for their team leader, a tall woman with a heavy offworld accent, to send a pair of her fastest runners ahead to the camp to retrieve their things. She and the other seven escorted the two of them through the remaining section of the gorge. Aside from a polite greeting and her orders to the two guards she'd sent to their campsite at the notch, she spoke little and neither Adela nor Billy bothered to ask what was happening.

As they neared the end of the gorge, the walls became lower and spread farther apart, and the air grew warmer out of the sheltering depth of the fissure, but the early sunshine had not yet heated the outback to what they had become accustomed to. In a few hours, it would be stifling.

Adela wasn't sure what she had expected to find once they got there, but it certainly wasn't the fully outfitted landing shuttle they now saw glinting in the morning brightness. Several people, all of them in uniform of one variety or another, milled about at the base of the thing. It was easy to see, even at this distance, that most of them were armed.

The shuttle itself was large, of a type that could easily transport a hundred or more passengers. This craft was of no design she had ever seen before, but the markings clearly showed it to be a commercial vessel, not one belonging to the Imperial fleet. She felt a moment's anxiety that something was dreadfully wrong, that somehow they had been lured out under false pretenses, but she quickly discarded the notion. If anyone flying a ship this size had wanted to do them harm, they could have easily done so already from the air while they were still in the notch.

Her fears were further calmed when, as they drew near enough to see clearly the faces of those at the base of the shuttle, she saw Eric himself anxiously pacing. The others, she now saw, were armed military personnel, their uniform markings identifying them as the Emperor's personal guard. Eric waved to them as they approached.

"I'm glad that you're together," he said. "It saves a great deal of precious time." He embraced his mother in greeting, exhaling in a sigh of relief that told her that finding her here was more than something he considered a mere convenience. There was something behind his words that almost sounded like he hadn't really expected to find her at all. As they parted and he vigorously shook Billy's hand, she also noted that he was in full uniform, and even wore the Imperial sash. "Come inside, both of you. We need to talk."

The three of them were escorted inside, where the shuttle's similarity to a commercial vehicle came to a jarring halt. While the vessel's design might originally have been for commercial use, this ship proved to be no less than a movable Imperial Court, the commercial markings on the hull obviously intended as disguise. Adela once more felt her nerves twitch. Something serious was happening here. Why else would her son fly halfway around the planet in a disguised ship to discuss something that couldn't even be mentioned over normal, secure Imperial communications links?

Eric took them to a room that appeared part briefing room, part office. As such, the room looked similar to many others Adela had seen aboard Imperial craft that were alternately used for informal meetings or simply to get necessary work done. There was a study area with a desk, complete with a manual data terminal, set off to one side of the room; a long table with comfortable padded chairs was arranged on the other. On one wall, the one nearest the table, was a large mural that must surely be a holoframe. There were amenities here as well: a plush leather sofa and a pair of matching high-backed chairs surrounding a low table with two silver trays. One of the trays held various bottles and glasses, but it was the other tray that demanded her attention; it held, judging from the rich aroma she'd noticed upon entering the room, a steaming pot of coffee and several cups.

"I'm sorry for all of this," Eric said at last, once the escort had been dismissed and the three of them were alone. He pulled the sash over his head and tossed it casually across the meeting table as he headed for the sofa, unbuttoning the tight collar of his jacket as he did. He poured coffee for all of them, passing the delicate china cups around as he filled them. Replacing the decorative silver coffeepot on the tray, he approached the table and pulled three chairs out for them.

Adela could barely stand it. "Eric, what's—"

"Please, watch this before you ask anything else."

Eric took the centermost of the three chairs and faced the mural, which immediately faded from view at his silent integrator command, to be replaced with a soft blue field. The Imperial crest, with a sequence of numbers below it, occupied the image's center. The numbers were meaningless to Adela, except to indicate that what they were about to see was a recording as opposed to a live transmission.

For some reason, Adela was not the least surprised when Jephthah's image faded into view.

"This isn't pleasant for me." Jephthah's voice was still as deep and commanding as she remembered, but somehow he sounded almost repentant as he spoke. He looked tired, troubled, and seemed almost nervous as he gazed from the holoframe. She also noted that the reactionary was not as well dressed as he usually was, and gave the appearance, with his open-collared shirt and slightly disheveled hair, that this transmission had been done in a hurry with little preparation. There was even a sense of desperate urgency about it. From what she had learned about Jephthah, Adela was convinced that any tone or underlying message put forth in one of his transmissions was not only intended, but most certainly rehearsed.

"My friends, we have reached a crisis point in our existence. I have warned the Human Worlds for so long about the threat presented by the Outsiders that you might think I would take pleasure in what I am about to show you." He lowered his head, shaking it slowly, and took a deep breath before continuing. "Please believe me when I tell you that nothing that has happened, although it justifies even the very worst of my fears, gives me even the slightest amount of satisfaction. Let me warn you, too, that what you will see in the next few minutes is not pleasant to behold.

"You may recall that several months ago I spoke to you of an alien, a Sarpan scientist who had somehow coerced our own scientists to allow it to be placed into cryonic suspension. This alien, along with its human companion, had been taken to a research station on Mercury, in Sol system, to await the day when the grand project to save Earth's Sun neared completion."

Jephthah turned away briefly, then continued, a self-conscious look on his face. "I admit, this particular alien had been instrumental—working alongside humans—in not only helping to perfect the scientific procedures developed by Dr. Adela de Montgarde, but in the discovery of the very nature of wormholes. It is to this alien we owe a debt of gratitude, for without its help we might never have developed wormhole spaceflight.

"Its name was Oidar, and because of its contribution to human science we gratefully—if naively—assented to its request to be present for the conclusion of the greatest human endeavor of all time. But that was our fatal mistake. You see, we allowed our own gratitude to blind us. We allowed ourselves to consider this Oidar's contribution a gift, rather than the self-serving ploy it was: a device intended solely to gain our trust."

Jephthah's image faded in the recording and was replaced with a picture of a small, cratered planet that looked like nothing so much as some forlorn moon.

"This is Mercury," Jephthah continued as the image rotated and centered on the desolate planet's south polar region. As the image zoomed in, Adela recognized the research facility located at Chao Meng-fu. "It is the innermost of Sol system's nine planets, and location of four 'sunstations' critical to monitoring the finishing stages of Dr. Montgarde's glorious project. What you're

going to see was recorded at the station you're looking at now.
I apologize if the recording is blurred or difficult to follow; the
high angle of the surveillance cameras used to document these
events did not offer an optimum viewing perspective."

The overhead shot of the sunstation was replaced immediately
with a stationary view of a modest, sparsely furnished room. As
Jephthah had warned, the recording-within-a-recording had been
made from a wide-angle lens placed near the ceiling, which gave
the entire picture an ethereal feel. Objects nearest the lens, like the
simple chair almost immediately below it, appeared grotesquely
out of shape. The upper portion of the chair's backrest was
seemingly three times the width of the seat and legs beneath it.
Even the room itself twisted into a trapezoidal shape that seemed
to fan out from the viewpoint of the surveillance lens.

There were two cryosleep tanks at the far side of the room,
although in the fish-eye image they seemed to curve upward over
a sloping floor. One of the tanks was dark, sealed and obviously
unused. The plastiglass lid of the other had been removed, and
now rested against the wall. There was a man in a lab coat near
the open tank who was busily engaged in what Adela recognized
at once as a reawakening procedure. She had certainly experienced cryosleep enough to know what it was like. There was
something unusual about the man's actions, however, in that he
had a pressure bottle tucked under one arm and appeared to be
spraying the contents into the cryotank. Littering the floor were
several smaller bottles, plainly empty, that Adela recognized as
juice packages. If the occupant of the tank had already consumed
that much rehydrant, then the cryosleep wake-up procedure they
were watching must be fairly well complete. He abruptly dropped
the sprayer apparatus and set the bottle aside, then leaned into
the tank, helping someone inside to sit up. The image suddenly
froze.

"We've already confirmed the man as Dr. Templeton Rice,"
Eric said, a silent integrator command causing the paused recording to zoom in to the center of the picture, highlighting the tank's
occupant. "Mother, you worked closely with Oidar. Is that him?"

Adela looked closely at the image. "I . . . can't be certain. The
angle makes it . . . Can you correct it?"

Eric concentrated as he requested the necessary adjustments
from the playback computer. The image tilted suddenly, "un-
bending" itself into an almost normal still frame.

Adela gasped. The alien appeared near death, his face frozen
in what looked like a desperate attempt to merely draw his next

breath. His skin was an unhealthy-appearing gray-brown, not the vibrant green-brown normal for a Sarpan of his age. More disturbingly, his skin looked dry and brittle, and the gill slits on each side of his face drooped limply despite the wetting-down he had just received. The nictitating membranes on his eyes, halted mid-blink in the still image, appeared cloudy, gummy.

"My God," she whispered, the tone of her voice confirming what Eric had asked. "What have they done to him?"

The recording switched to its original angle and resumed playback with Rice helping the alien up to a sitting position. "Easy! Not too fast!" he said desperately. "How do you feel?"

Oidar turned to face his friend, barely able to keep his bobbing head erect. He blinked several times and managed to grasp the man's forearm with a shaking webbed hand. "Temple . . .?" His voice was little more than a croaked whisper, barely audible.

"Yes, it's me! I'm right here!"

"Temple . . . my friend. This one is . . . pleased . . . to see you." Oidar gave a weak attempt to imitate a human smile, an unnatural expression for the Sarpan that Adela knew had been learned only through long hours of painstaking practice.

There was a sudden pounding, which drew Rice's attention to a point directly below the camera lens. The pounding shifted to splintering, and he jumped to his feet just as the door burst open at the bottom of the image, seemingly "downhill" from where he stood. Thick smoke billowed through the room, while pieces of the doorframe itself were sent scattering about the floor. There were several loud discharges; with each, a small hole exploded in the wall behind Rice.

"No!" Dropping to one knee, Rice pulled a weapon of some sort from his belt and fired at whoever was attacking him, the gun making an exaggerated puffing sound that was almost lost in the commotion—a needle gun. He fired twice, his aim true in the close quarters, and two bodies came into range of the camera lens as they fell to the floor, unmoving. There was a good deal of scuffling and shouting from somewhere outside the pickup range, but no one else appeared. After a moment, Rice tucked the gun back into his belt and tended to the alien, who, although still shaky, was obviously recovering. His coloring was already improving, and his eyes were beginning to look slightly clearer than before.

"Come on, Oidar," Rice barked, helping the alien out of the tank and up onto thin, wobbly legs. As Oidar steadied himself against the side of the tank, Rice yanked at the wires and tubing that stretched from the tight-fitting cryosuit and stockings back into the tank itself, ripping them loose. A few of the longer dangling wires he then tore from the suit, ignoring the others. "Listen, we've got to get to the evac pods. Can you walk?"

Oidar didn't answer, but started moving almost immediately. His gait was slow—one foot, carefully but unsteadily placed before the other—but with Rice's arm around his reed-thin waist, within a few steps he seemed to reacquire a fair sense of the balance he'd lost during his two-hundred-year sleep.

"Good; that's good." Without taking the supporting arm from around his friend's waist, Rice swept at one of the soldier's bodies and grabbed the man's weapon with his free hand. "Here," he said, handing it to Oidar. "Take this and hang on to it." None of them got a good look at it before he moved under the camera, but it was clearly a projectile weapon considerably more deadly than the needle gun that had put to sleep the two who had burst into the room. Just before disappearing under the surveillance camera, Rice grabbed the other man's gun as well.

Abruptly and without warning, the image suddenly changed to one that was oriented from a handheld video pickup. The carnage it showed nearly turned Adela's stomach as Jephthah's voice-over continued.

"Unfortunately, there were no other surveillance cameras that could record the events that occurred next. However, it is all too easy to show you the results of what happened."

The handheld camera showed the entrance to the cryosleep chamber from the corridor, the shattered fragments of the doorway still hanging around the edges of the image. There were the two uniformed bodies, lifeless and bleeding, a pool of dark blood beneath each.

A quick cut to another jerky handheld shot. This showed the results of a different exchange of weapons fire. Two bodies lay crumpled on the floor, one reaching up and hanging from a remote console as if she had been gunned down while calling for help. Both wore lab coats, although from the grotesque position of the bodies Adela couldn't identify them as any of the scientists she had met during her visit to the sunstation. The woman had been shot—three times, judging from the triangular pattern of bloodstains on her white coat—in the back; the other in the face at close range.

Another quick cut to what appeared to be a vehicle hangar or storage facility of some type; there were a couple of small caterpillar transports here, as well as a dismantled short-range surface hopper that looked to be undergoing repair. There was another body; this one was neither a soldier nor scientist, as his greasy coveralls attested, but rather an engineering tech. He had also been shot in the face. A small plastic case and a scattering of tools spilled at his right hand indicated that the man had been taken by surprise.

Another quick cut, this one to what was unmistakably an evac-pod hatch. The status lights above the hatch blinked red: empty. There were four bodies here, all of them Imperial soldiers. From the position of the bodies, it looked like a full-scale firefight had taken place here.

The image cut again, this time to a tight shot of Jephthah. His face was pained, saddened, and in this close-up view it looked as though he hadn't slept in quite some time.

"I apologize if what I've just presented has repulsed you. Seeing it again, now, I am just as sickened as the first time I saw it. I am truly sorry.

"But, after thinking long and hard, I decided that it was necessary to present it as I did, for, as I said at the beginning, the Human Worlds have reached a turning point." He lowered his head dramatically once more, as if to emphasize the crisis.

"Dr. Templeton Rice, a close associate of Dr. Adela de Montgarde, and the Sarpan astrophysicist known as 'Oidar' have murdered the entire crew—Academy scientists, Imperial soldiers, even the civilian support personnel—of the sunstation at Chao Meng-fu in order to make their getaway. The events leading up to their escape were documented by the Imperial forces stationed there, and will be accessible on the public nets in short order, if they are not already, to those with access clearance. Before he himself was brutally killed attempting to prevent the liftoff of the evacuation pod, Lieutenant Jerzy Koll, the officer in command of the Imperial forces at the sunstation, thoroughly documented Dr. Rice's actions preceding his illegal takeover of portions of the station, as well as the murder of the two Academy scientists who trusted him."

Jephthah lowered his head again, not looking at the camera as he concluded, "This entire treasonous misadventure—the reanimation of the sleeping alien, the certain theft of centuries of hard-gained research, the murder of several innocent people and, ultimately, an escape to parts unknown—was clearly planned, to an exacting degree, by Dr. Templeton Rice, who thought nothing of casually slaughtering his own friends, researchers who wanted only to achieve success in their worthy goal of saving the home-world of all humanity."

There was a long pause then as Jephthah stared out from the recording once more. So long, in fact, that Adela and Billy almost thought that it had concluded. Suddenly, Jephthah's face turned to a visage of rage as he addressed the camera, his voice rising as she had never heard it before.

"Isn't it time we had some answers!" he bellowed, pounding his fist forcefully, loudly, somewhere outside the video pickup. "Why haven't we heard from our Emperor? It should be painfully evident, even to the most skeptical, that the Sarpan present a threat of unimaginable magnitude. They *fear* us! They *envy* us! They covet our knowledge, and they covet our accomplishments! How is it possible that a trusted colleague of the Emperor's own mother, Dr. Adela de Montgarde, can plot something of this nature for years without his knowledge?"

He lowered his voice, his eyes narrowing, his features taking on a curious mien. "And just where is the honorable Dr. Montgarde?" He snorted contemptuously, a suspicion-filled smile appearing on his lips. "I, for one, thought she was to be instrumental in bringing the project to save Earth's Sun to fruition. Instead, she is nowhere to be seen. Is it possible that she has more to do with what happened on Mercury than we know?

"Speak to us, Emperor of the Human Worlds! You have led us well for so many years. Do not forsake us now in our time of great need."

The recording ended abruptly, fading instantly from the holo-frame upon completion. The screen remained dark; Eric didn't bother to replace the mural. Adela's hands were shaking as she set her cup down, the fine china chattering against the saucer, her coffee now cold.

"How much of what we just saw was true?" she asked softly, emotionlessly. "And how much was lies?"

"For the record," Eric began. "All personnel at Chao Meng-fu were killed except for Rice. I personally reviewed the report from the sunstation only five hours ago, and can tell you that although Rice certainly is responsible for some of what we just saw, any deaths he caused were in self-defense. Despite the weapons they had with them, the pair of them could not have done all of this. Contrary to what he said, there were other surveillance cameras at the station that should have recorded some of what occurred, but those that showed anything other than Rice and Oidar mov-

ing through corridors were either conveniently destroyed by gunfire, or were, for some reason, off-line."

Billy cleared his throat and leaned back heavily in his chair.
"I've been in a firefight before, in close quarters like those we
saw," he said, his voice deadly serious. "There's no way trained
military personnel, outnumberin' Rice the way they did, could've
been so completely overwhelmed. I just won't believe it."

"I won't either," Adela added. "I know Rice, and it's hard
enough to accept that he could do it even in self-defense, much
less as an aggressor."

Eric paused, then said, "And Oidar?"

"You can't be serious, Eric. Did you see him?" She shook her
head in disbelief. "I don't care what this lunatic claims, or what
he shows in his damned recording, either; it was all Oidar could
do to even keep himself erect."

The Emperor nodded thoughtfully. "The gun we saw Rice give
Oidar was found just outside the cryosleep chamber, unfired.
This recording was carefully presented to give a specific idea that
they shot their way out of the facility, murdering everyone who
might have been able to stop them or contact the Imperial
Court."

Eric poured himself coffee, then took the cup with him as he
rose and crossed to the far side of the room to stand in front of
the holoframe. "I'm sure you both realize why I couldn't discuss
any of this with you over the handlink. We suspected it for a long
time, but it's certain now that Jephthah has people within official
Imperial circles. He also has access to Imperial communications.
He could not have obtained any of what you just saw without
both." He paused, holding the steaming cup with both hands,
sipping gingerly at it. The hush in the room was palpable.

"We know that Koll was one of his people; the faked records
could only have been done by a commanding Imperial officer.
What isn't apparent in the recording is what the investigating
team found: Koll was killed, executed, *after* the pod left. Medi-
cally speaking, the time frame is clear, which means that Koll was
sacrificed by whatever operative Jephthah had there to accomplish this. Frankly, even though it's been made to look like they
used the evac pod to rendezvous with another ship sympathetic
to the Sarpan, I believe that Rice and Oidar are being held by
Jephthah. Why, I don't know."

Eric said nothing more, and seemed to concentrate on the cup
cradled in his hands, deep in thought. Adela thought perhaps he
was using his integrator to receive additional information and

was connected even now to the Imperial computer net, although he gave no sign that such was the case.

"Eric . . ." Billy said, breaking the silence. "We've been mates a long time now. What is it you're not tellin' us?"

Adela had been thinking along the same lines, and nodded in agreement. "All that you've said, everything we've seen so far, as terrible as it is, has just been a prelude, hasn't it?"

"You're right." Eric approached the table and half sat, half leaned on the edge. He set the cup down, and looked at each of them in turn.

"There was another broadcast, following this one by only a few hours. He even did something he's never done before: He used the same transmission source." Eric snorted contemptuously. "He must have really been in a hurry. Or thought he was so far ahead of us that we couldn't trace him as quickly as we did. In any event, we intercepted and blocked it." He sighed heavily. "I suppose he'll find out soon enough that no one outside the highest circles of the Imperial Court heard him, and he'll rebroadcast the address from another source—not much I can do about that." Eric pulled out one of the chairs on the side of the table opposite the two of them and sat wearily, regarding them each with a weak smile.

"The contents of the second transmission prove beyond doubt that he has somehow breached the Imperial net, as every bit of information in it came from a single communication, coded for my consumption only. No other Imperial communication could possibly contain the information since that time, since I personally had not yet released any of the contents to even my closest advisors between the time I received it and the moment he made his second transmission. However, as the contents of his broadcast contain more of his histrionics than usual, I won't bother playing it for you." He breathed out heavily, mentally preparing himself for what he was about to say.

"I don't need to tell you the kind of hysteria Jephthah has managed to cultivate over the years. Distrust of the Sarpan was always there, going back to some of the regrettably deadly encounters we had with them during first contact. Even an attempt to kill Father and me years ago, when I was barely a teenager, was made to look, at the time, like the aliens' work. This latest business at the sunstation tells me he's ready to advance to the next level of his campaign of hatred. Unfortunately . . ." Eric breathed out suddenly in frustration, his cheeks puffing. She noticed for the first time just how exhausted he was. "Unfortunately, the timing of what he's orchestrated on Mercury couldn't possibly be worse.

"Mother, Billy . . . the stakes in whatever game he's playing have just jumped a thousandfold. A survey vessel, the *Paloma Blanco,* commanded by Gareth Anmoore, has filed a report stating that they have just discovered a third intelligent race on an Earthlike world orbiting Tsing 479. That was the subject of Jephthah's second broadcast."

The news out, Eric relaxed visibly in his chair. Adela watched her son, studied his face, and in his eyes saw the struggle of emotions within him. She got the feeling that the two of them were the first people he had personally told, although other members of the Imperial Court and Academy of Sciences must certainly know by now because of Jephthah's intercepted broadcast. And as the thought struck her, she couldn't help but feel a little bit closer to this son she had never really known. For him to have thought so highly of her, his mother, and of Billy, his best friend, to tell them first confirmed the initial impression she had had of him upon awakening: This leader was one who put *people* foremost in his thoughts, not *Empire.*

"That's incredible," she breathed, unable to think of anything else to say. Billy said nothing, but Adela could tell that he was contemplating the significance and potential repercussions such an announcement would have on the Hundred Worlds following the years of xenophobic propaganda Jephthah had spread. She watched as Billy glanced at Eric and their eyes met. Something was being exchanged there, she knew, a wordless understanding shared only by those who had led others. "Incredible," she repeated.

"Nah," Billy said, facing her. "It was bound to happen."

Eric nodded agreement. "He's right. We've already met our first intelligent race, the Sarpan, centuries ago. Since then we've found life of some kind almost everywhere the Empire has grown. Considering the rate of expansion we're seeing as a result of the wormholes, the only truly incredible thing is that we've not found other intelligent life before this."

Eric paused, rubbing his eyes. He concentrated for a moment, then regarded them once more. "I have instituted new restrictions on communications involving all activities at Tsing 479. A partial 'blackout,' if you will—no descriptions or accounts of the survey work being done there will be sent outside of that system; even at that, I've restricted all intership transmissions in-system to contain only the most basic of information. But please," he said, holding both hands up before him, "don't think that I want to stifle the news of this discovery. It's too late for that, even if I thought there would be any useful reason to. It's just that I want nothing more about it in Jephthah's hands for him to distort and use for his own goals."

Eric stood, a silent integrator command returning the lights in the room to normal, as he looked down into their faces.

"There are very few people whose trust I can absolutely count on in this, so I intend to rely on family more than anything. Imperial protocol be damned. I've already contacted Lewis aboard his flagship and Brendan at the Academy; Cathay is out-of-system, but I hope to hear from her shortly. They will be my eyes and ear at Tsing. In the meantime, I've assigned a working suite to each of you here on the shuttle, and have routed Captain Anmoore's complete report to the system under your personal IDs." He hesitated, licking lips that had gone dry. "Mother, Billy—I need your help. There are no two people I trust more than the two of you, and I want you there to make some decisions for me. Work closely with the others, review everything without putting it through the comm net, then give me your recommendations. I'll back up any conclusions you make."

"You've got it," Adela said instantly. "Jephthah is using my name and my friends to further his propaganda. He's corrupted everything I stand for. Of course I'll do anything I can to help you in this."

Eric smiled. "Thank you, Mother." He turned to his friend, who fidgeted uneasily in his chair. "Billy, you once served my father as Imperial legal liaison. Working closely with my mother, your contributions to the Empire were indispensable; the mission to bring Pallatin back into the Hundred Worlds would not, *could* not, have succeeded without you. I need for the two of you to go to Tsing as soon as—"

"No! I . . . I can't bloody go right now!" Billy was on his feet, his chair nearly tipping over backward as he rose. He paced desperately, literally wringing his hands, his face a frantic mixture of indecision and anguish as he swung himself around to face the Emperor. "Eric, please; don't ask me to leave now!"

Eric said nothing at first, then nodded thoughtfully. "All right," he said simply. There was no anger in his voice, but it was impossible to hide his disappointment. Behind the words, however, Adela knew that he truly understood. "I know you're in the middle of something very important to you, and I respect that."

He crossed to the desk and pulled a data stick from among

several in a cuplike container, then inserted it into a slot in the desktop terminal. He hesitated as he gave a silent integrator command, then withdrew the data stick. He retook his seat and handed the stick to his friend, saying, "This is Captain Anmoore's report; take it with you. I'd like you to be as fully informed as to what's happened there up to now as possible, and would appreciate any ideas you can contribute on the situation." He paused, a thought occurring to him.

"In fact—since Brendan and Lewis will probably be on their way to Tsing before Cathay's back in-system, maybe I could send her down here. As a legitimate Imperial authority and my personal representative, she could assist in any official capacity you need to deal with local government. Could you use some help?"

"Well . . . I'm gonna have a lot of work ahead of me here," he answered, thinking over the offer. "Yeah, I could use the help."

"Then consider it done." The Emperor of the Hundred Worlds rose. "Listen, Billy: What is about to begin at Tsing 479 will last some time, I'm afraid. Please don't think that I'm trying to pressure you when I say this, but whenever you finish your work here, we can use you any time you can get there." He smiled warmly and held out his hand. "Good luck, mate."

Billy accepted his friend's hand, and Adela saw the beginnings of the broad grin she knew so well.

"Thanks, mate."

THIRTEEN
Captives and Captors

Rice's head throbbed as he struggled to sit up. He lay there, frowning sourly at the cottony taste in his mouth as drops of nausea-induced sweat trickled down his scalp. He blinked rapidly, resting the back of his left wrist on his forehead, and felt a sharp, unexpected scraping. He blinked at his arm and saw that he was wearing a stiff, plastic medimonitor bracelet. He stared dumbly at it, trying to decipher the readings, but his churning stomach forced his eyes closed again.

The first attempt to sit resulted in little more than his bending his head and upper body forward before falling dizzily back against the cushioning softness. The room was spinning even before his head hit the pillow, and he closed his eyes tightly, willing the nausea to go away. His insides finally stopped twisting long enough for him to slowly open his eyes and examine the objects nearest him. On each side of the bed was a guardrail with a keypad membrane running the length of the smooth surface. The keypad on the left matched the one his right hand still gripped tightly following his ill-timed attempt to pull himself to a sitting position. He squinted at it, trying to force his eyes to give him a nonblurred image, then thumbed one of the keys. There was a slight hum at the skin of his back and the top portion of the bed rose slowly, smoothly until he was almost sitting upright.

He managed to swing his legs over the side of the bed and looked around, still fighting off the light-headedness he felt, longing for the comfort of lying horizontally again. *In a minute,* he promised himself, trying to shake the cobwebs from his brain. *As soon as I figure out where the hell I am, I'm going to lie down and sleep for a month.* The lights in the room were at a low level, and Rice—eyelids still fluttering involuntarily—did his best to make out the surroundings in the dimness.

Obviously, he was in a hospital room or, at least, a room whose sole purpose was the medical attention of its occupant. Three of the walls were featureless, although there was a door in the wall directly opposite the foot of the bed; the fourth, to his immediate right, was nearly all glass extending from floor to ceiling. Or maybe not glass. It could have been a nonpermeable shield that divided one long room into as many separate smaller ones as were needed. From the edge of the bed—and he was not yet confident enough to attempt standing nearer the clear wall for a closer look—he couldn't see much in the adjoining room, which was completely dark. However, he could make out a light-colored shape that might be another bed. Above it blinked readouts similar to those on the tall headboard above his own.

His head clearing, he turned to study the array of monitoring equipment behind him, the various winking lights corresponding to the data collected by the medimonitor on his wrist. Standard stuff, mostly, he decided. But among the readouts he recognized one that explained the cottonmouth feeling as well as his dizziness and disorientation—he was on medication.

There was another readout, this one a simple red panel with the words CALL INITIATED. Whatever program was monitoring him had obviously included a subroutine to alert—whom?—that he had awakened.

The door opened abruptly and Rice turned, squinting anew at the bright light flooding into the room from the corridor. He released his grip on the rail long enough to shield his eyes, and saw a figure silhouetted in the doorway.

"Hello . . .?"

"Ah, Dr. Rice," he said pleasantly, entering. "I'm glad you're back among the living. Watch your eyes. . . ." He paused, looking ceilingward. "System, bring lights to normal level at the rate of ten percent per minute." The lights rose gradually, revealing a strong, handsomely groomed man in a white medical technician's jacket. "How are you feeling?"

"I feel . . . well, to be perfectly honest, I feel like hell." He sagged back into the bed and leaned against the upright mattress, the movements setting his head to spinning again. "But I don't know where I am, or how I got here."

"I'm not surprised. You took quite a ride in that evac pod." The man sat on the edge of the bed and loosely took Rice's wrist in the age-old gesture all doctors used to check a patient's pulse.

But the touch of the man's fingers on his wrist seemed wrong. He couldn't really be reading his pulse, unless—Rice felt suddenly foolish, realizing that the man was not taking his pulse at all, but rather must have been checking the medimonitor on his arm. But if he was doing that, Rice wondered, why wasn't he comparing the bracelet with the readouts on the headboard?

"You're at the medical facility on the orbital habitat *Curtis*," he went on, interrupting Rice's thoughts, "midway between Mercury and Venus. Your evac pod was picked up two days ago by a short-haul passenger shuttle from the Venusian reclamation colony and towed here—we're the best-equipped medical facility this far out from cislunar space. You drifted just over three weeks before they found you crossing into a transit lane; by accident, as it turns out, since no one was looking for you there. After you escaped the mutiny at the sunstation. You must have—"

"Oidar!" The mention of the sunstation snapped Rice's mind to crystal clarity. "Oidar, where is he?"

The doctor paused uneasily, his eyes not meeting his. "I'm sorry, Dr. Rice." He glanced into the darkened room and exhaled heavily, puffing his cheeks. "Well . . . how do I tell you this? The evac pod you used to escape was programmed with different survival modes to react to both short- and long-term situations.

After a preset number of hours or days, the life-support system introduces stasis-inducing gases into the atmosphere to assure the survival of the occupants until they can be picked up. I'm sorry, but the alien's biology was incompatible with the stasis. After three weeks . . . Well, there wasn't anything we could do." He turned to the darkened room again, and Rice now comprehended what was in the other bed.

"But that's not right!" Rice tried to get out of the bed and get a closer view of the next room, but the doctor's gentle, yet firm, hand on his shoulder prevented him. At the doctor's urging, he remained sitting up in the bed, collecting himself. "That can't be right. As soon as we were safely in the evac pod I sent out a distress call; for that matter, an emergency locator signal activated automatically the moment the pod fired. We should have been found almost immediately."

The doctor shrugged somberly. "I'm not sure how those things work, but there *was* a general alarm and search ordered right after you escaped. There were military personnel at the station, right?"

Rice nodded, still trying to figure out what had gone wrong.

"I heard that your escape created enough of a diversion for them to regain control of the station, putting down the mutiny. They immediately contacted Imperial forces, but your pod wasn't on the trajectory it should have been. Maybe in all the shooting, could something have been hit?"

Rice stared at him blankly. "There wasn't any shooting in the pod bay."

He shrugged again, smiling. "As I said, evac pods aren't in my area of expertise. What I do know is that after your pod's trajectory took you out of Mercury orbit, you weren't even close to where they were looking. You're lucky you crossed a commuter lane when you did. Stasis is a tricky thing; you probably would have been all right until you were found, but there's no telling just when that might have been. How long did you drift before long-term survival mode put you to sleep? Was the alien all right until then?" There was a tiny, high-pitched beeping that caused him to glance at the timepiece on his wrist before silencing the sound with a fingertip.

Rice hesitated. "I . . . I don't know. We made it to the pod bay, and I distinctly remember getting us both in—Oidar was still groggy from cryosleep and had a hard time negotiating the hatch. I remember that. I secured the hatch. . . . I remember checking through the hatch window before rotating the pod for ejection to see if they'd caught up, but the pod bay was still empty. . . ." His voice trailed off and he eased back into the pillow.

"And then you hit the autosequencer to eject the pod, right?"

Rice concentrated, gnawing absently at his lower lip, but he just couldn't place his actions after securing the hatch. Frustrated, he turned on his side to gaze into the darkened room, but the lighting on his side was now at full brightness, and he saw only his reflection; the clear wall must have been glass after all. "I guess I did, but . . . why can't I remember?"

The man turned to Rice, speaking in a low, reassuring voice. "You hit the autosequencer right after you secured the hatch. You lifted off smoothly, but the pod was damaged and carried you out of orbit and nobody heard your Mayday. After several hours of drifting, the stasis kicked in." The doctor smiled then, rising from the edge of the bed. "I wouldn't worry too much about it. It'll all come back to you soon enough, I'm sure." He glanced at his watch again. "I imagine you're hungry. You've been sleeping off the stasis for nearly forty-eight hours now."

At the suggestion, Rice felt an insistent gnawing at his stomach he hadn't noticed before, but he still didn't feel like eating. Was Oidar's lifeless body lying in the darkened room behind the shield?

"Maybe later."

"I think you'd feel better if you ate something solid." Again, his voice was low, his words measured.

The persistent growling in Rice's stomach increased, and the thought of a hot meal began to sound appealing.

"Yeah," he replied. "On second thought, I guess I am pretty hungry."

"I thought so." The smile was back as he headed for the door. "I'll have an orderly bring you something." He touched the door plate, then turned back to Rice, his face serious but compassionate. "Again, I'm sorry about your friend." He nodded to the darkened room, his lips a tight line of remorse. "You did a brave thing trying to get him out of there. I just wish there was something I could have—"

"No," Rice interrupted. "It's all right. You did what you could, I'm sure. Thank you, Doctor . . .?"

"Rapson."

"Thank you, Dr. Rapson."

Rapson smiled again as he left, the door sliding shut behind him.

Alone once more, Rice turned and stared into the darkened

room at his right, trying desperately to penetrate the gloom that lay ominously beyond his troubled reflection.

Rapson waited but a split second after the door slid firmly closed before turning sharply to another door just a few meters down the corridor. He barely slowed his stride as he thumbed it open.

"Well?" he asked, entering the dimly lighted room. There were several chairs here lined up in a double row facing a long plasti-glass wall. Other than the chairs, the room was bare. "You watched that whole charade; what do you think?"

Rihana Valtane stood before the glass, arms folded in front of her, and stared at Rice. The man lay on his side in the bed, still gazing unknowingly into what he thought was a clear window. "What kind of game were you playing there at the end?" she demanded. " 'I think you'll feel better if you eat something.' " Rihana snorted. "You asked me what I think; all right, I think you let playing doctor go to your head."

If Rapson was put off by her affront, the sly smile on his face didn't show it. "Just call it 'bedside manner.' " He approached the clear wall and stood next to her, observing Rice in the next room. The scientist had turned away from the window and now lay back in the bed. The door in Rice's room opened, admitting Poser, wearing a white medic's coat and carrying a tray.

"Dr. Rice," Poser began, his words easily heard in the observation room. "I'm sorry to have kept you waiting. I hope you find the food to your liking." Rice nodded gratefully for the meal and allowed the "orderly" to set the tray on a support table extending over the bed, then thanked him. There was a bit more mundane banter as Poser made a show of examining the readings over the bed. Instructing Rice to press the call button should he require anything, Poser turned politely and left.

"I needed to see for myself if he was buying it," Rapson said finally, watching Rice dig hungrily into his dinner. "If I could make him feel three weeks' worth of hunger less than twelve hours after he left the sunstation, then I'm sure I could convince him of the other things I was feeding him as well. But let me ask again: What do *you* think?"

Rihana nodded agreement. "Yes, then. I think he believes the story you just gave him, just as he believes he was looking through a window at his dead friend a few moments ago and not at a one-way projection." She paused, raising an eyebrow. "But what happens when he starts asking questions? He's not just going to languish in that bed forever."

"But you forget, dear Rihana," Rapson replied smugly, "that I don't *need* him forever." With that, he turned away and crossed for the door.

"What now?"

Rapson stopped, his hand paused over the opening plate, and regarded her. "I was notified a few minutes ago," he said, tapping the face of his watch, "that Jephthah's address about the discovery at Tsing, the one Imperial forces blocked earlier this afternoon, has been rebroadcast—unimpeded, this time." He thumbed the door open and exited the room, then headed in the direction of the lift that would take them out of the detention area of Rihana's disguised yacht. He left the door open for her to follow.

"*Damn* him!" Rihana spat under her breath, not caring if he heard or not, then—checking her anger as best she could—hastened after him.

As she came up beside him, he continued as if nothing had happened. "I've gotten all the recordings of the alien I need for now, and will have them edited and reassembled for Jephthah's next broadcast the same way I did the Drew Hatton interview. In the meantime, keep them both healthy at least until you hear back from me."

"Until you—" She stopped dead in the corridor, shouting at his back, "And just where in hell do you think you're going?"

"Well," he called back over his shoulder as he reached the lift door and pressed the call button. "I wouldn't exactly call it 'Hell,' but right now I think I can be much more effective at Tsing 479 than I would be sitting here with you, waiting for something to happen."

"Now wait just a minute! What am I supposed to do while you run off to Tsing? If you think I'm going to just stay here and play baby-sitter for these two—"

The lift doors parted, cutting Rihana off, and he stepped inside. "But my dear Rihana," he said, turning to face her, his hands clasped almost casually behind his back. "I have more important things to attend to." There was just enough time, before the doors slid shut again, for him to flash her one last condescending smile.

Rihana could barely hold her fury back and stomped her foot so hard on the deck plate that the sound echoed throughout the now-empty corridor.

"*Damn* him!"

PART FOUR

THE GATHERING STORM

All your strength is
in your union, all your danger
is in discord.

—Henry Wadsworth Longfellow

FOURTEEN
Transit

W hat do you think she'll be like?"

Commander Lewis Wood turned to face the newcomer on the empty bridge of the Imperial flagship and felt, as he often did, that he was looking in a mirror. Although the other man was smaller, more wiry than he, his sandy blond hair, fair complexion and high cheekbones were a near match. Only the expression behind the deep blue eyes was different; where his own radiated an intensity and power common to those who aspire to command, the other's shone with the eager curiosity of a man of science.

"Good morning, Academician," he said genially, and removed his uniform jacket from the first officer's seat at his immediate right. Tossing it over the back of a swivel chair at one of the nearby display stations, he indicated the empty seat with a wave of his hand, then, noting the other man's drooping eyelids, added, "Can't sleep either, Brendan?" The tone of his voice indicated that he already knew the answer.

In spite of his small frame, Brendan fell heavily into the cushioned seat and wordlessly surveyed the deceptively small control center of the powerful starship. Most vital ship's operations were carried out elsewhere, with the bridge reserved for command functions only. As such, the absence of lower-ranking Imperial officers made the room feel truly deserted. The ship was in "night cycle," and the bridge lights had been dimmed to give the psychological effect that it was actually night. Their jump completed, duty cycles on board had been matched to a normal day length on Tsing IV. In the two weeks it would take to reach the Tsing 479 system, crew and passengers would be acclimatized to the day/night cycle of their destination.

"How can you stand it down here?" Brendan asked finally, still looking around in awe at the myriad display screens. "I'd think that if you wanted to be alone, you'd be considerably more comfortable in your quarters, among familiar surroundings."

Lewis smiled at his younger brother. "These *are* my familiar surroundings, Bren. I'm as comfortable here as you would be squirreled away in some research lab back at the Academy."

"Yes. I suppose you're right," Brendan agreed, conceding the point. Just as the two men shared many physical features, so, too, did they share certain personality traits. Chief among them was the fact that each was most at ease when encompassed by the trappings of his chosen profession. Lewis, as Supreme Commander of the Imperial Military Forces, felt most at home here on the command deck of the *Scartaris,* the flagship he had helped design. The lateness of the hour and the ever-present level of anxiety caused by the upcoming mission notwithstanding, he was honestly relaxed and contented here. Brendan, on the other hand, was loath to even pull himself away from the Academy of Sciences, and felt distinctly out of place no matter where he was on board the imposing vessel.

"So, what do you think she'll be like?" Brendan asked again. "Are you as nervous about this whole thing as I am?"

Lewis nodded. "Ironic, isn't it?" A frustrated smile softened his expression somewhat. "A madman has half the Empire whipped up into xenophobic frenzy, the discovery of another intelligent race threatens to give legitimacy to 'Lord' Jephthah's rantings, and nearly every available Imperial ship is converging on some tiny world in an unexplored sector only recently connected to the Hundred Worlds by wormhole. And what am I sitting up half the night worrying about? Our grandmother. What is she like? I haven't the slightest idea."

Lewis stretched cramped arms and legs out before him, then stood. Had they both been on their feet, the commander would have been several centimeters taller than the young Academician. He paced the bridge aimlessly as he went on.

"Speaking to her over the tachyon link gives about as much insight to a person's character as a holo recording does. I don't know about you, but I can never get the full measure of someone until I see them face-to-face, and look into their eyes." He stopped pacing, his body neatly silhouetted in the dim lighting in front of one of the display screens. "But Bren, I'll tell you this: I think I like her. There's so much of Father in her; and she reminds me so much of Cathay."

"What about Juliana?" The question was spoken softly, cautiously.

Lewis turned to face his brother, his features unreadable in the dim light. "I was only eleven years old when she was killed," he said soberly. "You and Cathay were, what? Seven and three? Do you really think I remember any more about her than you do?" He dug his hands into his pockets and turned away again, making a show of studying one of the displays. "I've seen recordings of Mother, too, and frankly . . . I think we have more in common with Adela de Montgarde than we do with her."

Brendan considered this for several long, silent moments. "There's one thing I do know," he said tiredly, sinking deeper into the first officer's chair. He let his arms hang loosely over the armrests, and leaned his head, eyes momentarily closed, against the backrest. "I agree with Father: With everything that's happening right now, I think there's a good chance her life would be in danger anywhere else *but* here. I'm glad she's coming, and I'm looking forward to meeting her."

The older brother was quiet for almost a full minute, then said finally, "Me too, Bren."

She reminds me so much of Adela, Billy thought as he watched Cathay playing with the group of Aborigine children. The youngsters had been engaged in playabout, shrieking with joy at simple games of tag or toss. But when she joined them she taught them several more games from her own childhood, even though she shared not a single word of common language with many of these children. Indeed, the children were from different parts of the continent and spoke several languages, but all of them shared one language in common: the language of laughter.

She had been waiting to meet him here but he had come early, and stood now at the top of a slope watching her cavort with the children below. The children were a disparate mixture of colors and sizes—their skin ranging from golden brown to dark chocolate, their hair from shaggy blonde to jet black—and still, they shared this common bond. But it was Cathay who had brought this bond about. The children had been wary of one another, at first, as had their parents and families when the tribes first began coming together here. But while the adults of the tribes worked hard day and night to form a common relationship with Billy and

the others, it was Cathay who had taken the many confused and
frightened children and given them a reason to be friends.

There were seventeen tribes represented here so far, their hutlike wurlies scattered randomly around the valley floor at the spot
that had been selected for the corroboree. When the day arrived
for the celebration, however, there would be hundreds.

"Billy! Hello!"

He turned his attention to the playabout, and saw Cathay
waving excitedly up to him. She had arranged the children in two
lines facing each other, their hands joined. From time to time
there was a gleeful shout and a child would break away from one
line and run at top speed to the other, trying to burst through.
More often than not the attempt ended in a wrestling free-for-all
of children piling on top of the running child before he or she
joined their line and the game repeated in the other direction.

"Watch this!" Cathay called up to him. "And pay attention,
because your turn is next!" She laughed in delight and ran from
her line to the other, trying to burst through. As before, the effort
ended in a giggling, squealing mass of brown and black that
kicked up a massive cloud of dust. The tussle over, the children
jumped up and ran back to their lines, leaving Cathay sitting in
the dirt, exhausted, her hair tumbling over her face. "All right,
Billy!" she shouted. "Your turn to get trampled!"

"Nah, not bloody likely!"

"Oh, yeah?" She stood and slapped at her clothes, sending
clouds of reddish dust flying. "We'll see about that!" And with
that she sprinted up the slope, tackling him to the ground—much
to the delight of the watching children below. They all called up
to her in a cacophony of different tongues, waving for the two of
them to come down. She untangled herself from Billy as they sat
up on the dirt and waved back, sending the children returning to
their playabout.

"I don't think . . . I'll ever . . . walk again," she said, trying to
catch her breath. She lay back on the ground, supporting herself
by her elbows, and turned to him. Her face was smeared with dust
and grime, and the filth on her sweat-soaked shirt and bush
shorts was indescribable.

"Have I thanked you for what you're doin' with the children?"
he asked. "Keepin' them occupied and happy is a big worry off
their families."

"You mean," she asked in mock seriousness, "that what I'm
doing is work?" She let out an exaggerated sigh. "Oh, well. I
guess I'll have to stop having fun, then, ay?" She blinked her eyes

several times, then broke into a smile. And as she did, somehow, even the dirt on her face failed to diminish the beauty she had gotten from Adela.

Billy returned her smile and leaned over to retrieve the object he'd dropped when she tackled him. "I wanted to show you something," he said, handing it to her. It was a length of wood not quite a meter long, its dark surface intricately carved with cryptic markings.

"Is this the letter stick you told me about?"

He nodded. "There are more than seven hundred languages among the Aborigine. Seven hundred! And yet, the headman of each tribe can read this." He ran his hand respectfully along the carved surface as she held it, his delicate touch clearly showing the respect he felt not only for the artisan who did the work, but for the tradition and importance that lay behind it. "It tells of what we're doin' here, and asks for representatives to come to corroboree."

Cathay looked at him oddly, her head tilted as she regarded him.

"What?" he asked, noticing her expression.

"You've changed." She sat upright, cross-legged with the letter stick across her lap, and turned to him. "You're happy again."

"I'm pleased that things seem to be workin' out, yes."

She looked out over the valley floor at the smoke curling from one of the previous night's bonfires. "It's all coming together here, Billy. You've infused them all with the same feeling you have for keeping in touch with your heritage. It was always there, all along; but it was you who awakened it in them."

"You're right, I am happy." He reached out to her and brushed some loose sand from her cheek and chin. "And I'm happy that you're here."

Her smile broadened, and she took his hand in hers, squeezing tightly.

"Cathay! Cathay!" They looked below to where the calling children were, and saw that their numbers had swelled by another dozen. Apparently another tribe had arrived. They squealed and jumped, calling for her to come down and show her games to the newcomers.

"Would you take me to your special place?" she asked abruptly, lowering her eyes almost bashfully. "The hidden pool in the gorge? I'd like some time for just the two of us, to talk and to enjoy the quiet."

"Of course. I've been wantin' to show it to you, but there just hasn't been—"

"Cathay! Cathay!"

"Tomorrow," he finished, helping her to her feet. "I need to see that these letter sticks go out, and . . ." He gazed down at the valley and saw several Aborigine milling about the new arrivals. ". . . it looks like there's more to welcome."

She grinned at him, delighted at their plans, and sprinted down the slope to the jumping children.

Billy watched her go, the warm smile still on his face.

The Imperial landing bay on Luna had changed little in two centuries. The rational part of Adela's mind knew that every aspect of the operations here had certainly been updated over the years, every component and mechanical system replaced countless times to handle the constant comings and goings of official traffic. But visually, as she walked across the enormous landing grid toward the waiting spacecraft, the huge dome looked exactly as she remembered it.

The ceiling was fully four hundred meters above her, and it was necessary to look closely to make out the separation lines between the movable doors at the top of the dome and the gently curving walls that swept upward to meet them. There were several catwalks regularly spaced on the walls and the lighted windows of numerous workstations, viewing rooms and technical facilities glowed brightly on the various levels.

Below the lowest of the catwalks were the spectator galleries, used only occasionally to view the arrival or departure of important Imperial visitors or dignitaries. The galleries were all empty now, her departure for Tsing unannounced and, hopefully, unnoticed. Not that anyone seated in the darkened galleries would be able to tell one member of her party from another as they walked—the landing grid was so large that she was still unable to read the name or designation on the side of the big Imperial jump ship waiting for her at its center.

Adela distastefully regarded the other four people who walked silently at her side. There were two men and two women, each dressed in nondescript utilitarian coveralls that looked more like government issue than personal choice. Similar to her own, the only differences that set their outfits apart from hers were the coloring and the high collars covering their throats. Although they walked casually, handbags or jackets slung nonchalantly over a shoulder or tucked under an arm, she knew the four were scrutinizing the surroundings with the utmost care. She did not know their names, nor would they have identified themselves had she asked. Each wore clothing accessories and hairstyles that might or might not be concealing their true appearances. Meeting them only moments earlier, she didn't even know what their voices sounded like.

These four were among the Emperor's most elite division of the Imperial Protection Corps. Ready to die instantly to protect her, they would also just as quickly kill anyone they felt presented a threat to her. Eric had not even discussed their inclusion among the members of the mission headed to Tsing; he had, instead, merely told her of their presence in such a way that left little doubt his decision was irrevocable. Boarding the ship last, they would surreptitiously take their places among the hundred other Imperial and scientific personnel already on board. Although she suspected she would never be able to recognize them again, she knew that at least one of them would be near her at all times.

She had bristled when Eric informed her of their presence, saying she had no need or desire to have personal bodyguards. Eric had smiled at that, maintaining that their role was closer to that of lifeguards, before immediately changing the subject to another aspect of the mission and permitting no further discussion on the matter.

Billy had called them "deathguards."

I wish you were going with me, Billy, she thought, remembering their conversation of the day before. *I know you have a lot to do, and I understand why you have to do it. But . . .*

Adela stopped, ignoring the four as they each overreacted to her sudden movement. *But what . . .?* she asked herself again. *What is it I'm afraid of?*

Regaining his composure, the man nearest her smiled warmly and gently took her arm.

"Are you all right, Doctor?" he asked, his voice certainly disguised by the electronics she knew were installed in the specialized collar of his coveralls. The next time she spoke to him, in whatever capacity, she was confident his voice would be different.

"I'm fine," she said, and resumed walking. "I just thought for a moment that I'd forgotten something." He nodded politely, but said nothing else. The other three, having paid what seemed little heed to their brief chat, fell smoothly into step.

Her thoughts turned again to the deep trepidation she felt about this trip. Was it because Billy, upon whom she had relied so heavily in the past, would remain behind? A part of her was torn between helping her son by going to Tsing, and staying here to help her friend. Then, too, there was the fact that at Tsing she would meet her grandchildren for the first time. Despite the seriousness of the mission to investigate the discovery on that faraway world, Eric had admitted how pleased he was that they would be together. Adela, on the other hand, was uneasy with whatever expectation Eric's sons—and Eric himself, for that matter—had of this imminent "family reunion."

But what bothered her most was that once this mission was completed, she would return to Earth, would return to . . . what? No loving Javas would be waiting for her this time, as he had when she and Billy had been sent to Pallatin. Instead, she would return to a world she barely recognized, and a society where half the population hated the very mention of her name. And what did she have to show for it? If only she had stayed with Javas when she had the chance, instead of . . .

"Watch your step, Doctor." The attendant standing at the foot of the entrance ramp held out her hand for the carry-on bag over Adela's shoulder. She handed it over absently, gazing up at the huge spherical jump ship looming above her. She had paid no heed to it as she walked, completely absorbed in her thoughts, and realized she had never even gotten a good look at it.

Two of her gloomy IPC companions were already at the top of the short ramp and disappeared quickly inside, while the other two went up with her and the attendant. It was likely these two would be with her at least until the ship lifted off.

A man in uniform, the markings identifying him as a high-ranking crew member, greeted her warmly at the top of the ramp. "Dr. Montgarde! It's indeed an honor to have you aboard the *Kiska*. My name is Darrly, Second Officer."

"It's good to meet you," she replied. Her two shadows remained silent, and Darrly pointedly avoided making eye contact with them. The man was clearly under very strict orders as far as the two IPC operatives were concerned.

"I'll have your bag sent along to your quarters, if that's all right." Without waiting for a reply, he nodded to the woman, who disappeared down the corridor. "We'll depart within the hour, but once we break orbit the captain has arranged a tour of the ship for you before you enter cryosleep."

"I won't be going into cryo this trip," she said suddenly, the words coming out without thinking. Until this very moment her plans had, in fact, called for riding most of the trip out in the tank, but she suddenly changed her mind. "I've slept enough of my life away."

The two Imperial protectors looked instantly nervous; obviously, her sudden reconsideration changed their plans, too.

"But . . . but the captain led me to understand that you would . . ."

"It's all right, Mr. Darrly. I'll speak to the captain directly about it." The sudden decision felt good, and the apprehension nagging at her only minutes earlier had been somewhat subdued by it. "Now, if you'd be so kind as to show me to my quarters. I'd like to unpack a few things before my tour of the *Kiska.*"

Rihana Valtane was as furious at this moment as she had ever been in her life.

"Are you saying, even *hinting,* that I am not permitted to leave my own ship?" She felt a wave of angry fire spread slowly across her face, down her neck. The very thought that another person could make her react this way would certainly cause her to become angrier still, she knew, and she fought against the distasteful feeling as she sat in one of the room's two viewing chairs. "Is this what you are saying to me, Krowek?" Rihana Valtane, used to controlling others, did not like being controlled by something so mundane as ordinary emotion. But to be controlled by this man! The words came out in a veritable hiss through gritted teeth.

"Not at all, Mistress Valtane." He smiled, his features composed and businesslike. Like Rapson's at its most persuasive, the man's smooth, self-assured voice seemed to radiate confidence and authority. "I'm merely reminding you of your role in things at the present time. Until Mr. Rapson returns, or until either of us receives updated instructions from him, you are to keep your two guests safe and secure."

"I see. And just what is *your* role in things 'at the present time,' Mr. Krowek?"

His smile broadened, subtly transforming his demeanor from confidence to indifference. "My job, Mistress, is to see to it that you do your job."

It was a testament to her strength of will that she managed to keep from strangling the person nearest her—which would certainly have been the hapless aide, Poser—much less keep her voice calm. But instead of allowing herself to succumb to the vehemence welling up within her, she crossed her legs calmly and concentrated on the look of approval that passed fleetingly over the face staring back at her from the holoframe. The single look told her what she wanted to know: that the man she was speaking with was weak, which reaffirmed that she was better than he. She took pleasure in the fact, then used that pleasure to further mollify her anger.

Who is this man, she wondered, *and why didn't that damned Rapson tell me about him before now? Just how much does he know about what we're doing here and about our ties to Jephthah? For that matter, just how close to Jephthah is this fool?*

She leaned slightly in her chair, purposely allowing the skirt of her outfit to hike moderately higher, showing off her legs to their best advantage. His reaction was the same as before: a look of lecherous approval. To her mind the man had just proven himself to be so far beneath her that he was barely worthy of her contempt and, as such, he might be easily manipulated. All it would take is a bit of effort on her part, and a little time.

"Very well, then," she concluded. "I suggest that we both set about doing our jobs."

Rihana thumbed the armrest of her chair and Krowek's image faded, to be replaced with an exterior view showing his tiny ship. Not even a ship, really; it was merely one of Rapson's shuttles, the same one he had used for their rendezvous, left behind after he had departed in his own yacht.

The small craft remained oriented on her ship, its laughably minimal weaponry—verified several times by her crew's scans—trained on the yacht. Krowek had made no threat, and there was no indication that the weaponry was powered up, but it was clear that he fully intended her to remain on her vessel. The little shuttle couldn't hurt them, could not even inflict much damage, in fact; but it could do enough to keep them from moving freely at maximum speed and efficiency.

"Bastard!" she spat. "Poser!"

"Yes, Mistress?" The aide came from his usual place near the door.

Rihana stood, hands on hips, and stared at the diminutive shuttle. "Wait a few minutes, then contact our Mr. Krowek and invite him to dinner. And inform the crew in the lower bay that the shuttle will be redocking."

Poser nodded, then disappeared from the room. Scarcely ten minutes had passed, however, before he returned, an uneasy she's-not-going-to-like-this look easily readable on his mousy face.

"Well?" she demanded before he could speak. "What is it? What did he say to you that has you so obviously on edge?"

"Mistress, I . . . am afraid I did not speak to him. Not exactly." He tried to smile when he saw her look of disapproval, but failed miserably. "I was only able to reach an interactive message retrieval system. I tried several frequencies, but the automated message was the same each time."

"And what was the message?"

"He said that, ah, he would only receive your call if it was made by you. Directly." Poser shrank back, but it wasn't clear if the move was intended to put himself out of striking range or to put him closer to the door in the slim hope of being dismissed. He need not have bothered, as her surprising reaction led to neither.

"I see our Mr. Krowek likes to play," she chuckled, genuinely amused. "All right, then. Place the call for me, and let us see what happens."

Poser concentrated, his integrator making the necessary connections. After a few moments, the holoframe glowed and Krowek's image appeared.

"Mistress Valtane, it's so good to see you again. Although I'm forced to admit that I hadn't expected to see you again so soon as this."

"I'm sure you didn't." She crossed to the viewing chair facing the holoframe and sat, noticing as she did that his features changed subtly to the same look she had seen before, a mixture of appreciation and downright leering. Her disgust for him raised a notch as she realized the man was even shallower than she originally thought. "In any event, since we both seem to be stuck here for roughly the same purpose, I thought it might be nice to get to know one another. Please, won't you be my guest for dinner this evening. I'm sure you would be much more comfortable with the facilities I can offer here aboard the *Tiatia,* than on that cramped shuttlecraft of yours."

He flashed the ingratiating smile she was coming to loathe. "But Mistress, I'm perfectly comfortable where I am. And as to your offer of dinner, I'm very grateful but I've already eaten. Thank you anyway."

"Surely, there must be some comfort I can offer. Perhaps I can arrange to have something sent over, then?" She turned in her chair. "Poser, please see to it that after-dinner refreshments are shuttled over to—"

"No," he said simply, cutting her off with the single word. "That won't be necessary either. In fact, until the situation changes, or until we receive further instructions, the two of us should not be on the same vessel. Now, if you'll excuse me, there are some matters I need to attend to." He leaned outside the pickup range of his sending unit, and his image faded away.

Rihana was silent for several minutes as she considered what Krowek had said, then: "Now, what reason could there possibly be for us to avoid being on the same ship? Poser, come sit down." She indicated the other viewing chair.

The aide was startled and, while not exactly distressed, was nonetheless wary of her motives as he took the offered chair and sat stiffly with his hands clasped in his lap, his back not touching the chair.

"What is your impression of Krowek?" she asked bluntly, all her usual airs forgotten for the moment. Oddly enough, the moment she spoke to him on a one-to-one basis, Poser, too, seemed less rodentlike in his own movements. Discussions of this type between them were rare, but when they occurred the two of them immediately took on a no-nonsense demeanor. "The way he acted, how he spoke and looked. Anything you can recall."

"I don't recollect anything out of the ordinary, Mistress. Although . . ." He shook his head weakly, his brow furrowed in thought. ". . . he reminded me no small amount of Mr. Rapson himself."

Rihana leaned back in the chair and pulled absently at her lower lip. "How about the way he talked, how he formed his sentences?"

"Again, he reminded me of Mr. Rapson; although there's nothing specific I can put my finger on."

She nodded slowly, thinking, then said, "Did you see the way he looked at me?"

"I . . . I'm not sure what you mean." He stiffened in the chair, his nervousness returning.

"Please!" she snapped. "You know exactly what I mean. You have seen the look I'm referring to a hundred times over the years." She rose and paced for several moments, again pulling absently at her lip. "Access the communications log and run back the recording of the first conversation, triple speed, sound muted. Put it in edit mode, as I wish to mark two five-second segments."

Poser complied and the holoframe glowed again, Krowek's

image animatedly moving through the message up to the point where he had glanced at Rihana's obvious attention-getting movement.

"Mark."

The playback continued for several moments.

"And . . . mark." The recording ended shortly afterward. "Now, connect and play the two segments back-to-back, normal speed."

Poser complied. The holoframe glowed with Krowek's image centered in the frame at the exact moment Rihana had crossed her legs. There, again, was the approving look, a tiny shift of his head, a downward then upward glance of his eyes, a tiny curl at one corner of his mouth. The computer had blended the segment smoothly with the next marked portion. It showed the same leering look of approval, but the two segments were more than just the same mannerisms made by the same man at different times—the two segments were virtually identical, as if the same segment of the recording had been played twice.

"There, do you see what I mean?"

"They're . . . the same. But I don't see the significance in that, Mistress."

Rihana nodded, still considering the possibilities. "Can you overlap them? Play them at the same time?"

A look of concentration more intense that usual spread over his features as he set up the proper playback parameters. The holoframe glowed again; the segments replayed.

"If there had been any difference between the two, there should have been a double image at some point. They're identical, aren't they?"

"Yes, identical." He cleared his throat and straightened contentedly in his chair. Was that a genuine smile on his lips? "I . . . also took the liberty of checking timing, lighting intensity, and angle of pickup. There is no difference, not even infinitesimal, that I can detect between the two."

Rihana raised an approving eyebrow. "Well done. Now, find the same segment from my second conversation with him and overlay it atop the two we just viewed. Same analysis."

Poser complied. After a few minutes, he said, "The results are the same, Mistress."

"That sneaky bastard," she whispered so softly under her breath that Poser had to strain to hear. "Can you scan for life signs aboard the shuttle?"

A look of comprehension appeared behind Poser's eyes. "I'm

sorry, but the *Tiatia* is not equipped for that. However, I believe I can . . ." His voice trailed off as his brow furrowed once more. Rihana waited in uncharacteristic patience. Then, after several minutes, "Mistress, I'm sorry it took so long—I had to reroute the proper scan circuits—but, there can be no one alive on board the shuttle. All life-support systems are on standby. Internal temperature settings in all passenger sections read well below zero."

"The sneaky bastard," she said again, louder and almost appreciatively this time. "We have been talking to a computer-generated representation. He has plainly altered his image, but no wonder 'Krowek' reminded you of Rapson." On one level, Rihana was furious with herself for being taken in so completely; but on a deeper level, she admired the intricacy of the ruse. She made a mental note to ask Poser to outfit a similar system for herself—after she had dealt with Rapson regarding this act of subterfuge. "System!" she barked, forgoing Poser's assistance. "Connect me with the master pilot's quarters."

It took a moment, but directly a bleary-eyed woman's image appeared in the holoframe. She clumsily tangled herself in the sheets as she swung herself to the edge of the bed, struggling to clear the sleep from her mind. "Yes, Ma'am?"

"Moyan, I want the *Tiatia* ready to move on a moment's notice."

"Yes, Ma'am." The woman was now wide awake and already pulling on her clothes. "Do you have a specific destination that I can enter into the—?"

"I will keep you informed."

"Yes, Ma'am. I'll have a duty roster ready for your approval as soon as I—"

Rihana thumbed the image out.

Poser cleared his throat again, the annoying habit alerting Rihana that he wanted to say something. Their discussion closed, both had returned to their usual role patterns.

"Yes, Poser?"

"Mistress, shall I make preparations for departure?"

Rihana laughed, the pure, natural sound surprising the man more than anything his mistress had done in some time.

"No, not yet. Let's sit here for a while and play with our new toy."

FIFTEEN
Discovery

Gareth Anmoore strained at his side of the heavy rectangular slab of gray-brown stone. The faces of the other three crew members lugging the burdensome rock—the huskiest men the landing party could offer—were beet red with exertion, the muscles and veins in their necks and shoulders standing out in marked contrast to their sweaty skin. All had removed their shirts, but even that gave them little relief as they worked in the hot sun.

"Easy! Easy!" A survey member, geologist Vito Secchi, rushed forward and grasped the slab next to Gareth. "Set it down on its edge, over here. Then flip it over so I can examine its underside. Careful! Watch your feet!"

Gareth's voice came in nearly unintelligible grunts. "Take it—*unhh!* Take it easy, Vito. We're not about to—*aaah!*—hurt your precious rock."

The five men let the slab down on its side as gingerly as they could, then allowed it to fall over so the underside was exposed per the geologist's request. Secchi almost leapt onto the slab, studying it for whatever minutiae had originally excited him about it. The image reminded Gareth of a cat curiously pouncing on an intruding insect. A shout for similar help came from the other side of the dig site, and Gareth waved the three big men over as he sat heavily in the freshly turned dirt, leaning back on an elbow.

"Was it really necessary," Gareth puffed wearily, "to do this right now?" He pulled his shirt from the waistband of his pants and wiped it across his forehead, the sweat mingling with dirt to form a pasty, claylike whitish coating on the side of his face. He looked around him at the dig, watching as more than a dozen filthy men and women worked at numerous tasks on every side of the five-meter-wide man-made crater. Secchi himself, although he had done a minimal amount of the actual lifting and carrying, seemed to be the dirtiest. "You could at least have waited on the big stuff until someone brought down a null-gravity harness."

The two had been friends for years, but when Secchi turned to face him, a sudden worrisome expression crossed the man's face.

He straightened over the slab, saying, "I'm sorry, Captain; but finding this here I just—"

Gareth's hearty laugh cut him off. "Vito, come on. Lighten up a bit." He stared at the geologist, watched as the troubled expression changed to one of better cheer. "And drop the 'Captain' stuff when none of the freshman crew are around."

A sudden, bright flare over Secchi's shoulder, high in the southern sky, caught his attention: the braking rockets of yet another ship inserting itself into orbit around the newly popular planet. He wondered idly who was on this one. The Emperor's two sons had already arrived in the system, and he expected them to make a personal inspection of the base within a few days. Perhaps it was Adela de Montgarde herself, come to take over authority here in her role as the Emperor's official representative at Tsing. He felt a surge of excitement at the prospect of finally meeting the woman he'd heard so much about all his life.

Whoever it was, once in orbit the ship would be invisible to the natives, who possessed little optical technology. Still, he hoped again that the natives—concentrated most heavily in the planet's northernmost landmass—wouldn't notice the increased low-altitude activity in the skies above the southern hemisphere where South Camp, the planetside base, had been set up.

"We get more company every day, Vito," he mused, sitting upright in a cross-legged position. "When do you think you might tell me exactly what it is you're looking for here?"

"Metal." The geologist didn't look up from the slab.

"I know that." Gareth liked Secchi, but if there was anything about the scientist that did get on his nerves it was his way of explaining things in shorthand. It didn't help that Secchi's face, hidden behind a thick, bushy black beard, was virtually unreadable. "The metal concentration in this entire region was easily detectable, even scanning from orbit. What's so special about this particular site?"

Secchi sat back on his haunches and let his breath out in one long, slow sigh. He took a rock hammer and struck a corner of the slab, easily and neatly chipping off an angular fist-sized chunk, then tossed it to Gareth. "Take a close look at it."

Gareth turned it over several times in his hands. It was gray-brown, indicating that it was of the same material as the slab from which it came. He hefted the piece in one hand, guessing that it weighed a little more than a kilo and a half, a bit heavier than he might have expected. Like most of what had been dug up, it was covered with tightly packed dirt closely matching the color

of the rock itself; but looking more carefully at the clean side that
had been in the interior of the slab before being chipped off, he
could see dark blotches running through it.

He scraped experimentally at one of the blotches with a grimy
thumbnail. "Is this the metal you mean?"

Secchi nodded.

"What about it?"

The geologist glanced up, making sure that none of the other
team members were within earshot.

"I don't think it's from here," he answered simply, raising his
thick, dark eyebrows.

Gareth considered this new bit of information gingerly, careful
not to infer more from Secchi's words than he was offering. "All
right," he began directly, handing the chunk back to the other
man, "so it's not from here. Is it meteoric in origin, or could the
natives have brought it? Even though there's little evidence
they've explored much of this hemisphere, they could be responsible for it being here."

Secchi shook his head and took a seat on the slab, putting his
back to the others as he spoke. He dug a battered handheld data
pad out of a vest pocket and automatically wiped a layer of dirt
from it with his hand, then punched a few keys before passing it
over to Gareth. "I've positively identified each of those metals,"
he said, pointing to the handheld. "Most are common; it would
be unusual to find them here, but it's conceivable they could have
been brought here by the natives."

"But the last three listed here?" Gareth tapped at the readout
on the handheld's tiny scratched screen.

The geologist shrugged. "They're not from here," he repeated.
"At least, not in those combinations or amounts."

"So they *are* meteoric, then." He gave the handheld back and
stood up, brushing the dirt from his pants, then retrieved his shirt
and pulled it over his head, frowning at the way the damp garment clung to his sweaty skin as he tugged it into place. "Interesting, but hardly worth the silent treatment you've been giving me
about this dig site."

"Gareth?" Secchi leaned forward, his elbows on his knees, and
looked up at him. "This isn't rock," he said under his breath as
he tapped at the slab with the chunk he still held. It crumbled
slightly at the impact. "It's clay, baked at high temperature as if
it had been fired in a pottery." He kept striking the slab with the
smaller piece, breaking it up into a pile made up of dissimilar
shapes and sizes, then ran a finger through it and fished out a

darker piece, which he held out in the palm of his hand. "Look at this closely."

Gareth scrutinized the offered piece, turning it over in his hand with a fingertip. The piece was smooth and globular, not a broken fragment as he had first suspected. Holding it between thumb and forefinger, he spit on it, then wiped it on his already filthy pants. "It's a bit of metal that's been melted," he said finally. "That's obvious; but I don't see the significance."

"Whatever hit here wasn't a meteorite," Secchi responded, standing and sweeping an arm around the shallow hole. "The temperatures were just too high." He took Gareth by the arm and led him several meters away, up the side of a gradual slope that overlooked the area. From here they could see the shuttle and the prefabbed shelter that had been erected for the survey team here at the dig site, as well as the larger, more permanent dome in the distance that served as the main base on the planet. From this vantage point even Gareth, whose knowledge of planetary geology was weak, at best, could tell that it had once been a basin or lake bed.

"A couple thousand years ago the climate was a lot different," Secchi began. "It was still pretty cold and damp around here. I can't be sure just how much water there was, but there was plenty of mud and wet clay filling this depression. A meteorite hitting here—the tight, dense mass that it is—would have buried itself in the muck quite nicely; mostly in one piece, at that, if it wasn't too large. But whatever hit here tore itself apart on impact, and burned hot enough to melt everything that wasn't incinerated entirely."

"Big meteorites don't do that?"

"Sure, the really big ones do. But one that big would have left a massive crater; this is a natural water basin. What hit here, though, wasn't that big, not nearly big enough to generate the temperatures needed to make these." He reached into a pants pocket and pulled out a handful of irregularly shaped metal globs similar to the one Gareth was turning over and over in his fingers. "I've found them everywhere." He poured the pieces back into his pocket and walked to a spot just above them, then scanned the depression in the landscape.

"The way I see it, something crashed and burned here. It must have been fueled, too, because the trees and scrub that would have grown around here at the time couldn't possibly have been responsible for the amount of heat it would have taken to bake the clay like that." He indicated the slab. "Then it explodes, slinging molten metal everywhere. A few millennia of drying out and the rest of the clay solidifies with these nice streaks and veins of molten metal in it."

Gareth thought the geologist's speculations over carefully for several minutes, then said, "Maybe the natives here once had, then lost, a higher technology. Maybe this is a relic of something fairly common a long time ago, but has been forgotten because of . . . hell, I don't know. Maybe they went through a 'dark age' here, just as Earth did, and lost everything. Is that a possibility?"

The other man shook his head. "I'm not an archaeologist, so I can't say for certain, but my guess is no. The metals are just too rare to come from here in these quantities." Secchi sighed heavily again and looked at the moon Big One, just now rising over the far horizon. "I suppose—and this is a real stretch, mind you— they might come from up there. If their technology had been far enough advanced, they *might* have mined it up there . . ."

"But?"

He paused before answering. "Look, I did the orbital spectrographic scans of both moons myself, and then we both went over them. These aren't captured bodies with differing compositions; they're made of the same stuff you'll find here, in roughly the same proportions. You won't find any more of this stuff up there than you will down here."

A shout from below reached their ears. Gareth could see someone waving up the slope at him. Even from this distance, he could tell from the newcomer's unsoiled clothing that the man had just arrived at the site from South Camp. He reached for his belt, cursing softly under his breath when he realized he'd left his handlink down at the dig.

"We'd better get back. My guess is that someone on whatever ship we saw braking a while ago is trying to reach me." He turned to leave, slipping the metal glob into a pocket.

"Gareth, wait a minute," Secchi said, grabbing his sleeve. "I'm not sure you follow what I'm saying here. If you want to find the source of whatever hit the ground down there, you're going to have to look somewhere else. It's not ours—or the Sarpan's either, for that matter. This was here a long time before either one of us was flying. And it wasn't anything the natives are capable of. I'm sure of it."

Gareth Anmoore laughed humorlessly. "Oh, I follow you

perfectly, Vito." He turned and started hiking back down the slope.

"I'm just trying to figure out how in the name of God I'm going to break the news to everyone up there in orbit that we've found signs of yet another intelligent race out here."

SIXTEEN
Arrivals

Captain Tra'tiss, commander of the Sarpan vessel *Cra Stuith,* was middle-aged, judging from the predominance of brown in his skin coloration. A trio of silver bobs adorning the gill slit on the left side of his face—an indication that he had spawned three times in his life—was further indication the alien was probably no more than nine or ten standard Solar years old. At his side stood another alien, his moist skin the brighter green shade of a Sarpan youth; this would be his first officer. The younger alien sported only a single silver adornment on his gill.

Tra'tiss glowered from the screen, tapping slowly, rhythmically at the corner of his wide mouth with a long, webbed finger. The alien's facial expression was unfortunate, in that all Sarpan looked as though they were perpetually scowling. The hand gesture, however, conveyed considerably more information about his mood. According to what Brendan had told him to look for prior to this communication with the alien ship, the subtle tapping motion indicated that the alien was in a state of what he'd described as "frustrated thoughtfulness."

The two commanders—one human, one alien—were in what the aliens referred to as a "contemplation phase" in their negotiations, a maddening but necessary feature of most peaceful discussions with the Sarpan during which they remained silent for long periods of time. Audio had been turned off on both ends of the conversation while they waited, although video had been left active.

"He's still considering his options," Brenda said aloud while the control-bridge audio pickup remained off. "He's trying—all simultaneously, mind you—to reflect on several things: Mainly, he's deciding whether or not you're lying to him; but he's also planning an emergency escape, weighing potential armed responses to any actions you might take as well as their repercussions, comparing the value of staying here at Tsing versus monitoring everything that happens here from a safer vantage point outside the system . . . not to mention wondering what you and I are talking about right now." Brendan paused and almost smiled. "At the same time he's probably juggling work assignments for his crew, fuel consumption from his last three jumps, and how long it's been since he was 'in the water.' But don't let any of this fool you; he's still giving you his full attention. Nothing you say or do in this discussion will slip past him. You can count on it."

"They're magnificent creatures," Lewis breathed softly in true admiration. "They're so orderly, so efficient in their scientific and military dealings; so competent in everything they do. And what you've told me about their parenting/learning process, the way they can pass on intimate knowledge to their children through touch . . ." Lewis frowned angrily, shaking his head. "To think that damned paranoid madman is poisoning the minds of so many people about this gentle race."

Brendan regarded his brother. "You almost sound more like a scientist than the commander of the Emperor's flagship. However . . ." His face grew serious. "Although I agree with everything you've ever said about Jephthah and his campaign of hatred, this 'gentle race,' as you call it, is quite formidable. And secretive. We know little of what their goals are regarding much of anything—we never have, much less what they want here at Tsing."

"I know that," Lewis snorted. "And I know how serious a meeting with them—here! now!—is to the Empire. Can I help it if what Jephthah has done angers me?" Realizing that he had sat bolt upright during this last, he settled back in his seat and lowered his voice. "You want a military commander's opinion then? All right: I'm not really sure I blame them for wanting to protect themselves, Bren. I imagine they've seen every transmission Jephthah's made, just as we have. And now here they are at Tsing, sitting smack in the middle of what must appear to them to be half the Imperial fleet. As to why they're here, I believe what he just told us two minutes ago—they're here for the same reason every other ship is. The discovery of a new race must be every bit as important to the Sarpan as it is to the Hundred Worlds."

The bridge filled suddenly with sound from the holoscreen as audio from the Sarpan ship was restored. Lewis nodded to his first officer, at his right, to likewise reactivate the audio pickup on their end.

"Commander Wood," the alien began formally in a surprisingly human-sounding voice. "My advisors inform me that everything you have said about the Imperial ship *Paloma Blanco* is true. It is indeed a minimally armed scientific vessel. So." The Sarpan paused, nodding in a way that indicated he had come to a conclusion. "I accept your offer to remain in rendezvous status with the science ship until your arrival. However, what assurance do I have that our safety will be guaranteed until such time as you do arrive?" He tilted his head questioningly, the silver bobs on his gill slit twinkling in the dim light of his bridge.

"Captain Tra'tiss," Lewis responded in the same formal manner the Sarpan officer had used, "I have contacted an Imperial military ship already near your location, and have given orders to enforce a blockade around both your ship and the *Paloma Blanca*. No other vessel—Imperial, Sarpan or private—will be permitted near either. However . . ." Lewis paused, raising an eyebrow in a facial expression that Brendan had explained carried more importance to the Sarpan than any other human gesture. "I must stress just how important it is for the *Cra Stuith* to remain in a defensive powerdown for the duration. Both your ship and the science vessel will be surrounded in a defensive field of our making. You are not to initiate defensive actions of your own. I cannot stress this strongly enough."

"So." Tra'tiss nodded, a slight narrowing of his eyes the closest thing to a different expression Lewis had seen on the alien's face during the entire conversation. "This one wonders: Is this arrangement truly for our protection? Or is this an attempt to make it easier for you to exercise control over us?"

You do come to the point, don't you? Lewis thought. "Believe whichever you wish, Captain," he answered bluntly. "But understand that I can guarantee you no protection unless you agree to, and accept, these terms. Understand further that should you violate our agreement before my arrival, I will have the blockading vessel take offensive action. On the other hand, if you choose not to accept my offer, I must insist that you depart this system. Frankly, there is too much happening here for which I will be responsible in the foreseeable future; I simply cannot compromise my own effectiveness by tending to the daily whereabouts of one Sarpan ship among dozens of others already in system. Please understand that I am prepared to back this up." He paused a beat, then added in the best Sarpan inflection he could muster, "So?"

"So," Tra'tiss answered. There was a long hesitation on the alien captain's part as he weighed the options. Tra'tiss stared directly at him, nictitating membranes blinking occasionally as he considered Lewis' proposal. "Very well, Commander Wood. I accept your offer. My first officer tells me that an Imperial craft is approaching and should arrive in a few moments. The vessel has been scanned at a tonnage of ninety-three-point-four thousand, Imperial. Is this the ship of which you spoke?"

"Yes, Captain. That would be the *Dana Gordon,* a destroyer-class ship. Make them welcome when they arrive."

"Very well," he repeated. "I will cooperate in this regard." He seemed about to break the connection, but raised a webbed finger. "A question." It was a statement, more than a query in itself, and Lewis frowned, hesitating, not understanding that the Sarpan had just asked permission to speak to him about a different subject.

"Yes, Captain?" Brendan asked. He shot his brother an apologetic glance, but turned back to the screen immediately. "What do you wish to ask of us?"

Tra'tiss continued to address Lewis, the one he considered to be in authority, despite Brendan's interjected remarks. "This one has been informed that Adela de Montgarde will attend this discovery. It is my sincere hope to meet with her on a formal basis on behalf of my government. Is it possible for you to make a request of your superiors to arrange this?"

"I cannot speak for Adela de Montgarde," Lewis said. "While I have been in contact with her ship, I do not yet know of her priorities upon arrival."

"It is true that she will be the Emperor's official representative here, so?"

Lewis frowned again, this time at the thoroughness of the alien's information. "Yes. That is true."

"In that case, Commander Wood, I would like to make an official request of you, the highest-ranking Imperial officer presently in the Tsing system, for a formal meeting with Adela de Montgarde. I have entered my intentions to make this request in our log." He tilted his head as he gazed at Lewis. His facial expression changed subtly—was he actually smiling? "Or should I also make a formal request through my government?"

He looked up at Brendan, standing at his side, and thought, *They're not only formidable and secretive, they're crafty.* "No," he answered. "A formal solicitation won't be necessary. I'll relay your request to her personally."

At that, Tra'tiss' face *did* change as his froglike eyes widened noticeably. "You will speak to her yourself?"

"Yes."

"This is possible?" Tra'tiss was nearly incredulous. "You may speak to she who can rebirth a star?"

Lewis hesitated, his brow furrowed in confusion at the Sarpan's reaction. "Yes, of course."

"Commander Wood," Brendan broke in, "is the eldest grandson of Adela de Montgarde. I am certain he would be happy to arrange a formal audience for you with Dr. Montgarde. . . ." He paused, then added meaningfully, "Assuming all goes well during your rendezvous with the *Paloma Blanco,* of course."

Tra'tiss said nothing, but it was clear he was newly impressed with the status of this human commander. Judging from the looks on the faces of those on board the *Cra Stuith* bridge, the feeling was shared equally among them.

Lewis felt suddenly that his brother had taken the conversation away from him and was about to say something in an attempt to regain control when his first officer touched his sleeve, then whispered in his ear. He nodded to the man, then regarded the holo-screen once more.

"Captain Tra'tiss, the Imperial vessel *Dana Gordon* is within shield range of you now. Are you prepared to go to defensive powerdown?"

"It is done." Tra'tiss nodded to one side, and his image winked out.

Lewis breathed a sigh of relief, then dismissed the bridge crew with a wave of his hand. They wouldn't arrive at Tsing IV for another fifteen hours, and he wanted everyone to get as much R & R as they could before then. They would most certainly see little relaxation once they were in orbit around the troublesome new world.

"I'm glad that's over," he said when they were alone. "The last thing I needed right now was a confrontation with the Sarpan." He swiveled his command chair to face Brendan, his demeanor suddenly more pointed than before. "Why did you insert yourself into my dealings with the alien just now? I thought I made it clear what your role was to be any time you were on the bridge. I won't have you undermining—"

"In his view, I didn't," Brendan retorted firmly. "In the Sarpan hierarchy the captain's aide or first officer is a literal extension of the captain himself, frequently speaking for him, sometimes even finishing his sentences."

"I already have a first officer!" Lewis was on his feet, staring down menacingly at his brother. "And *he* knows full well what his duties are!"

Brendan put both his hands before him. "Lewis, please! Let me finish. Tra'tiss thought my response to his question was the role you had assigned me for this particular communication with them. He doesn't know who I am and he doesn't care; all that matters to him is that—in his eyes—you had trained me well." The easy smile returned to his face, and he almost laughed aloud as he added, "To the Sarpan way of thinking, my butting in made you look good."

"I see," he said grudgingly. He remained silent a moment and allowed the last remnants of the anger he'd felt seep away. Indicating that Brendan be seated in one of the vacant chairs, he retook his own. "Tell me: Why was he so impressed with my relationship to our grandmother?"

"The Sarpan almost worship her." He plopped into the communications officer's seat and unbuttoned the collar of his Academician's tunic. As Lewis regarded the action, it occurred to him that he hadn't even noticed that Brendan had worn the official Academician's garb for the communication with the Sarpan commander. As a military man, he had frequently looked down upon the sciences during his career, but as he took stock of Brendan's contributions so far on this mission, he realized he could stand to learn much from his little brother.

"She accomplished something of near-religious significance for them when she proved she could control the inner workings of stars," Brendan continued. "That, in itself, would be more than enough to earn her a revered place in Sarpan history. But when wormhole travel was developed as a direct result of her work— For a race with a life span of only ten or fifteen standard years, to suddenly have the ability to travel between stars in a single lifetime is something we humans can barely imagine."

"Well, if having a certain amount of celebrity status with the Sarpan makes our job here any easier, then I'm all for it." There was a chirp from the room system, and Lewis raised his chin, speaking into the air: "Yes?"

"There is a communication from Captain Anmoore of the *Paloma Blanco.*"

"Put it through." The holoscreen glowed, showing a confused-looking Gareth Anmoore. He was in full regulation uniform, something Lewis had already come to learn was unusual for the survey-ship captain, although it was plain from his appearance that the jacket had been hastily donned. "Captain Anmoore, is everything all right? What is the status of your rendezvous with the Sarpan ship?"

"Everything is fine, Commander. But . . ." His voice trailed off, and he seemed almost perplexed.

"But what?"

"Sir, if I may be so bold—what did you say to them? To the alien captain, I mean?"

"How's that?"

"Captain Tra'tiss, sir. He contacted me right after concluding his communication with you, and . . . well, he's offering a trade of goods and Sarpan delicacies, engineering data, use of their recreation facilities. Sir, for lack of a better description, he's acting like a giddy schoolboy."

Lewis turned to Brendan, smiling for the first time since being contacted by the Sarpan ship earlier that afternoon.

"Celebrity status, indeed," he replied sanguinely.

The name on the ID badge clipped to the pocket on the left side of his work shirt read BODISEE. The patch and stripes on his sleeve identified him as a maintenance tech, first class. His thumbprint was his passkey, even though the plastiskin print had been applied weeks ago. Since "Bodisee" did not exist before the ship left, he could have used his own thumbprint with the Bodisee name, but had chosen not to. He never used anything of his own, even when there was no way to trace it to him, when he could come up with a suitable fiction.

There was the sound of a door sliding shut some distance down the corridor, and he glanced at his watch. *Right on time,* he thought.

After a week's travel to reach the wormhole that would take them to Tsing IV, the excruciating jump itself, and nearly two more weeks as they approached the planet, he had had more than enough time to memorize the IPC officer's routine.

He shouldn't have been able to, of course; the IPC prided itself on training its operatives to thwart observers attempting to do exactly what he was now doing. But he had been here numerous times in the past month, always at the same time, always doing the same job—a standard check of the monitoring station in corridor nine, level six, starboard. The monitoring stations recorded access and egress to the corridors, body weight, walking speed and a dozen other descriptions of anyone using the corridor—in all, a normal security precaution implemented on Imperial ships carrying VIPs. The data were sent automatically to the central computer system, but daily manual checks were also made to each monitoring station aboard the *Kiska* to compare readings with the central computer, as well as to check for any signs of possible equipment tampering.

The schedules and check routes of each maintenance tech were switched at random, and he could never be certain what day he would be at this particular monitoring station, but it was a fairly simple matter to arrange to be here at the same time whenever the name Bodisee came up on the roster to check corridor nine, level six, starboard. Each time he was here he would linger as long as he felt safe until he saw the IPC man, noting carefully his appearance, clothing, gait, and anything else he could discern about him. In turn, the agent came to know and recognize him.

He had selected this IPC man carefully, and had considered himself lucky that his body size matched the other man's as nearly as it did. As it was, he had been forced to fast almost the entire trip to insure that his weight matched the man's even more closely.

He had arrived early enough that he already had the panel removed when the IPC agent rounded the corner and approached his position. As always, he felt the man's eyes almost dissecting him as he worked, but he only smiled the man's way before turning back to the monitoring station's open access hatch.

He waited until the man was barely two meters away before touching the button of the tiny explosive charge he had secreted in the cuff of his left sleeve. The charge carried little impact, but generated a satisfactory noise and just the right flash of light and amount of smoke. Deftly tucking the spent charge casing back into its hidden pocket in the cuff, he threw himself sharply against the opposite wall, acting dazed and disoriented, and allowed himself to crumple to the floor.

It pleased him that the IPC man had not made an effort to instantly come to his assistance, but had instead dropped to a defensive position, a previously hidden firearm now held steadily, unerringly in his direction.

"Freeze!"

He feigned confusion and, although he made no moves the IPC agent would consider threatening, he did not obey the man's order. "Wha—what happened?" he offered weakly, and made a show of trying to sit upright. He stared at his hands, blackened from what he knew would look to an unsuspecting observer like an electrical burn, and blurted, "My hands! God, it hurts!"

The man lowered his weapon slightly. "Listen carefully. I'm going to help you. I'm going to approach you slowly, but my weapon will be on you at all times. Do you understand?"

"Please!" he begged, giving the act everything he had. "Help me!"

There was a moment's hesitation as the man made a decision; then his hands moved quickly to put his firearm away, so quickly that it wasn't immediately apparent where he had hidden it. "Look, I'm going to help you stand up," he said, moving to his side. "I want you to put an arm around my shoulder and I'll get you to the end of the corridor. There's a terminal there and I can get you some help. Do you understand?"

He nodded vigorously, teeth clenched in a visage of pain. He was pleased, again, at the IPC man's trained response: Anyone else would have left him here and run unencumbered to the nearest terminal for help and then returned to his side, but the man's indoctrination demanded that in a potential danger situation such as this, he could not leave him here unattended and, more importantly, unguarded.

The man helped him to his feet, and as he threw his arm around the agent, he let his thumbnail drag sharply across the back of the man's neck.

They had taken only a few unsteady steps down the corridor when the IPC agent stopped abruptly in midstride. The man gasped sharply, painfully, and pushed himself away from him, his eyes wide in bewildered panic, and tried desperately to steady himself against the corridor wall. He fumbled uselessly for his weapon with hands gone suddenly clumsy; then, as his gyrations became even more intense, he clawed frantically at his chest, knocking his ID badge off and sending it skittering across the smooth floor. His futile efforts lasted but a few moments before his movements halted and he slumped into a lifeless heap on the floor, his face frozen in horrified shock.

The man known for the last three weeks as Bodisee went to work instantly. There wasn't much chance of being discovered— not in this corridor, not at this hour; he already knew that from weeks of careful observation—but he hurried nonetheless. He stripped off his shirt and pants, then removed the dead man's coveralls and put them on. The fit was snug, but passable. He carefully adjusted the collar.

"Hello. Check, check, check."

He applied a little more pressure on the collar, then, "Check. Check." He nodded, satisfied that the tone-shifting electronics of the collar made his voice match that of the IPC man. The new voice pattern would not fool a system scanning for a specific ID, he knew; but then, the IPC agent's natural voice patterns would certainly not be in the system anyway. On the other hand, the voice match would be more than good enough for human ears.

That taken care of, he took a last careful look at the man's face, then ran his fingers through his own hair—which he had gradually changed in the last week and a half to match the IPC agent's light brown—to part it on the other side. He had already altered his eye color and skin tone.

Done, he thought, then crossed to the still-open access hatch, where he retrieved a zippered pouch about the size of the palm of his hand, and took from it a small pair of metal heat cutters and a thin bag. He shook the flimsy bag open and pulled it over the body of the IPC man, wrestling him inside; then, removing the ID badge and slipping it into a pocket, he tossed in Bodisee's discarded outfit. Just before sealing the bag he reached inside with the cutters, flicked the heat switch and neatly snipped off the man's right thumb. There was no blood—the tool's heated cutting edges instantly seared the wound closed. He dropped the severed thumb into the pouch, sealed it and slipped it into a pocket; the cutters he tossed inside with the body. There was a wafer pad located at one of the upper corners of the bag, and he squeezed it between thumb and forefinger until the bag began to shrink, opaqueing as it did. The man who just a few moments earlier had been William Bodisee watched, arms folded before him, completely unaffected by the grisly sounds emanating from the lump at his feet as the constricting bag grotesquely drew the body into a compact, shapeless bundle.

It took a grunted effort to lift/drag the plastic-enshrouded body, but he managed to move it to the open hatch, where it was then a simple matter to slide it into the recess behind the wall and replace the access panel. He would remove the body later at his leisure, but for now this would suffice.

He checked the corridor for any signs of a struggle, being especially mindful to check the spot where the man had died, but found nothing, other than the agent's ID badge on the floor several meters down the corridor, to indicate that anything had happened. There was still a faint odor of smoke in the air from the tiny explosive charge, but that would be gone soon enough.

He glanced at the timepiece on his wrist, pleased to see that less than three minutes had elapsed since he had taken the monitoring station off-line. The normal check routine took between five and six minutes, so no alarm would be raised in the central system by the station at corridor nine, level six, starboard.

Bodisee would not be missed. At the duty shift's end the maintenance tech supervisor, checking the *Kiska*'s computerized duty logs, would find that William Bodisee had been transferred to life support. The supervisor wouldn't mind, since Bodisee's work had been neither good nor bad, merely average. Bodisee had been close to no one, no crew member had become his friend; he had spent most of his time, in fact, blending himself inconspicuously into the background during the voyage to Tsing. It was doubtful if anyone aboard the jump ship would even remember him at all if questioned, much less recall anything of the intimate details of his appearance, his habits, or his lifestyle.

Not surprising, since he had never really existed in the first place, but it had still been a great deal of work to live under a false persona in the underbelly of a busy, crowded starship.

But he was an IPC agent now, a person who, almost by definition, did not exist. It would be even easier now, for once the *Kiska* had departed Luna, the four IPC agents assigned to the voyage had blended into the crew and passengers with established IDs and job descriptions unknown even to their fellow agents, IDs that would stand up under any scrutiny, unlike Bodisee's had he been anything but exacting in his efforts to hide in plain sight.

Quickly finishing his check of the monitoring station, he put it back on-line with his plastiskin thumbprint when he was done, and took one last look around the corridor. He retrieved the agent's ID badge and glanced at it, noting that he might want to alter the picture slightly to match his own face more closely. Reading the name on the badge, he almost chuckled out loud. *Hanson,* he thought, *an easy name to remember—it almost matches my own.* Then he turned and calmly walked in the direction of the lift that would take him to the crew level.

There, the grisly item inside the pouch he now carried in his pocket would admit him to his new quarters.

The *Kiska*'s lounge was a spartan facility, more a multipurpose gathering area than the intimate restaurant-like atmosphere she had seen on other ships. The lighting was too bright, the scattered tables offering little seclusion for crew and passengers desiring a quiet moment alone together. The decor, such as it was, was minimal and almost sterile. There was no music, although it would have been easy enough to ask the room system to provide it. The room lacked an overall sense of warmth, lacked the feeling of friendliness that should be central to the only place of relaxation offered the passengers.

It's almost like a military vessel, Adela told herself. *The only thing missing is that everything's not tinted the same color.*

The room was large enough, with seating at the long circular bar and the tables that could easily handle a fair-sized crowd. Maybe that was the problem; maybe if the room was smaller or partitioned in some way into separate seating and dining areas, a feeling of intimacy would lend itself naturally to the surroundings as they were.

"I'll bet I know what you're thinking."

Adela turned, startled, to find the man at the next table staring at her.

"I'm sorry," she said to him. "What did you say?"

He stood and raised his eyebrows in a way that asked "May I join you?" as he picked up his glass and moved toward her table.

Adela felt a sudden rush of uneasiness sweep over her as he approached, and looked around the room at the other patrons, thankful for the first time that the light levels were too high. Among them must certainly be one of the damned IPC death-guards Eric had assigned to watch over her. She had hated the thought of them coming on this trip, even after they had blended themselves in among passengers and crew. The fact that they had all adopted new identities upon boarding, and that she no longer recognized any of the four people who had embarked with her, made it even worse—she frequently found herself gawking in unnecessary suspicion at total strangers, trying to determine if they might be the ones following her, the ones watching her every move.

But now, with this man standing here, weaving slightly from side to side after obviously having had too much to drink, she found herself hoping that someone at one of the closer tables might be looking out for her welfare right now. A few people had heard his remark or had seen him walking over, and had turned their way out of idle curiosity. But among those who were staring back at her table now, all wore high-collared coveralls or tunics; there was no clue for her there.

"I said that I know what you're thinking," he continued, snapping her attention back to him. "My name's Zaklin, but everyone calls me Zack. May I?" Not waiting for an answer, he pulled out the chair opposite her and sat. "You're wondering why everyone in here is so boring. And why it's so damned quiet in here. You'd think there's some kind of funeral ceremony going on in here, huh?"

"I'm sorry, Zack, but I really don't feel like company right now." She smiled at him, hoping he'd take the gentle hint and go away, but no longer felt so afraid of him. Now that she had a closer look at the man and had a name to hang on him, she decided he was harmless, and she could simply get up and leave if she needed to. She felt foolish for the apprehension she'd felt only a few seconds earlier.

Zack grinned at her response, and seemed about to try another approach when a surprised look of recognition spread over his features.

"D—Dr. Montgarde!" he sputtered, nearly toppling his drink as he jumped to his feet. "I—I'm sorry, I didn't realize it was you!"

"It's all right," she replied calmly. This wasn't the first time her identity had caught someone off guard, and it wouldn't be the last time she wished her celebrity had not made it so difficult to just be herself. "It's just that I'm a little tired, and I'm afraid I really wouldn't be much company. But thank you for—"

"The lady asked you to leave." The newcomer had his hand solidly on Zaklin's shoulder. "I think it'd be in your best interests to do just that."

"Everything's fine," she assured him, rising. "He was already leaving."

"I was! I was leaving!" He wriggled free of the man's grasp and retreated hurriedly to the other side of the big room, looking over his shoulder repeatedly to make sure he wasn't being chased.

"Are you all right, Doctor?"

"I'm fine," she said, smiling gratefully. "He really was leaving. But thanks anyway." She looked the newcomer over. He was tall, clean-shaven, with curly light brown hair that fell just short of the high collar on his duty uniform—the ever-present coveralls favored by the crew. He must have just come off duty, as he still had his ID badge clipped to his pocket. The name next to his picture read HANSON, KAL. The color coding on the bottom of the ID badge was bright orange, indicating he was a member of ship security. Just what she needed, another bodyguard. At least this one was off-duty.

He smiled warmly back at her. "I hope I didn't scare him too badly." There was an amiable chuckle underlying his words, and she got the impression that he had been a little unnerved himself by his actions. Apparently, aiding damsels in distress was not something he did every day. "I don't think he'll bother you any more tonight, though. And judging from the condition he was in, he probably won't even remember this tomorrow." He looked in the direction in which Zack had disappeared, then back to Adela. There was an awkward silence as he searched for something else to say.

"Would you like to join me?" she asked, sparing him further embarrassment.

His smile returned, and she admired the warmth in his face.

"Oh, uh . . . No, thank you. I wasn't fishing for an invitation," he said, almost bashfully. "I, uh, just heard the commotion over here and wanted to be sure you were okay. Good night." With that, he nodded politely and turned away, threading his way through the scattered tables and chairs. Looking past him, Adela could see that there was an empty table in that direction with a single unattended dinner, barely touched.

She watched him as he sat at the table with his back to her and resumed his meal, thinking, *If I had to choose someone to watch over me, it would be someone more like him, and not those damned mercenary IPCs.*

"I don't want them following me, Eric!" Adela shouted into the holoframe at her son. "I feel like I can't make a move, can't do anything without trying to find that one face among the people around me who's a trained killer, ready to open fire at a moment's notice." She turned her back on the holographic image of her son and paced frantically across the floor of her plush stateroom. "I've researched them, gone through the files. The IPC doesn't hesitate to murder innocent bystanders right along with an assailant if it's the only way to stop an attack on their assigned . . . 'dependents.' "

"I'm not going to dismiss them, Mother," the Emperor countered. "It's for your own safety."

"I don't care!" She stopped pacing, and spun around to face Eric. "I feel like I might as well lock myself into this room. How about if I ask Darrly to have the door welded shut for the duration of the trip to Tsing? Would that please you?"

Eric exhaled heavily, searching for the right words. "I am not going to remove them," he reiterated, his voice indicating the finality of his decision. He stared silently from the screen for several moments, his image distorting slightly in the real-time tachyon link. He started to speak, but his words and the slight movements he made slowed to molasses thickness until the computers could correct the signal and alert him to begin his sentence again. "When you were on Pallatin—when I was still a boy, long before I ever met you—do you remember the long recording I sent telling you about how Javas had taken me to Earth to protect me against an assassin? About how the very man responsible for murdering a close associate of Father's rode happily along with us on our own shuttle, without our knowledge? I won't let that happen to you. If you truly reviewed the files on the history of the IPC and their purpose, then you can understand why I personally created them when I became Emperor."

Adela stood facing the holoframe, arms dangling limply at her sides, and said nothing for a moment. Then, bluntly, her voice almost a whisper: "Don't you understand? I feel like I'm suffocating."

Eric sighed again. "Once you've arrived at Tsing I'll discuss with Lewis—based on their own post-jump reports—the need to continue IPC surveillance. Not before. I'm sorry that you disagree, Mother." His patience worn thin on the subject, he stared obstinately from the holoframe. "Is there anything else we need to discuss?"

The room fell suddenly cold and silent.

"No," she replied emotionlessly. "I don't think there is."

"All right, then." He attempted a smile, with little success. "Take care." The Emperor's image faded away.

Adela fell heavily into the chair facing the holoframe, thinking, *Where are you? Are you in the room next to me? Above or below me? Are you watching me now, listening to my every word even as I talk to your Emperor?*

"Damn you!" she shouted to the confining walls around her, hoping that the IPC agents were monitoring the room. "Damn you to hell!"

She sat motionless in the chair for nearly half an hour until deciding, on a sudden impulse, to reactivate the holoframe.

"Ma'am?" the softly feminine system voice inquired.

"Set up a real-time link to the *Scartaris* at her current coordinates at Tsing."

It took several minutes for the correct links to be made before the system confirmed that a solid connection had been established. "Ready." The voice that emanated from the system this time was different, indicating that she had indeed reached the ship now in orbit at Tsing. "To whom would you like to speak?"

"Connect me with Commander Wood."

A pause. "I'm sorry, but direct communication to Commander Wood must first be arranged through—"

"System, interrupt," she said, cutting off the *Scartaris'* security programming. "Scan files for my voice authorization code."

Another pause, then, "One moment."

A full minute passed before Lewis' holographic image appeared in the frame, his tousled hair and the casual pullover he wore indicating that he had been trying to get some rest. The dark circles under his eyes made him look like he needed it, and Adela felt a moment's regret for calling him so hastily.

"Grandmother?" He blinked at the brightness in the room around him as a look of sudden concern flooded over his features. "What—? Is everything all right there?"

"I'm sorry, Lewis, for the intrusion," she said contritely. "I should have considered the difference in time when I—"

"No, no; it's all right." He shook his head tiredly and waved a hand to dismiss the transgression. "We've been on local time since exit," he said, smiling warmly. "It's good to get the chance to talk to you. I'm looking forward to meeting you—personally, I mean, not on the link. . . ." He paused, wrinkling his brow wearily as he tried to remember her flight schedule. The mannerism reminded her of Javas. "Let's see, you'll be here in just a few days, if I'm not mistaken."

"That's right. I'm looking forward to getting to know both you and Brendan, too." She hesitated, unsure how to proceed. "Lewis, I'd like to ask a favor of you. Since we're almost there, would it be possible for you to recall the IPC agents your father has assigned?"

His face suddenly turned dour, taking on the same obstinate appearance Eric's had displayed earlier.

"Father told me weeks ago to expect this," he replied bluntly. "We had planned to discuss this once you had arrived, but he said it would ultimately be my call. But frankly, I agree with him." He pursed his lips momentarily, but his eyes never blinked as he stared out of the holoframe.

"No. I will not recall the IPC team."

SEVENTEEN
A Change of Plans

I'm being drugged."

Dr. Templeton Rice sat morosely in the only chair his room offered, his head leaning dejectedly against his fist. The room was comfortable and nicely appointed, considerably nicer than the recovery room in which he had awakened two days earlier.

He hadn't intended to say the words aloud, although he spoke so softly that anyone not within a meter of him wouldn't have noticed he'd said anything at all. He assumed he was being watched, or at least monitored audibly, but he didn't think his slip could be heard by the room system. If he was wrong, well, he'd deal with it.

How much time had really passed since he'd been here on the orbital? He had seen little of the medical facility, let alone any other portion of the orbital habitat. This room, part of a suite that also included an exercise chamber, a small examination room, an office workroom and the connecting corridors, had become his entire world. Not disagreeable if he were spending a short amount of time somewhere, especially in a hospital, but just how much time *was* he spending here? He looked around his room for any telltale sign that would give him some clue, but found nothing. Everything was in its proper place as far as he could tell, nothing changed from day to day. He rose from his chair and walked aimlessly, restlessly around the room, touching and moving objects at random looking for—what? Cobwebs? Dust outlines around the objects that would indicate just how long it had been?

There was no clock, no calendar, no terminal he could use even to time his own pulse, much less the passage of hours or days. There was a room system, of course, but it served only to control the environmental aspects of the room and would not grant him access to the main system. There had been no communications from outside, no news broadcasts, nothing that could indicate the passage of time.

He looked at his hands, turning them over and over, rubbing them together.

It seemed as if only two days had passed since his talk with Dr. Rapson, since he'd learned of Oidar's untimely death. But it didn't feel right, not at all. Somehow he knew that a longer time had passed, but there was nothing he could seize on that would prove it, even to himself, other than his own feelings. But even as he struggled with the thought, another feeling kept nagging at him: If he really was being drugged, if he was being kept asleep for long periods of time, what was the motive? Why would anyone want to deceive him in that way?

And still, he knew deep down that more than a few days, maybe even weeks, had passed. The doctor had said he'd been in stasis for three weeks when his pod was picked up. He'd been in stasis before, and how he had felt when waking up two days ago seemed right for a drug-induced stasis like the one that would have been part of the pod's emergency system. . . . But it was hard to believe then, as it was now, that that much time had passed while he drifted in the pod. Maybe the time he'd spent here on the orbital station was accurate, and the time Rapson had claimed he drifted in the pod was a lie.

He fell heavily into the chair, the seat still warm from sitting in it moments earlier, and rubbed at his neck, stiff with tension and stress. *Why would someone convince me I was asleep for three weeks, when I wasn't,* he thought, *and then try to make me believe only two days had passed while I slept for a much longer period of time?* He rubbed at his throbbing temples with both hands. It didn't make any sense.

He leaned back in the chair and stared again at his hands, examining his fingernails. He had trimmed them himself shortly after waking up. After talking with Dr. Rapson and getting a good solid meal, he had showered and shaved. He remembered distinctly how refreshing it had been to wash off the stink of stasis, to remove the grimy stubble from his face. It had all seemed so real.

But his fingernails . . .

He experimentally dragged his fingertips across his face. He had shaved that morning, as he always did, and his fingertips played smoothly over the skin of his cheeks. He brushed his nails against his cheeks, noting the soft scratching sound, then delicately rubbed a thumbnail against the more sensitive skin of his lips. He repeated the action with his other thumbnail, then with each of his nails in turn.

They were too smooth.

Having trimmed them only the day before yesterday, they

should still be rougher, with sharper edges—he had not used a nail file, only clippers. He held both hands before him, his fingers curled over his palms. His nails were just too nicely done, almost manicured.

It was possible. If someone was keeping him out for days at a time but wanted him to think he was adhering to a normal routine, it would be a fairly simple matter to trim his hair and shave him twenty or so hours before bringing him around. That way, he'd wake with what appeared to be a normal day's growth of beard and shave himself, noticing nothing unusual, just as he had done these last two "mornings." But his fingernails were different. If they were to convince him that only two days had elapsed, they had to carefully trim his nails in such a way that he wouldn't notice that more time had passed.

But why?

He rubbed his neck again, trying to work out some of the kinks that kept developing there.

He leaned back in the chair again and closed his eyes. Maybe he was going about this backward. Maybe, instead of trying to figure out why someone would have a motive to keep him asleep, he should concentrate on why someone wouldn't want him awake. If weeks had truly passed, what would he be doing now? Surely he would be long gone from this facility, probably back on Luna or at the Academy. He might even be back at work at the sunstation with a new research team, or at least be making plans to rebuild his team and restart work on Mercury. He would certainly have filed a complete report on the deaths of Julie and Boscawen during the mutiny at the sunstation by now, and been debriefed by Imperial security. But if only two days had passed, there wouldn't have been time for any of that—he'd merely be near the end of a short hospital stay, assuming that everything else would take place as soon as he could be picked up.

Was that it? Was he being fooled into thinking only a few days had passed so he wouldn't insist on contacting the outside? So he wouldn't suspect he was being detained for an extended period of time? He nodded. It made sense, except for one detail: If they wanted him quiet and unquestioning, why not just keep him in a drugged stasis around the clock? Why not put him in cryosleep, for that matter? That way he wouldn't be a burden at all; no subterfuge, no intricate shaving and nail-trimming schemes, no careful isolation from anything that would tell him the time. They wouldn't even have to feed him. Unless . . .

Unless they thought they might need him for something on

short notice. But what? "Maybe it's time to find out," he said under his breath.

"System!" he called, getting to his feet. There was a confirming chirp. "I'm not feeling very well. Could I please summon Dr. Rapson."

"I'm sorry," came the synthesized reply, "but he is unavailable at the moment. Can you describe your discomfort?"

"It's my stomach. I don't think it's anything serious; just a bit upset, is all."

"I will notify one of the other physicians immediately of your request."

Fine, he thought, moving into the corridor. Since leaving the recovery room where he first awoke, he had been given considerable freedom in his limited area, although the access doors at each end of the corridor were kept locked at all times. There was an examination room adjacent to the exercise chamber, and he tried to find something in it that he could use as a weapon. He kept his movements as inconspicuous as he could, hoping that if he was being watched it would appear he was just looking for something to relieve his upset stomach. The cabinets were locked, thumb-keyed, as were all the drawers. There were some lightweight plastic glasses stacked on the countertop, similar to several he already had back in his room, but he doubted if one could be broken into pieces suitable enough to use to threaten someone.

The brief search of the office proved just as fruitless. Like the examination room and his bedroom, the only things he could use as weapons were objects that he might throw. Frustrated, he decided to return to his room and find something that he might at least be able to conceal. But as he passed the darkened exercise chamber, he had a thought.

His muscles had been stiff since awakening and he had used the equipment here several times, and knew the machines and the layout of the room. He stepped inside and, guided only by the sparse lighting from the opened doorway, quickly approached the weight machine. There was a sliding pulley system on it that adjusted the amount of resistance, and his fingers easily located the adjustment handle, sliding it to its lowest setting. He felt one of the thin weight cables, satisfied at the amount of slack that was there, and managed to work it free of the pulley. The tension on the meter-long cable now completely relieved, it was a simple matter to unhook each end and pull it out of the machine. He coiled the cable and slipped it under his shirt, tucking it carefully into the waistband of his pants, and left the room.

"Are you all right, Dr. Rice?" It was the orderly, Poser. He had just entered the corridor through the locked door at the far end, and carried a small plastic tray with a carton of fruit juice and a glass. "Why were you in there in the dark?" he indicated the exercise chamber.

"Oh." Rice turned in the direction of his room. "It's my stomach. I thought maybe if I walked around a bit I could shake it. Didn't do much good, I'm afraid."

"This will probably be more effective in settling your stomach," he said once they were back in his room. He set the tray on the table while Rice sat in the chair, then did a perfunctory taking of his pulse, glancing at the readout on a handheld he'd produced from a pocket of his white coat. He did not, Rice noticed, wear a watch. He also checked his temperature, peered into each of his eyes, and pressed on his neck just beneath his ears with his fingertips.

"I think you'll be fine," Poser continued. "You'll recall that Dr. Rapson mentioned how dehydrated you had become by your ordeal aboard the pod. You should be drinking more fluids, especially since you are spending so much time on the exercise equipment." He opened the container and filled the glass, handing it to Rice.

"Thanks." Rice took the offered drink and sipped at it gingerly. "I'll try to remember."

Poser smiled and turned to leave, picking up the tray as he did, and Rice followed him to the door.

"When will I be able to leave?" He sipped cautiously at the juice again, careful not to swallow too much in case that was how they were drugging him. If they *were* drugging him.

"I'm afraid you'll have to talk to the doctor about that."

"Can I see him?"

"I'll be seeing him in just a little while," Poser said, his smile just a little too practiced, a little too plastic. "I can tell him myself that you're ready to get out of here."

Rice returned the smile. "Thanks, I'd appreciate that." He lifted the glass to his lips again, but instead splashed its contents into the man's face, catching him completely off guard. He staggered back against the doorframe, eyes blinking in shock, his hands wiping at his face. Rice reached under his shirt, and in one smooth motion uncoiled the cable and looped it over Poser's head, pulling the ends tightly behind the man's back as he pawed frantically at the cable now digging into his neck, and dragged him into the corridor. Poser was able to get his fingers under the cable and managed to loosen it a bit, choking loudly as he gasped desperately for air.

Rice knew that they had to be watching him closely now and moved with his kicking, struggling burden as fast as he could down the corridor, grateful that the little man was so light. He didn't loosen his grip on the cable around Poser's neck until reaching the locked door that would admit them into the next corridor.

"Open it!" He jerked backward on the cable, letting him know he meant what he said. "Open it! Or so help me I'll strangle you!"

The orderly continued digging at the cable cutting into his neck, too terrified to do anything more than struggle.

Rice nearly lifted Poser off the ground and slung him against the doorframe. He gripped both ends of the cable in one hand and pushed the man face-first into the wall, pressing against him to hold him there while pulling at his arm with his other hand. Each time Rice pulled Poser's arm free, the hand would snap back to Poser's neck as he tried to get his fingers under the constricting cable around his throat. Rice finally got a firm grip on Poser's wrist and slapped his hand against the opening plate next to the door, but the palm wasn't flat against the plate and the door didn't open. He tried again with the same results. And again. But the man's flailing made it nearly impossible to even hold him still, much less control the angle of his hand.

But with each passing second his struggling lessened, and Rice realized the man was blacking out. He eased back on the cable and felt the gasping Poser beginning to slip to the floor like a rag doll. Leaning almost his full weight against him to keep him upright, he then flattened his hand against the plate, making sure the man's thumbprint was centered on the scanning mechanism. The door slid obediently aside.

Concentrating more intently on just drawing his next breath, Poser put up little resistance as Rice dragged him down the corridor to where another door would admit them to the next section. This time he was able to get the door opened on the first try.

The section they entered was similar to his own in that it was arranged like a suite of rooms, although one wall had been re-placed with a single sheet of dark plastiglass that reflected the two of them as they moved quickly through in the direction of the next doorway. When he took a careful look at the door, Rice began to feel lucky for the first time since deciding upon his little revolt—it was a lift entrance. If he could just access the lift, he could then use the terminal sure to be inside it to find the location of the orbital's escape pods. He might yet be able to make it out of this.

But as he flattened Poser's hand on the opening plate, it glowed red. Someone aboard the station had caught on to what he was doing and had disabled the opening plates to Poser's thumbprint.

"Damn!" He loosened his grip on the orderly, allowing him to sink to the floor, still gasping and clutching his throat. He turned to run back the way he had come, but the door they'd just come through slid abruptly closed.

That's it, then, he thought cheerlessly, leaning out of breath against the wall opposite the pitiful man at his feet. *It was a good try, though.* It occurred to him, however, that now he would at least find out what was going on. If he wasn't being kept here under some pretense, there certainly wouldn't be so much security in place to keep him here. At least he'd managed to establish that.

The opening plate suddenly changing from red to green caught his eye. He grabbed Poser and jerked him to his feet, encircling his forearm around his neck. There wasn't time to grab the cable on the floor, but the diminutive man's weakened condition had so thoroughly worn down his resistance that it hardly mattered. Rice backed down the hall with his impromptu hostage, putting some distance between himself and the opening lift.

He wasn't sure what he had expected to see when the doors parted completely. A dozen armed security officers, guns leveled in his direction, bursting forth from the lift would not have surprised him at all. But what he saw there he could never have imagined: a single woman with flowing copper hair, dressed in a gown more befitting an Imperial ball than the hospital section of an orbital station. As she came forward, gracefully and with no small amount of practiced poise, he realized just how beautiful she truly was—but just who *was* she?

"Let him go," she said simply.

Rice tightened his grip around Poser's throat, setting the little man to gagging once more. "I don't think so. If you come any closer, I'll break his scrawny neck." He continued backing away from her. "I mean it. Either you let me into that lift, or I'll kill him."

She almost smiled at that, but didn't slow her pace as she approached. "Let him go, Dr. Rice."

"You're not even armed!" he shouted at her, feeling his

advantage slipping. "What the hell kind of place is this? You're not going to stop me without security to back you up."

"I don't need security, and I don't need a weapon. I knew that before I came down here."

"How could you?"

"Poser told me."

"He *told* you? How did . . .?"

Rice stared down incredulously at the man locked tightly in his grip. His face was twisted in agony.

"Let . . . me . . . go . . ." he managed to gasp between clenched teeth. His face was beet red, his bloodshot eyes wide in terror.

Rice had already traveled the length of the corridor and felt his back touching the closed door behind him.

"Listen carefully, Dr. Rice—"

"No, *you* listen! I want access to that lift, and if you or Rapson follow me or hamper me in any way I *will* kill him."

She did smile then. "No, you won't. And unless you do kill him, or at least render him unconscious, you'll find you won't get very far. He has an implanted integrator and can control every system aboard this ship." She paused, allowing her words to sink in. "That's right, Doctor; this is a ship, *my* ship. Not an orbital."

Rice nodded, beginning to understand as the pieces started falling into place. He tightened his grip around Poser's neck, saying into the man's ear loudly enough for the woman to hear, "Listen to me, friend: Either you escort me to an escape pod or shuttle, or I'll strangle you right here and now. Do you understand me?"

Poser tried to reply, but the best he could manage was an unintelligible gurgle.

"Believe me, Doctor, your strangling my personal aide would be no great loss." At that, Poser's eyes widened even further, if that were possible. "But before you do, I think you should see something." She walked toward him, stopping in front of the long expanse of plastiglass. "System!"

There was a pause as the security subroutines in this area recognized her voice pattern. "Yes, Mistress?"

"Lock in to the shield wall in suite D, level four."

"Ready."

"Remove opacity and audio dampers."

Rice suddenly realized, as the wall became transparent at her order, that it had not been plastiglass at all, but rather a generated shield. But it was what he saw inside that stunned him.

The interior of the modest-sized room on the other side of the shielding resembled nothing so much as a small greenhouse. There was a low plastic couch in the center, a small table set to one side. There was also a cabinet against the far wall next to an open doorway that led to what Rice assumed to be a bathroom or galley. There was no other furniture. The rest of the room was filled with plant life of every variety he could imagine. The very lighting of the room itself glowed green as it filtered through the myriad growing things.

The audio dampers off, he could hear the sound of insects as they buzzed around the room, as well as the steady dripping of water falling among the leafy plants. There were other soft, melodic sounds he couldn't quite identify, but as he listened more closely he realized what it was: Sarpan music, emanating, apparently, from a speaker system somewhere inside. The room must have been incredibly hot and humid, because the walls, furniture, even the ceiling light grids ran wet with moisture; the air itself was a steamy haze.

A naked figure with skin of glistening brown appeared in the doorway, undoubtedly drawn to the living area by the sound now emanating from the corridor. The being had apparently been unaware of their presence until the very moment he entered the room, and came to rigid attention when he saw that the shield wall of his room had unexpectedly become translucent. He stared out at them, his large eyes wide in shocked surprise.

"Oidar!"

The alien came fully into the room, tilting his head at them. He blinked the nictitating membranes in astonishment as he recognized him. "Temple? Is it you? You are alive?"

Before Rice could do anything else, the woman strode defiantly up before him. "Doctor, I'm sure you recognize the Sarpan-normal conditions that are being maintained on the other side of this shielding. You can credit those conditions for keeping your soggy little friend alive." She paused. "System!"

"Yes, Mistress?"

"On my mark, wait fifteen seconds then discontinue current special environmental settings in place in suite D, level four, and dissolve the shield wall at the same location. . . . Mark." The corners of her mouth turned up into an almost sadistic smile. "Well, Doctor, kill my aide if you'd like; but if you do not release him in the next few seconds you will condemn your friend to death." She took a few steps away from the shielding and leaned casually against the wall on the opposite side of the corridor. "We can all watch as he dries out right here on the floor in front of us. It's your call."

Rice released his captive and let the man fall, nearly sobbing, to the floor.

"I thought so," she said, the slightest hint of disappointment in her voice. "System, cancel last directive."

EIGHTEEN
A Change of Mind

S he is known as Rihana Valtane," Oidar said. "I have been treated well at her hands. The small male, I believe, is her water tender; he is called Poser. However, this one has no way of determining the truth of these things." He tilted his head in an apologetic manner. "Do you know of her, Temple?"

"Yes, but not from personal experience," Rice replied.

Oidar nodded slowly, his face assuming the familiar pouting expression that indicated he was deep in thought. "So" was all he said as he tapped a webbed forefinger against his lower lip. "So."

The Sarpan's speech patterns and mastery of English were old-style, Rice noted. In the last century, the aliens had come to master vocal communication quite handily; but Oidar, asleep for so long, awoke with his speaking patterns intact. Somehow, that was a distinct comfort to him, something solid to grab on to, something *known* in this situation where so many things remained unknown. It was even a bit relieving the way Oidar used his old nickname. Rice regarded his old friend, and felt good about Oidar's condition for the first time since pulling him out of the tank back at the sunstation on Mercury. Although his skin was still the dull chocolate brown of Sarpan old age, Oidar's eyes were bright and inquisitive, and his face reflected the image of the young scientist Rice had known so many years ago. The severe dehydration caused by cryosleep might have made him look older, but Rice could feel that Oidar was just as vital now as he was then.

The Sarpan occupied most of one side of the low couch, reclining in a characteristic position Rice had come to recognize over the years as the most comfortable pose members of his friend's race could employ on furniture designed expressly for human frames.

Rice ran the fingers of his hands through his dripping hair, plastering it back across the top of his head, then wiped uselessly at his face. Licking his lips, he tasted only his own salty sweat. He had shed all but his undershorts before entering Oidar's room, leaving the rest of his clothes in a pile on the other side of the shield wall, where they would remain dry. Sitting upright on the other side of the couch, Rice was grateful that Oidar had draped a large woven throw over the back of the couch in deference to him, but he was careful nonetheless not to allow his bare back to touch any of the exposed plastic of the couch itself.

The room was a veritable steam bath, and he was forced to reach again for the tall glass of water on the table, wondering if it was the fifth or sixth full glass he'd downed in the two hours they had been left alone by their captors. The water had been cold when first drawn from the tap in the room's tiny galley, but was now approaching room temperature. He set the container back on the table and, shooing away a pesky dragonfly-like insect, refilled it once more from the pitcher Oidar had provided.

"Rihana Valtane was once married to Javas, long before he became Emperor," he went on. "Long before our project began." Rice mused at how it all seemed like ancient history, and yet how most of it was part of his own lifetime. "Several years after being ousted from the Imperial House, she had a son conceived artificially from an ovum fertilized by Javas, and attempted—with the help of a religious cult leader from Earth—to kill both Javas and Eric. Fortunately, it was Eric himself, then just a boy, who prevailed . . . at the cost of her own son's life. I wasn't even involved with the Sun project yet. I had not even met Adela de Montgarde, for that matter, when it all happened; but I always got the impression from what I'd heard over the years that she had a personal vendetta against the Imperial House."

"She is an enemy, then?"

Rice shrugged, but immediately remembered the Sarpan's weakness for understanding human body language. "Dr. Montgarde warned me of her before going into cryosleep, as did Academician Bomeer before his death. But to my knowledge she hasn't shown much interest in Imperial affairs since, choosing instead to utilize the many technological developments that have come about to increase her material wealth and position among the interstellar trading Houses. At that, she's been quite success-ful; respected, even." Rice paused and wiped again at his face and neck with the back of his hand. "Next time," he said jokingly as he reached yet again for the water, "you're putting on an E-suit and coming over to my place." He drank, frowning at the water that was now almost as unpleasantly warm as the room itself.

Oidar let the quip pass without comment, then, still tapping idly at his lower lip, replied, "So. If she is who she claims to be . . . ?" In typical old-style fashion, he let the unfinished question hang in the thick air.

Rice nodded, finishing his friend's incomplete thought. "Yeah, what does she want with us? That's just what I've been wonder-ing. We're being used for something, that's certain." Rice looked around the room, studying the ceiling first, then walls. Thinking silently for several long moments before coming to a decision, he stood. His head spun dizzily for a second, and he realized that he would have to get out of this heat and humidity before much longer.

"I'm sure you're listening," he called out aloud, having no doubt they were being monitored. "So what is it, Mistress Val-tane? What do you want with us?" Rice waited patiently for an answer, but no response was forthcoming. "The two of us would like to talk to you about a couple things," he said, just slightly louder this time.

Nothing happened for several minutes, but when light filled the corridor outside Oidar's room he knew he had been heard. Some-one was coming—the angle was wrong to see who it was, but he had no doubt it would be Rihana Valtane.

"Of course I have been listening," she said testily when she reached the shield wall. She was dressed more casually than when he had first seen her a few hours earlier. Instead of the gown, she now wore a tailored sky-blue pant suit of a design that seemed more sensible—and more comfortable—for life aboard a star-ship. Her copper hair had been pulled back, and was fastened behind her head with a jeweled clip just above the collar of her outfit. The man Poser was with her, but this time he offered no pretense of being a medical aide. In fact, his attire matched hers rather closely in both color and design. Rice could see, when Poser turned his head to watch his mistress, a slight bruising above his collar from the rough handling Rice had given him earlier. As he studied the pair, it occurred to him that the gar-ments almost had the appearance of being uniforms, or at least as much of a uniform as this headstrong woman would ever deign to wear. He had to admit, however, that it did lend her a certain air of authority that had been missing—despite her obvious command of the situation—at their last meeting. Rice wondered idly if she had consciously altered her appearance in this way solely for his benefit.

"I appreciate the candor of your conversation with the alien over the last few hours," she continued dryly, "although I found myself becoming quite wearied with the actual discussion itself. I'd hoped to gain some insight as to how much you already knew, but you chose instead to talk mostly about the progress of the Sun project." She sighed disappointedly. "That's what happens, I suppose, when you throw two scientists together for any length of time. Frankly, scientific talk, especially when it's little more than an update of what he's missed over the last two hundred years . . ." She jerked a thumb in Oidar's direction. ". . . bores me to no end."

"Fine," Rice snapped back, rising. He approached the shield wall and stood before her, hands fisted rigidly at his sides, and glared defiantly into her eyes. "Let's talk about why we're here instead. Oidar has confirmed that we've been detained here for nearly three weeks, although you've done your best to convince me otherwise. I want to know what you want with us. To start with, why was I drugged?"

She looked the scientist up and down as he stood brazenly before her wearing nothing but his underwear. A brief, sly smile appeared on her lips and she raised an appreciative eyebrow at what she saw. "You do not seem to be any the worse for your treatment," she mused. "Don't bother asking any questions, as I intend to tell you only as much as I've already decided you should know at this time. But, as it is now obvious that you *have* been deceived, and that you *are* indeed being detained, I have decided to inform you of your general situation." She smiled again, and Rice noted just the hint of several tiny wrinkles at the corners of her mouth and eyes as she looked at him. "I anticipate that you won't much like what you'll hear, however."

She turned to leave, kicking at the pile of clothes at her feet. "Get dressed," she said in a voice clearly accustomed to giving orders. "I'm afraid you might prove too much of a distraction to me in your present apparel."

She nodded curtly to Poser, and a vertical section of the shield wall between them immediately became fuzzy. The hazy rectangle remained attached to the wall but extended itself quickly into the room, passing over Rice until he was enclosed in a tall boothlike structure that would form a shield airlock. The airlock coalesced at his sides and back; then the front wall dissolved completely, allowing him to exit Oidar's room. One of the insects had been caught in the airlock with him, and it buzzed away down the corridor. Once he stood dripping before her, the airlock shrank back into the wall and disappeared.

Her face twisted in disgust and she turned away, her hand to her nose. "See to it that he bathes!" she shouted as she walked briskly to the lift doors at the corridor's end. "I won't have my office smelling like some damned swamp."

Rihana Valtane had not yet arrived when Poser admitted him to her "office." The diminutive man took a position near the door through which they had just entered, hands behind his back, and stood at relaxed attention as he awaited the arrival of his mistress. Almost ignoring Rice, he held his chin up and stared absently off into the distance in such a way that made his nose appear more prominent than usual. His face reminded Rice of some kind of weasel.

Oidar was right, he thought, staring at the aide. *You are little more than a water tender.*

"Where is she?"

Poser turned with a surprised, incredulous look that wordlessly asked "Are you talking to me?" visible on his face.

Rice tried again. "I thought I was to meet with Mistress Valtane. Where is she?"

"Mistress Valtane will be with you in a moment, Doctor," he replied. "She is in consultation with the pilot of this vessel at this time, and deeply regrets that she must keep you waiting any longer than is necessary."

Yeah, right.

Rice filled the time by more closely examining the room in which he now found himself, concluding that Rihana Valtane's office was, without a doubt, the most plush quarters he had ever seen aboard a ship of any kind. He suspected that the Emperor's own ship was not so marvelously adorned. Designed as a combination study, lounge and command center, the room had obviously been furnished with the thought that she would be spending a great deal of time here.

The plush seating was considerably nicer than any he had ever beheld in a working office, and spoke as much of her vanity as did the other fine appointments. He couldn't be certain, but the tapestries that hung on the facing wall might just be genuine,

ancient Persian rugs, although he had never actually seen one
before other than in library holofiles. There was a holograph
frame here, of course, that occupied an entire wall of the office.
Displayed on it was an old artwork, depicting a noblewoman
holding a small carnivorous animal. The woman in the painting
was the very picture of innocence and grace, her gentle smile able
to lure any man into her confidence. The minklike animal, meanwhile, exuded a vicious, predatory stare, and appeared ready to
attack without mercy upon command. While he had no idea what
the work was called, or what artist had rendered it, he could
definitely see—based on what he knew of this woman—why this
particular work would appeal to her. The two subjects of this
single work were but two sides of Rihana Valtane.

On one side of the room, before a vast oak-paneled shelving
unit, was a desk workstation. There wasn't much on the desk
other than a small manually operated terminal and a few items of
a personal nature: a blue crystalline figurine of a winged goddess,
a leather folder, a gold cup containing what he assumed to be
blank data sticks for use with the terminal. Paneled doors set into
the shelving unit behind the desk were parted, revealing what
looked remarkably like . . . was it a wet bar? Surely, this woman
had better things that she could—

"Sit down, Dr. Rice."

He whipped around, startled by her sudden entrance, and was
barely able to step out of her way as she swept arrogantly past
him and took a seat behind the desk. She glared at him a moment
as if sizing him up, then pointed to the single chair facing the
desk. As he took the proffered seat, Poser—the ever-obedient
servant that he was—scurried over to stand behind her as if
playing out the part of her personal shadow.

"Pay attention," she said curtly and without preamble. "I only
want to tell you this once. I shall leave it up to you as to how you
explain any of this to your alien friend." Rihana leaned forward
on the desktop, momentarily steepling her hands in front of her
face in thought before going on. For just the briefest of instants,
Rice got the distinct impression that she was just now making up
her mind even as she spoke. She must certainly have been considering what she was about to say for some time, but he was
somehow convinced it was only now that she had resolved to
carry through whatever plans she had for them.

Rice said nothing, waiting.

"You are correct in assuming that you and the alien have been
taken for a reason," she began directly, and as she spoke, he

noticed that she had unexpectedly dropped all airs of superiority. For the moment she was being uncharacteristically blunt with him. He reminded himself, however, that if she was truly being honest it was undoubtedly in her own best interests to do so, and not his. He wondered if it was the gentlewoman from the painting who addressed him now, or the cunning animal. "I am working with someone who sees an advantage to using you and the Sarpan scientist to achieve certain goals. While I couldn't care less about the nature of these specific goals, I, too, see an advantage to cooperating with him in this matter." She paused, tilting her head questioningly at him. "Do I make myself clear, so far, in this regard?"

Rice nodded silently, knowing full well that it was pointless to ask the woman anything just now. Better, he decided, to save any questions he might have for later and let her proceed at her own pace.

"Good. Now, understand further that my agreement with this individual has been breached in a manner not to my liking. I have given the situation more than enough time . . ." She hesitated again, raising an eyebrow in his direction. ". . . keeping you drugged for the duration as you have correctly surmised, to allow my, ah, 'partner' enough time to come to his senses and honor our pact. Unfortunately, he has not done so. Therefore, I have decided that the time has come to proceed in a manner I feel best, to salvage what I can from our agreement."

He considered her words carefully, then asked, "As your personal plans change, do your plans for the two of us change, too?"

She smiled in appreciation at his insight. Or perhaps it was the blatant nature of his question that appealed to her.

"Frankly, Doctor, I don't yet know just what I'm going to do with you. But believe me when I tell you that I would not hesitate to blow the both of you out the nearest airlock if the idea appealed to me. No one knows you are with me; no one even knows with any certainty that you are still alive. Discarding you and the alien at this very moment would not, in a million years, be traced back to me." She smiled then, the gesture actually containing what seemed a bit of warmth. "However, I don't intend to do that just yet, as you might still prove valuable to me." She leaned back in her chair, swiveling idly from side to side. "Please, don't think I mean you harm; however, if I can't make a profit from you in some manner—I might just as easily set you down someplace where you won't get in my way until long after I've had time to establish myself elsewhere."

"And what if we don't cooperate with you?"

"Not cooperate?" She laughed lightly, truly amused by the question. "Doctor, you do not even know the exact purpose for which you were taken. Just what is it that you think you might refuse to do?"

"I . . ." Rice began feebly. "I assumed our abduction has something to do with Adela de Montgarde's project to save Earth's Sun. I know you once tried to prevent the project from—"

"You know nothing!" she retorted, cutting him off. "I never cared a whit about the project. My alliance with forces opposed to the project was an alliance of convenience that benefited me at that time." Her face broke into a haughty smile. "If I had wanted merely to disrupt the project, that would have been quite simple. My goals were different. But that is a matter best left in the past, with little relevance to what we are discussing now." She hesitated, her sapphire eyes penetrating his. "I ask you again: In what way are you threatening to withhold your cooperation?"

Rice tried to reply, but could think of nothing to counter her question.

"Go on a hunger strike if you want," Rihana continued with a casual wave of her hand. "Flop down on the deck and refuse to move unless carried, spend your hours screaming for help down in your quarters—it doesn't much matter to me. Remember, the original reason for which you were detained has evaporated along with my former partner's desertion. I have no immediate plans for you other than to keep you a while longer." She leaned forward again, adopting once more the unpretentious manner of before. "Your choice, I think, is simple: Give me no trouble and your stay with me can be a pleasant one. The *Tiatia* is very nicely outfitted, as I'm sure you've noticed by now. I'll be happy to have you moved to a stateroom for the duration of your stay, if you agree to 'behave yourself.' "

Why not, he thought. "Fine; I won't give you any trouble. I'm not ungrateful for your hospitality, but I think I'd just as soon stay as close to Oidar as possible."

Rihana shrugged. "Whatever. I'll see to it that more comfortable accessories are installed in your current suite. However . . ." Her face softened, and an almost demure smile appeared on her lips. "If you should change your mind about more comfortable quarters, don't hesitate to let me know."

"Mistress . . ." Poser's face looked concerned.

"Not now," she snapped. "In the meantime, Dr. Rice, feel free to return to your suite. You'll find that you now have unrestricted access through the corridors connecting your suite to the alien's. Please don't kidnap anyone to open the locks."

Poser cleared his throat loudly. "Mistress, I am receiving a level-one query from Mr. Krowek. He demands to speak with you immediately."

"Yes, I'm sure he does. Tell him I am unavailable."

"I already have, Mistress, but he insists—"

Poser stopped abruptly as the painting in the holoframe dissolved, to be replaced with the image of a man in a neatly tailored business suit that looked as out of place as Rihana's earlier attire.

"Why are you moving your ship?" he demanded. "You agreed to make no attempt to navigate without first consulting with me!"

Rihana was instantly on her feet, the expression on her face a combination of disbelief and outrage. Her nostrils flared as she addressed the image in the holoframe. "Would you mind telling me how in hell you obtained direct access to my comm net, Krowek?"

The man sneered contemptuously. "It's unimportant right now. Answer me: Why are you moving your ship?"

Rihana ignored his question and turned instead to her aide, making no effort to lower her voice. "Poser, please reconfigure the entire comm net and all ancillary functions on the *Tiatia* capable of being accessed by an outside source. Do it at once, and use a random-code generator." She turned back to the man she called Krowek. "You know, I wondered how long it would take before you noticed," she said bluntly, just the slightest hint of humor beneath the words. "Very well, then. I wanted to see just how sophisticated your monitoring systems were, so I ordered my pilot to move the *Tiatia* in ten-centimeter increments. I must admit, I am quite impressed you noticed so quickly."

"More game playing." The response was almost a sigh. "Please stop all movement of your ship until Mr. Rapson has given us further instructions."

"And suppose I do not?" Rihana came around from behind her desk and stood before the holoframe, her arms folded defiantly over her chest. "You don't possess the weaponry on your little ship to even attempt to stop me from going anywhere I please."

The man in the image paused, apparently unprepared for her refusal.

"Suppose I decide to have my pilot power up and leave? What would you do?"

"Please stop all movement of your ship until Mr. Rapson has given us further instructions," he repeated, almost exactly as before.

"Now who is playing games?" she spat back. "You are nothing more than a holographic representation prepared by our dear Mr. Rapson, who, for reasons known only to him, has seen fit to leave me out of whatever endeavor has taken him away. Frankly, Krowek, I'm tired of it—I'm tired of playing accompaniment to someone who refuses to take me fully into his confidence. I'm tired of sitting here motionless in space while my interests lie just out of my reach. I'm tired of acting as nursemaid to these two scientists—one of them a damned alien!—while I wait for his 'instructions.' "

Rice squirmed uneasily in his seat, remembering her earlier offhand remark about the airlock.

"And most of all, I am tired of talking to his animated puppet. System!"

"Yes, Mistress?"

"Connect me with pilot Moyan, simultaneous with the current transmission here on my screen."

A window opened up in the upper corner of the holoframe, and a young woman appeared. "Yes, Mistress?"

"Implement the travel orders I gave you immediately."

The woman nodded, and the window shrank out of sight.

"I'm leaving, Krowek. You can tell Rapson—if you're programmed for it, that is—that I have no further use for him." She spun about, drawing a finger sharply across her throat, and Poser obediently blanked the holoframe. "Now might be a good time, Doctor," Rihana began, turning her attention back to him for the first time since the holoframe had come to life, "to return to your quarters. Since I have need of Poser for the time being, I'll have one of my stewards escort you down to level four so that you may—"

The room went black for a split second, then was bathed in dull amber light from the emergency illuminators built into the wall and ceiling. Before anyone could move, there was a sudden violent jerk that sent Rihana hurtling through the air in his direction, slamming into him as his chair toppled backward, spilling them both across the floor. Furniture, objects from the shelves, even the heavy desk were suddenly being tossed around the room like kindling. There was the sound of a faraway explosive impact, somewhere above and behind him, that caused the entire ship to shudder ominously, then other smaller explosions that seemed to emanate from several directions at once. Each was followed by an accompanying shudder or shaking. One particularly violent blast sent them both tumbling through the holoframe, and Rihana's head hit the plastiglass viewport behind it so hard that he clearly heard the impact above the sounds the ship was making.

"Poser! What's happening?" Rihana grasped her forehead, smearing blood down the side of her face. Her hair had come undone, and quickly became matted with blood and stuck together in a disgusting mass against her neck.

"Poser!"

There was no answer.

They untangled themselves from one another just as the normal lighting came back up. The sudden appearance of viewport, until now hidden by the activated holoframe, gave the disconcerting perception that a gaping hole had just opened in the side of the room. The ship was quiet again.

"Are you all right?" Rice asked, helping her to her feet. She ignored him, pushing him away.

"System! Connect me with Moyan!"

The holoframe remained empty, but the sound of the *Tiatia*'s bridge filled the room. Obviously, the visual mode of the holoframe had been disabled by whatever had happened; just as obviously, they could tell from the sound emanating from the bridge that it was in a state of turmoil.

"What's our situation?"

"Mistress, I . . . We've had a hull breach; in the docking bay, I think. It's been locked down, and we're otherwise intact. I'm still assessing damage."

"What happened?" she demanded. "Was it the shuttle? Did it fire on us?"

"I'm . . . not sure. But—" There was a loud cry from somewhere on the bridge, and the sound of scuffling as people rushed to help whoever was screaming. The sound died away as the person was either tended to or carried out. "I'm sorry, Mistress. It was the shuttle. . . . As we were powering up, it . . . it just rammed us without warning."

"But the detonation—we felt it up here."

"Yes, Ma'am. The fuel tanks on the shuttle exploded violently on impact. I can't explain it."

"Can we move?"

There was a long pause, then: "I don't know, Mistress, but I wouldn't risk it until we can check out hull integrity and propulsion systems."

"Damn." Rihana thought for a moment, then, deciding there was little more to discuss, said, "Keep me posted. System, comm off." She wiped at her forehead again, the blood from the superficial wound already clotting. "Of course he didn't fire on us." She spoke aloud, to no one in particular, her voice more angry than shocked. "He didn't have to. The shuttle itself was all the weapon he needed. Poser!"

Again, the aide didn't answer.

They both turned to where he had been standing before the shuttle had rammed them, although that portion of the room barely resembled its original appearance. They found him near the doorframe, the heavy desk pinning him solidly against the wall. Rice immediately started tugging at the heavy piece of furniture. Rihana stood motionless, almost in shock, staring at Poser's crumpled body behind the desk.

"Give me a hand here!" Rice grunted, trying to snap her out of her morbid reverie. "Come on!"

She turned her attention to him finally, her eyes blinking as though she were lost. "What?" Her voice was shaky, uncertain.

"Get over here!"

Rihana moved slowly, as though drugged, and gripped the edge of the desk opposite Rice. She tugged once, halfheartedly; then again, harder this time. Then, as if she finally comprehended what she was doing, her face assumed a visage of sheer determination, her knuckles whitened and she pulled against the massive weight with all her strength.

They coordinated their efforts, and the desk pulled away a few centimeters, allowing Poser's inert form to slip to the floor behind it. They heaved again, then again, until finally they had it clear of the wall.

Rihana circled the desk immediately, but it was obvious to both of them that their efforts had been for nothing. Poser, his chest crushed when the desk slammed him into the wall, was unmistakably dead.

"Oh, Poser." Rihana stroked the little man's cheek with her hand, and attempted to rearrange his disheveled hair with her fingertips. She said nothing else until she stood and turned to Rice a few minutes later.

Rice looked into her eyes and found there a variety of emotions, each of them threatening to tear her apart as it fought for dominance. But in that mixture, two emotions stood out above all the others. One was clearly a sense of rage that ran through her unabated. As it coursed through her, the muscles of her face tightened, and she clenched and unclenched her fists into tight balls at her side. The other emotion was simpler—pure, undiluted hatred. As he regarded her, it was almost as if she was unaware that he was staring intently at her, unaware that he was even in the room at all. She raised her eyes to look at him at last, and as she focused her gaze, he could sense her bringing her tremendous rage under control.

But as she spoke, it was also indisputable that the feeling of hatred would be a permanent part of her being for some time to come.

"Rice . . ." she began, her voice calm and unemotional. "Would you like to know who Rapson is, and exactly why you and the Sarpan were taken?"

NINETEEN
Corroboree

C athay lay back on the rickety cot, wondering each time she moved on the rusted, loudly complaining frame if the whole thing might collapse under her. If it did, at least the thin mattress Billy had unrolled over the frame for her would cushion her fall. There was only one thick, scratchy blanket on the cot, and that she had folded into a makeshift pillow, allowing what buttons remained on the surface of the worn, lumpy mattress to press into her back. It had made for several sleepless nights until she became used to it, but she had registered no complaints—this mattress, and the cot itself, for that matter, were considered luxuries by many of the people who had gathered here for the celebration.

Her hosts had done their best to make the humpie livable, with limited success. The structure was a hutlike affair of corrugated metal left behind untold years earlier when the diamond mine that had once thrived here had been abandoned. As she stared up at the humpie's curved ceiling, she could see areas where the metal had corroded—almost all the way through in spots—and she wondered idly how many of these structures had originally been here, and how this one managed to survive all these years.

Destroyed by weather, torn apart piece-by-piece by scavengers or razed by the mining company when the land no longer gave up its glittering treasures; she had no clue why this one sad little building remained.

A metal and glass lantern, nearly as rusted and ancient-looking as the humpie itself, hung from a loop of rope on a metal hook set into the center of the low ceiling. Swinging slightly from side to side, it cast odd dancing shadows over everything in the cramped quarters. The old chemically fueled lantern was inefficient, and occasional tendrils of dark, sooty smoke curled from the top of it, which accounted for the blackened appearance of the upper third of the lamp.

There were no windows, although a louvered grating in the rear allowed the chilly night air to waft in, causing the tattered canvas tarp that served as a door to flutter gently. The interior remained cozily warm, however. She ran her hand along the rusty surface nearest the cot, and felt heat still radiating from metal warmed by a Sun two hours set. Drawing back her hand, she saw that her fingers were red-brown with a thin coating of rust. She touched a fingertip to her nose and, closing her eyes, inhaled deeply; the metallic scent was earthy and comfortable, the tang mixing pleasantly with the odor of the lantern and the aroma of wood smoke from the bonfires downhill from the humpie.

She kept her eyes closed and listened to the sounds of the corroboree drifting through the louvers behind her: the steady, rhythmic beating of clapping sticks; the deeply droning *gibba-yerruh, gibba-yerruh, gibba-yerruh* of the didjeridoos, long pipe-like wind instruments frequently larger than the men playing them; the thumping of a hundred men stamping their feet in unified jubilation; even the occasional whirling buzz of the bull-roarers favored by the young boys of the various tribes. There were hundreds of Aborigines, representing dozens of tribes, who had gathered here at Billy's invitation. All were still involved in the festive ceremonies, which promised to last well into the next day.

A soft beeping abruptly drew her attention, and she reluctantly opened her eyes. Using the bed for a seat, she leaned over the battered wooden crate that served as a makeshift desk at the foot of the cot. The words ARGYLE DIAMOND MINE, stenciled darkly on one side of the crate long ago, were just barely visible on the surface of cracked, dry wood. Cathay lightly touched the flat-screen tablet she had propped up there, and the screen obediently came to life with a steady blue glow that contrasted strangely with the dull yellow light from the lantern. In the center of the blue field was displayed the Imperial crest. She saw her own reflection in the glossy plastic, and was startled by how unkempt she looked. Her long brown hair was a tangled mess, and she quickly pulled it back over her shoulder, twisted it into a tail and tucked it down into the collar of her blouse. As far as tidying her appearance, that would have to do. Satisfied, she touched a square on the lower corner of the screen marked Receive, leaving behind a tiny red-brown fingerprint on the plastic.

"Daddy, thank you for getting back to me so quickly," she said cheerfully when Eric appeared. He looked well, and it was good to see him again. He was in the study of the family estate, and she could see the morning sunshine streaming in behind him through the opened doors leading to the balcony. "I hope I'm not disturbing you. I know it's still early morning there."

"Hello, sweetheart," the Emperor said warmly from half a world away. "Don't worry about the time; I've been up for hours. Is everything all right there?"

"Everything is fine. But I might be difficult to get hold of for the next few days, so I just wanted to check in with you; it's been some time since we last spoke, and I wanted to fill you in on what's been happening here."

"In that case, then, I'm glad you did. How are things progressing? Is Billy pleased with what's happening there?"

"Oh, Daddy," she replied, feeling her smile broaden as she relayed the news. "It's even better than we could have hoped for! There are more than a thousand people here, with tribal groups represented from as far away as Kalgoorlie, some two thousand kilometers on the other side of the Great Sandy, to Brisbane and Tamworth, more than three thousand to the southeast. We even had a letter stick returned by one of the southern tribes that— Wait a moment. . . ." She reached to one side of the crate and retrieved a length of wood perhaps half a meter in length, inscribed with cryptic markings, and held it before the flatscreen's video pickup lens. "Billy says it was returned by a tribe in Tasmania, accepting our invitation, although I haven't met them yet."

"I'm impressed."

"They *all* share Billy's concerns; they have for years, but never had any way to channel their efforts to do anything about what was happening here. Now they have.

"These people are so beautiful, Daddy. Their art, the unfettered way they dance and celebrate, their love and affection for their families, the very simplicity of their lives. Even the names of their tribes sound like songs! The Bunuba from near Derby, Billy's own tribe—the Arunta—the Tiwis from Melville Island, the Mia Mia, the Murinbadda, the Tindaya." She paused, nearly out of breath, then added softly, from her heart, "I am so grateful that you asked me to come to Australia. We're doing something wonderful here."

Eric's smile mirrored her own, and as she studied her father's face she saw a twinkle in his eyes that she had not seen there in some time. "You sound very happy, Cathay."

"I am, Daddy." She grinned like a child, and saw in her reflection in the flatscreen that she needn't have worried about her appearance. Her face positively glowed. "I'm happier now than I've ever been in my life."

"And I'm happy for you," he echoed. "Your smiling face is truly one of the nicest things I've seen in days." He shifted in his seat as he prepared to change the subject.

"Things are heating up at Tsing, as you might expect," he went on, his face serious. "I suspect it's getting downright crowded about now. I've authorized no fewer than twenty-two new ships to enter orbit around the planet itself, as well as allowing another even dozen to take position elsewhere in the system. The Sarpan have a ship there, but they seem to be behaving themselves—I don't think we'll have any problems from them. And, of course, Brendan and Lewis are there, as is your grandmother." His smile returned as he added, "She's looking forward to seeing you when you wrap up there in Kimberley at the end of the month."

She didn't comment on his last statement, but instead asked, "And Jephthah?"

Eric shrugged. "Nothing. He's been quiet for weeks."

"Well, that's good news—it's about time we got a break from him. Although it just makes me think he's working on something bigger than he usually does, what with all that's happening at Tsing."

The Emperor nodded, sighing in reluctant agreement. "I hope not, but you're probably right." He looked to one side, as if called. "Well, I have to go. Take care of yourself, and give my best to Billy."

"I will, Daddy. I love you."

"I love you, too, honey."

The flatscreen faded back to the familiar blue field and crest. A fingertip tapped lightly on the screen winked the power off.

She sat there for several long moments and stared morosely at the blank flatscreen on the crate. "The end of the month," she muttered. "Just two more weeks."

Cathay rose and crossed the few steps to the door, drawing back the canvas, and gazed down at the corroboree going on below her. She pulled a thin jacket from a peg by the door and walked out into the night, her nostrils filling with the pleasantly acrid smoke from a score of bonfires. As far as she could see, the entire area was laid out in steplike plateaus left over by the mining company as they stripped the ground of the diamondiferous ore that once lay beneath it. At one time, nearly a third of Earth's annual diamond production had come from this very spot. But that was centuries ago, and the played-out landscape had been given back to the Aborigine and allowed to return to its natural state, leaving a beautiful vista of man-made steps.

In the distance she could just barely make out Lake Argyle, still filled so soon after the wet season, the moonlight glinting off its tranquil surface. Out of sight over the horizon, the Ord River flowed up past Wyndham into Cambridge Gulf, and from there northward into the Timor Sea itself.

She hadn't bothered to bring the lantern with her, but it was easy to see here. The many fires, combined with the full moon and the lantern light spilling from the humpie, cast a pale light that made walking in the outback at this hour less difficult than it would otherwise have been. Pulling the jacket on and pressing the front closed, she walked to one of several large rocks and sat down. Below her, the corroboree had reached a crescendo, and she watched in rapt fascination for nearly half an hour without moving. There were bonfires everywhere, and around each a different dance was in progress. Here and there were knots of tribesmen sharing tales or trading small belongings and crafts. And among it all, engaged in every manner of Aborigine play-about imaginable, were the children. In and around the hundreds of scattered gunyahs and wurlies erected by their parents, they ran, jumped, and shouted gleefully among the bonfires and make-shift dwellings.

Would these people ever have survived without Billy? she wondered. In the basic sense, they would certainly have "survived" as far as their lives were concerned, but would their culture have endured? The values Billy held, the values he was so shocked to see disappearing among many of the Arunta, were still strong in at least some members of nearly every tribe. And in a few truly special cases, there remained a handful of tiny clans—particularly in the most remote regions of the Great Sandy and Nullarbor Plain—that still lived almost untouched by Earth's evolving culture.

But what Billy was doing—*No,* she corrected herself, *what we are doing*—was to bring them together, to let them all know that memories of the Dreamtime endured among them all, no matter the tribe, and that the Song Lines still connected all Aborigine across the great physical distances separating them. Weeks from now, when all that remained of this corroboree would be scattered piles of ashes where the bonfires had once blazed, the message would be carried back to their homes, their peoples, that it did not matter how many Aborigine abandoned their heritage. Because that heritage would outlast their mortal lives, and be waiting for them when they all met again in the Dreamtime.

Cathay didn't know why—there had been no sound, no hint of movement that caught her eye—but she looked to one side, and was startled to see a goanna lying on the ground next to her. The lizard was good-sized, nearly a half meter in length, and it was clear that it had been recently killed. So intently did she gaze at the goanna that when the Aborigine standing a few meters behind it became apparent to her it seemed as though he had suddenly popped into existence out of the very air around him.

Her heartbeat, which had quickened considerably at the surprise, slowed, and she rose and nodded in greeting. She felt no fear of these people.

Like most Aborigine, he was thin, almost gaunt, and exhibited a full head of thick hair. The man was old and yellow-eyed, the whiteness of his hair matching the thin beard that traced the line of his jaw and chin. He wore nothing but a headband and a thin red strip of cloth around his waist with thinner strips bundled decoratively in a dangling mass below his navel that afforded him little coverage. He was armed: In one hand he carried a spear and woomera, while a boomerang was tucked into one side of the waist belt. It was clear that he had been part of the celebration, as he had decorated his body with smears of white ashes that ran like stripes down his chest and legs. His expressive face had been framed in smears of white and red.

There was movement behind him and she saw that he was not alone. A nearly naked woman—his lubra—and three young boys that must have been their sons stood silently by, waiting. All three boys assumed the stance typical of desert Aborigine: balancing gracefully on one foot with the other placed on the opposite knee, they reminded Cathay of nothing so much as resting shorebirds.

They, too, carried spears and boomerangs, and had decorated themselves in a manner similar to their father's.

And there, off to the side, stood Billy.

"G'day," he said, almost formally, as he came forward to stand next to the man. It was evident from the single statement that his presence was for the benefit of this family, and that Billy was acting as intermediary. His feet were bare and he wore no shirt over his denim jeans. He, too, had decorated himself with a tracing of white ashes, but he must have done it some hours earlier, as the markings had been rubbed and smudged almost completely off.

"His name's Namajira," Billy continued. "His people are called Yagga, 'The Quiet.' " He extended his hand in her direction as he turned to Namajira and said by way of presentation, "Cathay Wood."

"Tananana turu-etya?" the old man inquired reverently.

Billy spoke a few words and Namajira nodded in understanding and respect, then bent to pick up the goanna and held it out before him.

"He wants you to accept his gift," Billy explained softly. "But, as a sign of his esteem for you, he can't walk toward you. You must approach him."

"Thank you." Cathay came forward and accepted the offering, ignoring the trickle of the dead animal's blood that ran down one wrist and forearm.

A big, pleased grin broke out on Namajira's face, and he nodded again before rejoining his family. Without a word, the five of them turned and made their way back down the slope toward the corroboree, never looking back.

Once the family was out of sight, Billy relieved her of the goanna. "Here, I'll take that. Sorry about the mess," he said, indicating her hands. "You don't have to really eat it. Although as far as wild tucker goes, it cooks up better'n most."

"No; it's all right. 'No worries, ay?' " She wiped her hands casually on her already dirty bush pants. "What was it he said?"

"He asked if you were the *turu-etya,* the 'fire-person.' I only know one or two dialects other than my own, but I think I've learned that word in at least a hundred tongues in the last month." He removed a canvas sack he had slung over his shoulder, a tucker bag, and dropped the goanna inside, shaking his head in amazement. "You know," he said, "about a third of the people down there only have a limited knowledge of science and technology, much less current events, and yet word of your presence here has spread among them all."

"I see." She turned, sitting once more on the rock, and stared down at the bonfires again. Billy joined her, sitting cross-legged on the ground next to her. "They think my grandmother is a Sky Hero."

"And you, in turn, through her." Billy chuckled softly in the moonlight. "Ah, it ain't so bad. You get used to it."

She had been concerned that the honor represented by the gift the tribesman had just given her had been ill-placed, but looking at Billy's face stretched into its characteristic grin erased any misgivings she might have felt.

"Thank you, Billy." She reached out her hand and placed it on his shoulder, feeling the strength in the muscles beneath his dark skin. "You almost always seem to know what I'm thinking at any given moment, and then you always say just the right thing."

He reached across his chest and took her hand in his. His hands had become callused in the time she had come to know him, but his grasp was warm and gentle. He rubbed the back of her hand against his cheek and lightly kissed her fingers.

"It's part of m'job," he said whimsically, grinning up at her. "But I like the work."

Their attention was drawn to a particularly noisy dance taking place at one of the nearer fires, and they both watched wordlessly for several minutes. The air was getting chillier, but as long as Billy held her hand, she didn't mind the cold.

"He still thinks I'm leaving at the end of the month," she said at last. "I spoke to him barely an hour ago, but I didn't have the strength to tell him I wanted to stay. I've already talked with Brendan and Lewis about the possibility of my staying here. I know I have their support for any decision I make in this, but . . ."

Billy nodded in comprehension. "Will you be goin' then?"

She turned away from him and gazed out over the fires, not answering for several moments. "No," she replied finally, not taking her eyes from the activity below. "What we're doing here is every bit as important as what's happening at Tsing. I know that now. I'm just not sure what more I could offer there."

Billy said nothing in response, leaving her for the moment alone with her thoughts, but she knew he agreed. They had had long conversations, some late into the night, about what was being accomplished here, and they both agreed that the task was nowhere near completed.

"I'll let Brendan and Lewis know right away, while I try to work up the courage to tell my father. Besides . . ." She started to say something else, then thought better of it. Instead, she turned and kissed him warmly, drinking in the mixed scent of smoke and outdoors that she associated with him. She pulled away reluctantly and rose, smiling softly down at him, and let her fingers slip from his grasp.

"I'll be back in a few minutes." Cathay walked quietly over to the humpie, pulled back the canvas door and disappeared inside.

Billy turned back to the corroboree below him, reveling in the guttural, rhythmic music sweeping up the slope in his direction. A soft wind came up from the south, carrying with it the howl of a dingo baying at the moon as it rose still higher in the night sky. He closed his eyes and tilted his head back to the heavens, listening to the dingo's Song, and noted the other sounds of the night: a bird, the occasional buzz of an insect, the incessant chirping of crickets.

And then, from the humpie, came another sound, faintly audible over the fanfare of the celebrants. But unlike the natural sounds of the outback, this one was obtrusively artificial, man-made:

The beep of a flatscreen tablet being set into communication mode.

TWENTY
A Little Knowledge

Adela shivered, thrusting her hands deep into the pockets of the hooded parka they had given her down at South Camp. The air had grown steadily colder as they ascended the rise, but it was neither the dropping temperature nor the unremitting wind whistling through the trees that chilled her—the vigorous hike they had been on for the last fifteen minutes had actually sent a trickle of sweat down her back. Rather, the chill she felt as they waited here for the xenoguide to return was from the anticipation now coursing through her. Trying to control her excitement, she wished again that security reasons had not prevented the landing shuttle from touching down closer to the edge of the river valley.

The night here on Tsing IV was very dark, and with only three members of her party using hand lamps—again, an ironclad precaution taken for the sake of secrecy when traveling at night on the surface—the going had been slower still. Adela could have waited until morning, of course; but after the many weeks of anticipation since learning of the discovery here she knew sleep would be nearly impossible. If she did grow tired, she could always nap once they arrived at their destination, as the shuttle was not scheduled to pick them up until late the next morning.

Looking up through the treetops, she could see that neither of Tsing's two moons was in the sky at this hour, and the only natural glow as they neared the edge of the woods was the faint light of the stars overhead.

A bird called loudly from a tree somewhere up ahead of them on the trail, its night cry strikingly similar to that of an Earthly owl, and drew her attention back to the ground. There was a sudden rustling in the branches and leaves above them, followed again by the same night cry as the large bird soared gracefully overhead in search of a less-traveled perch to rule the darkness.

"Is everything all right?" Adela asked Captain Anmoore as she waited anxiously for Hannah Cee to return.

"Everything's fine." Anmoore smiled broadly. "The day Hannah stops fretting the little details like this is the day *I* start worrying." He waved an arm in the direction of the top of the rise. "I've been keeping a watch of at least two people posted at the observation deck around the clock. They're in charge of maintaining the equipment we keep here, as well as monitoring the camo-shielding that's in place and just keeping a general eye on anything interesting that happens. They know we're coming, of course, but Hannah always goes ahead to warn them that it's us. She's afraid they'll hear us approach and alarm them unnecessarily, thinking it might be a native hunting party or something like that. It's a courtesy, really, more than anything else; but the loneliness can get you pretty jumpy when you're down here all night, and they appreciate it."

"I see. But wouldn't they think the same thing—that it's a native, I mean—when they hear her coming up on them?"

"Hear Hannah coming?" He chuckled aloud. "You don't know Hannah."

Almost as if to prove his point, Hannah appeared without warning at the front of the line of hikers. Again, Adela was struck by how out of place the middle-aged woman was as part of a scientific survey team. In the pale glow of the hand lamps, the shadows that played over her deeply lined face, gray-tinged hair and quiet mannerisms made her look more like some Academy-bound philosopher than an expert xenoguide. Even the heavily threadbare brown parka she wore stood out from the others of Imperial issue, although Adela had to admit that the woman's personal clothing allowed her to blend in to the forest much more than their own brightly colored coats would ever allow. Jogging silently back to their position in the line, Hannah smiled apologetically at Adela, her weathered face wrinkling pleasantly.

"Captain, could you please review security procedures for our guests?" she said. When Anmoore nodded, Hannah immediately returned to the front of the line, and they started trudging slowly up the rise once more.

"More security measures?" Adela asked.

Anmoore shrugged, but made no attempt to apologize. "Don't let her abrupt nature put you off, Doctor. Believe me, the secrecy with which we move around down here can be maddening at times, but it's all important, even the little rules." He quickened his pace briefly and said something into the ear of the man ahead of him, who then moved past her down the line and spoke softly in turn to each of those bringing up the rear. Presumably, he was relaying the same safety precautions Captain Anmoore was about to tell her.

"You can't see it yet because of the camo-shielding, but from that tree we're only a hundred meters from the observation deck." He indicated a fat tree just up ahead and to the right of the trail. "At night, no open lights are allowed past that point, and there's to be no talking day or night from there until inside the deck. And no weapons of any kind, but that almost goes without mentioning. That's it." Hannah, just now passing the tree, extinguished her hand lamp. Anmoore followed suit with the light he carried immediately after, as did the last person in the line. "Watch your step now," he added under his breath.

The footing was smooth, though steep, as they walked along in silence. Fortunately, the tree cover was thinner here and the faint glow of starshine was sufficient for them to navigate along the path.

There were ten of them all together, their number evenly divided among personnel from the *Kiska* and from the science station already established at South Camp in the southern hemisphere. Hannah was in the lead, followed by two station members whose names she did not recall, and Gareth Anmoore. Following immediately behind her in line were First Officer Darrly and three others from the *Kiska* crew—two men and a woman. Adela knew little about the three save their names, and she wished she had gotten to know them better, as one of them must certainly be one of the IPC deathguards Eric had sent along from Luna. Each of the three had a legitimate reason, according to their duty assignments, for being on this trip, and each had done or said nothing out of the ordinary, but she realized that one of them was merely acting out a role in being part of this excursion. The thought made her nervous, as did the fact that whoever it was certainly carried at least one deadly weapon at the ready.

She wondered briefly if Captain Anmoore knew, then decided he most likely had not even been informed of the IPC presence. The deception bothered her.

"Here it comes," Anmoore whispered, drawing her attention back to the task at hand.

Adela followed his extended arm and saw Hannah Cee's faint outline disappear into what obviously must have been a holographic projection of a line of trees and brush. The woman behind her similarly disappeared, as did they all one at a time. Once inside the projection, Adela turned back. She could see the others following her up the trail, although it was evident from the amused looks on their faces that from their vantage point still on the outside of the camo-shield it must have seemed that she had just vanished. The shield was, apparently, one-way. She also noted that she could no longer hear the shuffling of their feet in the leaves or any other night sounds familiar to the forest, and assumed the shielding was also programmed with an audio damper.

The inside of the camo-shield had been cleared of most plant growth, making the short climb up the hard-packed dirt to the top where the "observation deck" was situated a fairly easy matter. The deck itself was a prefabricated structure of plastic panels forming a long platform perched on the edge of the rise overlooking the valley. From the size of it, there should easily be enough room for the ten of them, and then some. They were only a few meters below it, but from this angle she still couldn't see anything or anyone on it from here.

"There's a cubicle of solid shielding that surrounds the edges and top," Anmoore explained as they climbed the last few steps. "Any portion of it can be opaqued for privacy or when the sun comes up over the valley—I've been here at sunrise, and believe me, Tsing 479 can be brutally bright sometimes when it's at the right angle. Of course, we've got the whole thing set for translucency for your viewing pleasure this evening."

He smiled warmly, and it suddenly occurred to Adela why he had not minded personally escorting her down here in the middle of the night: He was as excited about the discovery here as she, and unquestionably felt a certain sense of pride to be the one to show her the town. She found herself liking this man more and more.

"Now, if you'll just step this way."

Hannah had already reached the crest of the hill and had entered the shielding; there was a tall rectangular outline where the opening had appeared, and Adela ascended a short set of steps leading up to the deck itself. The two men who were assigned to monitor the deck waited on either side of the "door"; one of them, the name JONATO above the breast pocket of his coveralls, extended his hand to steady her as she came up. His face positively beamed as he welcomed her inside. Clearly, her arrival had been eagerly anticipated.

Once inside, she saw that one side of the platform had been walled off with solid panels, and she assumed that sleeping quarters and personal facilities for visitors, regular observers and maintenance personnel were located there. The interior of the long cubicle that constituted the observation deck glowed softly, and Adela trusted that from the outside the one-way camoshielding prevented its detection while at the same time allowing proper visibility for anyone working here. There was a low sound she noticed upon entering—a steady, soothing hum that she couldn't quite place until she realized it must be the power and shield generators beneath the floor. Looking around, she noted a surprisingly large amount of furniture here as well—two worktables, several chairs, a number of low cabinets placed against the panel walls. But it was the far shield wall, the one facing the valley, that captured her attention. Fully two dozen cameras, recorders, and measuring devices of all manner had been arranged there, all of them oriented on what lay below that edge of the deck.

She approached the edge slowly, the vista spread across the river valley below appearing a bit at a time. As she saw it, she caught her breath audibly.

"Jonato," Anmoore said. "Would you please dim the lights so Dr. Montgarde can get a better look at our little town?"

The young man complied quickly, putting the room in darkness.

"My God," Adela breathed. "It's incredible."

Despite the lateness of the hour—locally speaking—thousands of lights glowed in the darkened town, almost giving it the appearance of a starlit sky. Some of the lights moved slowly through the town, occasionally disappearing behind buildings in one spot and suddenly appearing in others, and were undoubtedly lanterns being carried by the natives or mounted on vehicles. Most of the lights, however, seemed fixed and must have been windows or house lights; but as she studied the entire scene she detected a pattern in the way that some of them had been laid out. "Street lights?"

"Gas," Anmoore replied in confirmation, his voice low in the darkness. "From what we've been able to learn, they have a rather extensive system of underground lines down there. While we've found evidence of the same thing in a few other towns, it seems that only the larger communities like this one have gone to such lengths."

A broad, dark band that would be the river wound around it all, producing a sharply defined boundary to the town itself on the side nearest them. Lifting her gaze to the far side of the town, she saw that the lights became more widely separated as the area delineated gradually from the tightly packed urban dwellings to the surrounding countryside. In all, it was magnificent. Beautiful.

"Incredible," she said again. "What are you calling it?"

Anmoore plainly had not expected the question and he blinked in surprise, glancing around at Hannah and the others. "To be honest, we've not called it anything. We'd given names to a number of landmarks and features as we surveyed them when we were still in orbit—" He hooked a thumb in Jonato's direction, then nodded at the valley below. "It was Jonato who picked the name 'Cascade' for that river, for example. But once we actually came down and verified the existence of the natives, we more or less dropped the practice in hopes we could learn local names. Obviously, we've not been able to do much of that yet." He shrugged, a hint of embarrassment in his mannerisms. "We've just been calling it 'the town.' "

"That's a shame," Adela said, regarding the twinkling lights once more. "It's almost too lovely to just keep calling it that."

"All right, then," he replied, his friendly smile reappearing. "Pick a name for it."

Adela turned to him. "That wouldn't be a breach of protocol?"

"Protocol?" He laughed pleasantly, drawing the attention of the xenoguide. Hannah didn't join in his laughter, but there was a twinkle in her eyes that was unmistakable. "We've never gone in much for 'protocol' on the *Paloma Blanco*. Oh, we've put some pretty strict rules and regs in place regarding the situation here at Tsing, and we've rigidly adhered to some fairly explicit guidelines from Luna, but when it comes to discovering a new, previously unknown intelligent civilization—there *is* no protocol."

"I don't know," she said. "Maybe I'd better speak to Brendan—to Academician Wood first. The Emperor has given him complete authority in matters regarding the natives."

He came over to stand next to her. "Listen, Doctor," he said frankly, all traces of humor gone from his voice. "We wouldn't even be here if it were not for you. Without your efforts, without the Sun project back on Earth, the technology of wormhole travel would most likely not even exist. If anyone deserves the right to name the first town discovered here, it's you. Besides," he continued, his smile and easy manner returning, "I've spoken to Academician Wood since his arrival and have gotten a fairly good measure of how he feels about your involvement here." He raised an eyebrow, his voice a near-whisper. "Do you really think the Academician would disagree with any name you chose?"

Adela grinned. "No, I suppose not." She gazed down on the quiet scene and thought about what the town and its inhabitants represented. To Jephthah and those he had been able to reach, she thought somberly, it was a threat to humanity itself. But to her, and to the countless others as enraptured with the discovery as she, what was occurring here was the very essence of knowledge. "I have no idea what it looks like in the daytime other than from the recordings. But the way it looks right now," she said wistfully. "The lights . . . If I could call it anything I wanted . . . I'd call it 'Jour Nouveau.' It means 'New Day.'"

"I am not looking forward at all," Anmoore said bluntly, "to what Jephthah's reaction is going to be to any of this. We saw his harangue on the discovery itself; we've seen everything he's done, for that matter. . . . Believe me, you miss out on a lot when you're out on a survey vessel like the *Blanco* for years at a stretch. I suppose that's why we tap into the tachyon nets for *any* kind of public communication, just to feel a little less disconnected from the rest of the Hundred Worlds. Anyway, we've managed to intercept just about every broadcast he's made." His face turned sour and he sighed heavily in disgust. "What he said about you was just, just—"

"It's all right," Adela interjected, sparing him the explanation. "I've come to terms with his lies. That's why I'm here."

Anmoore nodded. "I'm glad you are."

A hint of gray had appeared over the mountains to the east of Jour Nouveau, and Adela realized the two of them had been talking for several hours. As she looked into the quiet valley she could see that many individual pinpoints of brightness still twinkled through the gathering mist as it rolled in off the river, but here and there lights began to wink out with the approaching light of dawn. A new day in Jour Nouveau.

Only three of them remained in the main room of the observation deck to greet the dawn, although Hannah had dropped out of the conversation some time ago, and now snored softly in her chair. Judging from the way her head had lolled to one side against her shoulder, Adela mused, she would have a stiff neck for certain when she awoke.

The rest had long ago drifted off one by one into the personnel quarters to get some sleep. Adela tried not to speculate on whether the IPC agent who had surely accompanied them was sleeping soundly with the others or was, even now, watching them, listening to their conversation. After weeks of trying to get used to the fact that one of them was always somewhere nearby, ready to protect her, she still had trouble putting the role of the dreadful deathguards into any kind of reasonable perspective, much less out of her mind.

Which one are you? she asked silently of the three sleeping *Kiska* crew members in the other room. *Pritsik? Hanson? Doss? Which one of you would kill, without remorse, everyone here if you thought it necessary to carry out your orders from Eric?* Pritsik and Hanson were both a part of ship security—too obvious. Doss? But the anthropologist seemed to be exactly what he claimed to be. *Stop it, stop it, stop it! I'm making myself crazy with this.* She shook her head in frustration, making up her mind that her first order of business when she met with Lewis face-to-face would be to demand their immediate removal. . . .

The xenoguide shifted noisily in her chair, drawing Adela's attention away from the IPC, and she said softly so as not to wake up Hannah, "I've read and seen everything you encoded into the *Paloma Blanco*'s records and sent back to Luna before the blackout was instituted, as well as the contents of the hand-delivered data stick waiting for me when we exited the wormhole. Brendan and Lewis have already scheduled a full session for the four of us later today, but what else can you tell me about them?"

"Well," he began, clearing his throat. "Understand that they have no electronic communications, no radio, not even wired communications that we could easily monitor. Everything we know about them has been obtained in one of two ways: spectrographic and photographic data collected from orbit and from long-distance observation posts like this one, and a concerted search for artifacts in uninhabited areas. Without electronic interaction of any kind—no electricity!—there's no way to tap into their records, if they have any, or their day-to-day communication. We have gotten lucky in a few areas, however."

"Luck is good," Adela put in pleasantly. "It's long past time we started having some."

"Agreed. We have a full physiological make up on them, or at least on the males. We discovered several bodies in a harsh, remote area about eighty kilometers to the southwest. Fortunately, they were in good shape and we obtained as complete a pathology on them as we could have hoped for, save inviting one of them to come in and have a seat while we poked and prodded at him.

"You'll also find hours of recorded conversations that were picked up right here." Anmoore pointed to a piece of tripod-mounted equipment behind Hannah's chair. "We keep that shotgun microphone in place outside the shielding during the daylight hours, pointed directly at the most exposed areas of the harbor down there. The *Blanco*'s computer has been working on some of it for weeks now with limited success, but hopefully the linguistic specialists you've brought along from Luna can make use of the recordings to redo the software. But we have managed to get an understanding of a smattering of their language. The river, for example—It's called 'Quittanika,' which translates roughly to 'Speed-Flow,' according to the computer. The name seems to fit, though; when it's daylight you'll see how fast the water runs." Anmoore chuckled lightly, one eyebrow raised, and added as an afterthought, "Of course, we're recording mostly deckhands and sailors down there, so the reference of any words we've been picking up may be skewed in a direction we'd rather not anticipate."

Adela joined his laughter. "Well, when we do finally get to talk to them, I suppose we'll be well stocked with the latest ribald jokes—not that we'd understand the humor."

Sounds of movement and an occasional voice filtered into the deck from the personnel area and she glanced at her wrist, realizing that the morning shift for this day's observation of the natives was about to begin. Adela let her tired eyes scan the horizon and could see the first rays of sunshine streaking the sky over the far mountain range. She stretched, feeling fatigued for the first time since arriving at Tsing. She would have to get some sleep soon, like it or not; and she had certainly imposed on Anmoore enough. One glimpse at the man's face revealed the reddened eyes and dark circles that must certainly reflect her own. Stifling a yawn, she asked, "The bodies you found; what happened to them?"

Anmoore didn't answer, but instead rose and gently shook Hannah's shoulder, rousing her. "Hannah, could you see to it that everyone heading back to South Camp is ready to go in forty-five minutes?" She nodded, rubbing at her face. Then, still half asleep, she moved unsteadily into the adjacent quarters. Anmoore returned to where he and Adela had talked through the night, but did not sit. He stared dolefully down at the river, the waking harbor already a buzz of activity.

"They had been killed by a raiding party," he said, his voice matter-of-fact. "You saw the first recordings of the airships? The ones we made our first day on the surface?"

Adela nodded that she had.

"The inhabitants here are very aggressive, almost warlike. There's very little association between population centers. Larger communities like this one—with their solid economies, established trade routes and manufacturing centers—are incredibly protective of what they've achieved. Pirating appears to be quite common in exposed regions, as is outright aggression against neighboring regions. From what we've been able to determine, what could best be described as a 'city-state' located some two hundred kilometers to the southwest had sent a scout party here, to what purpose is anybody's guess—information gathering, outright spying, who knows? Those charged with defending *this* city-state discovered they were out there and, trailing them for days, dispatched the two airships after them. They slaughtered them mercilessly before they had a chance to return to their own people." He stared down at the harbor, easily visible now that the bright morning sunshine had burned away the mist, and watched a heavily laden steam-powered vessel as it headed out into the center of the river before plying slowly northward. "We followed them, and recorded the whole sordid episode."

There was a loud burst of laughter from the personnel section of the deck, and one of the *Kiska* crew—Hanson, if she remembered right—came out, his face beaming. He went to the chair, bent down, and retrieved the hood of the xenoguide's parka from where it had fallen while she slept. "It's out here, Hannah!" he called back. "I told you no one hid it from you again." He nodded to the two of them, then went back into the sleeping quarters, calling teasingly ahead of him, "Now will you stop tearing up the bunks looking for it?"

Anmoore laughed as the man left the room. "They love ribbing her," he explained. "She's so serious all the time. I try to get her to lighten up, but she makes such a good target for them. Now they've got your folks doing it, too. It's all in good fun, though, I assure you; they all have the highest respect for her abilities out here in the woods."

"You've got a lot of good people working here with you," she said candidly once they were alone again. "They've obviously made friends very quickly with mine." She paused, then returned to their discussion of the airship recording. "Has the recording of the raid been sent to the *Scartaris*?"

He had draped his own parka over the back of the chair during the night, and he shook it once before pulling it on over his shoulders. "Absolutely not." His words were blunt, his tone almost irate, but it was plain that the anger was not directed at her. "I won't take that chance. I'll give it to Commander Wood personally when we meet, along with the full report of what we've found at the dig site at South Camp. If you'd like, I can make a data-stick copy that you can review on the *Kiska* before the meeting. Could you imagine what Jephthah could do with something like that?" He shook his head at the thought, then pressed the front of his parka closed. "I'm going to take a quick look around outside."

Anmoore smiled politely and produced a keypad from a pocket, touching a button on it to open the shielding before slipping it back into his parka.

Adela sat alone in the observation deck, watching the river traffic as Jour Nouveau prepared for another day. The occasional sounds of good humor from the personnel section did nothing to improve her mood.

PART FIVE

TO FEAR THE LIGHT

The mind will ever be
unstable that has only prejudices
to rest on, and the current will
run with destructive fury
when there are no barriers
to break its force.

—Mary Wollstonecraft

TWENTY-ONE
Breaking Silence

The cylindrical airship held steady, hovering directly above the small band of Tsing natives it had trapped in the meadow below it. There were six of them, all caught in the open as they tried to run for the protective cover of the woods on the other side of the wide field. The second airship had effectively cut off their route of escape at the edge of the tree line, while this one had followed their path and came up from behind, neatly trapping them in the open. As the battle unfolded, the other airship had moved into a closer support position and now hovered halfway between the fighting and the tree line, ready to come about in whichever direction it might be needed. The dark green and brown of its flanks could just be seen at the very limit of the camera's field of view, the red markings on the side of the cylinder barely visible.

Those on the ground fired projectile weapons upward at their attackers, with little result: Their hand-carried weapons simply lacked the power necessary to present any serious threat to the airship at its current altitude.

The four Tsing natives in the basketlike gondola suspended beneath the bulk of the cylinder, on the other hand, held a distinct advantage in their attack. As the image zoomed in to give a closer look at the underside of the gondola, it was clear the airship's purpose was for fighting. The slender muzzles of four downward-firing guns extended through openings in the bottom of the gondola itself. It was difficult to tell, but by the way the thin barrels disappeared inside the openings periodically or wavered as they sought their targets, the guns could be hand weapons designed specifically for the purpose of aerial assault.

The picture swept dizzily downward and oriented once again on the hapless natives defending their position below, the shaking and wildly tilting image an explicit indication of how nervous the camera operator must have been at being this close to the fighting. It centered on one of the natives who had just fallen, the blood flowing freely from a wound in his left shoulder matting the fur of his upper arm. As he screamed out in pain, another of his comrades bent to his side and ripped back his clothing to get at the wound; then he, too, cried out as he was similarly felled. Unlike his downed companion, however, he dropped silently to the ground, where he lay unmoving as the other continued to call for help. The four natives still on their feet persisted in their ineffectual assault on the airship, deaf to his agonizing cries.

Directly, they, too, fell to join the others.

The gunfire halted; the scene grew quiet save for the cries of the first native to fall and the steady thrumming of the airship's steam engine. The camera swung upward again, revealing the four passengers of the airship leaning over the rim of the gondola in an attempt to get a better look at their handiwork below. One of them, the fur on his face and arms a shade of gray-brown much lighter than that of his three younger shipmates, nodded vigorously, then stood upright and slapped the nearest of his companions gleefully on the back. The wild chattering that ensued among them was indecipherable, but it was clear that the four were rejoicing over their good fortune in battle. The smallest member of the gondola crew gesticulated animatedly to the other airship, which slowly swung around in their direction.

The image zoomed closer as the four discussed what to do next. The older one, seemingly in charge of this endeavor, addressed the others, prompting an excited showing of hands. He put his own hands on the shoulders of one of them, whose face beamed proudly. The chosen native shucked off the top of his uniform and played a length of rope out over the side of the gondola, while the others set about altering the airship controls in such a manner that it sank gradually, smoothly to a point about twenty meters above, and to one side, of those felled on the ground below. The airship held its position and the crew watched as the shirtless native scrambled over the side and easily slid down the rope, dropping to the ground several meters from where the others lay.

The native pulled a small weapon from the waistband of his

trousers and pointed it at the bodies as he cautiously approached. The field of view tightened on the bloodied clearing as he drew near, such that it was easy to see that the shirtless one would meet with precious little resistance from those lying on the ground. Of the six, only one—the first to fall in the ambush—still moved; and he had lost too much blood, and was in too much pain, to even rise to his feet.

The native from the airship kicked at the first of the bodies as he neared, knocking one of the dropped weapons aside. He bent nearer the body, then put his weapon to its head and pulled the trigger with a single, sharp *crack!* Apparently determining that the next body was lifeless, he ignored it as he moved on to the next, repeating his actions. *Crack!*

At that, a sudden strangled scream of protest came from the one member of the ground party still obviously alive. The shirtless one swung around and aimed the weapon at him as the downed, bleeding native tried to raise himself up on one elbow, chattering frantically, unintelligible at his assailant. The attacker shouted back at him, then let loose with an unmistakable sound: a hearty, ruthless laugh that would have been understandable in any language. He shouted again, then spun about and put a projectile into another of the bodies, which—apparently still alive—jerked grotesquely. He then did the same to another, before turning back to the remaining member of the party.

The camera zoomed in closer as he pressed the muzzle of the gun into his victim's forehead and shouted several more words at him. The native was fear-stricken, his expressive eyes wide in abject terror, his mouth working silently as he undoubtedly tried to beg for his life. There was one last *crack!* and he was thrown violently backward, thudding heavily into the ground, and moved no more.

As the image began to fade, the last thing that could be seen in the recording was the shirtless one lifting his arms skyward, dancing among the bodies at his feet. A cry of triumph came from him, then, as he called out to his fellows in the airship above him. They, in turn, called back to him in a ritualistic song of conquest and waved to the other airship, whose occupants responded in kind.

The image cross-faded to Jephthah, the frame tight on his face. His eyes were moist, his brow furrowed in concern.

"It's loathsome, is it not?" he asked, his eyes almost pleading. "This is the new 'civilized race' discovered at Tsing that the Emperor would seek to hide from you. A race of brutal, aggressive killers that make the Sarpan seem unthreatening by comparison. They live for aggression, their sole aim in their miserable existences to prey upon their neighbors, to take what they have, while at the same time protecting what they already possess." He paused, an ironic half-smile appearing briefly on his lips as he shook his head disgustedly. "Is it any wonder why the Emperor would keep this secret from you?"

The image panned back, revealing Jephthah to be wearing the familiar casual suit that was his trademark. He sat in a swivel chair at a terminal screen mounted into a desktop, the small room and his surroundings nondescript. The broadcast, as always, could have originated anywhere.

"You're probably wondering, as you think back over the recording you have just viewed, what threat these aliens represent to us. They are, after all, technically backward to such a degree that they could pose no serious danger to even the most ill equipped of the frontier worlds. Why, they don't even possess *electricity* yet, much less the means to take their unbridled aggression off their own world. In that aspect, then, you would be correct to look with derision upon these primitives.

"But think a moment longer," he said, leaning forward on his elbows. "What exactly might this race be like if they possessed a sufficient level of technology to move them out to the stars?" He paused, giving his audience sufficient time to contemplate the rhetorical question. "Well, consider their differences from the Sarpan: Where the cold-blooded Sarpan share little in common with us as far as what they need in the way of creature comforts, these 'Tsingers' share a common biological heritage with us humans. Where a Sarpan would die quickly, horribly, were it to stroll the surface of a human world, a Tsinger is a mammal that enjoys the same air and temperature range as we do. Their children are born warm, and must be raised to adulthood in a family unit. Their basic sense of sight and sound; their diet, mating habits, commerce, even their architecture; all are similar to ours.

"The Sarpan have always been a threat to us, because they perceive us to be a threat to them. And while they have always been desirous of our knowledge and our technology, they have never fully coveted the life we lead because of the physical requirements of their amphibious biology.

"But the Tsingers are not amphibians! They are like us!" He slapped both hands flat on the desktop and stood, leaning intently forward. "They are warm like us, and enjoy the sunshine like us. They give birth and suckle their young like us. They are adaptable to all but the harshest of the Human Worlds. Imagine," he said portentously, "the threat they would pose to you, to your children, if they moved out among us."

Jephthah retook his seat, lacing his fingers together in front of him. "But they cannot, because they are weak . . . for now; even a schoolboy would find their technology to be laughably crude. But they *are* intelligent. Take the airships you saw in the recording, for example. How could they be powered by steam engines, and still be light enough to achieve lift? They found a way, utilizing their abundant mineral resources to concoct a simple, gas-fired method that produces ample amounts of steam without requiring enormous wood or coal boilers. They are not to be underestimated."

"But they are weak now," he repeated. "Would it not be better to deal with this threat *now,* rather than wait until they are able to develop a higher level of learning or, worse, receive it as a gift from our shortsighted Emperor?"

TWENTY-TWO
Containment

The holoconference chamber on board the *Scartaris* reminded Adela a great deal of the Imperial residence in Kentucky, which, in turn, evoked a memory of how the Empire used to be. The semicircular ring of ten sculptured couches, the manner in which the room was laid out, even the subtle decorations that adorned the walls all spoke of an era long gone. And yet, it shouldn't have been a surprise to her that Lewis, a son of House Wood—given free reign to design the facilities of his flagship as he saw fit—might choose to fondly mimic what he saw in the place where he grew up.

She remembered many such conferences, held in holographic facilities much like this one, in the early days of the project back on Luna. The Imperial Court was still in the process of being moved from Corinth to Earth's Moon, and her beloved Javas served as acting Emperor while his father traveled from the former Imperial planet. Javas would sit by her side then, either in actuality or holographically, along with Bomeer and his fellows from the Academy of Sciences, Commander Fain of the Imperial fleet, and Emperor Nicholas himself as he approached Earth aboard his starship.

The faces and temperaments, not to mention the mind-sets, were far different now as she looked around the room; but there was much here that was familiar, and in that familiarity she found a sense of belonging, a sense of place.

The conference room was far from filled to capacity. Later, following the conclusion of this meeting, the chamber would be boisterous with the collected voices of a parade of holographically invited attendees of every imaginable stripe—captains of starships now in Tsing system; scientists and researchers engaged in study of the controversial planet spinning below them; experts on anthropology, biology, geophysics, law and a hundred other disciplines.

Now, however, there were only three people physically in the room. Brendan and Lewis, ironically seated next to each other in a manner that recalled their counterparts Bomeer and Fain so many years earlier, were at her right. Eric's real-time holographic image meshed smoothly with one of the couches directly across from the three of them, as did Captain Anmoore's image at her left, and only at those times when the computer was unable to correct the transmission speed of the tachyon signal from Luna was there even a hint that the Emperor of the Hundred Worlds was not actually seated in the room with them.

There were three generations represented here, it suddenly occurred to her. At another time, she thought, it would be pleasant for the four of them to be gathered in the same place, to enjoy each other's company without the overwhelming pressures of the coming difficulties. For now, however, she would have to content herself with this holoconference, and leave thoughts of familial pleasures aside for the moment.

"I first viewed the recording of the airship raid at Captain Anmoore's planetside facilities, at the dome down at South Camp," Adela was explaining, "right after returning from seeing Jour Nouveau for the first time. I viewed it again at the planning session with Lewis and Brendan, then again, in private, in my cabin aboard the *Kiska*. I've seen it one other time since . . . twice, if you include Jephthah's broadcast of it."

"I see," Eric said, turning to Gareth Anmoore. "Captain, are you certain that at no time was it ever transmitted ship-to-ship?"

"Absolutely, Sire." Anmoore was nervous as he addressed the

Emperor. He'd had no way of knowing, before this meeting began, that the Emperor of the Hundred Worlds himself would be taking part until he actually saw Eric sitting across from him in the room. "Not even a scrambled data transfer was attempted. I simply didn't want to take the risk of it being intercepted by an outside source."

Eric nodded in understanding. "I appreciate your efforts, Captain. Unfortunately, this man has penetrated much more deeply into Imperial workings than anyone could possibly have anticipated. Understand, however, that I don't hold you in any way responsible. You exercised all normal care, as well as a number of precautionary measures on your own initiative. I appreciate your diligence." He allowed a smile, then said, "In fact, based on what Dr. Montgarde has told me, and the official reports from the commander and the Academician, your work there has been exemplary. I have already entered a commendation for you and each member of your crew into the record. Please convey my personal thanks to your people as well. That will be all for now."

"Thank you, Sire." As his holographic image began to fade from view, leaving the seat next to her own empty, Adela saw a look of pride radiate from Anmoore's face.

"I've checked the distribution of the recording," Lewis put in. "Copies now exist in the computer systems of seven ships besides the *Scartaris* and *Kiska,* as well as in the main system at South Camp. The distribution was by hand only, on my orders, to those with a legitimate need to have it, and took place over a period of eight days." Lewis sighed, shaking his head sheepishly. "The recording was ID-coded, of course, to the recipients. But if the coding was broken, as it obviously was by someone, then any one of literally hundreds of people could have accessed it over that time period."

Eric stroked his chin in thought, and the look on his face told Adela that he was consulting his integrator, undoubtedly computing the possibilities of how the security might have been breached. At this moment he might be reviewing duty rosters, personnel lists, work assignments, ship-to-ship transfers and anything else occurring over the eight-day period in question that might have allowed someone to come into proximity of the recording.

"I think the number is more accurately in the thousands, son." He pursed his lips in silent thought, his own deep sigh echoing, almost exactly, the mannerism his eldest son had used moments before.

As he contemplated the situation, Eric's image flickered once, then nearly froze. He had gestured with his hand just before he had spoken, and it now moved in exaggerated, jerky slow motion as his likeness stretched oddly. Another bout of flickering told her that his transmission matrix was being reassigned by the tachyon dish computer to find a more favorable link. Fortunately, the interruption was brief.

"I will *not* permit him to make another of his broadcasts!" Eric burst out abruptly once the link had been reestablished. The new link was not as firm as the other had been, and although the time distortion had been eliminated, his likeness now seemed fainter, less distinct.

There was fury in his voice, and it occurred to Adela that she had never before seen in him the blaze of anger that now flashed in his eyes. In one way it lent him an air of strength, an attitude of vitality she had never previously witnessed in him; at the same time, it suggested weakness, in that his emotions could be so passionate as to threaten his composure. She could not tell for sure which of these two was closer to the truth; there was so much about this man—her own son—that she had never experienced during all her travels and long years of sleep, and she simply did not know him well enough to make that determination.

"I can no longer allow him to go on poisoning the minds of people already frightened by years of his hatred. For so long, now, it has been a nonstop effort merely to correct his lies, countering his efforts by spreading the truth. It was all I could do. To the both of you"—he nodded at Lewis and Brendan—"and your sister, I owe a debt of thanks for your efforts. You can take comfort that until now only the weak-minded have fallen for this man's lies." Eric paused, anger still simmering just below his words. "But now, with the discovery there at Tsing, he is using this new, young race to make his hate even more appealing to those who would already accept his views; and the fear of the unknown more uncomfortably real to those whose minds tremble at the thought of all things new and strange. And if he were to obtain the *Paloma Blanca*'s report of the crash-and-burn site at South Camp, or if he already has and decides to make some twisted version of it public before we've been able to determine exactly what it is . . ." He almost literally shuddered at the thought.

"I have yearned for years to put an end to his stupidity, but have always found myself powerless to do so. Jephthah has been a phantom who dwells everywhere, and nowhere, at the same time. Unable to stop him, the best I have been able to do is to chase after the effects of his passing."

He paused again, his face changing. Where before anger and frustration were evident on his features, now a sense of relief, even satisfaction appeared behind his eyes.

"Now, however, I finally have the means to stop him, at least for a time. And, ironically, it is he who has provided the means. Lewis, have you accounted for all ships currently in the system, as I asked?"

"I have, Father," he replied. "There are now fifty-nine Imperial ships of varying classes in the system. I've assigned a signature code to each. . . ." He touched a button on the armrest of his couch and a three-dimensional representation of the solar system appeared in the center of the ring of couches. The G-class star that was Tsing 479 was at its heart, the orbits of the eleven planets ringing it filling the void above the floor. Scattered throughout the holographic image was an arrangement of several dozen bright red dots, and a smaller quantity of green ones. While the red dots were evenly distributed throughout the system, all but one of the green points of light stayed well beyond the limit of the planet farthest from the star. Floating next to each dot was a corresponding code number.

"Imperial ships are indicated in red and, as you can see, nearly half are in the vicinity of the fourth planet itself, either in orbit or at the Lagrange points. Others are concentrated in tighter solar orbits or are taking station at the other planets in the system." Lewis stood, walking into the projection. "The green dots are Sarpan ships. However, only one Sarpan ship, the *Cra Stuith,* is actually 'inside' the system at the present time." He leaned into the image, pointing at a solitary green pinpoint near Tsing IV. "The commander has been given local authority here from his homeworld, and he has agreed that all other Realm vessels will be kept just outside the orbit of number eleven."

"Can you trust him?" Eric asked sharply.

"Yes, Brendan and I both agree that he'll stick to his word."

"They have a stake in this, too," Brendan added by way of agreement with his older brother. "And as long as they're permitted to have a presence here, they'd just as soon keep everything else back a safe distance." He smiled, arching an eyebrow. "With everything they've been hearing the last few years, I'm not so sure they trust *us* all that much. I imagine they feel safer with this arrangement; outside eleven's orbit they're not sitting in the middle of a fleet that outnumbers them five to one."

Lewis nodded. "They're more than satisfied for the moment with just the one ship in orbit." He retook his seat and touched the armrest again to cancel the display. The vista faded immediately.

"Excellent."

"Eric, there's something I don't quite understand," Adela said. "You suggested a minute ago that Jephthah himself had given you the means to stop him. How?"

"His last broadcast was, as always, traced to Mark-89. But since no Imperial ship has left the Tsing system within the last eight days—and we're all agreed that that's when the recording of the airship raid must have been accessed—it could *not* have been delivered to him. We can be reasonably certain, then, that his broadcast must have originated where you are." The Emperor hesitated, then added simply, "Jephthah must be there right now, with you, on one of those fifty-nine ships."

Adela gasped. *Of course,* she thought incredulously. *It makes perfect sense. He has to be here.*

Somehow, she felt dirty, as if someone had violated her in a personal way. She shivered, rubbing at the gooseflesh on her arms, and fought the unreasonable urge to look over her shoulder.

"Wait a minute," Lewis said. "Every transmission that's been sent from here has required personal authorization from Brendan or me. Anything transmitted without authorization would be detected, automatically coded, and flagged for our attention. There's no record of his address coming from here, any more than there's a record of the code for the airship recording being sent out-system."

"Nothing on Imperial channels, you mean," Adela stated candidly. All heads turned in her direction. "What if he recorded his address—and don't ask me how he managed to find the facilities to accomplish that—then sent it out as a scrambled message through a Sarpan frequency to whatever method he uses to rebroadcast through this 'Mark-89' heading of his? Closed Sarpan transmissions can't be monitored or intercepted—could doing something like that be possible?"

All were quiet for a moment, until Brendan leaned forward, his finger wagging the air excitedly in front of him. "Yes. It's extremely possible." His brow furrowed as he eagerly thought it through. "Making the recording itself is easy—" He scanned the room, his gaze coming to rest on the comm terminal on the wall near the entranceway. "Anyone could do that at any comm terminal, even that one right there. Once it's recorded, he doesn't send it through the terminal, but dumps it instead to a data stick and takes it with him. At his leisure, he scrambles it any way he wants, encodes it and sends it on a handlink through the nearest Sarpan dish, which in itself isn't that difficult—the Sarpan have a fairly widespread presence, albeit it a limited one, throughout the Hundred Worlds. Then he just sits back as the encoded programming directs it along whatever circuitous route he wants to send it on before it appears to originate from Mark-89. The best part is that the addresses have all been short enough that a scrambled, encoded broadcast would barely register a blip even if the Sarpan *were* monitoring for it. It's brilliant in its simplicity."

"Pardon me," Lewis sneered at his brother, "if I don't seem to admire all of this as much as you obviously do."

"Forget it," Eric snapped. "Brendan's right. It *is* ingenious, and we've all been fools to let it slip past us so easily. However, it makes what I've decided to do to contain him somewhat easier to arrange." He glanced to one side, a faraway look momentarily visible in his eyes. "I've just given the order to institute a total quarantine of Tsing system. No ship traffic in or out of the wormhole, and no transmissions of any kind to be sent out-system. How long will it take to set up a jamming net at your location?"

Lewis whipped a handheld data pad out of the breast pocket of his jacket and pressed the keypad several times. "There are fifteen Imperial ships in a wide enough solar orbit to assume jamming positions in . . . thirty-six hours at the outside. I can have a partial net up in a fraction of that time, however."

"Good. Do it. In the meantime, there are . . ." He lingered a moment, concentrating. "There are twenty-two ships at the wormhole, ten on this side of the gate and twelve on yours. I want full defensive posture instituted there. You're more familiar with the abilities of your commanders than I, so assign them as you think best."

"Yes, sir."

"And, Lewis—I mean that *no* ship is to leave. See to it that any attempt, made by any ship, is unsuccessful."

"I understand." The young commander nodded solemnly. "I'll chose my commanders well."

"But what about the Sarpan?" Adela asked urgently.

Eric allowed the corners of his mouth to curl upward slightly. "I think that once I've explained to them how Jephthah, the main threat to a continued alliance with the Realm, utilized their own facilities to accomplish his goals, they'll be more than willing to join us in this effort. In any event, we'll know soon; I've just sent a request for a formal audience with their leader, the Guardian."

A brief silence fell over the room.

"There's one more thing I'd like to discuss," Adela began. "The deathguards you've got following me around. I want them recalled."

"No." Eric's answer was immediate, his tone unequivocal. "I want them in place now, more than ever."

"They're suffocating me!" She pulled back, then, leaning heavily into the couch and gripping the armrests in an effort to control her own anger. "I find my travel requests delayed or speeded up to accommodate them. I'm placing others in danger when they're with me in a crowded situation. I suspect every one I see of following me or staring at my every move. I won't have it anymore, Eric!" Adela glared at her son. "I've even made one of them; her name is Andina—or at least that's the name she's using—and she's masquerading as a steward, of all things, on the *Kiska.*"

"Mother—"

"No!" she said, standing firm. "Eric, I need to move freely if I'm to be any good at all to you here. Don't handicap me in this way."

Eric said nothing for a moment, then: "All right. I won't recall them, but I'll order their status changed to level two, the same level as the agents assigned to Lewis and Brendan." Both men straightened in surprise at the words. It was apparent that neither of them had been aware that they, too, were under the surveillance of IPC guards. "They'll still be looking after your safety, but you'll be free to move about without a 'shadow.' And since you've seen through her cover, the agent you identified as 'Andina' will be reassigned. Will this be acceptable?"

"I suppose it'll have to do."

"Good, as it's as far as I'm willing to go in this matter . . ." He looked at each of them in turn. "With any of you."

A quiet sense of finality came over the conference room. Lewis stared intently, unbelievingly, at the image of his father, waiting for him to continue. Brendan, meanwhile, squirmed uneasily in his couch. Clearly, the thought that Eric had assigned IPC agents without their knowledge had affected both of them quite profoundly.

"You all have things to do," he concluded. "I'll let you get to them. In the meantime, I'll contact Cathay and explain what's happening there so she can make her travel plans accordingly. Lewis, I'll have her go directly through you before the jamming net is in place, so that her ship may be escorted through the blockade at the gate."

"Of course" was all the young commander replied.

Lewis and Brendan exchanged a brief glance, Adela noted. What was it they weren't saying?

"Good luck, all of you. In a few hours, you'll be on your own." Eric's likeness faded from the couch.

"System . . ." Lewis said, already on his feet. His fingers flew over the keys of the data pad. As he addressed the *Scartaris* net to arrange travel orders for the list of ships scrolling on the handheld's tiny screen, Brendan busied himself at the comm terminal. Neither looked at her.

There was another comm terminal located on the opposite wall, and while she waited for the two men to complete their business, she made a few calls of her own to organize everything she wanted to accomplish before the jamming net was in place. The last call she placed was to Anmoore, to arrange to accompany the next survey team in its search for artifacts in the westernmost section of the main northern landmass where some promising finds had been located.

The academician had already concluded his conversation when she bid good-bye to the captain, and was about to leave the holoconference room before she managed to stop him at the door.

"Brendan, if you have some time, could I talk to you a moment?"

He turned back to her, standing warily in the entranceway, and met her eyes. Brendan was not much taller than she. "Of course." He smiled warmly, but it was clear he would rather have continued out the door. Across the room, Lewis noticed the two of them together and hurriedly completed his business, then signed off the system and joined them at the entranceway.

"Good," she said. "I can ask you both. What was that a moment ago? When your father mentioned Cathay you both became apprehensive. The link had weakened at that point and I don't think he noticed it on his end, but I was sitting right next to you."

Brendan glanced at Lewis, nodding.

"She's not coming," the older brother replied directly. "Father doesn't know yet."

"She feels there's a considerable amount of work still to be done in Australia," Brendan added.

"I see." Adela nodded, considering the news. "I'm disappointed, of course; I was truly looking forward to meeting her, and her input will be missed, but it shouldn't pose too much of a problem as far as what we're doing here is concerned. And if Billy still needs her help, then that's the best place for her to be. But why hasn't she told your father? He's counting on her being here."

"She's afraid to," Lewis offered. "Father's concerned with her safety, as he is for all of us, and was counting on us all being together. 'Strength in numbers.' She knows that and doesn't want to worry him unduly. And . . ." He paused and looked at Brendan.

"And she's fallen in love with Billy," his brother finished. "She doesn't want to leave him."

"Oh."

An unexpected emotional rush shot through her that she couldn't understand. *What is it I'm feeling right now?* she demanded of herself. *Why am I reacting like this?* Privately, her thoughts were spinning, but aloud she asked, "What's wrong with that? Billy is your father's closest and dearest friend; surely she doesn't think—*you* don't think—he'll disapprove?"

"No, but . . ." Brendan shrugged. "It's the timing of all of this. She's afraid Father will think she's putting her own needs ahead of what's happening here, ahead of what he's asked us all to do."

Of course she's afraid, Adela reasoned. *She's being presented with the same decision I was when I chose to go into cryosleep: her own happiness, or her goals.*

"Timing be damned." Adela smiled inwardly. It felt good. "She's made the right choice."

She spoke a while longer to the two men, but directly all three went about their separate tasks. Hours later, back aboard the *Kiska,* she attempted to reach Billy with no success. He and Cathay were in the bush, she was informed, and would not, in fact, be available until long after the jamming net was in place.

Adela sat alone in her cabin and enjoyed the quiet, wondering if the IPC agent on duty was even now being told of his or her new status. She hoped so.

The hour grew late and she yawned, stretching out on the comfortable sofa as she thought back over the day's affairs, trying to sort out her feelings. As pleased as she was with the turn of events enabling them to silence Jephthah for the time being, and of the welcome change in the status of the deathguards, she found her thoughts drifting, unbidden, back to Billy, back to Earth.

"System," she commanded softly, sitting up on the sofa and straightening her appearance.

"Ma'am?"

"Prepare to record a message for out-system delivery."

The room lights increased to a level sufficient for a clear recording as she sat in the chair before the holoframe in the corner. A tiny red light glowed faintly above the pickup lens.

"Ready to record, on your signal."

She cleared her throat softly. "Go." A confirming chirp told her the recording had started.

"Hello, Billy," she began, uncertain of exactly what it was she needed to say. "I'm sure you will have talked to Eric about everything that's happened here by the time you receive this, so I won't go into it now. I just wanted you to know that I'm pleased to hear how well things are progressing there. I'd be less than honest if I said your presence here wasn't missed—there's so much to see here, so much I'd like to share with you! The people I'm working with on the *Paloma Blanca,* they . . . well, they understand the same thing about our goals here as you do there in the outback. I know what you're doing there at Kimberley is so very important, not only to you, but to the proper order of things. I suppose I've always known it, but I think it's only since I've been here, and have seen how these people hold valuable the same things you and I do . . . that I've realized how much what you're doing means to you.

"I've also recognized that what you're doing there is so very similar to what's happening to the Empire. I know you're struggling to have your people hold on to the best of their old ways at the same time they move into a very different future. The difference between our situations is that your people see it all so clearly; I truly wonder if the people scattered among the Hundred Worlds will be so fortunate."

Adela hesitated, carefully forming her words.

"I know about Cathay's decision, Billy." Another pause. "Don't worry about Eric's reaction to her staying there with you. You know him as well as I do, better than I do. He's a good man, a reasonable man; and he'll understand. He'll *worry* about you both. . . ." She smiled reassuringly into the lens. "But nothing

would please him more than the two of you being together. I
know it pleases me. She's a lucky woman, Billy; very lucky. I'm
so happy for you. For both of you. Good luck."

Adela ended the recording, addressed it and encoded it for
immediate transmission. "System, please bring lights to thirty
percent," she said, moving back to the sofa. She sat there, unmoving, hands folded in her lap.

I am happy for him, she thought. *I truly meant it when I said it.*

She lay back on the sofa, resting the back of her arm on her
forehead. She was happy for Billy. Helping the Aborigine to
restore their faith, to "reconnect their Song Lines," as he had put
it, was the realization of his fondest dream. And the thought he
and Cathay were in love sent a profound sense of family through
her very being, along with the awareness that the union would
bring her closer to both of them.

But why did she suddenly feel so all alone?

TWENTY-THREE
Friends, Through All

You are *not* our enemies," Eric insisted. The Emperor of
the Hundred Worlds stood on a tiny island of solid
ground jutting out of the water amid a lush, misty jungle
that was more swamp than forest. An enormous insect more
closely resembling a dragon than did its Earthly namesake
buzzed curiously around him, then flew into his chest only to
reappear, confused and disoriented, out the other side of his
holographic image before disappearing into the distance. "I am
as concerned with Jephthah's crazed propaganda as you must be,
and desire nothing so much as to see it ended, once and for all.
Will you help us with this?"

"We were your enemy once." The Sarpan known as S'Senoh,
Guardian of the Waters, swam closer to Eric, raising himself to
a sitting position waist-deep in the murky pool. He idly played his
webbed fingers across the surface of the water at his sides, nictitating membranes blinking in Eric's direction. The dark brown,
leathery skin of his forehead wrinkled oddly with each blink.
"Could we not be your enemy again?"

"You were our enemies many, many years ago," Eric admitted. "But that was a darker time when both our races had just begun venturing into space. Our races were young, inexperienced, and easily frightened by what we found as we moved out among the stars. Had our paths crossed at a later time, perhaps the blood spilled between us could have been avoided."

"But the blood was spilled; it is mixed here in the water with me now." As if to demonstrate, S'Senoh dipped cupped hands beneath the surface and lifted the water to Eric as it seeped through his fingers. "Do you not see it?"

"I know. The blood of my forefathers is a part of my history, too."

"So?" S'Senoh asked. "Could this spilled blood not bring about the same . . ." He stopped, his mouth moving silently as he tried to form the right word. ". . . animosity . . . between us, now that it has been fed by the Human Prophet?"

"The man is not a prophet!" Eric replied, frustrated. "He is little more than a selfish opportunist, and speaks for no one other than himself. Can you not see that?"

S'Senoh sighed, expelling the air heavily through his nostrils. "Can you not see that individuality is as alien to us as a dry nest?"

"You are wise, Guardian," Eric acceded, "to recognize and understand this difference between our people. I ask forgiveness for my outburst."

The alien nodded, accepting the Emperor's apology. "However, my query remains: We have been blamed by Jephthah for all manner of atrocities. The lost human colony at Zephyr; the burning of a city on 82-Delta; and my ears still burn with human voices crying out 'Remember the *Sylvan!*' "

"I know you were not responsible for these acts, and have done my best to correct the record in your behalf."

"And still, many humans believe. I ask yet again, Emperor of the Human Worlds: We were your enemy once; could not . . . Jephthah's . . ." Again, he struggled for a word of the proper context. "Could not his 'propaganda' turn humanity against us again? Could not more blood join me in this water?"

Eric regarded S'Senoh carefully. Although the elder leader did his best to downplay his fear, he was truly concerned with what might happen should a united humanity turn against the Sarpan. And why shouldn't he be afraid? Humanity had, after all, almost wiped out his race centuries earlier during the First Contact Wars that had raged between their races.

"But we were a different people then," he said. "Both of us,

humanity and Sarpan. We conceitedly thought of ourselves as
Terrans then, and had settled far fewer than a hundred worlds.
We were eager to extend humanity wherever we could, and to let
nothing stop us from doing so. You called yourself Rak in those
days, and your only goal was to spread out among the stars, to
increase the size of your water at all costs. You looked down
upon any life you found, and considered it beneath you—just as
we did." Eric shook his head in genuine sadness at the history.
"Both our peoples were stupid, shortsighted." Eric sat on the
mound, pulling his knees up before him as he leaned closer to
S'Senoh. "We have both matured."

The Guardian looked away, considering everything Eric had
said. High in the misty sky behind him, the lowermost of his
world's twin suns began to dip below the tree line. As it did, Eric
noticed all around him that the sounds of myriad animals and
insects had grown stronger, louder as they prepared to great the
approaching night.

"So." S'Senoh, his decision made, turned back to him again
and nodded. His head tilted in a posture of assent, the setting
suns glinted off the nine silver bobs on his left gill slit. "I accept
your offer to strengthen our alliance in this cause. I will contact
Captain Tra'tiss personally and instruct him to cooperate fully
with your male spawn Lewis Wood."

"Thank you," Eric said simply. "I believe that united in this,
humanity and Sarpan can show to one and all that this man's
hatred is unfounded, and that he is to be shunned."

"Let us hope so." S'Senoh hesitated, and seemed to concentrate on something unseen below the surface of the pool. "May
I ask something in return?"

"Of course."

"She who will rebirth the star of your homeworld is near the
Cra Stuith, is this not so?"

"Yes. Adela de Montgarde is there."

"So." The Guardian seemed uncertain, as if he was self-conscious about what he wanted to ask. "I am correct in thinking
that she is from the same water group as Lewis Wood and yourself?"

"Yes. She is my mother, and the grandmother of both Commander Wood and Academician Wood."

S'Senoh nodded, pleased that his information was correct.
"Captain Tra'tiss will spawn soon. It is his wish to meet with her
for first touching. Would this be possible?"

Eric considered the request with absolute earnestness. Much of what the Sarpan were, as a race, was passed on through touch, father to spawn. Knowledge, instincts, a sense of unity, and many more things less tangible passed in that way from one generation to the next. Only under the rarest of circumstances had the Sarpan allowed a human to touch their spawn, only rarely had they considered a human to be of such importance as to want their young to be imprinted with their thoughts.

"I cannot speak for she who is my mother, nor can I command her in this. As you noted earlier, humanity is a race of individuals, each in charge of his or her own destiny. However," he said, "knowing her as I do, I am certain that she would consider it an honor to share first touching with your captain's spawn. I will speak to her of it."

"This one is most grateful." The Guardian stood, water dripping noisily from his naked body. Eric had been surprised at the alien's age when he first noted the number of silver bobs he proudly displayed, but it wasn't until now, with S'Senoh wading slowly toward him, that he realized just how old and frail the Sarpan leader truly was. He was thin, almost emaciated, and was clearly long past bequeathing his Guardianship to another. Eric rose, regarding the old one with a renewed respect. "Perhaps one day, when this present difficulty is ended, we, too, shall touch."

S'Senoh stopped before him and extended his hand, palm toward him, in the ritual of touching. Eric responded in kind and held his own palm against the alien's.

Their palms did not truly touch in this holographic setting. The symbolic gesture would have to suffice, for now.

S'Senoh said a few words softly in his native tongue, and the misty swamp dissolved around Eric, leaving a dimly lighted holographic display chamber. It was foolish, Eric knew, since he was never on the Sarpan homeworld, but the room suddenly felt colder.

You are a wise leader, he thought, alone once more in the vast, empty display chamber. *Maybe someday you and I will meet. I would consider a touching with you to be a great honor indeed.*

TWENTY-FOUR
Surprises

The dome at South Camp was in an uproar. A torrential downpour had sprung up almost without warning, catching the surface teams by surprise. It was all they could do to move as much delicate equipment into the dome as possible, while covering the rest with plastic tarps. All around Adela there were people running, shouting, and trying to do a hundred things at once.

The fact that the weather change was a surprise was not entirely true, however. The meteorological data from any one of a dozen ships orbiting the planet were available, but with the activity both on and above Tsing IV increasing on a daily basis, the information never managed to find its way to the officer of the day at the dome. Even now, Adela could hear the OD bellowing on the far side of the dome as he corralled yet another equipment-laden transport in from the storm.

"I've found it, all right." Vita Secchi's image beamed from his portion of the holoframe, his shaggy growth of beard bobbing animatedly as he spoke. "The probe's on its way, but I want to get down there and check it out myself as soon as possible. It's about five hundred meters down, but it's definitely the source of the metal we found at South Camp. And there's more of it. A *lot* more of it."

"Please, Vito. One thing at a time." Gareth Anmoore, standing at Adela's side, raised a hand to slow the energetic geologist down. "You'll have to excuse Dr. Secchi, but I share in his enthusiasm. I think this is what we've been looking for."

"But how is it that you've just now located it?" Brendan asked. "I understood that both moons had already been thoroughly scanned."

"They were. Dr. Secchi did two complete orbital surveys. I personally reviewed his findings." A pleasant grin spread across his face. "However, Vito has a tendency not to give up when he's convinced of something. Geologically speaking."

Adela felt someone brush lightly against her back, and was not surprised to see that a small crowd of combined personnel from the *Kiska* and *Paloma Blanco*, as well as from other ships that had sent specialists down, had gathered behind her and Anmoore to learn whatever they could of this latest news.

The holoframe seemed nearly as crowded as the dome. Unlike the fully equipped holoconference room aboard the *Scartaris,* the frame installed at South Camp was fairly basic and little better than a large, wall-mounted flatscreen. Vito's transmission from the survey ship in orbit occupied the left third of the frame, while Brendan and Lewis shared the rightmost portion. An orbital shot of the surface of Big One, the two-dimensional picture centered on a series of overlapping craters, filled the middle portion. Telemetry numbers scrolled along the bottom of the center image, which appeared—as the probe sending back the picture continued to lower itself gently to the surface—to be gradually zooming in on the largest of the craters.

"Captain Anmoore's right," Secchi verified. "We scanned both of them, top to bottom. Problem was . . . we weren't meant to find it."

The was a sudden hush among those who had gathered to listen in to the holoframe, then a steady rising of soft voices anxious to offer thoughts and opinions among themselves about what the geologist had just said. The three-way link was confusing enough, but the clamor of personnel still coming and going in the dome's main chamber, the raging storm outside, and the growing crowd around them all contributed to make the conversation even more difficult to follow.

"The whole deposit is shielded," he went on. "From most angles, we read nothing but loose regolith or solid rock, which is the reading anyone scanning Big One was supposed to get, I think, either from orbit or a planet-based observation point."

Lewis rubbed at his temples. "I'm not sure I follow this. Are you saying that whatever this metal deposit is, it's being deliberately hidden?"

An unassuming why-didn't-I-think-of-that look spread over Secchi's face. "Uh, I hadn't really thought it out that far . . . I've just been mainly concerning myself with trying to get some measurement of the extent of the deposit and its exact location below the surface. I never really stopped to think about *why* it wasn't readable." Someone leaned into his portion of the image and tapped at his shoulder, and Vito nodded. "Oh, I can give you the playback now. We have a few minutes before the probe touches down anyway."

The center of the holoframe blinked, the display switching to a sweeping overhead view taken from one of the many sensorsats in orbit around it. The surface zipped along, giving the same view one might see of the ground from a standard aircraft, except that in this recording dots and smears of color appeared and disappeared as various ore and mineral deposits came within range of the spectrographic equipment on the satellite. A sequence of numbers sprang into the image at each occurrence.

"This is a portion of a typical scanning sweep. You can see that it's cataloging every geological trait it's been programmed to find. The metals we've been looking for, the ones from the crash-and-burn site, pop up occasionally. . . ." He paused, waiting. "There! There's one right there. Did you see it? Anyway, although the metals were present, for the most part the scans found them only in the same proportions as they naturally occurred on the planet itself."

"For the most part," Anmoore emphasized.

"Right!" Secchi blurted happily, the level of excitement in his voice climbing. Although Adela noted that Lewis' expression clearly showed his desire for the geologist to get on with it, she couldn't help but share in the scientist's delight. "But I found one trace signature . . ." The picture changed to a still image, similar to the view the descending probe had been sending back. ". . . where I didn't expect to find it. It was still too small to be the one we were looking for, smaller than a lot of other deposits I'd already recorded, for that matter, but it was out of place based on the earlier scans we'd completed of the region.

"So I did a third overhead scan to verify where it was, and found a series of fissures leading out from the impact site of these craters . . . here." A yellow circle appeared over the area in question. "Keep in mind that all the survey work to this point has consisted of straight-down scans from directly overhead; that's normal procedure. But look at the left side of this crater, the big one in the center." An oblong circle appeared at the indicated depression, starting at the center of the crater and tracing an area to the rim; then another thin line, not quite connected to it, snaked far out along the featureless surface. It looked like a tadpole shedding its tail. "There seems to be one large fissure, mostly in the lower portion of crater wall, that extends several kilometers to the west. It goes underground, though, as soon as it crosses the crater wall, then reappears on the surface only periodically."

"I see," Adela said, realizing what he was getting at. "You think you managed to get a brief reading through the fissure itself?"

"That's it. But it was just dumb luck, honestly. Past the crater wall the fissure is only a few centimeters at its widest—on the surface, that is."

The playback changed yet again, but this time it was an angular shot that allowed the horizon to scroll beneath the sensorsat, the view a pilot might see from the front of an aircraft, versus a passenger's downward view. As before, there were the scattered color flashes and their associated spectrographic readings.

"We programmed five separate passes over the site, the scan set for the angle you see now, with no luck. But, on number six . . ." The view showed the gently rolling landscape, the big crater dotting the very edge of the horizon. The surface scrolled by, bringing the eastern rim of the crater closer until it passed beneath them, slowly revealing the interior. There wasn't much to see—the deep shadows inside hid half the crater floor and the entire inside portion of the western rim wall. But as the angle increased, there was a sudden brilliant flash of white light at the base of the rim wall that sent a veritable avalanche of numbers cascading down the screen. Then, as the image neared the rim wall, the flash disappeared, as did the readings. The center of the holoframe returned to the overhead view of the descending probe, still in the final stages of its landing phase.

No one in the crowd spoke, leaving only the sounds of the vehicular traffic wrapping up work on the far side of the work area, and the steady drumming of the rain on the surface of the dome.

Lewis nodded thoughtfully, understanding the implications, while Brendan hurriedly tapped at his handheld, undoubtedly checking the numbers that had just flashed on his screen aboard *Scartaris.*

"If I got the numbers right . . ." The academician started under his breath. "No, wait a minute. This can't be accurate."

"Ninety-eight thousand, five hundred metric tons, Imperial standard." Secchi positively beamed. "I've run the numbers ten times." He waited as long as he could, then, looking like he was going to burst, blurted, "Can I go down?"

"I say yes," Adela offered firmly, then looked to Anmoore. He, in turn, regarded the two men aboard the flagship, his eyebrows raised questioningly.

Brendan set the handheld aside and leaned back into his couch, hands steepled in front of him.

"Well?" Lewis said. "It's your call. Is this the proof we were looking for?"

"I think so," Brendan said finally, evoking a not-quite-silent *"Yes!"* from Secchi, whose portion of the holoframe immediately winked out. The man couldn't move fast enough to get ready.

"All right, then." Lewis leaned forward. "You have my authorization, Captain." Brendan rose from his own couch and said a few words into his brother's ear. Lewis nodded. "I agree," he said to Brendan, who promptly left the image. Then, to Anmoore, "Academician Wood, along with an assistant of his choice from here, will accompany you to the surface, and will act as team leader. What he says, goes. Is this satisfactory?"

"Of course."

"Good. Let's keep this one small. No more than eight people for this first trip. The Academician and whoever he brings make two—"

"I'm going," Adela said excitedly. "I won't miss out on this."

Lewis knew better than to argue with her. "Choose the remaining five members of the party as you think best, Captain, but I'll insist that two of them be from security."

Adela bristled. The motion did not go unnoticed by her grandson.

"If it makes you feel better, Dr. Montgarde," he said formally, "you may decide the security personnel." He stood, signaling that there was nothing more to discuss. "Select your team and get going. By the way, it may surprise you to know that I'm as anxious to find out what's down there as you are. Good luck." He nodded encouragingly, but his eyes lingered a moment on Adela as the right side of holoframe faded, a hint of worry behind them. Only the probe landing sequence remained, and now expanded to fill the entire frame.

"All right, people!" Anmoore shouted, clapping his hands to get their attention. "That's all the excitement for now, so let's get moving here." He had a headset hanging loosely around his neck, which he pulled over his ear; then he spoke into his collar pickup. As he talked, he watched the general milling-about as everyone returned to what they were doing before the three-way conversation, occasionally waving and pointing directions to one group or another.

Prsently, he pulled the headset off and let it dangle from his neck again, and turned to Adela.

"Vito's probably already waiting in the shuttle bay, I suspect," he said pleasantly. "I'm sending Hannah with you, of course; and a vac tech named Lan Heathseven. He's had years of experience working in hard-vacuum environments, so pay attention to anything he tells you. With his knowledge of equipment and engineering he should be able to handle any of your physical needs. Besides, if this metal you find turns out to be something like, say, a working spacecraft, I want his opinion on it. Security's up to you."

"Lucky me." Adela turned, scanning the ID badges of the personnel nearest them for bright orange. She spotted one, pleased as she recognized the face of the man who wore it. "Kal— Kal Hanson! Can you come over here for a moment, please?" He waved back, and as he approached she glimpsed another orange badge. "And you," she called to the woman. "Yes, with the short red hair."

"Hello, Doctor," Hanson said, coming up. "Good to see you again."

The woman also greeted her politely. Adela had never seen her before, and assumed that she must have been one of Anmoore's people.

Adela explained what she wanted, much to the delight of both of them. Admittedly, there had not been much for security to do down here other than accompany the occasional trip to the observation deck or to one of the remote dig sites. Even then, their responsibilities usually leaned more toward their paramedical and evac training—used, so far, in only a few rare instances on this gentle world—than to outright armed protection. These two were clearly anxious for the opportunity to go along.

"Wait a minute," Anmoore said, looking Hanson over as he pulled the headset on again. "We may have a problem." He spoke a few words into the collar pickup, then asked, "How tall are you, Hanson?"

"A hundred ninety-one and a half," he replied, just the slightest suggestion of concern on his face. He stood straighter, a bit more tense. "Is something wrong?"

Anmoore spoke again to his unseen listeners, thanked them, and pulled the headset off again. "Yeah, I'm afraid so. Normally, standard issue, shield-reinforced pressure suits are fine for vacuum work, but I'm not taking any chances. Hard suits only this trip." He shrugged apologetically. "Sorry. You're too big for what we have on hand."

"Oh, well," he answered agreeably, his features relaxing. "Maybe next trip. Good luck, Doctor; hope you find what you're looking for."

"Thanks. Me, too."

He nodded politely, then headed off in the direction he had come.

"Actually, I'm a little disappointed," Adela confessed, once he had disappeared into the crowd of workers. "He's one of the few people in security I knew I could trust."

"That's understandable. Well, you can trust Cannin here," he said, confirming that she was from the crew of the *Paloma Blanca.* "I'd trust her with my life. I have, in fact, on one or two occasions. Right, Mike?"

She laughed at his reference. "I suppose so . . . if you consider shore leave a life-threatening situation."

"Anyway, if you'd like, I can pick the last team member."

"That would be fine," Adela replied. "I appreciate it."

"Well, that's it then. Mike, why don't you go see if Waltz is doing anything tomorrow afternoon, and if not tell him to give me a call as soon as he can. Oh, and Lan will be going with you, too."

Cannin's face brightened. "I was hoping the two of us could get away for a while." She nodded a wordless thank-you, then headed to the far side of the dome in search of the other security tech.

Anmoore looked around, and noticed that the interior of the work area had brightened considerably: With the bay doors opened wide at either end of the dome, the rays of diffused sunshine that were just now beginning to sift through the cloud cover told them both that the storm had broken.

"Off the record . . ." he said soberly, turning back to her. There was a stern, no-nonsense look in his eyes she had never seen in him before. "I won't allow an IPC on any survey team I send out."

Adela stared at him in abject shock. "Wha— You mean Hanson? But how did . . .?"

"It's not important." Anmoore's voice was filled with anger, and he stared away, not wanting to meet her eyes. "Look, I know you had nothing to do with it; and I've only known about him for a short time, or I'd *never* have allowed him to accompany us— armed!—to the observation deck." He lowered his head, checking his anger, and a shout from a woman driving a cargo lifter caught his attention. He walked in her direction, and although Adela couldn't hear their conversation, she saw him point to a group working at one of the shuttles making the run to the western dig site.

"I didn't know," she shouted over the whine of the lifter as it pivoted away. "I thought he was all right. I mean, I thought he was just normal security. I only knew the IPCs were here, following me; I didn't know who they were. I'm sorry."

"Forget it." He waved his hand, dismissing the whole episode, but Adela couldn't help but feel that she had lost some measure of Gareth Anmoore's respect. "You'd better take care of whatever you were working with before the interruption." He nodded over his shoulder at the holoframe. "We're heading up to the ship in an hour. I won't be going on the trip with you—I can't fit into our hard suits any better than he would—but I do want to pilot the shuttle down to the surface of Big One."

"All right," she answered. "I'll see you on the pad, then." They smiled at each other, a certain degree of tension still between them; then she turned away and headed in the direction of the temporary office suite they had set up for her in the working section of the dome.

"Hey!" He called after her, waving. "You *have* worked a hard suit before, haven't you?"

Adela waved back, pretending that she hadn't heard what he said, and continued on her way.

TWENTY-FIVE
The Last Emperor

E ric, Emperor of the Hundred Worlds, knew nothing of Adela's preparations.

The jamming net in place, and now made even stronger with the assistance of the Sarpan ships at Tsing, he had no idea what was happening there. A means had been devised, at Lewis's suggestion, to channel information back to the Imperial Court; but it involved a complicated series of coded, hand-delivered missives sent through the wormhole. Once through the wormhole and outside the area of quarantine he had prescribed, the scrambled reports could then be sent through the tachyon dish, but they would still be dated. In the meantime, then, he waited.

However, the reports he *was* receiving, those from elsewhere in the Hundred Worlds, were not good. Not good at all. Jephthah might have been silenced for now, but his last broadcast had been much more effective that even he could have hoped. Unrest and anti-alien sentiment was increasing on a score of worlds, demands for full dissociation from the Realm had been sent by the governing bodies of a score more; there had even been scattered incidents of violence on a few worlds against visiting Sarpan scientists, scholars and diplomats. Everything hinged on what was happening at Tsing. And all he could do was wait.

Just like when my father used to wait, he thought, experiencing for the first time some of the pressures that surely must have affected Javas' rule. On reflection he realized that he felt useless, unnecessary—almost impotent as he anticipated some word, any word from Lewis on what was happening at Tsing since the jamming net was closed.

He was at Woodsgate, on Earth, on one of the balconies adjacent to the study that had been used by so many Emperors before him. No sense in sitting on some figurative throne up at Luna, he'd reasoned, when there was little to do but . . . just sit. He stood now on the west balcony looking out over the Kentucky hills that blended gracefully, mistily into the blue mountains in the distance. The Sun was just now setting, the sky streaked in brilliant hues of crimson, scarlet and orange, and he watched the brightly burning orb as it slowly dropped behind the wooded mountains.

A bright, square outline appeared in the air high above him, and he looked up to see a controlled entrance gate opening in the shield dome that protected the estate. A tiny shuttle appeared, easily maneuvering through the opening before it touched down lightly on the receiving pad in front of the house. A familiar round form waddled out to the craft and, after a few moments, trundled back to the house with a long, narrow bundle as the shuttle lifted off again and disappeared through the opening.

"Billy told me once that he stood on a beach and cursed you," he said ruefully under his breath, returning his attention to Earth's bloated, sinking daystar, "for bringing this all upon us. How much different would our lives have been had you not decided to die?" Eric stood there, leaning with both hands on the elegant carved railing. "Was he right to curse you?"

Eric felt/heard a signal in his head and turned his back on the waning brightness. Walking slowly, deliberately back into the study, he closed the double doors behind him as if to shut out the Sun, and in that single, trivial gesture imagined that he had some small power over the damned thing.

He took his customary seat behind the enormous wooden desk that his grandfather, Emperor Nicholas, had commissioned, built from golden oak taken from the backwoods surrounding the family estate in all directions. He played his hands across the polished surface. *This is real!* he thought, tracing a fingernail along the deep grain of the wood. *This simplest of nature's creations is more real to me now than any of the trappings of this . . . this 'Empire.'* As he ran his hand along the desktop, he spied the flower. The intensely red blossom was embedded in a solid block of plastiglass, and had belonged to Javas. He picked it up and stared at it—the magnificent petals magnified by the curved surface of its crystalline container—marveling at nature's design. It was from a firebush, a flowering shrub native to his grandmother's homeworld, Gris, but his father had never told him the significance of this particular bloom, nor why he had asked on his deathbed that it always remain a part of this study, for however long the Emperors of the Hundred Worlds used it. As he stared at it, Eric wondered, not for the first time, what the fragrance of this flower smelled like.

The thought was interrupted by another summons somewhere in the back of his mind. The integrator signal, as always neither quite heard nor felt, had been automatically issued by the monitor system built into the richly carpeted and appointed corridors of the old estate to alert him that someone was approaching the study.

"Come in, Fleming," he called out, not waiting for the Master to knock. The door opened, and the ruddy, jowly face of the House Master peeked timidly into the study.

"Sire," he said, waddling his considerable bulk into the room. He carried a long object gingerly in both arms and approached the desk respectfully, holding it out in front of him once he stood before the Emperor's desk. The cylindrical parcel had been wrapped in old-fashioned brown paper, secured with a length of rough, stringy twine. "It has arrived."

"Thank you, Master Fleming."

"Sire." The House Master bowed so deeply that anyone who did not know him intimately might have expected him to topple over under his own weight. He turned to leave.

"Wait."

Fleming turned tentatively to face the Emperor, a look that

wordlessly, plaintively asked "Is there some way in which I have displeased you?" evident on his round face.

"Do you know what this is?" Eric asked as he noisily peeled back the paper to reveal a length of dark wood.

Fleming shook his head vigorously, his cheeks jiggling at the motion.

"It's a letter stick." He tapped it against the edge of the oaken desk with a sharp *clack! clack!* sound that reverberated sharply through the room. "It's nothing more than a simple, straightforward means of communication employed by an ancient race of noble people. This one contains but a few words; a simple, heartfelt message that would take only two sentences in our own language." The Emperor closed his eyes and held the stick to his nose, inhaling deeply of the rich wood scent that emanated from the freshly made carvings. "I'm sending it to Billy and Cathay down in Kimberley." He smiled, opening his eyes. "All it says is that I am so very happy for them, and that I dearly love them both. That's all, nothing more.

"But do you know that it took a dozen historians of the Imperial Court to research the correct design, then another dozen Court linguistics experts to determine the proper language, syntax and character set." He turned the intricately carved stick over and over in his hands, his fingertips gingerly exploring every nook and cranny of its ornamented surface. "It took yet another dozen Court artisans to get it to a point where the linguists could then present it back to the historians once more, who, in turn, could then return to the artisans for still further revisions on the final design." He pushed back a stack of plasticine folders and set the stick reverently in the center of the felt-and-leather blotter on the desktop.

"Dear God." He turned to face the House Master, his eyes moist and glistening in the last piercing shaft of sunshine streaming through the curtained double doors. "Is this what we've come to, Fleming? An Empire that requires thirty . . . 'technicians' to accomplish a task that any humble tribesman could have done—can still do!—in a few minutes' time? Is this all we are?"

"Sire." Fleming's voice was strong, tempered as he took the chair facing the desk. He sat, not waiting for his Emperor's permission, and addressed him man-to-man, as an equal. It was an action Eric had never seen him take before, an action he had never imagined the man was capable of taking on his own.

"The Masters of this House have always spoken plainly when it was required," he continued, the emotions within him rising.

"Over the years the Masters consulted one another frequently—as a young man, I spoke to, and was guided by, McLaren, the Master who tutored and raised you here at Woodsgate in Emperor Javas' stead. He, in turn, served well to consult and learn from Master Montlaven, your own father's surrogate. And so on, and so on." He raised an all-encompassing arm and swept it through the air to take in their surroundings. "Sire, there is no business that has transpired in this House that has not been passed on in such a manner, over each successive Imperial generation, to the next Master."

Fleming bit his lower lip, tears suddenly welling up in his eyes to flow freely down his ample cheeks. "Think you that I am as blinded as not to see that . . ." He gasped for breath, forcing the words out. "Your children do not wish to follow you! Think you that I do not already realize that I am to be the last Master of this House?" he yelled at the top of his lungs. He leaned forward, his face falling into the palms of his hands as he sobbed openly.

Eric said nothing for several moments, and remained staring in mute helplessness at the Master sitting opposite him. He knew that what this man had just done in his presence was so very much more than a personal humiliation, and he was deeply ashamed for having been responsible for it. He had turned to this man in conceited self-pity over his own failings, seeking some consolation, and had in turn brought this once proud man to his knees.

"Master Fleming," he said resolutely, rising and circling the massive desk to stand next to the leather-bound chair. "You—along with McLaren, Montlaven and all those who came before you—have served this House well. It is to your credit that this antiquated Empire has held together as long as it has." He held out his hand, and Fleming stood to accept it, his grasp firm and sure.

"Believe me when I tell you this . . ." Eric went on, his words coming from the heart. "There is nothing that you or I have done to precipitate anything that has happened. And just as you feel an overwhelming sadness that comes with the realization that the Masters of my family have reached their end, know, too, that I feel the same about my own destiny. Being the last Emperor is a fate I would wish on no man, any more than you would wish your own fate on another. What has happened to bring this about is a thing that could neither have been helped, nor avoided—we both know that to be true. And yet it is a thing for which the last of the line always assumes the blame."

"I can hear the voice of Master McLaren in your words, Young Prince," Fleming said earnestly, releasing his hand at last as a twinkle returned to his eyes. " 'Young Prince.' Do you remember when I used to call you that? It was, oh, so very long ago." He inhaled deeply, his thick chest heaving outward beneath his robe, and sighed wistfully. "Sire, I remain your servant until you no longer require me." The Master bowed deeply again, and left the study without further word.

Closing the study's enormous oak doors solidly behind him, he left Eric, the last Emperor of the Hundred Worlds, alone with his thoughts in the rapidly darkening room.

"Sire!"

The frantic cry echoed hollowly throughout the corridors of the Wood estate. "Sire!"

Eric sat bolt upright on the leather sofa, momentarily disoriented, and rubbed at a neck gone stiff from resting against the arm of the sofa. What time was it? He looked around the room, but there was no light in the study save the pale grayness of the full moon shining through the opened double doors. Had he opened them before lying back on the sofa? Just what was happening here? He shook his head in an attempt to clear the cobwebs from his mind.

"Sire, are you all right?" Fleming burst into the room, his outline silhouetted hazily in the lighted doorway. Behind him, five armed Imperial Guards appeared. "System! Bring the lights in this room to full!" The rotund man moved quickly, much more quickly than Eric would have thought possible, and was at his side in an instant. "Sire, we must get you to the shelter!"

The Emperor was on his feet now as Fleming grabbed him by the shoulder. The strength in his grip, like the speed he had exhibited moments ago, surprised Eric. As the Master tugged wildly at his arm, the five guards trotted into the room and took positions at each window, only to be followed by several more.

"What's happening?" Eric paused then, his attention drawn to a steadily descending whine from somewhere outside the study. He tried to go to the window, but was stopped by a handful of well-meaning guards. Over their shoulders, however, he could see the lights of a descending shuttle as it eased itself down onto the landing pad in the yard below. Even in the moonlight he could see that the markings on the side of the craft where not of Imperial origin.

"The House security has been breached," Fleming cried frantically. "You have to get to the shelter *now!*"

Eric nodded. "All right, then. Let's go."

He allowed the Master to lead him from the room and into the corridor, where twenty more guardsmen waited to escort him to the shelter beneath the estate.

"A gate opened in the shielding without warning," Fleming explained as they walked, filling him in on what was happening. "There was nothing security could do to stop it. They even tried to project a secondary shield, below the first, to no avail. Whoever is controlling the main shield has also disabled the backup measures." They marched down the main hallway, then turned into a lesser corridor that led to a level containing myriad guest rooms.

"Have we been contacted?" Eric demanded.

"No!" It was clear that Fleming was frightened, but as he dragged Eric along it was just as clear that it was for Eric's safety that the Master feared. "There has been no communication of any kind."

The guardsmen in the lead entered the first of the guest rooms, which was in reality the entrance to the high-speed lift that would take him a full hundred meters beneath the lowest level of the estate. The lift doors were already open, and he entered along with Fleming and four of the soldiers. The rest took up posts on either side of the lift as the doors slid shut. The moment the doors pressed closed, it felt as though the floor had fallen out from under their feet. Less than two minutes later, the Emperor was ensconced in the heavily armored quarters that served as the House main security shelter.

The shelter was more than just a single armored room, however. It was a suite of rooms capable of housing the Emperor, each member of his family in residence, the House Master, and—in the antechamber through which they had just come—sufficient space to barrack a squad of Imperial guards. The main living room was comfortable, even ornate, and it was clear that it had been regularly maintained, as it was immaculately clean. There was even fresh fruit in a large bowl on the dining table.

Eric had been in this room once, as a child. As he often did in those days, he had reprogrammed House security and entered the room, playing here for hours as though it were his private home. As usually happened, McLaren—almost always one step ahead of his schemes where the House computers were involved—had caught him. He had not been punished, however. Instead, McLaren had spoken to him as an equal, explaining in all deadly seriousness the purpose and importance of this room. He remembered lying awake that night, thinking that, had the circumstances and timing been wrong, his actions might have cost the life of his father. Not only did he immediately stop hacking the security areas of the House computer net, but he had not set foot in the room since.

"Can you access the House system through your integrator, Sire?" Fleming's voice was a continual, rattling wheeze as he tried desperately to catch his breath. Although they had been here for several minutes, his face was still beet red from the exertion of their flight from the study. He wiped ineffectually at his sweaty neck and face with a handkerchief. "Try it."

It hadn't occurred to Eric that the integrator might have been affected by the security breach as well. He concentrated, and was relieved to find that his integrator was working perfectly. It returned him little useful information, however, other than confirming what they already knew: The shield dome had been breached in some unknown way, the attempt to erect the secondary shielding had failed for some unknown reason, a shuttlecraft of unknown purpose and origin had touched down on the estate's front landing pad. Nothing more.

A silent command brought the holoframe in the corner of the room to life, and the image of the Imperial Guard commander appeared. The man had his back to the lens when it activated, but he whipped instantly around and regarded the Emperor the moment he heard the connection go through on his end. The name YEANY was stenciled above the breast pocket of his flak suit.

"Sire!" He nodded curtly in way of greeting.

"What's happening out there with the intruder, Colonel?"

The man started to reply, his mouth working soundlessly. "Nothing!" he finally managed to say, shaking his head in disbelief. "Nothing at all, Sire. It's just . . . well, it's just sitting there. I—"

Yeany was abruptly interrupted as a full squad of guards—undoubtedly just roused from their bunks at the alarm—trotted into the image for his orders. He ignored the Emperor for a moment and turned to send them in groups of four to different areas of the estate grounds, then turned back to the lens and continued as if the interference had never occurred. "I've set up a defensive perimeter around the vehicle itself, and have brought

House guns to bear on its engine housing. But, Sire . . ." He trailed off, uncertain how to continue his report.

"Yes, Colonel? What is it?"

"Well, Sire. Our scans show there is no weaponry of any kind on the vehicle. No shielding is in place, and the scans show that power levels for the vehicle's shield generator are not even on standby."

"And the occupants?"

"This class of vehicle has facilities for ten passengers. We've pinpointed a total of only five heat sources on board, however, two of which have to be flight crew."

"I see. Keep me informed." Eric blanked the screen. "I don't understand any of this," he said angrily, turning to Fleming.

Before the Master could respond, however, the holoframe glowed again, displaying the flight deck of the mysterious shuttle-craft. There was, as Colonel Yeany had predicted, a two-person flight crew. Both women busied themselves, if Eric's guess was correct, with resetting the shuttle power sequence for emergency liftoff and ignored him entirely, if they even saw him. The image then pulled back to reveal a demure, if conservatively dressed, Rihana Valtane seated behind the flight crew in a plush chair that only she could have designed. She smiled when she noted the look of recognition on his face.

"I don't believe it," Eric spat, approaching the holoframe for a better look. "Master Fleming, did I ever tell you about the time my bastard brother tried to kill me?"

Fleming was as much confused by the question as he was by the sudden appearance of the woman in the holoframe. "I have heard the tale, Sire," he said, still wiping at his brow. "As I understand it, Emperor Javas' eldest son attempted—"

"This woman raised an assassin of my own blood," he said, cutting off the hapless servant, "who tried to kill both my father and me, and then claim the throne for himself so that *she* might rule through him." He crossed his arms in front of him and reveled in the feeling of pure loathing that swept through him at this, the first face-to-face meeting with his father's former wife. After the disappointments he had experienced in the last twenty-four hours, this raw, primitive emotion felt refreshingly good.

"What the hell do you want, Rihana?"

He had seen and heard enough recordings of this woman to know what she was like and, as such, he was taken completely by surprise when she answered.

250 Ben Bova and A. J. Austin

"Hello, Eric," she said. Instead of the haughty tone he expected, her voice was straightforward, unpretentious. "I apologize for the dramatic entrance, but I did not wish to waste the time it would have taken to go through the proper channels. I doubt very much you would ever have agreed to talk to me anyway."

Eric snorted, turning back to take a chair facing the holoframe. Fleming remained silent, but out of the corner of his eye Eric could see that the agitated man continued to dab at his neck and forehead with the sodden handkerchief. "And what makes you think we have anything to discuss now?" he asked brusquely. "I can't imagine how you linked into the House comm net, but I can just as easily shut it down."

"If you would like to know," she offered, "I have had the ability to breach Woodsgate security for years. At great personal expense, I purchased the access codes for the shield control, both primary and secondary, years ago; but understand that I never bothered to use them. Until now. As to the House comm net . . . you gave me access to it yourself when you activated it through your integrator a few minutes ago, when you contacted your guard commander." She smiled again, this time allowing a hint of arrogant pride to show through at her abilities. "So shut it down if you like. But I'll only reactivate it again, and I'll keep reactivating it until you either talk to me or open fire on me." Rihana paused, a tilt of her head sending her copper hair tumbling over one shoulder. "You can always do the latter in any event, so why not at least hear what I have to say first?"

Eric stared back at her, playing a fingertip along his lower lip. He said nothing for a full minute, then turned abruptly to Fleming. "Open the room."

"But Sire!"

Eric was on his feet, a moment's concentration through the integrator sending a House-wide command to disable all security measures between the shelter and the main level. The seal on the vaultlike door on the far side of the room popped open with a soft hiss.

"I'll see you in five minutes," he snapped at Rihana, "on the lawn. I won't have the likes of you setting foot inside this house."

Not bothering to blank the screen, he strode to the heavy door and pulled it aside, exiting the room with Fleming at his heel. The rotund man talked to himself worriedly and wrung his hands as he tried to keep up with Eric's quickening pace.

The surprised guards fell back at the sight of the Emperor the moment he swept through the parting lift doors. They milled about, weapons hanging loosely at their sides as they tried to figure out what to do. Several called aloud for their commander, unsure even whether to stay at their posts or follow Eric as he stomped down the corridor to the main foyer. Colonel Yeany, alerted by one of the guards at the lift, met him in the foyer.

"Sire!" He made an ill-conceived attempt to block Eric's path, but thought better of it and stepped out of the way at the last moment. "I can't allow you to endanger yourself in this way."

Eric stopped at the main door, leaning against it with both hands as he caught his breath. Standing there, his arms outspread, he felt his sweaty palms slide as he pressed against the centuries-old oak. His heart beat as though he had just run a kilometer. Not bothering to turn back to look at Colonel Yeany, he said evenly, "I want every weapon trained on her. If she moves, kill her. If I call out in alarm, kill her." He did turn then, his back pressed for support against the solid bulk of the massive double doors, and lowered his gaze to stare at the Guard commander. "If nothing at all happens, and I merely turn around and ask it . . . kill her."

Yeany nodded, swallowing audibly.

Eric tugged at the doors, flinging them inward to bang loudly against the side walls of the foyer, and walked out onto the ornate steps leading to the front lawn of Woodsgate. He stood there a moment, allowing the cool night breeze to play over him, then wasted no further time in descending the staircase and walking out onto the glistening, dew soaked lawn illuminated as bright as day from a hundred floodlights directed at Rihana's shuttle. He crossed the distance to the shuttle in but a few seconds, and stood waiting at the side hatch.

There was a popping depressurization as the hatch opened, the sudden movement bringing to Eric's ears the sound of countless weapons being armed and pointed at the shuttle entrance. The door fell down smoothly to become a short set of steps extending to the ground. Rihana was waiting in the opening and stepped down the ramp the moment the hatch touched the dew-laden grass.

"Five minutes," he said.

She nodded. "I'll make it worth your while," she replied, and as she did two more figures appeared behind her in the shuttle's entrance hatch. One was human; the other, wearing a shiny, protective E-suit and bubble helmet, was Sarpan. "And as a show of good faith, I've brought along some friends of yours."

"Temple?" Eric managed to say. "Is it you?"

"Yeah, it's me. Hello, Eric." He smiled broadly, and started down the ramp, helping Oidar negotiate the narrow steps. "Can we get him into the House? It's been a long ride."

Eric waved behind him, but Master Fleming had already ordered several of the guards in his direction to give the two newcomers an escort inside.

Eric watched them in silence as they helped Oidar up the steps to the main entrance, then turned back to Rihana.

"Now that that's been taken care of," she said, her trademark arrogant smile back in place, "would you like to know who Jephthah is?"

The Emperor of the Hundred Worlds was nervous, for the first time in his life since accepting the office on the death of his father. He sat rigidly in his chair and straightened the Imperial sash across the front of his full dress uniform, and wondered how Javas would have handled what he was about to do. For that matter, would his father—an Emperor in a different time, with different expectations of himself—have even considered the actions he was about to take?

There was only one other person in the room with him, and at this moment he would have wanted no other. Master Fleming stood off to one side of the study, well out of range of the pickup lens.

He carefully reviewed in his mind what he wanted to say. The time had come to set the record straight regarding the so-called mutiny at the sunstation on Mercury, as well as to clear Templeton Rice's good name. Now that he and Oidar were on board a starship, headed toward a rendezvous with the Sarpan flagship as his personal emissaries of goodwill to the Guardian of the Waters, perhaps at least some of the anti-Sarpan sentiment could be allayed. And with the information provided by Rihana, he would announce that an Empire-wide warrant had been issued for the man Rapson, although he also planned to admit the truth—that the chances of finding Rapson anywhere but at Tsing appeared remote. All this, and more, he would tell in this address.

"Ready." The softly feminine voice of the House system informed him that the recording was set. Through the integrator, he activated the sequence.

"Citizens of the Hundred Worlds," he began. "I have news

both grave, and hopeful." He looked into the lens, his eyes never blinking.

"But first, I wish to announce that I have decided to go to Tsing 479."

TWENTY-SIX
Fissure

The landing craft touched down gently, Gareth Anmoore's steady hands on the controls.

"Stay strapped in for a minute," he called back from the flight deck on the other side of the bulkhead from the passenger cabin. His voice was tinny over the intercom speakers set into the ceiling.

"There's even more fissuring on the surface than we thought, and I want to be sure our footing is secure before I initiate shutdown."

The so-called hopper shuttle they had used for the trip down from the survey ship was one of the most basic means of short-range transport, and Adela marveled that even after two centuries, the hoppers had changed little. Although this particular craft was a "working craft" as opposed to one dedicated to tourist transport, the passenger cabin was both spacious and comfortably appointed with everything from a self-contained entertainment system to a small galley. Two rows of plush seats ran the length of the forward portion of the cabin, five in each row. Each seat featured a viewport flatscreen that simulated a window, as well as a program screen recessed into the back of the seat in front of it. The only thing that set this hopper apart from strictly passenger craft were the equipment lockers behind them, also arranged in an orderly row down each side of the cabin.

"Not bad," he said over the descending whine of the engines as they shut down. *"Not bad at all."*

"Yeah," Secchi countered jokingly to Adela over his shoulder, leaning across the surprisingly wide aisle. "Not bad for an old guy who hasn't actually flown in years."

"I heard that, Vito. . . ." The door to the flight deck opened,

admitting Anmoore into the passenger section. Behind him, through the opened door, Adela could see the copilot going through standard postflight routines. "You feel like walking home?"

"Oops! Didn't know this thing was in two-way." Vito rapped on the flatscreen with his knuckles and laughed, the pleasant sound almost a giggle. The man was so excited about this trip that his good humor had been irrepressible. "Sorry, boss."

The cabin broke into laughter and good-natured ribbing at Vito's expense, with everyone joining in except Hannah Cee. The xenoguide, occupying the seat in front of her, did not like to fly, and looked positively green. Vito reached into a shirt pocket and produced a small vial of pills, handing them to her. "You left these in the ready room upstairs before you got inside," he said under his breath. "I saw them sitting there and thought you might need them." She accepted them and smiled a silent thank-you, and he turned back to the merriment as everyone unstrapped, stood, and stretched. Hannah downed a couple of the pills, then, noticing that Towsen, the academician/geologist Brendan had brought along, looked as bad as she felt, offered the vial to him.

"The more time I spend around these people from the survey ship," Adela said to Brendan across the aisle as she unstrapped herself, "the more I find myself liking them."

"They're hard workers," Brendan agreed, fumbling with his own belt. "They not only seem to take genuine pleasure in what they do, but they really care about each other and enjoy each other's company. That's rare." He finally managed to unclick the catch on his restraining strap, and nodded in Anmoore's direction as he added, "He's a good man, and a good leader to inspire such a combination in those under his command."

"All right, people, listen up." At Anmoore's words, the laughter died away and all gave him full attention. The cabin now quiet, Adela could hear a metallic thrumming: From what she had been told, the sound would be that of the hover platform being lowered to the surface beneath the hopper.

"As far as the actual exploration of the fissure is concerned, Hannah's in charge; what she says goes. For anything involving safety, Mike and Waltz are in charge and what *they* say goes. Got it?" There were sounds of assent all around, and he nodded at the two security people. "You two want to go ahead and get everything unlocked and do an initial check of the suits? Thanks."

Kent Waltz and Michaela Cannin, or "Mike" as everyone

seemed to call her, headed immediately down the aisle, opening each of the equipment lockers as they moved aft.

"No one leaves the platform without Hannah's permission. In fact, I want all of you to try to stay on the platform unless you have to go on foot. But if Hannah says it's all right, you travel in the following order: Hannah and Mike will take the lead, followed by Vito, Dr. Montgarde, Academician Wood and Academician Towsen. Then Lan in the worksuit, and Waltz bringing up the rear." He lifted his chin, trying to see Waltz as he dug noisily into the interior of one of the lockers. "You hear that, Waltz?"

"Waltz brings up the rear." The security man's voice echoed hollowly in the locker.

Anmoore walked down the aisle and sat on the armrest of one of the middle seats as he addressed Brendan, Towsen and Adela. "These hard suits are pretty standard, and aren't much different from anything else you've used, but watch it out there. The suits are heavy, but remember that even with the extra weight you've still got only point-two *g* out there, so be extremely careful about jumping and bouncing around if you do go any distance on foot. I've seen more than my share of people take a jump and turn over in 'midair,' only to land on their head or back. Try it and you'll find out why they call these 'hard' suits. You'll have bruises for a week—if you don't break something." He looked from side to side at the others. "And the rest of you—no showing off," he said soberly. None of them laughed; the time for joking around would come later.

"Anyway, if you should fall don't worry about it. The suits have a skin-shield emergency system, so even if the suit does breach you should be in good shape. Even if you do lose your balance, just make yourself comfortable on the ground until Mike or Waltz can check out your suit and help you back up. Don't even bother trying to stand up on your own." He looked around at the six of them, then at the two by the lockers. "Any questions? Good, let's get going."

Moving to the aft section of the cabin, the eight of them slipped into the EVA undersuits from the lockers, with Waltz and Mike checking them all—and each other—for proper electrical connections and hose placement. They then grabbed what other gear they would need and descended a narrow ladder into the suit room in the lower level.

There were ten hard suits here, all mounted front-to-back along each side of the lower chamber in a way that reminded

Adela and Brendan of the ancient metal armor that lined the Grand Hall back at Woodsgate. But where the old battle regalia on Earth carried with it a sense of foreboding and lethality, these looked more like a double line of comically parading snowmen, a perception enhanced by their shiny white plastic coating. The only color adorning the suits, in fact, was a series of painted rings around the knee and elbow joints of each one—red striping on the left arm and leg, and corresponding green rings on the right. Each featured pin-spotlights mounted on either side of the helmets, and yellow lenses studding the perimeter of the upper and lower sections of the suits to make everyone in the party easier to spot from any direction in dim lighting conditions. Save for hookups for the snap-on life-support packs on the rear torso, and emergency air and power input jacks on the front, all but one of the suits were otherwise identically smooth and unadorned.

The oddball suit was mounted in front of the others and must have been the "worksuit" Anmoore had said Lan Heathseven would use. On inspection, Adela assumed it must have been the one he always used, because unlike the other suits with their tape-strip name tags, his was the only one with his name permanently stenciled on the plastic in large, black letters. Also, where the regular suits got their snowman look from a system of interconnecting spheres that made up the helmet, upper torso, lower waist, and arm and leg sections, the helmet and torso of his suit were a single ovoid that made it look like a walking egg as much as anything else.

Despite the whimsical appearance, it was easy to see why it had been called the worksuit: All manner of tools and implements were set into recessed niches across the front and sides of the torso, as well as on the upper thighs; he might *look* like a walking egg in the suit, but Heathseven would function as a walking toolbox. And, according to what the vac tech had told her on the trip down, it was filled with electronics designed for everything from diagnostics to field measurements. Even the segmented sleeves of the suit were bulkier, allowing him to withdraw his arms into the torso itself to operate the instrumentation located there. Fortunately, Heathseven was not a large man; all the equipment in the suit didn't leave much room for the occupant.

The five members of the group from the *Paloma Blanca*, familiar with procedure and apparently used to having a "regular" place in the suit lineup, went directly to their own gear as they chattered among themselves. Adela, Brendan and Towsen, meanwhile, were forced to look for the hastily applied name tags that had been affixed to the front and back of the hard-suit helmets to identify the ones that had been sized and selected for them back up on the survey ship.

"Everybody in," Anmoore said, starting an odd display of strenuous climbing, grunting, and stretching as eight people donned the surface gear. Just before pulling the upper portion of the suits down over them, Adela saw Mike and Lan steal a quick kiss.

With everyone helping each other, getting into the protective gear took the better part of ninety minutes, even with the added assistance of the captain and the copilot. At last, however, the eight of them stood in a semicircle and allowed Anmoore to conduct a final check of the hard suits and the suit-to-suit and suit-to-ship comm links. That done, the pair scrambled back up the ladder and sealed the upper level, preparing the suit room for pressure purge.

Adela watched and familiarized herself with the readings of the heads-up display in the lower front of the helmet—matching the readings with those appearing on the display screen near the hatch—as the atmosphere was pumped out of the room.

While they waited for the room to cycle, she noted that unless their name tags were visible or the angle was right to see through the helmet visors, it was going to be difficult to recognize anyone but Heathseven once outside, so she made a point of studying what little telltale differences she could find among them. Heathseven was obvious. Secchi's bright orange gear bag looped around the waist of his suit made him stand out, as did similar equipment pouches carried by the others. There was a long, dull scratch on the torso of Brendan's suit. Towsen carried nothing that would distinguish him from the others, but that in itself made him stand out, she realized, just as the depressurization procedure completed and the hatch fell gracefully, noiselessly open.

"Let's go," called Hannah's voice from inside her helmet. "I'll meet you under the nose. Watch your step, please." With that, she loped easily to retrieve the hover platform from its position beneath the hopper itself.

They filed out onto the surface, some of them gripping the equipment pouches around their waists to keep the contents from bouncing, and carefully maneuvered to the front of the hopper. Anmoore had been right, Adela noted, in his warning on the difficulties of walking. While the others strode easily under the low-gravity conditions, she, Brendan and Towsen were forced to

steady each other as they got used to it. With each step, there was
a subdued *vrrrrr-click!* audible throughout the suit from the
servo-assist motors located in each of the suit joints. After a few
minutes, however, she grew so accustomed to the subtle noise
that it became unnoticeable.

It was beautiful here. She had never, in the whole time she lived
on Luna, gone out onto the surface in anything other than a
pressurized vehicle. And while she had worn EVA suits before, it
had always been only for precaution on a ship, not for surface
excursions like this one. Gazing out across the crater, she could
see the deep, airless shadows that stretched out from every rock,
every rise on the crater floor. Tsing was low in the sky, and the
long shadows were so thick as to be impenetrable. There were
thousands upon thousands of smaller impact craters everywhere,
and as she examined the powdery regolith at her feet, she could
even spot some tiny pockmarks only centimeters in diameter.

As the *Paloma Blanca* regulars spoke among themselves, she
pressed the comm bar with her chin to put the open channel on
standby and switched to a secondary channel, then held up three
fingers to her companions and waited for them to chin their own
comms to the proper frequency. "Is that the fissure over there?"
she asked, pointing to a dark, angular blotch barely visible inside
one of the deep shadows lining the rim wall. "I can't tell for sure."

"That's it," Brendan assured her. "It's closer than it looks, too.
The brightness, all the shadows—it's throwing my depth perception off."

"I can't believe this," she breathed, hearing the awe in her own
voice. "I never thought it could be this strikingly beautiful."

"Me, too." The voice was Towsen's, and carried with it the
same sense of wonder she felt. He waved and signaled that he was
switching back to the open channel, then moved slowly off to one
side to examine an odd arrangement of jagged talus, gingerly
placing one foot in front of the other as he bounced toward the
pile of rocks.

"I went outside once, back on Luna," Brendan reminisced.
"Father took us on one of those rare outings—the kind where
everything is so perfect that you always wish it could last forever." His pleasant chuckle at the memory buzzed in the helmet
speaker. "Of course, when you're a child you always wish that
just about everything can last forever."

"I remember the same kinds of outings with my father," Adela
said, recalling a similar experience. "On Gris."

"Anyway, it was just the four of us. I was, let's see . . . I was ten; that would have made Lewis fourteen and Cathay six. The whole thing was a birthday surprise for me—I had begged for years to be taken out onto the surface and he finally relented. Cathay was thrilled, and as I recall Lewis put on a show of complaining the whole time because he was missing out on something his Academy friends were doing. He never fooled Father, though; he was just as glad to spend time with him, away from Woodsgate and the day-to-day affairs of the Court."

"It sounds lovely, Brendan. I wish I could have been there."

He sighed. "But then it was back to being the Emperor. And while we saw Father regularly, it was more than three years before all four of us did something together again. Oh, well." Adela couldn't tell for sure, but somehow she felt he had just shrugged inside the hard suit.

"Sorry to break in, Academician," said Towsen apologetically. He must have heard the last of what Brendan had said, but if he had intruded on the private moment, he didn't let on. "They want us all back on the open channel."

"Pay attention, down there," Anmoore called from the flight deck above them. He waved once, then pointed to where Hannah was smoothly bringing the platform around, settling it effortlessly to the ground. The hexagonal platform had a low railing that ran all the way around it save for an opening just large enough for them all to climb aboard. Once they stood together on the platform, Anmoore admonished, "Three hours, that's all I'm allowing for this first trip. Ninety minutes in, and ninety minutes out. I'm setting the time . . . now. Check your heads-up."

Adela and Brendan glanced down inside their helmets, confirming that a countdown timer had started, the softly glowing numerals ticking down the remaining time.

"Good luck, everyone."

Hannah powered up the platform and they moved freely away from the hopper, the silhouettes of Anmoore and the copilot still on the flight deck diminishing rapidly as they increased their distance.

As they entered the gaping fissure, Hannah slowed the platform and turned on the floodlights mounted on the underside, orienting them in such a way as to sweep the steady beams around the opening. There was still a good bit of natural sunshine from outside, but the bare rock face was dark, nonreflective—darker, in fact, than the rock on Luna—and seemed to drink in the light as she played the beams around. One by one they each turned on their helmet pin-spots to better cut through the gloom, careful not to turn around into each other's faces and inadvertently blind one another. Heathseven, meanwhile, had a combination spotlight/video pickup mounted at the top of his helmet, and activated both, although any hope of getting decent images in the heavy gloom seemed unlikely.

"Mr. Secchi?" the xenoguide asked, bringing them in closer.

The geologist reached into his bag and produced a hand scanner. He pointed it at the rock, and then down into the blackness ahead. "There's no metal here, but the readings from inside remain steady. They match what we got from the probe, all right." Vito scrutinized the bare stone with a geologist's eye. "It looks okay to me, but I'll have a better idea once we're in a few meters." The platform eased forward into the fissure while Vito looked carefully around, examining everything he saw. "All right, hold it here." The platform slowed to a stop and hovered roughly twenty meters into the crack. After several minutes, Vito said, "It's solid; there hasn't been any breakdown action in here for centuries. I say go."

"Captain Anmoore," Hannah said, "we are going to proceed on in now."

There was a soft click as he manually keyed his microphone back on the shuttle. As he did, she heard the background noise of the copilot moving around, as well as some nondescript music. "Fine. I'll be listening." He clicked off and the open channel was silent again but for the soft breathing of the others.

The platform sailed smoothly, evenly into the tunnel, and the last bit of light from the opening disappeared. There was little discussion as they moved along, just the infrequent remark from Vito concerning the readings he was getting, or an occasional exclamation directing their attention to one rock formation or another.

The fissure continued in a nearly straight line, tall and narrow, and rose to a pointed, cathedral-like joint that ran the length of the tunnel like a backbone. The floor below them—when they could see it—was littered with thousands of tons of sharp, jagged breakdown. As she gazed at the passing jumble below her, Adela speculated idly if the platform had been fully charged before being loaded underneath the hopper.

"Look there." They followed Waltz's outstretched arm and could see a thin shaft of sunlight coming from above at a point where the fissure did not quite meet at the top.

"I'll bet that's where I picked up those initial anomalous readings in the first orbital scans," Vito offered. "There should be a couple spots along here where the scans got through."

A half hour passed—the moment duly noted by Captain Anmoore back on the shuttle when he called their attention to the time and reminded them of their deadline—and there had been little change in the fissure. They seemed to have angled down in their forward motion a bit, taking them farther away from the surface; and from time to time the width of the fissure grew broader in some spots and more narrow in others. Towsen was the first to notice that the deeper they went, the less breakdown there appeared to be below them. At the same time the fissure became considerably wider and more rounded at the top, and started to look less like a crack, and more like a tunnel or cave.

"Slow down a minute," Vito said unexpectedly. "I'm getting confused here."

Hannah brought the platform to a stop, and Towsen glanced over the geologist's shoulder at the readout on the hand scanner. The readings showed nothing at all ahead except the ever-present rock. "The metal's gone. What happened to it?"

Vito cursed under his breath and handed the scanner over to Towsen, then pulled another instrument from his bag. Although slightly larger than the other, it looked otherwise identical. It, too, showed that the readings had vanished.

"What the hell—?" He looked frantically around at the tunnel, trying to find some clue as to why the readings had stopped. Gripping the platform railing with his free hand, he leaned over as far as he dared. "I can't see anything at all down there."

There was a soft click, accompanied again by the faint strains of music as Anmoore started to say something on the suit-to-ship link, but he thought better of it and clicked out again.

Hannah turned away from the controls momentarily. "Can you give us some more light?"

"Watch your eyes, everyone." Mike pulled a magnaflare from her pouch, looped it into a length of cord and snapped it to life, then slung it over the side to let it dangle a few meters below the platform. Waltz did the same with a second flare, and then again with a third. The tunnel became bathed in light.

Although there were no unusual features to be seen, they now had their first good look at their location.

As they had suspected, the structure of the fissure had changed radically. Instead of the craggy, irregular rock surface, the nearly vertical sides tapering to narrowness at top and bottom, the tunnel was now smooth and fairly oval in shape, wider from side to side than from ceiling to floor. And therein lay the biggest surprise: Until now the bottom of the fissure had been a break-down-filled crack that was, reasonably, tapered in much the same manner as the ceiling had been. But it was clear that the area below them, and as far as they could see along the length of the tunnel ahead and behind them, was flat and nearly level. The platform hovered motionless at a point roughly thirty meters from the ceiling; the floor was about a hundred meters below.

Although no one said it out loud—verbal confirmation would have been unnecessary—it was now obvious that the tunnel, or at least this portion of it, had been hollowed out of the rock artificially.

"I am going to set the platform down," Hannah announced. "Please grip the handrail."

They lowered smoothly, but at a point about halfway down Towsen and the geologist became simultaneously excited.

"Hold it here!" he shouted to Hannah. "It's back!" Vito compared his reading with that on Towsen's unit, and sure enough, both once more detected the enormous mass of metal that was their goal. "I don't get this at all. What was blocking it?"

At Vito's request, she experimentally maneuvered the platform higher, whereupon the readings once again disappeared. They tried a side-to-side motion at their present height, then again at varying distances from the floor, and found that nothing could be read in an area extending sixty meters down from the ceiling, and from wall to wall.

"Maybe the scan signal is deflecting somewhere up ahead," Brendan suggested as the platform resumed settling to the bottom of the tunnel, "in such a way as to block the scanner from certain angles? The ceiling *is* a lot higher off the floor here. . . ." He stared upward, adding, "Or maybe there's an ore pocket or something up there the scanner can't read through?"

The xenoguide held the platform a meter off the bottom and waited for the two security people to retrieve the magnaflares before she allowed it to thud silently to the floor. The two pulled small, funnel-shaped collars from their pouches and snapped them to the flares, turning them into effective spotlights, and pointed them above their heads.

"No, I don't think it's an ore pocket." Vito extended the scanner ceilingward, with Towsen doing likewise with the other unit. "No, that's not it."

"But wait a minute," Adela interjected. "You said yesterday, when most of us were still at South Camp, that this metal deposit—whatever it is—was shielded, maybe even deliberately. Could we be at the edge of the shielding?"

They looked at each other, then up again at the ceiling. As before, there was nothing to see.

Vito moved toward the opening in the railing, ready to hop off the platform.

"Wait." Hannah's command, her tone firm, stopped him before he could move through the opening. She motioned to Mike to follow her and the two stepped down to the tunnel floor. "It is quite solid," she reported after a brief examination.

"But soft," Mike added. "Feels almost like a layer of sand beneath my boots." She dug into her pouch, but could not find what she wanted, and turned to Heathseven. "Lan, throw me a stick or something."

The vac tech unclipped a short rod from the side of his leg; there was a grip on one end, a small hook on the other. "Catch," he said, tossing it her way.

She easily snagged it as it tumbled in a slow-motion arc in the low gravity, then pulled at the ends, showing it to be a telescoping tool of some kind. She kicked at a portion of the soft floor, then dug deeper with the tool, scraping solid rock several centimeters below the sandy covering.

"All right," Hannah declared finally. "You may come on down, one at a time. But stay close together."

Once on the floor they noticed almost immediately that it sloped at a gentle angle, downward, back in the direction from which they had come.

Click. "That's one hour, everybody. Thirty more minutes and you're at the halfway mark and time to head back. Not a minute more. Be careful." *Click.*

"Mike? Waltz?" Vito called from the far wall several meters farther down the tunnel where the platform had settled. "Can you bring those spotlights over? Bring the camera, too, Lan." He stood leaning close against the rock wall, his back to them. "The rest of you might want to see this, too."

They strode over to him, the hand-carried lights sending dizzy, dancing snowman shadows everywhere.

"Look here," he said, once they were gathered at the spot. He traced a gloved finger along what looked like a scratch in the rock face. The scratch was perfectly straight and ran from the sandy floor up along the curved face toward the ceiling. It probably went all the way over the top, although it grew too difficult to see.

"Can one of you take a light and trot over to the other side, then see if there's a similar mark, directly across from this one?"

"Got it." Mike took her light and bounded gracefully across the floor, calling back over her shoulder once she reached the opposite wall, "Yeah, there's one over here, too, going straight up just like that one. I can't see how high up it goes, though."

"Shield lines?" Adela asked.

"That's my guess." Vito stepped away from the wall, tilted back as best he could in the restricting suit, and stared up. "It's up there, all right. Good thing we stopped when we did—another fifteen or twenty meters and we would have smacked right into it."

"Not that we were going that fast . . ." Mike offered, rejoining the group.

"You people are starting to break up a little bit." Anmoore's voice, scratchy and static-laden, buzzed in their helmets. Adela noted that they had turned the music off. "Can you move back to the platform?" They turned, as a group, back down the tunnel. Before following, Waltz knelt down carefully and embedded the end of the spotlight flare into the sandy floor in such a way that the light shined upward along the curving wall.

"You've got any theories, Vito, I'd like to hear them."

"It's the impact craters, Gareth, out there where you are. There was a series of impacts a long time ago, big ones, that cracked the surface badly enough in some places to be seen from orbit, as well as creating the fissure we followed in to get here. I'm pretty sure this tunnel we're in now was already here when it happened." He paused. "Glad I wasn't. When those things hit they raised the terrain up, then dropped it again. That's why this whole thing is at an angle—I'm betting this tunnel used to be level."

"And the lines on the wall . . .?" Adela looked back at the spotlight tracing its beam upward. "That's where the shielding originally was, right?"

"I think so." The geologist looked around again at the tunnel. "I think this area used to be—" He turned to Towsen. "What do you think, Academician? Forty, maybe fifty meters higher when it was originally cut out of this rock?"

"He might be right, Captain. Whatever is generating the shield is still farther up ahead, but the tunnel is sloping upward. The generator may be near or even at its original position, forming the shield in the original place . . . up there." He pointed at the ceiling. "In spite of where the tunnel now is."

"How much time would it take to find the source?"

No one knew what to estimate. Finally, Hannah spoke. "It will take longer than before. I do not think it is a good idea to use the platform, not after we almost ran into that shielding up there. We will need more time, Captain."

"All right, then, but do it on foot. Don't fly the platform past the shield line. I'll give you all an additional half hour." A blinking from the heads-up display caught Adela's attention, and she saw that the countdown timer had jumped back by thirty minutes. "I noticed you were starting to fade out a bit when you were on the other side of the shield line. I want a couple of you to stay at the platform; you'll be closer to those who go in and can relay what's happening back to me."

A few minutes later, with Waltz and Towsen staying behind at the platform, Adela and the others moved up the gradual incline toward what they hoped would be the source of the shield, as well as the metal readings that had precipitated this expedition.

"Captain said he's already lost you," Waltz reported when they had gone about a hundred meters. "You getting me all right?"

"You're coming in fine, Kent." Mike turned back, staring down the sloped floor of the tunnel, but could not see the two men or the platform lights. "Let us know if we start fading out on you, too."

"Will do, but your signal's nice and strong."

As they went on, it became apparent that the angle of the floor was getting steeper. Adela checked the countdown timer, noting that if they didn't find something in the next fifteen minutes they'd have to turn back. Maybe they could push it, though, since it would be easier, faster going back downhill to the platform.

"Look there."

Everyone swung their lights in the direction Hannah had indicated, the beams falling on more breakdown, filling a series of faults running across their path. They spread out, examining the obstruction, and could see that the cracked and broken stone ran up the side walls, as well, and across the ceiling where vertical fissures extended beyond the reach of their lights. On the other side of the breakdown, however, the lights revealed that not only did the tunnel become perfectly level again, but that it also appeared to widen considerably. They played their lights over the pile, looking for a way across.

"This is where a fault line ran through," Vito said. "Everything this side of the fault line was lifted up and then slammed down hard after the meteorite impact, tearing everything up and lowering the level of the tunnel. That side over there was probably shaken up a good bit, but it stayed where it was."

"Over here! I found an opening."

They followed the beam of Mike's spotlight and saw that, yes, there was a fairly level, clear pathway through the rubble. She stood aside as Hannah went through.

"Wait here. I will tell you when to follow." The footing was loose, uneven, and she was forced to take her time, but she emerged on the other side with slightly more than ten minutes left before they had to return to the platform.

"Come through slowly," Hannah called back, a slight edge to her voice. "When you are through, move quickly to allow the next person room to get clear of the rocks, but do not proceed further."

"What is it?" Adela asked. "What do you see?"

"We have but nine minutes remaining now, Doctor; do not waste time."

They came through one at a time, and as each emerged, there was soft gasp or comment made to the others already through. Bringing up the rear, Lan Heathseven was nearly ready to burst with anticipation.

What they saw there when they were all through the breakdown had more than made the trip worthwhile. There, in the center of a huge circular cavern cut from the solid rock, was an enormous, round structure, low and roughly cylindrical like a fuel storage tank, only much, much larger. It did not appear to be a spacecraft, or even movable as some of them had speculated on the ride here from the *Paloma Blanca,* but from here no one could tell for certain. There was a circular door or gate in the side of it, near the floor of the cavern, that appeared closed or sealed, and randomly placed around the perimeter of the thing was a series of dark depressions, almost like funneled openings that seemed to lead into the interior. The surface of the thing reflected an unmistakable metallic silver-gray in the beams of their lights.

"I *knew* it!" Vito shouted gleefully. "I knew the metal at South Camp came from here. Hannah! Can we go closer, or at least close enough for Lan to get some good video?"

She thought a moment, shooting a glance at the countdown timer in her helmet display. "All right, but Mike and Lan only; everyone else is to stay here."

"Hannah!"

She started to protest, but then relented. "All right, but get on with it; we have only five minutes and then back we go."

Mike pulled out another magnaflare and snapped it to life, wrapped a reflective collar around it to make a spotlight as she had with the others and passed it over to Vito. The glare shone momentarily through his visor, and Adela saw him squinting and grinning like a boy.

"Hey, in there," Waltz called from back at the platform. "You want to let us in on what you found?"

"We'll let you know when we figure it out," Vito chortled, then he and Mike approached it slowly, holding the spotlights out ahead of them, while Lan walked a few meters to their right to get a clear shot of it with his helmet camera.

There was a sudden sparking at the ankle joint of Mike's left leg, and a scream of pain vibrated through the tiny helmet speakers.

"What happened?" Adela started to move forward, but Hannah stepped in front of her.

"Mike! Come back now, all of you!" she bellowed, then turned to her and Brendan. "The rest of you, back through the rocks!"

Adela wanted to turn and go, but she felt frozen where she stood.

Mike tried to spin around toward them, but she lost her balance and stumbled to her knees, her forward momentum carrying her another half meter closer to the structure. As she fell, the servo motors in both shoulders exploded, followed by the units in each of her elbows. She pitched forward in dreadful slow motion and hit the ground, the force of the impact sending a severed arm spinning toward Vito and Heathseven, blood splattering across the chest and visor of their suits. She lay there, then, silent and unmoving. No sound at all came from her helmet pickup.

"Mike!" Vito dropped his spotlight and started moving to his left.

Hannah shoved at Brendan, trying to get him into the breakdown. "Stop! Don't go near her!"

"What's happening in there? Hannah?" Waltz paused, then, "We're coming in!"

"No! Stay there!"

Vito made it to Mike's side in two bounds, but as he leaned down to her body his right shoulder exploded, followed by his left, sending him tumbling to the ground, where his spinning body blew apart at the knees, hips and ankles.

Adela pushed Hannah aside and tried to run to them, but in the

unaccustomed gravity she lost her balance in the first few steps
and fell to the ground far short of the two bodies.

"Grandmother!" Brendan got to her at once, grabbing her
solidly by the arm to help her up and, at the same time, prevent
her from running into whatever it was that had just killed the
others.

Heathseven stood there dumbly, helmet camera pointing at the
mangled bodies, unable to move either forward or back. "Mike?"
The single word was a paragraph. In her helmet speaker, Adela
thought she could hear the man sobbing.

At that moment, from a point somewhere atop the structure,
a bright light glowed that illuminated the cavern as brightly as the
Sun.

TWENTY-SEVEN
Contact

There was no apparent source of the light, just a steady,
bright radiance emanating from the top of the cylinder
that, considering they had just spent the last two hours in
darkness, was almost blinding in its intensity.

Nothing moved. There was no sign that they had been attacked.

"What's happening in there!"

"Waltz! You're not helping; stay off the open channel!" Hannah took a few steps closer, stopping about three meters from the
grisly sight of her two friends. Like Adela, she could plainly hear
the sobbing on the open channel. "Lan? Are you all right? Are
you injured in any way?"

"Wha—what?" The hard suit did not move, but the cavern was
so bright now that they could easily see his features as he turned
to the xenoguide. His face was pale, and tears welled up in eyes
that were round and unblinking from shock.

Adela took a step toward him, Brendan still at her side. "Lan,
are you hurt?"

"Hurt . . .?" His brow furrowed in confusion as he concentrated on the question, and he sniffed loudly. "Uh, no. No, I
don't think so."

"Listen to me carefully, Lan," Hannah said softly. "Do not move any closer to the structure. Do you understand?"

"Yes."

"We need your help, all right? Can you help us?"

"I don't know. What can I . . ."

"We need you to use some of the systems in the worksuit. Is it functioning?"

He sniffed loudly again, the simple conversation taking his mind a bit away from the shock. "Let me see. . . ." The hard suit moved slightly as he wriggled his arms out of the sleeves and into the torso. "Yeah . . . it all seems to be working."

"Very good, Lan. I need for you to scan everything within a twenty-meter circle around you. Look for weaponry—complex alloys, electronic components, trip wires, anything at all."

"There's nothing solid, but . . ." He sniffed again, wiping at his face with the back of his hand. As he spoke, his voice was still agitated over what had happened, but the edge of shock that was there a few minutes earlier was beginning to diminish. "I'm getting . . . a power-field reading that runs like . . . like a curtain from wall to wall across this side of the cavern nearest the mouth of the tunnel. I can't get a reading on what it is, but it doesn't really seem to be defensive; more of a sensor field, I think. It's about two meters in front of me. Vito and Mike . . ." He hesitated, nearly choking on her name. "They . . . They're lying on the other side of it."

"Don't go near it."

"Lan," Brendan put in. "Can you get a power reading from the servo motors in . . . in the hard suits?"

A moment's pause, then, "There's nothing there. I'm not even reading the chemical composition of the power chips anymore."

"That's it," he said. "That's what did it. It's not a defensive field."

Adela motioned for Brendan to stay where he was and strode forward, slowing as she neared the bodies, then picked up the makeshift spotlight Vito had dropped and held it out to Heath-seven. "The power chips in these magnaflares are the same kind as in the suit servo motors, aren't they?" No answer. He was still staring at Mike's body. "Lan?"

"Uh, yeah. Or almost the same anyway. Power consumption rates and voltage are different, but they're the same composition and circuitry."

"Watch yourself, everybody." With that, she backed up a few steps and tossed the magnaflare spotlight in a high arc toward the mysterious structure. The light exploded, the pieces sailing on until they peppered the floor of the cavern some distance ahead.

"It's not a defensive field," she said firmly. "I'm sure of it." *Not that it does Mike and Vito any good,* she added silently. She gazed over at their bodies, and tried to think of them as empty, discarded suits, and not the two people she had come to know and respect.

"Waltz!" Hannah called, deciding that they were in no imminent danger. "Inform Captain Anmoore that we have taken two casualties. We would like to retrieve their bodies, and need a bit more time."

"All right." The man's voice was downcast. "Tell Lan . . . Tell Lan I'm sorry." The two back at the platform had heard everything, of course, but it was Hannah's confirmation that filled in what gaps remained and made it all real for them. There was a pause as Waltz relayed her request to Anmoore. No one moved; not a word was uttered as they waited for a reply. "Sorry, Hannah; Captain says no, leave them there for now. He's says to get out of there immediately."

Hannah cursed, the first time Adela had heard her do so, and looked ruefully at the two battered hard suits. "You heard him, everyone. Let's go."

Adela couldn't believe what she was hearing. "You can't just leave them here."

"We'll come back for them, Dr. Montgarde," she said. "Later; I will insist on it." She held up three fingers, and Adela switched hurriedly to the side channel. "He is right, Doctor. We have to get you and the academician out of here; and Lan, too. There's nothing we can do here right now. Please take Lan's arm—I am worried about him—and escort him back to the path." Her signal clicked off on the last word as she went back to the open channel and turned away, ushering Brendan toward the opening in the breakdown.

Adela turned away from the massive structure and put a gloved hand on Lan's shoulder. They stood face-to-face, the brightness in the cavern making it easy to see him inside the roomy, carapace-like torso. Although the suit still stood facing the field he'd detected, his head was turned away from her as he continued to stare at Mike's body.

"Come on, Lan."

He bit at his lip as he stared, his eyes unblinking. His arms were still out of their sleeves and he rubbed his face with his hands. "I should have been scanning for defenses as soon as we walked in here."

"This chamber is ancient," she said softly. "There's no one here; there hasn't been in hundreds of years. It wasn't even a defensive field. Lan, we'll come back, with more people and equipment, and we'll figure it all out."

He shook his head remorsefully, and began to slip his arms back inside the sleeves. Adela waited, watching him carefully for signs that he might be going into shock. It was then that she noticed the moving reflection in his blood-spattered visor.

"Adela . . ." Brendan said incredulously, his voice a whisper. "Look behind you."

A perfect silvery sphere floated there a meter or two over the floor of the cavern, about halfway between them and the structure, moving slowly, smoothly toward them. It looked like solid metal, its featureless surface so delicately polished that had it been motionless, it would have reflected the dull, gray rock-face stone around them in such a way as to be nearly invisible. Only its forward movement, which sent the reflected stone walls bending around its surface, gave it away.

They looked past it and saw that more spheres were coming from the dark depressions in the tanklike structure, dozens of them in all. Some came immediately toward them on exiting, while others reentered other depressions elsewhere on the outside of the structure. Their surfaces caught the light as they flew about, the color of the metal ranging from deep copper on some, to silver like the one nearest them, to bronze and golden on others.

"Do not move," Hannah warned unnecessarily as it came to a halt ten meters away. "Do nothing threatening."

One of the golden spheres peeled away from the structure and sped in their direction mere centimeters above the floor before arcing up and coming to rest next to the silver. Then another gold one, and another, followed by a crowd of others that flew in a loose formation across the floor to join those already holding position in front of them. There were fifteen altogether now hovering before them, all slightly less than a meter in diameter and virtually identical in every way. While still more of the floating spheres literally poured in and out of the openings, moving in every conceivable direction—hovering, circling each other, rising to near the ceiling and back—no more came to take up position with the others.

"Hello?" Brendan asked tentatively. There was no response or indication that he had even been heard, much less understood. Adela chinned the comm bar, trying the same thing on each of the hard suit channels, but with the same results.

"What are they?" she asked of the others. "Lan, can you get any kind of reading on them?"

The vac tech pulled his arms inside again, and looked intently at the instrumentation in the torso of his suit. "Let's see. . . . No, nothing there." He tried a number of settings with little luck, then, slipping an arm back into its sleeve, pulled a sensor node from its mounting on the worksuit and held it in their direction with one hand while he fiddled inside the torso with the other. "Let me try to—"

The spheres surged instantly forward, and as each passed through where they had estimated the sensor field to be, its surface shimmered and rippled as if the thing were a single, enormous drop of liquid gold. They all converged on him in seconds, milling and bobbing in a flowing metal cloud around him, swirling in wide circles on every side like so many bees around a hive.

"Hold still!" Adela shouted.

He turned off whatever instrument he'd activated and the whirling mass slowed instantly. All but one—the silver one that had first appeared before them—retreated to the same position they had held previously on the other side of the sensor field. Where they had hovered motionless earlier, however, now they undulated like a tight cloud of swirling balls.

"Did you get any reading on them?" Brendan wanted to know. "Did you have time to get anything?"

"I got something," he replied, keeping a cautious eye on the remaining sphere, which moved slowly up and down in front of him as if examining his every feature. "It looked like an energy signature similar to that of the sensor field up ahead."

"So they're mechanical, then? Controlled objects?"

"I don't . . . I can't say for sure."

The silver ball zipped away to the other group, stopping at the nearest of the gold spheres. The two touched briefly, joining with a slight lurch like two soap bubbles as they formed a protracted hourglass shape. They stayed that way for a second, revolving around one another, then stretched apart with a snap that sent a series of ripples through each of them. They both then darted back to Lan. As the silver orb hovered and "supervised," the gold sphere rammed itself onto Lan's handheld sensor node, flowing like a silver glob of glue up past his elbow.

"It's pulling me!" He jerked forward, stumbled, and yanked back hard against the pull of the sphere, managing to stop his forward motion. He held his own but a moment, however, as the sphere stretched out and tugged at him again. Unable to keep his balance, he flopped onto his stomach and was dragged along steadily by one arm, his boots digging little trenches that trailed behind him in the sandy floor. "*Unnnh!* My arm!" The sudden cry was filled with pain.

Adela was closest and lumbered at him, trying to throw herself across his legs, but missed him and floundered onto the ground, where she struggled with little success to get back up. She just didn't have the strength or size to get the hard suit to maneuver into an upright position.

Hannah and Brendan, meanwhile, were also running for Lan, but the xenoguide—more accustomed to low-*g* conditions and using the suits—was on top of him first. She dove for him and tackled his rear legs as they kicked helplessly, throwing her arms as tightly around them as she could, but it didn't help. Between his own frantic struggling and the dragging motion, she let him slip out of her grasp and tumbled to the side.

Brendan never even made it close as Lan approached the sensor field. "Pull your arm out of the sleeve!"

There was a flash of light from his elbow as his body started through the field, then an explosion that ripped the arm off and shattered the gold sphere into a shower of golden globules that rained down all around them. Lan, still tugging against the sphere when the arm blew, jerked back instantaneously and rolled away from he field as fast as he could.

"I'm okay!" He rolled neatly into a sitting position, a gaping hole in the right shoulder of the worksuit. As he bumped along the floor, there were more sharp groans of pain. "I— My arm's broken," he said through gritted teeth. "I managed to get it out of the sleeve in time, though, and the skin-shield's snapped on. But I'm all right."

The silver sphere hovered over them a moment as if surveying what had happened, then swooped back to the others, where it again touched and separated with the nearest of the gold orbs. This time, however, that sphere touched one of the others, separated, and each touched a different one in turn until all had joined with at least one of the others, whereupon all of the gold spheres flew to wherever a piece of the destroyed sphere had landed on the sandy floor. They each dipped down to a shimmering fragment and blotted it into itself like a sponge soaking up water

droplets on a tabletop. Every visible scrap retrieved, they retreated to the cylinder, and began another touching-separating-
touching sequence that was repeated over and over among every
sphere in the vicinity. The silver sphere stayed behind, floating
slowly over to take a position safely above their heads. Once
there, it merely hovered in place, for all the world seeming like it
had decided to just watch them all from a safe distance.

Brendan and Hannah assisted Adela to her feet; then the three
of them helped Lan to stand upright in the damaged worksuit.

"Mother of God . . ." It was Waltz's voice.

They spun about to find the hover platform sailing over the
breakdown, the security man at the controls. Towsen hung
tightly to the railing. "Academician! Are you all right?"

Waltz lowered the platform to the ground as smoothly as
Hannah had. "Get on!"

They helped Lan to his feet, careful not to jostle him too much,
then climbed up through the opening in the railing and held on
tightly as he powered the unit immediately off the cavern floor,
and out into the darkness of the sloping tunnel.

As Waltz piloted, the rest of them looked somberly back at the
two bodies they were forced to leave behind. The silver sphere
hovered above the bloody, broken hard suits until they disappeared over the edge of the breakdown, then popped up over the
rocks and followed at a discreet distance as they made their way
out of the fissure.

Hannah made a full report to Anmoore as they flew steadily
on, but other than that they said little to one another. None of
them spoke of Mike or Vito, and none were able to take their eyes
off the sphere as it followed them.

Looking behind them as they were, they were taken by surprise
when the platform emerged into the sunlight again. The platform
sailed on to the hopper without incident, landed smoothly in the
dusty regolith near the open hatch, and the six of them filed back
into the vessel.

An hour later, hard suits removed, vacuumed and stowed, and
Lan's arm treated and splinted, all six of them—along with Anmoore and the copilot—packed into the darkened flight deck and
gazed out on the surface, where the silver sphere floated a few
meters above the platform parked in front of the hatch on the
side of the hopper. From time to time it would sweep across
the surface to examine one feature or another, then zip back to
the platform.

"What now?" Adela asked.

Anmoore sighed heavily, shaking his head. "I've already called the *Blanca*—called them at the first sign of trouble, in fact. And I've given a full report to Commander Wood. They're sending another ship, a big lander."

The sphere floated upward, sailing in to a point a bit less than a meter away from the hardened plastiglass canopy of the flight deck. It moved back and forth a few times, as if trying to peer into the darkened cabin, then glided back to its familiar position over the platform.

"In the meantime," he concluded, "we just sit and wait."

TWENTY-EIGHT
Introduction

I won't permit it," Lewis said. He had remained aboard the *Scartaris* and, although work being done by the combined survey teams at South Camp and elsewhere on the planet continued unabated, the commander had placed the ships of the Imperial fleet on standby alert status following the events in the Big One fissure. "After what happened down there, I would think you'd agree."

"I don't think we were attacked," Adela countered, looking around at the others. Only the copilot, ordered by Anmoore to remain on the flight deck in case they needed to lift off in a hurry, was absent from the hopper's passenger cabin. "We stumbled into a sensor field that explosively overloaded the power chips in the joint servos of the suits. It was accidental. And since we've had a chance to go over the readings from the worksuit, even Lan agrees that there would have been no indication of danger even if it had been detected."

Lewis raised an eyebrow. "That sounds like a damned effective defensive system to me. It convinces me even more that you need to stay right where you are and do nothing until the lander gets there. In the meantime, you don't even know what the sphere is. How do you know *it's* not a defensive system? It attacked Heath-seven, after all—"

"We don't know that it was attacking him."

"That's right," Lewis shot back. "It was just trying to take him for a friendly walk . . . through a field that would have blown him to pieces. Look, when the lander arrives and you've got some defensive backup of your own, then maybe I'll allow it."

"*Allow* it?" As her anger rose, Adela could feel the skin of her face and neck warming. She glanced at the others and saw that everyone in the cabin looked distinctly uncomfortable with the confrontation between the two. "Since when do I need your permission? I don't recall your father giving you jurisdiction over me."

He opened his mouth to say something, then thought better of it. Then finally, "That's true, that's true." It was clear to Adela, as it must certainly have been to everyone else, that he was just as angry as she. "Captain Anmoore, under no circumstances is anyone to leave the hopper until the lander touches down."

"Yes, sir." He seemed slightly embarrassed.

"Now, wait a minute! What are we here for if not to learn what's going on?" She pulled back, not at all liking the sound of her own voice.

"I'm forced to concur with her," Brendan put in. "The sphere is out there *now*. We've gotten as much as we're going to get from the worksuit readings we took in the fissure, as well as what we've been able do from in here. We've taken several hours of recordings of the thing as it comes and goes out on the surface, but that's the extent of what we can do inside the hopper." He hesitated, looking at Adela. "It might not still be there when the lander arrives. I think we need to get closer to it while we still can."

"No."

"Lewis, this is a science decision," he said bluntly. "And Father clearly left judgments of that nature in my hands. I wouldn't dream of telling you how to make a military judgment. It's no more my area than this is yours."

Lewis said nothing, just sat thinking for several long moments, and Adela wondered: Was he considering what Brendan had said, or was he trying to control his anger at both of them? "Towsen?" he asked at last.

The academician spoke up immediately. "Geology is more in my realm, Commander Wood; but I, too, feel that waiting for several more hours is unwise. The sphere has already disappeared three times. It's come back each time. So far." He shrugged.

"I suppose you agree, too," he said, regarding Anmoore.

"That *is* what we're here for."

Outnumbered and unable to come up with a suitable rebuttal, he finally assented. "All right, then. Captain, ignore my previous order. However, as before, you still make the calls." He started to go, then added for Adela and Brendan's benefit, "If you two get yourselves killed, I don't want to know about it. Good luck." His image winked out and the screens went dark.

"That's it," Anmoore said. "Let's get going before he calls back and reconsiders." He turned to Adela and Brendan, and motioned the others to circle around their seats. "What do you two have in mind?"

"Obviously, we need to get back outside with the worksuit; the instrumentation in it is the most sophisticated we have. Besides, it was the scanning frequency Lan used in the worksuit that made them all rush forward. As far as we could tell, it was the only thing they heard from us."

"We've tried sending it everything we can think of from the comm system here on the hopper," Brendan added. "But if it's picking anything up, it's not showing it."

Anmoore nodded at Lan. "Look at him," he said, pointing to the sling cradling the vac tech's arm. "He broke it in two places. He can't go out in the suit, and . . ." He looked quickly around at everyone. "I don't think anyone else here can fit in it."

"I'm small enough," said Adela.

"Wait a minute." Lan stood, looking down at her. "I'm not very big, but you're even smaller. You won't even be able to get your feet into the boots. You'll just rattle around inside it, hardly able to move. And in case you forgot, there's a big hole where the arm used to be."

"But the shielding will keep it intact. And I'll need to keep my arm inside anyway to run the instrumentation."

"Sorry, Doctor; he's right. Besides, I want to try something first that might be a little safer than risking going outside just yet."

Five minutes later, down in the suit room, they moved the worksuit to stand—empty—facing the hatch. The thing was massive, even in the lower gravity, and without operating it from inside with the servos assisting movement, it took three of them to bully it into an upright stance. Once it was in place, Lan, still remarkably facile using only his left arm, temporarily hard-wired the output jack into the comm terminal by the hatch.

"Slaving the worksuit instrument panel to the main control on the flight deck," Anmoore said, "we can remote every system it's got. This way, Lan—who knows the system inside and out—can still be the one running it. We can't walk it out onto the surface, but with the hatch open the sensors should be able to reach to the platform."

They retreated to the upper level and crowded onto the flight deck, some of them craning their necks to see the hatch as it lowered onto the surface, the others intently watching the two flatscreen monitors. One showed the pickup from the comm terminal next to the hatch, angled in at the worksuit. The other screen displayed the video signal from the helmet camera, the worksuit placement affording a straight-out shot of the descending hatch. A small cloud of dust kicked up as it thumped to the regolith, and the sphere moved slightly closer, as though to get a better look at what was happening.

"Good," Hannah observed as the others watched in silence. "Did not scare it away."

"All right, here goes." Lan pressed the membrane keypad on the control panel to activate the same instrument setting that had excited the flock of spheres back in the cavern. Instantly, the silver orb zoomed to a position in front of the visor of the worksuit. It hovered around it, moving first up and down, then in steady circles around the one-armed suit in a similar manner to what they had seen earlier, although the motions of this single silver sphere did not seem as frantic as the crowd of golden ones had.

It nudged experimentally at the torso, sending the worksuit rocking back and forth. If the thing had any notion the suit was different—empty now, and not controlled from inside as it had been in the cavern—it gave no indication. For that matter, they had no way of knowing if the sphere even comprehended that these were suits containing life-forms.

It circled to the right side and nudged the worksuit again, then swung up to where the arm had exploded off, giving the appearance that it was examining the damage to the suit. Plainly, then, it could tell that the suit was different, at least from the aspect that it had found something that had not been there before. It moved closer still, then pressed against the jagged plastic-and-metal fitting of the hole torn in the suit.

"What's it doing?" Adela and the others crowded shoulder to shoulder at the screen, and watched as the sphere seemed to shrink. "Is it . . .?" She watched a moment longer, then said, "It is. It's going inside."

As they stared, the sphere poured itself into the gaping opening at the worksuit's shoulder. They could see the silvery, floating mass through the visor as it undulated and reshaped itself down inside, falling from view into the lower part of the torso.

"I'm not believing this," Lan said, punching almost randomly at the keypad controller. "It's getting into the instrumentation." He pulled his good arm back and they all watched as system after system turned itself on and off. Several of the tools embedded into the outside of the worksuit, their catches released from inside, fell tumbling to the floor. One of them, a spot-welding rod, glowed white hot, searing the deck plate where it had fallen before it shut off.

The left screen, the one showing the helmet camera, winked out, as did the control keypad Lan had been using. "That's it, then," he groaned. "It got into the onboard computer."

At that moment the worksuit shuddered, the servos in the remaining arm and both legs activating simultaneously. Unable to remain upright, the worksuit collapsed in a heap on top of the spilled tools.

Anmoore reached for the flight-deck main control panel and angled the comm terminal's video pickup toward the downed suit in time to see a rippling silver blob ooze itself out of the shoulder hole and coalesce into its spherical shape once more. Free of the suit, it shot out the open hatch.

"There it goes—" Adela started to say, but stopped abruptly when the sphere bumped into the forward canopy, bouncing back with the force with which it had been flying. It came closer again, slower this time, and softly touched the plastiglass, spreading out and flattening as it pressed against it.

Anmoore reached for the hopper's shield generator control, his hand poised over the switch.

"Wait!" Adela put her hand on his shoulder. "It can't break the glass, can it?"

"I don't know—we don't know what it's made of; we don't even know how heavy it is. But if I get any significant pressure reading on the canopy, I'm popping the shield on and knocking it back to a respectable distance."

"I don't understand," Towsen said. "What's it trying to do?"

"Look at it," she said. "It almost seems like it's trying to come in the canopy the way it entered the worksuit." Adela put both hands against the cold inside surface of the plastiglass, and could feel just the slightest vibration. She turned to Brendan, a questioning look on her face. "Could something it did in the suit be making it act like this?"

Before he could answer, the center of the flattened sphere

pulled away from the canopy and then fell back against it, once, with a soft *slap!* that could be heard inside the flight deck. There was a short pause; then it pulled back again and hit the glass again, three times, one right after the other. Another pause, then three slower slaps. Then three fast ones again.

The sphere peeled itself off the window and hovered in front of the canopy, unmoving for nearly a minute. Then, attaching itself to the same spot on the window again, it repeated the routine.

"An SOS?" Adela breathed. "Is that what I'm seeing?"

"Yes," Anmoore verified. "It's an SOS, but don't ask me why."

"The last subroutine that ran in the worksuit's comm circuitry would have been the emergency sequence activated when the arm was torn loose and the skin-shield came on." They all turned to face Lan, who gestured with his good hand. "It's the automatic locator sequence. It would have been the last thing in memory when you all got me out of the suit."

Adela stood up to the glass, facing the sphere at eye level. She balled her hand into a fist and held it against the glass, then opened it palm out—three times fast, three times slow, three times fast.

The sphere came close again, extending a silvery tendril to touch the glass just opposite Adela's hand.

"I think it just said 'Hello.' "

They stood at the entrance hatch to the suit room, Anmoore with his hand over the opening plate. He nodded to Waltz, saying, "And one for Hannah, too." Waltz went to one of the equipment lockers and returned with two shield guns, handing one to the xenoguide. The weapon projected a shield force that could either—depending on its setting—gently shove someone back or hit them with the force of a solid, flying wall of steel.

Adela and Brendan bristled at the weapons, but did not protest Anmoore's decision to go into the suit room armed. It had been all they could do to convince him it was necessary to make direct contact with the sphere, in an attempt to find some way to link into whatever communication capabilities it had.

That the sphere could communicate there was no doubt. She had managed to use hand signs and flashing lights though the canopy to the point where all were in agreement that the sphere was either intelligent, or intelligently controlled.

"I don't know how much it picked up when it went into the worksuit computer," the captain was saying by way of explaining the precautionary measures. "Or what it's doing with the information. But I've got to assume that if it studied and understood the suit's working and life-support systems, it also understands what we are."

"Of course," Adela countered, "if that's true, then it also knows it could have entered on its own by interfacing the hatch opening plate from the other side while the suit room was still open to the surface. If it wanted to hurt us, popping this entrance hatch while the suit room was open and depressurized would have done it quite neatly." She looked at him evenly. "But it chose not to, waiting instead for us to let it in."

"Let's hope so." Anmoore pressed his hand against the plate, and the hatch fell inward. "I want this closed and sealed as soon as we're in," he said to Lan, Towsen and the copilot; then he turned to Hannah and Waltz, motioning for them to climb on down. He went down next, followed by Adela and Brendan.

The sphere hovered over the worksuit piled on the floor by the now-closed main hatch, but as the five of them stood facing it in a semicircle, it sidled closer, bobbing in the air in front of Adela.

"I can't imagine how it sees, but I think it recognizes me as the one sending the hand signals through the canopy." She turned to Brendan and he came forward. The sphere oriented on him as he neared, but then went back to Adela.

"Radar?" he posited. "Maybe sound waves, or heat readings, or even a scanning mechanism of some kind. At this point, it knows more about us just from that suit over there than we can even guess about it."

Adela raised her hand slowly, extending a fingertip toward the sphere. A bump rose in the silvery surface, forming a short tendril that reached out to meet Adela's finger.

"Oh!" She jerked her hand back, making Waltz and Hannah stiffen. The sphere did not move, but absorbed the tendril back inside itself.

"What?" Anmoore asked, waving the weapons down. "Was it hot? Did it hurt, or was there a shock? What?"

"It felt . . . I don't know, it tingled." She smiled sheepishly. "It didn't hurt; it just startled me is all." She reached out again, this time allowing the liquid metal tendril to engulf her finger. Her eyes widened and a brightness came to her face. "It feels like . . . like I'm sharing something with her."

Brendan arched an eyebrow. "Her?"

She faced her grandson abruptly. "Yes, I sense that somehow." Withdrawing her hand, she turned and paced back to the ladder, sitting on one of the lower rungs, and regarded each of them in turn. "It's not intelligently controlled, or even intelligent in the sense of some kind of AI programming." She shook her head at the gravity of what she had learned from the single touch. "It's a living being."

Hannah gasped, and Anmoore let out a low whistle.

"Are you sure?" Brendan asked. "How could you know that from just touching it?"

"You know that the Sarpan pass a part of themselves on to their spawn through touch—a sense of identity, customs, behavior patterns, personality traits. The touching ritual is very important to them, even among their dealings with us. I touched with Oidar, once, and got an idea of what it was like. But this—"

She rose and returned to the gleaming sphere, letting it envelop her hand in a softly spreading tendril. "It's cool to the touch, and feels like dipping your hand into a beaker of mercury—it moves to my touch, but I can feel the density of it. It *is* metal, by the way."

"A mechanical intelligence?"

She nodded wordlessly, her eyes closed.

"She's confused." Adela's brow furrowed. "I don't know. . . ." She pulled her hand away again, letting the living metal snap back from each fingertip like silver rubber bands. She crossed her arms and let her breath out in a long, slow sigh.

"What?" Anmoore asked.

"I just can't be sure. I get a sense that she doesn't know why we're here." Adela shook her head, frowning. "She doesn't understand why we're shaped this way, why our skin is so smooth."

Waltz chuckled. "And what are we supposed to be shaped like?"

"I just don't know." She turned to Anmoore. "We have to come up with some means to talk to her directly."

"Lan? Are you watching all this?"

"I sure am, Captain." The voice echoed in the small room from the comm terminal loudspeaker.

"When you used the sensor scan that set them off in the cavern, did you get any indication they 'heard' it?"

"No more than when we tried it when we remoted the worksuit an hour ago. They heard or sensed it somehow—you saw their reaction. But if you're trying to suggest some way to transmit and receive from them using it, I wouldn't know where to begin."

"Oh, well," Anmoore said. "Maybe when we get back up to the ship. Thanks anyway."

Adela approached the alien once more, her hand in front of her. "Let me try again to—"

She barely saw the silver tendril as it rushed at her head, flowing coolly, heavily over her face. Blackness and a numb silence gripped her as the living metal spread around and behind her cheeks, covering her ears. She gasped for breath and clawed at the tendril, but her fingers merely passed through the syrupy thickness of the alien and she began to see a series of sparks and fireflies as the lack of air started to overcome her. She fell backward, felt hands on her shoulders and arms.

I understand. The thought formed in her mind, and her mouth was suddenly uncovered, letting her inhale a desperate swallow of air, then another and another until the suffocating feeling left her. And with it went the surprised terror that had gripped her the moment the tendril had hit her forehead. She could breathe normally again, but the liquid silver still covered the rest of her face.

"I'm all right!" She had no idea if they heard her or not, but the desperate grip on her shoulders lessened, and she felt herself being lowered to a sitting position on the floor. . . .

The room was bright again. But Adela hadn't noticed when her face had been suddenly uncovered. She blinked at the strange light, dull and orange as it streamed through the opened window. There was a gorgeous sunset there, just visible through the draperies, and she saw a bloated K-type star hanging low on the horizon.

There was an odd, unfamiliar sensation at her chest and she looked down, stunned to find that she was suckling an infant. The shock passed instantly, and then she knew instinctively that everything was all right, that all was as it should be. She held the boy to her breast, stroking the tawny fur of his head and back, and kissed his tiny ears. He looked up at her with large, blinking eyes set above the tiny, bridgeless nose. His face was still furless and wrinkled, but he would have the coloring of his father in a few weeks. He pulled away, her nipple slipping from his mouth, and he yawned sleepily, tiny sharp teeth already beginning to appear in his gums. The mewling sound he made was warm and comforting as he yawned again and rubbed tiny, stubby-fingered paws on his face. His eyelids drooped a few times, then closed, and he fell into a deep sleep.

She pulled down her linen blouse, covering herself, and held him closer. As she rocked him in her arms, she felt his delicate breath on the light fur of her neck.

"Sleep, little Tanyo," she whispered. She hummed softly, a

lullaby she had learned when she was still a child herself. There was the thump of a door being closed down the hallway, and the sound of footsteps made in such a way that showed that whoever was coming did not want to wake the little nestling.

"Shhhhhhh . . ." she admonished when he came in.

He made an apologetic face and tiptoed over to her, sitting beside her on the divan and encircling them both in his strong arms. He nuzzled her, gently licking the fur of her neck and cheek, sending a feeling of love and warmth through her.

"I love you, Ettalira," he said, the scent of his breath sweet in her nostrils. "It's hard to believe that we leave tomorrow."

"And I love you." She rubbed her face against his, nipping lightly at his lips and ears, then said softly, so as not to wake the nestling Tanyo, "I wonder what kind of world we shall find?"

"As long as you and Tanyo are there with me, it will be a fine and happy world."

She smiled, and buried her face against his neck. . . .

"Grandmother?"

"Dr. Montgarde, can you hear me?"

She blinked and looked around her at surroundings that seemed cold, strange. The peaceful living room was gone, the glowing warmth that was the setting sun evaporated; her husband and baby were but memories. Seated on the floor of the suit room, she blinked up into four concerned faces, and behind them an improbable line of plastic snowmen. Looking down at her arms, she noticed that they were folded to her chest as if gently holding something protectively. Adela felt as though she had lost something precious.

A gleaming movement caught her eye.

"I understand you now, Ettalira," she said to the silver sphere. Adela rose, and smiled warmly at the alien. "Thank you for sharing your life, and your people, with me."

The sphere came forward. A round portion of the silvery surface perhaps three centimeters across flattened, vibrating.

"And thank you for sharing yours with me," she said in Adela's voice.

The holoconference chamber on the lander *Surtsey* was small, utilitarian, with only four couches. Still on Big One, Brendan, Anmoore and Adela listened intently, as did the image of Lewis from the *Scartaris*.

"First let me say that I am deeply sorry about what happened to your people," Ettalira was saying from where she floated between Brendan and Anmoore.

Although several hours had passed since the two of them had shared minds, Adela could still not get used to hearing her own voice coming from the silver sphere. As she watched, the sphere seemed somehow smaller, less threatening than it had when they'd first encountered it in the fissure cavern.

"We have hundreds of mechanical devices at the Home, powered in many ways," Ettalira went on. "But none have ever reacted with such destructive force. There was no way to anticipate, when the waking curtain was erected, that it would interact in such a way with the servo motors of your hard suits. For that matter, we had no reason to suspect that any life other than our own would enter the cavern."

"We will mourn our friends, Ettalira," Lewis said, his voice firm and strong. Adela enjoyed this moment to watch him "at work." It was the first opportunity she had had to see him in the role he loved so much, and she was pleased to see that he was a competent commander and authority figure. "However, we accept the unfortunate nature of what has happened as an accident that could neither have been anticipated, nor prevented. Even if the 'waking curtain,' as you call it, had been detected, its threatening nature could never have been foreseen. Eventually, something—or someone—containing a power chip of the type in the hard suits would have come into contact with your curtain. Perhaps our friends' sacrifice has, in some way, prevented an even greater tragedy. Let's speak no more of it."

"All right, then." The sphere bobbed in the air, the motion almost suggesting a nod. "However, I will join you in your mourning."

Lewis nodded back, a look of gratitude on his features. "Thank you." He straightened in his couch. "Dr. Montgarde tells me that you are an old race." .

"That's true," she said. "I would need to touch someone in the Home records to give you an accurate figure, since I've not needed to know how much time has passed since we left our world. To be frank, time is something that is hard for me to grasp anymore. To be sure, I can measure elapsed time—we have been in this chamber talking for three minutes, nineteen seconds, as you measure it. But the passage of time doesn't matter to me, since I was not alive until the waking curtain created me."

There was a silence, during which Lewis, as well as Brendan and Anmoore, sat upright.

"I'm not sure I follow you."

"Commander Wood, I have learned much from your grandmother about how you travel in space. Your ships are fast, much faster than ours—and the wormholes!" She paused, in awe of the very concept. "Our technology was not so advanced. My people, riding the seed ship, went out across this galaxy, colonizing hundreds of planets as we found them along our journey. But the voyage was too long, and too slow. It would have been foolish for us to go."

"Ettalira Tewligh never physically left Gatan, her world at the galaxy core," Adela explained. "Everything she, her husband and son were, was recorded and imprinted in their ship's core memory. The ship left—with no living soul on board—on a trajectory that would take it along one of the spiral arms, programmed to scan for appropriate systems with habitable worlds and alter its course to intercept them. Once in orbit around a candidate, the memory core determined the suitability of the planet and, if it was of a type that would support the Gatanni, then a waking call was sent throughout the ship. At that moment, hundreds of memory patterns were activated and encoded into these living metal spheres."

"And," Ettalira picked up, "we used recorded DNA and genetic patterns to construct living, breathing Gatanni, altered to adapt them to the specific conditions of each world. Then we imprint them with the recorded memories of those of us on the ship who would people the new world, and bring rise to a new civilization. Then I, and my husband, return to the ship and are absorbed into the core until we are created again."

"What you're saying, then," Brendan interjected, "is that you sent out a single colony ship, that colonized each world in the same way, with the same individuals? That you, or someone with your imprinted life and memories, has existed—still exists—on every world you've colonized?"

Ettalira moved into the center of the couches, regarding each of the men. "I perceive a sense of revulsion in your faces," she said in Adela's voice. "Understand that each world we colonize evolves on its own. We do not have interstellar communication, like you. Nor is the imprinting complete in the knowledge of how each society is created, or that a seeding ship has created them. Each new world, each new Ettalira Tewligh, her family and people, were free to develop on their own." She was silent a moment, then said, "Please; it is not so shameful a life. The person who I was has been dead for millennia; gone and forgotten on a world that I no longer would recognize. But with each *new* world we find, I live again. And so does my husband, and my nestling Tanyo, all over again."

"The natives on Tsing are not a separate intelligent species," Adela said. "They are the Gatanni. Their bone structure is slightly different to accommodate the difference in surface gravity from Gatan normal. Their eyes are smaller, better adapted to the G-type star. Their digestive and respiratory organs have been finely tuned to the ecosystem. But they are still Gatanni."

Lewis stood, pacing the small area around his chair. He would occasionally approach the limit of the holographic pickup and fade slightly as he trod back and forth. "So what happened here, Ettalira? The natives on the world below do not have a high level of technology. They are warlike, and unless some essence of cooperation develops among them, they are not likely to advance for a much longer time that your own world did."

"I don't know." The sphere moved to Adela, and floated at her side. "The work of reproducing our culture takes many years, and was underway while I slept. When all is ready, when the living beings are constructed and functioning, the landing ship returns for us to complete our role. The waking curtain responsible for killing your friends was to have created me and the others at that time to travel below to imprint our memories on the colonists. I have learned from Dr. Montgarde's memory that there is a crash site on the world below, many years old. I can only assume that this is the landing ship."

"I think I understand now," Brendan said, turning to the sphere. "You never were roused here on this moon, and your memories and customs were never given to the natives on the planet. The colonists that were designed and created for this world developed entirely on their own, then. They may have Gatanni origins, but their culture, their civilization, is unique to themselves."

"That's right."

There was an awkward silence, broken finally when Lewis retook his seat and addressed the room at large. "So what happens now?" he asked bluntly. "You have been awakened to find that your work was incomplete, and that the long journey of your seed ship came to an end here."

Ettalira didn't answer immediately, considering what he had said. "That's not entirely true," she confessed. "The seed ship would already have left, even before the living beings on the world below were constructed. You see, the ship itself is small. When it finds a suitable world, automated procedures gather the necessary ores and material from the candidate solar system, either on the selected world or from the other planets and asteroids in the system. They then construct, first, the Home, followed by all equipment needed to erect the colony, including a small landing craft. The main ship then departs, continuing along the galaxy arm, while those here in the Home are left to finish the work of peopling our new world. According to the updating I received when the waking curtain created me, nearly two thousands years, as you measure them, have passed since that would have occurred."

"I see." Lewis rubbed thoughtfully at his chin. "So your seeding ship had already come and gone, long before we even ventured out into space. I wonder how far it has traveled."

"And how many colony worlds it has settled," Anmoore put in.

"I have no way of knowing. None of us do who are left behind." She floated to the center of the ring of couches again. "Once the ship is gone, and everything in the Home is constructed, organic material is collected from the chosen planet and used to replicate living beings, who are transported to the surface and imprinted."

"That's incredible," Brendan said. "You construct living beings?"

"It isn't that difficult, Academician. I am a living being, made of metal and inorganics, mechanical in nature. Biological beings are but organic machines, not that different from the form I have now." She floated close to Lewis' image, her voice—Adela's voice—low. "For that matter, there is little difference among any living beings. Humanity is not that different from Gatanni, and the Sarpan share much with us both. The building blocks of life are the same."

"But what happens when you are done, when the new world is finished?"

"When our work is done, we are reabsorbed into the Home, which then shuts down and remains hidden for all time."

"The commander's earlier question still stands, Ettalira," Adela said. "You never completed your colonization. What do you plan to do now?"

"I don't know what happened on the planet so long ago that interrupted everything. An accident, a malfunction, a miscalculation; it no longer matters." There was a tiny sound, almost like a sigh. "But Adela, our work *is* completed. It's too late to interfere in the lives of those below."

"So you'll just . . . turn yourself off?"

"Yes."

"But that is such a waste," Brendan sputtered. "Why would you even consider such a thing?"

"Why should I not?" she replied, orienting on his couch. "Please understand, Academician, that I have lived a hundred times before coming to this world. I'm certain that I have lived a hundred times since."

"But why not stay . . . alive? There is much that we would like to learn from you, and a great deal you could learn from us."

"This form isn't permanent; it's designed to allow us to do what we need to realize our goals, but it is too energy-inefficient to last much longer than a few days. What you see here . . ." She rippled the surface of the sphere, the liquid silver undulating in waves around its circumference. ". . . is only temporary."

Adela regarded the alien carefully, studying her. "Looking at you a few moments ago, I thought you were smaller. I was right, wasn't I?"

"Yes. I have almost existed longer than I am designed to. This form is self-fueling, and is using itself up."

"Then construct a biological one," Adela said. "Consider this: If you had been successful here, if the landing ship had not been destroyed, there would be an advanced Gatanni culture here at this world. We would have discovered you then, and would have interacted and learned from each other. We can't do that with the inhabitants below; they know nothing of you or your past. Construct new living beings and imprint them."

Ettalira considered this for several moments, then addressed Lewis. "When Adela and I touched, I learned that there is a great fear of those not like yourself. Do you think it is wise, Commander, to further contribute to that fear?"

"I consider it unwise to turn away knowledge when it is available," he said without hesitation. "It is the absence of knowledge that feeds fear."

"Your offer is a generous one," she said. "But please remember that my time is limited in this form. Let me return to Home and discuss it with the others, although I'm fairly certain that they will agree. With your permission, however, I would like to suggest that only a few of us be imprinted at first. I think we should progress slowly in this."

"Very good." He turned to Anmoore. "Captain, would you please escort Ettalira to the lower level?"

Anmoore stood, nodding, and headed for the door with the sphere at his side.

"I have to admit," Adela said when the three of them were alone, "that you surprise me. I didn't expect your consent so quickly."

"Me, too," Brendan agreed. "You almost sounded like me a moment ago."

"Maybe I've learned from you; maybe I've learned from both of you. Besides, it's true." He stood and unbuttoned the high collar of his uniform jacket, then sat on the arm of the couch. "Jephthah isn't gone yet, only contained for the moment. If we ever hope to deal with the fear he's spread through the Hundred Worlds, we have to move before he does. Enlisting the Gatanni now, before he has a chance to twist this latest news—before he even knows!—gives us an edge."

Adela leaned forward, looking first at one, then the other of her grandsons. "Good. For once, then, the three of us are in accord."

"There's another reason I'm making this decision." He finished unbuttoning his jacket and removed it, draping it in front of him over folded arms. "I've received word from Father, relayed from one of my commanders at the wormhole gate. He's coming here—he's already on his way, in fact—and will arrive in less than two weeks. I want as much in place when he gets here as possible."

TWENTY-NINE
Working Relationship

In the days that followed, while they awaited the first of the biological Gatanni to be constructed, Gatanni spheres and humans worked together closely, often side by side.

A full information exchange was still taking place, with the entire Gatanni voyage—from the galaxy core up to Tsing—being made available to the Hundred Worlds. There were records of a thousand star systems, not just the ones that had been selected as life-supporting. The location of thousands more stellar objects, including nebulae, cometary bodies and rogue planets, even singularities that could be considered for potential wormhole transit points. Gareth Anmoore and Brendan coordinated efforts in this, seeing to it that the proper researchers received the information.

They disseminated the information carefully, almost always by hand-delivery to its intended recipient, to minimize the chances of it falling into Jephthah's hands. But they were forced to admit that his methods of acquiring information were unknown, and that none of their efforts might be effective in limiting what he found out. In the meantime, however, the quarantine remained firmly in place, and was certainly more effective than anything that had been done to date. There had been no broadcasts; the Sarpan intercepted nothing. Lewis had even suggested that Jephthah might already be aware that they had discovered his means of redirecting addresses through the Sarpan, and was no longer even trying. Perhaps he was biding his time, Lewis speculated, waiting until he could somehow get something outside the jamming net for rebroadcast by associates in other systems.

But so far, there had been no attempt to run the blockade at the wormhole gate. And although a small ship might not be detected if it left the system without going through the gate, Tsing was so far away from human space that the idea of Jephthah escaping that way was almost immediately rejected—there would be no human contact for any ship traveling between Tsing and the next human world for many decades, with no means of rejuvenation available. "His leaving that way would do us a favor," Lewis had said. "He would be so old when he arrived that no one would even remember him."

All the same, every ship that had entered the system was accounted for. No ship was found leaving.

In return for the enormous amounts of invaluable information given by the Gatanni, Lewis had freely given them access to a great bulk of Imperial knowledge—history, science, technology, astronomy.

The Sarpan had done likewise. Adela had spoken about it personally to Captain Tra'tiss aboard the *Cra Stuith,* convincing him of the importance of this sharing.

Tra'tiss had requested that she be allowed to touch with his spawn, and had invited her into his personal chamber. Only once had she touched with a Sarpan: the scientist Oidar, who was now, according to Eric's message to Lewis, on his way to rejoin his people. Like Oidar's had been aboard the science ship where he had served with Templeton Rice, the water chamber on the Sarpan ship resembled as nearly as possible their homeworld. A mixture of lush plant life and marsh conditions, augmented by holographically reproduced details, the water chamber was as close to being on their planet as she had ever experienced.

It was hot and almost unbearably humid there, and she had been grateful for the E-suit Gareth Anmoore had given her. Leaving the bubble helmet at the edge of the pool that dominated the chamber, she had waded out toward where he huddled in the shallows with his spawn.

The heat hit her face like a wave, and she turned the E-suit's thermostat lower, enjoying the cool rush of air escaping from the open collar ring.

Tra'tiss swam toward her, just below the surface like a terrestrial frog, his hands and arms swept back against his body while strong kicks from his legs carried him forward. Swimming up before her, he sat on the bottom and swirled his hands in a circular motion in the water at his waist. As she watched the splashing motion he made, she peered closer and noticed for the first time that he was surrounded by several tiny fishlike animals. They swam freely over and through the alien's legs, occasionally wandering slightly away before hurriedly wriggling back to join the others.

"These are my male spawn," he had said proudly. He reached for her hand and tugged at her gloves. "Can you remove these?"

Adela pulled off the gloves and tucked them out of the way into a loop on the suit.

"Now . . . like this." Tra'tiss cupped his hands in demonstration, then scooped up one of the tiny swimmers and poured the tepid water and the tiny Sarpan spawn into Adela's waiting hands.

The swimmer resembled the adult in many ways, although it still had a wide, flat tail and no rear legs yet. She could feel the slight pressure of the creature's tiny hands as it pushed itself up in her palms and studied her, tilting its little head in a typical Sarpan mannerism. He was "touching," learning something of her, although just what, she could not guess. It rubbed several times against her palms, then hopped into the water at her feet and wriggled back to rejoin the others at Tra'tiss' side. They greeted him with a touching ritual of their own, swimming and bumping against him and each other.

"I am honored," he had said, his face beaming as he watched

his children pass on what they had received from her. "This one is most grateful."

"Your ritual of touching," she had said, "is your very being. It is a way of becoming closer, much as you have become closer to humans by sharing knowledge."

Tra'tiss had understood perfectly, then, when she asked that he make Sarpan information available to the Gatanni.

THIRTY
Liaison

The air was warm here at South Camp, and Tsing, directly overhead, warmed the three of them even further as they looked down on the dome. A strong breeze blew from the north, carrying with it a pleasant salty tang even though they were a considerable distance from the vast sea that lay over the horizon.

The three sat on rocks far up the slope of the ancient basin, and from here could watch the activity going on below them. Brendan had removed his formal academician's tunic, just as Lewis had his officer's jacket, and both were slung over a low branch of the tree that shaded their perch.

"This will probably be the last time we'll be able to take this kind of break," Adela said, eyes closed and head tilted back to better enjoy the gentle wind blowing through her hair. "With your father almost here, I expect it'll be some time before any of us do much relaxing again."

Lewis chuckled agreeably. "So *this* is what 'relax' means."

She and Brendan both laughed at the remark, and as she thought about it, it occurred to her that this *was* the first time she had seen Lewis take a few minutes off from the hectic pace he had maintained in the long, difficult weeks they had been here.

"You call this relaxing?" Brendan asked, then pointed to the busy scene below. "I'm getting tired just watching them all down there."

He was right: South Camp was a maelstrom of activity. As they watched, they could see the workers at the dig site, still trying to piece together some idea of what had happened to the Gatanni landing ship. Among the human workers at the site, they could see a dozen shining globes of various metallic hues, all of them glinting brilliantly in the sunlight. They worked alongside their human companions, examining whatever was found. From time to time there would be a flurry of movement as something interesting was uncovered in the dirt, followed by a rapid touch-separate-touch sequence before one of the spheres flitted back to the dome to pass on the new tidbit of information to the spheres working there.

At the dome, meanwhile, a steady flow of vehicular traffic came and went. The information they had gathered here on the planet, combined with the Gatanni's perspective on the natives' development, had given them an understanding of Tsing IV and its inhabitants far superior to any they might have obtained had they studied this world for years by themselves. With the spheres volunteering to covertly observe them, their social structure, language, rituals and customs, even their games and pastimes had been observed and recorded, without their ever suspecting that their world was being visited.

Even the single Sarpan ship orbiting the planet had proven itself invaluable, occasionally sending an E-suited representative to the surface, who would take information back to the *Cra Stuith* for greater analysis, returning their findings and insights directly to the Imperial ships.

Adela reflected on what the cooperation had achieved, marveling at how smoothly things had gone, and at the same time she felt uncertain about the future. "We're still no closer to finding him, you know," she said, spoiling the light mood.

Neither man answered immediately.

"I'm so afraid he can still undo everything we've accomplished here."

"I'm not concerned," Lewis said, "for a reason that should be apparent. Look down there, and tell me what you see. You, too, Bren."

"I follow you," she replied before the academician could answer. "We're all working together. You want me to see the cooperation among our species, don't you? I agree: What's happened here has truly been wonderful. But do you feel that this, in itself, can defuse what he's done?" She shook her head, frowning. "I'm not so sure. Fear, as an emotion, is just too strong."

"But he's right," Brendan added. "Grandmother, the two of us have talked a great deal about this, in anticipation of Father's arrival. We feel that by emphasizing the relationship that has developed here, along with the incredible knowledge we've gained about what lies coreward on this spiral arm, we can counteract his lies."

"But there are so many lies, so many things he's blamed on the Sarpan. And now he's categorized the Gatanni natives here as even worse."

"But where is his proof?"

Lewis rose, and gazed out over the basin below. A hopper shuttle was approaching from the north, flying low over the treetops, and he followed its path as it settled on the newly constructed landing pad between the dome and dig site. A wheeled truck was waiting there to greet it as it touched down. "I agree with Bren," he said, reaching up and pulling his jacket from the branch, then slung it over one shoulder. "Other than all his years of accusations, and one stolen recording that he's presented woefully out of context, he has nothing."

Adela looked up at him. "But how can you be certain that he hasn't collected proof? He's been here for weeks; he did obtain the airship recording, after all."

"We'd better head back down. Looks like our company is here." He slapped his brother on the shoulder, tossing him his tunic. The three of them started down the slope, carefully negotiating the uneven terrain. "Bren and I have talked about that, too, and we want to present something to Father. We'd like you to make it unanimous."

"I'm listening."

"We know you feel that the native Gatanni should be left alone—we're all in agreement on that. We're going to suggest that the systemwide quarantine remain in place even after our work here is settled."

"And the planet?"

"Don't worry," Brendan said, walking around one of the larger bushes as they made their way down. "A presence will remain here. A permanent base can be set up on one of the moons. South Camp can continue in operation until the natives manage to cross the northern sea and reach this landmass, and then everything here will be moved up to the lunar base, and this area will be scoured clean, leaving no trace of our visit."

Adela thought about it for several moments. "I was thinking something along those lines myself; in fact, Captain Anmoore had suggested the same thing some time back. He's the one you want to run it, by the way."

"I agree," Lewis said. "He's the best man for the job. Anyway, almost every ship here will leave, one at a time, with each person on board being given a level-one background check. Jephthah is on one of the ships here now, with an identity that may be working fine for him in this hectic situation, but it won't hold up when the entire force of Imperial security sweeps through each individual ship before it leaves." He chuckled as he concluded, "Of course, that's going to take more than a few years."

"Giving us even more time to present a positive case for what we've accomplished." She nodded enthusiastically. "You've got my support."

"Good." He pointed ahead of him at a shiny sphere coming up the slope at top speed. It was on them in moments.

"Hello," it said excitedly in Adela's voice. Ettalira—or rather, the fifth temporary sphere that had been created with her memory imprint—was very small now, barely half the size of a newly created Gatanni sphere. She would need to transfer herself to another one soon. "They're here, and are anxious to meet you." With that, she zipped away, flitting down the slope like a silent hummingbird.

Fifteen minutes later, they stood facing the hopper shuttle, their attire rebuttoned and smoothed down in all official protocol. She suspected that even Gareth Anmoore, who piloted the hopper shuttle personally down from Big One, would appear at the hatch momentarily in his captain's jacket. Ettalira floated silently with the three of them.

Ringing the area behind them, meanwhile, was an excited crowd of onlookers, kept at a discreet distance by South Camp security. Everyone not on duty at the dome or dig site was here at the landing pad, and Adela suspected that more than a few of those in the ensemble had left their work uncompleted and sneaked away to be here for this. In the intervening space between them, a cloud of Gatanni spheres swirled and bobbed and touched with one another in excited anticipation.

Lewis lifted his handlink. "All right, Captain; I think everything's set."

The passenger hatch lowered and smoothly extended itself onto the paved surface of the pad, revealing Anmoore standing on the other side. He came down the short flight of steps quickly, a puzzled, worried look on his features. Directly behind him floated a silver sphere that sped immediately around him to Ettalira, whereupon they touched and completely absorbed into each other like two soap bubbles. When the two had become one, the sphere was just slightly larger than a newly created one would be.

"Commander," Anmoore said, nodding in greeting to the three of them. "Academician. Doctor."

"I don't understand," Adela said, her eyes on the united sphere. "Why was another sphere made for Ettalira? I thought—"

"I'm sorry, this isn't easy." He stood before them on the pad, looking back up into the hopper. "They didn't construct Gatanni. They made humans. I didn't know until I actually picked them up at the prearranged transfer site."

"What?" Lewis blurted. Brendan said nothing, and stared at Anmoore openmouthed. "And you didn't think it wise to alert me?"

"I'm sorry, sir." Anmoore stood his ground, straightening, and glared at him. "But do you think it would have been better to transmit something like this where it could be intercepted? Even a coded transmission?"

Lewis turned away and pressed a sequence of buttons on the handlink, whereupon the security personnel set about breaking up the crowd and sending as many of them as possible back to the dome and about their jobs. "You're right, of course," he said, turning back. "I regret my words of a moment ago." Then, to Ettalira: "What is happening here?"

She drifted forward. "While the biologicals were being constructed," she began, her words apologetic, apprehensive, "we had a great deal of time to study the wealth of information you've given us. We reached a consensus, back at Home, that Jephthah's influence has been too great. We feared that our appearance would aggravate an already serious situation for the Hundred Worlds . . ." She paused. "As well as for our personal safety."

"What is on the hopper shuttle then?" Adela asked, pointing up the steps. "Humans, or Gatanni?"

"They are both. And neither. While they are human in form, they have been imprinted with Gatanni memories and mannerisms. In such a way, they will be able to work closely with humans without causing undue resentment among those who would fear our alien form. Is this not a better, safer way to proceed for now, for this first step? Perhaps later, when your Emperor has had a chance to meet with us and review the situation here, he may give his personal authority for us to construct living beings more closely resembling ourselves."

"I suppose it will have to be acceptable for now." Lewis let his breath out loudly, frowning. "And I suppose it's better than constantly making new spheres every time one of you is used up."

"Maybe this *is* better," Brendan put in, eyebrows raised. He peered up into the open hatchway. "How many are there?"

"We constructed and imprinted four male humans, assuming that each of you would prefer a liaison designed specifically for you, taking into account your positions and functions, using genetic coding and DNA records from your medical files much in the way we construct adapted Gatanni. The imprinting is primarily Gatanni, but we have also seen to it that they received full knowledge of human ways and customs, much as I did when I touched with Adela. You will be able to interact with them as easily as you do with me. Perhaps even more easily, since each has been prepared individually."

"I see," Lewis said, putting a positive tone behind his words. "Well, let's meet them."

She flew into the hopper, reappearing almost immediately as the first of the Gatanni/humans started down the steps. He was of average height and build, with a tan complexion and wavy hair of light brown that hung shaggily over the collar of the standard-issue coveralls he had been given. Anmoore must have seen to that before they left Big One. He had a thick growth of beard that, like his hair, was in need of trimming. He smiled in greeting, and waved just a bit nervously as he descended the steps and eagerly shook their hands in turn once on the ground. His grip was firm, warm and distinctly human in nature. The nervousness seemed to dissipate quickly once he had been received, but he didn't seem inclined to speak.

Behind him followed another man, his complexion and hair a shade darker. He was somewhat shorter and stockier than his companion, but shared the shaggy hair and beard of the first. He joined the other and offered his hand in greeting, Adela noting that his grip was stronger, more muscular.

The last two appeared in the hatch together, and descended one behind the other. Each had shaggy blond hair and beards and the same fair complexion, but shared no other common features. These two were also the most dissimilar in size, with the first of the pair standing several centimeters taller. The other was easily the smallest of the four, his stance and features almost childlike. They joined the others at the bottom of the steps, waiting for them to move out of the way before stepping down to the concrete.

Ettalira started to present them individually. Beginning with the first to descend the steps, who seemed to be Brendan's liaison, she introduced him to the academician. Then Gareth Anmoore smiled and accepted another handshake from the next as that man was presented to him. Adela listened politely, waiting her turn, and noticed that the taller of the two blonde men was staring at her. This man, she reasoned, must be the one that was intended to accompany her. Like the others, he was in his youth, with an appearance that put his age somewhere between thirty and forty actual years. He seemed ordinary enough, but as she stared into his blue eyes, she saw something there that called out to her. She studied his face, searching for some reason why this total stranger, an alien at that, could affect her so, but his features and the nuances of his expression remained hidden behind the thick growth of beard— But the eyes. The eyes . . .

"Wait!" Her heart beat rapidly, threatening to tear itself from her chest. She went to the steps, nearly tripping the short man as she pushed past, and stood looking up at him. "What is this?"

He smiled broadly then, white teeth flashing in a grin she would have recognized anywhere.

"Hello, Adela," he said, the strong, mellow voice unmistakably that of Javas. "It's good to see you again."

Lewis was furious, and stamped back and forth behind his chair, not even deigning to look in the direction of the man seated next to Adela at the opposite end. "I refuse to accept the fact that you are my grandfather!"

"Do not accept it, then," he replied, the strength in his voice so hauntingly close to Javas'. "For I am not he."

"Javas is dead," Adela offered emotionlessly, turning to the man. He and the others had been offered grooming, and his beard was now gone, his hair neatly trimmed such that when swept back it just touched his collar. The resemblance to the former Emperor was now even more complete. "He is half a century dead."

There were four of them in the small workroom Anmoore had given them at the dome. Ettalira and the others had gone, taking with them the liaisons intended for the two brothers, and had left Adela, Lewis and Brendan alone to question this particular Gatanni construct.

"Then just who are you?" Brendan, seated on his other side, demanded.

"I don't have a name; none of us do. We were imprinted with all things that were Gatanni—knowledge, history, language—but given human personality traits and mannerisms."

"How can you have human personalities?" Lewis turned finally, slapping both hands flat on the table as he confronted him. "How can you look and sound like my grandfather?"

"Javas Wood's DNA recordings are on file, just as your own are. They were copied and replicated in me when I was built. I will, therefore, look and sound exactly like him; my eyesight, hearing, blood, cell type—everything matches that of Javas Wood." He turned to Adela, then, saying, "We got our first hint of human personality from you, through Ettalira, and recorded it; then added to it the personality of every human we've touched since you crossed the waking curtain. Our personality traits are a meld of all of you."

"No," Adela spat. "You act to much like him to be a . . . a mixture of random personalities. I don't believe you."

"I'm sorry." He turned to her, a remorseful aspect crossing his features. "I'm explaining all of this too fast, and leaving things out. I'm sorry," he repeated. He leaned forward on the tabletop, clasping his hands in a gesture that reminded her, yet again, of him.

"Why did you do that?" she asked, pointing to his hands. "Javas always used to do that when he wanted to level with someone. Why did you use that mannerism just now?"

He unclasped his hands and looked at them, chuckling softly under his breath. "I don't know, really; but believe me when I tell you that it wasn't a conscious action." He sat back in the chair, striking a pose that made Adela bristle. He noticed. "I did it again, didn't I? Understand that, unlike the other three with their random personality traits, I have received the partial imprinting of a single known human. I freely admit that."

"But why *his*?"

"Because Ettalira wanted to honor you, Adela. When she touched you, she felt every experience, every emotion, every memory of your life, just as you did hers. When they replicated me, she gave me the mannerisms and memories of everything you know about him, and shared with her." He reached out to touch her cheek with the backs of his fingers, but she pulled away before he could make contact. "Through your memory, I know what your skin feels like. I know what makes you laugh, and what makes you cry. I can search my mind and remember the flavor of a meal we enjoyed together, the touch of your hand against mine, or the way the scent of a firebush flower mixes with that of your hair. Do you still adorn your hair with a single red blossom from time to time? Do you still wear the silver chain with the agate pendant, Adela? When you're pensive or sad, do you activate the holographic representation of a Grisian forest and stroll quietly through it?" He hesitated, and held out his hand. "Do you remember this?" he asked, taking her hand in his and squeezing it gently three times, the way Javas used to at times when he wanted to say "I love you" silently, secretly, so that none in the Imperial Court would overhear.

Tears welled up in her eyes, and she took her hand away slowly. "You . . . are not . . . Javas."

"Not entirely, no." He regarded her, his eyes twinkling in the way she remembered, and brushed away a tear with a fingertip as it traced a line down her cheek. "But I could be, if you wanted."

"I have heard just about enough of this! He's not even human." Lewis was at the comm terminal, and banged the control with his fist. "I want station security here immediately."

"I am as human as anyone in this room, Lewis!" He was on his feet, glaring down the length of the table to where her grandson stood at the terminal, halted in midmessage. The way he reacted to this confrontation, and the way he spoke with strength and authority, was exactly as Javas would have done.

"Wait a minute." Adela's voice was soft, yet firm. *Why am I doing this?* she wondered. *What do I feel for this . . . man?* She pushed her chair back and stood, confronting her grandson. "Lewis, don't call security."

"Grandmother." He turned back from the terminal, his face incredulous. "You can't seriously be accepting what this man is saying?"

"No, I don't accept it." She inhaled sharply, letting the breath out in a long, slow sigh, and wiped at her face with the palms of her hands. "But what's the harm? Ettalira did this as a gift, out of friendship and gratitude; it won't hurt me to acknowledge that—to acknowledge him as such."

Lewis, disgusted, canceled his request and slapped at the terminal to shut it off.

Even though the landing pad had been all but cleared before the four Gatanni/human representatives disembarked the hopper shuttle, by the next morning word had spread throughout South Camp of the unexpected surprise presented them by the Gatanni. Half the reaction to what had happened was measured,

reasonable, with those already coming to terms with the unexpected turn of events going about their business. These were
mostly the younger members of the survey crew located here.
Those who were older, especially those who had received rejuvenation and therefore remembered Emperor Javas, tried whenever
possible to get a glimpse of him any time he was in the open
dome. They milled around him whenever he and Adela passed,
trying to confirm for themselves that it either was or was not him.

Finally, overcome by the crush of attention, Adela was forced
to leave the dome, walking out one of the big roll-up doors used
by the heavy cargo lifters.

Once outside, she leaned against the slanted metal sheeting of
the dome and reveled in the sudden, comparative quiet—the loud
vehicles going to and fro throughout the compound hardly reaching the level of annoyance the pressing crowd inside had accomplished—and enjoyed the heat that seeped up through her boots
from the baking pavement, as well as from the metal at her back.
Anmoore was here, along with his liaison companion, giving final
instructions to a survey team of both humans and Gatanni
spheres before they left for one of the western dig sites. The two
seemed to have hit it off and, as they took turns addressing the
assembled team, it looked as if they worked well together. They
bid good luck to the survey team, then started back for the dome,
waving to them as they approached. As always, this liaison, like
the others, touched frequently with the nearest spheres whenever
possible. The man had been groomed, as had the "Javas" liaison,
but had elected to keep a trim mustache.

"Where's your . . .?" Anmoore said when they came up to her,
then thought better of it and finished instead, "You're alone."

She nodded. "It was getting a bit too hectic in there. All the
hero worship."

"From what I've seen of the reception you've gotten wherever
you go, I would think you'd be used to that sort of thing by now."

Adela laughed, pleased at how Gareth always managed to say
the right thing at the right time. Just like Javas always did . . . Her
smile vanished, and with it the moment of good cheer she'd felt.
"It's just too hard to get used to. Tell me something," she said,
addressing Anmoore's liaison. "What happens to you when this
is all over? If this initial phase is successful, and more Gatanni are
created—true Gatanni, in your true form and without human
mannerisms and imprinting—what happens to you and the other
liaisons?"

He made a typically human expression of raising his brow and shrugging at the same time. "The four of us are more human, genetically speaking, than we are Gatanni. I don't have the identity of any Gatanni in particular, so I suppose we'll join you, if you'll have us." He turned questioningly to Anmoore in a way that told her the subject had not come up.

"Excuse us a moment," Anmoore said, indicating a refreshment cart several meters away. The man went to the wagon and selected a container of fruit drink, the look on his face a visage of delight at the unexpected flavor of the beverage. "You'd be surprised at how quickly they're developing their own personalities. I'll be honest: I find the working relationship we've developed to be more beneficial than I'd thought it would be. I can't speak for your grandsons—I haven't seen the academician since yesterday, and I understand that Commander Wood has rejected his liaison entirely. I sent him along with a team to the observation deck at Jour Nouveau."

"So, he's becoming more human," she said, hearing the tone of disbelief in her voice. "He doesn't even have a name, because they didn't bother to give him one. How human can he be?"

Gareth looked at her, then said, "He has a name now. He asked for one last night when I was showing him around the *Blanca,* and he was meeting everyone there. I had the computer scroll up a list of every name on the crew roster, and told him to pick any first name he liked. He chose 'Allie,' so that's what I call him." He hesitated, unsure of how to continue. "If he wants to join us, become a member of the crew when this is all over, he'll do so with my blessing." Anmoore looked over to where "Allie" was chatting with a group of off-duty personnel at the refreshment cart, then turned back to her.

"I hold you in very high esteem," he said. "So I'll give you the courtesy of speaking my mind to you." He cleared his throat loudly, looking away so as not to meet her eyes. "I not only revere you and your accomplishments, I've found that I like you even more than I thought I would all those long weeks we anticipated your arrival. Your reputation preceded you, of course, and it took some time for me to get over the awe with which I had always thought about you, but I finally managed to let myself relax around you, to consider you as something other than a legend. And once I did, I found that there was a real person there, with feelings and dreams just like the rest of us."

A small cargo lifter moved noisily by, and he waited for it to pass, using the few seconds it took to better form his thoughts. "Anyway, I found that you're someone I can be honest with. Do you know what I've seen in you since yesterday?" He waited a moment for the rhetorical question to linger in her mind, then said, "I see doubt, and fear of the unknown. I see the things we hate in Jephthah being reflected in your face, your words, your movements whenever he is around. Is this what you want?"

Adela looked at the pavement, not wanting to look him in the face. "Of course not. But he is not who he pretends to be!"

" 'He' pretends to be no one. He can't help how he was made, or what memories he's been given; that was Ettalira's doing, not his. Why punish him—and yourself—for that?"

"I don't know, Gareth." She glanced away, and saw that her liaison had come through the big cargo door, and was now looking back and forth, presumably for her. He had a flatscreen tablet tucked under his arm. "I just don't know. But he stirs so many feelings within me, feelings I've not had in so many years." She let out an ironic chuckle, still staring in his direction. "More than two hundred years, if you take a look at the nearest calendar."

He waved when he spotted them, and started in their direction. "Here you are. Captain Anmoore."

"Please—around the crew and in the dome, titles are appropriate, but we've become pretty informal on a one-to-one basis. It's Gareth."

"Fine." There was an awkward moment, as if Anmoore was waiting for him to give his own name, but all he said was "Gareth it is, then." He smiled broadly. "Mind if I steal the doctor away for a while? With everyone trying to get to us in there, we've hardly had a chance to talk all afternoon."

Anmoore assented reluctantly, and bid them both good-bye, heading back through the cargo door into the dome's main chamber.

"We have to get away from here for a few minutes," he said as soon as they were alone. "I have to talk to you."

"What's so important that we can't—"

"Please, Adela," he said, in a way that was so painfully familiar. "I'm not sure who to tell this to." He spied a small, all-terrain groundcar and headed toward it. A man with *Paloma Blanca*-issue coveralls was just finishing unloading the cargo rack on the rear of the electrically powered vehicle, and the moment he saw them he straightened, nearly dropping the last box to the ground.

"Dr. Montgarde! I—"

"We need to borrow this," she said, smiling, and patted the

hood of the still-running open-topped vehicle. "We need to check something out. Would that be all right?"

"Of course, Doctor. I'll sign it out for you myself."

She watched him trot immediately over to the dome, leaving the pile of boxes unattended where he'd stacked them, then turned back to find her liaison already in the driver's seat of the groundcar. "Do you know how to drive this?"

"*You've* driven one before," he answered, tossing the flatscreen into the back and engaging the controls. "So I can, too." The groundcar jerked forward, heading away from the compound. He accelerated the groundcar with the hand of an experienced driver, and seemed to know where he was going.

They rode in uncomfortable silence, the groundcar weaving expertly along the rough vehicle path worn into the landscape until coming to a tranquil glade near a moderate-sized body of water. The lake was all that remained of this basin, and occupied the lowest portion of the landscape. The setting, the tranquil water surrounded on all sides by trees, was a popular recreation spot for off-duty personnel. As she looked around the perimeter of the shoreline, in fact, she saw two or three groundcars parked some distance away to either side of them. On the other side, she could see the wake of a hoverboat as its occupants looked for a good spot to cast their lines in hopes of snagging the delicacies rumored to swim beneath the surface.

He turned the car off the path and parked it, hopping out and helping her step down. He reached back for the flatscreen, then took her hand and led her to a spot beneath a massive spreading tree at the water's edge. He sat, bringing his knees up before him, and set the flatscreen on his angled thighs, activating it with a touch of his fingertip to bring up the control window.

"Sit here with me," he said, patting the dry grass at his side. "I want to show you something."

Adela sat hesitantly at his side—not too closely—and watched him, almost scrutinizing him as he tapped at the screen.

"I was talking to one of Gareth's people when you left the dome," he said, still calling up the screen he wanted. At length a code number appeared in the center of a blue field on the screen, and he paused the display, turning to her. "She directed me to this recording, the most recent sent by this Jephthah person. I remember it, of course, because you have already seen it; but I never actually watched it for myself until now."

"Who are you?" Adela had asked the question almost without thinking.

"Who do you want me to be, Adela?"

She stared into his eyes and did not stop him as he leaned to her, reaching up to cradle her face in his hands, and kissed her gently. His lips were warm and soft as they met hers, his kiss exactly as she remembered it. But then, she recalled, he was imprinted with her memories—the kiss could be nothing less than as she remembered it.

"What did you feel, just now?" she asked.

"Good. I felt good."

She pulled back, leaning against the bole of the tree and gazing out across the lake. A trio of white birds, native snow sparrows, dipped across the surface and gracefully skimmed the water, leaving the tiniest of wakes behind them. As she watched them disappear into the trees on the opposite side, she thought for a moment that the birds reminded her of a dream she'd once had, but she couldn't quite place it. "What was it you wanted to show me?" she asked, changing the subject in an attempt to control the emotions coursing through her.

"Oh, I . . ." He turned back to the screen, obviously as emotionally affected as she had been by their brief encounter, then tapped at it to start the playback. The image of a native airship appeared, the recording the same one that Jephthah had last broadcast. He pressed the screen, rapidly scrolling through the sequence until the airship raid had concluded.

Jephthah's face was centered on the screen now. "This is loathsome, is it not?" the recording asked rhetorically. "This is the new 'civilized race' discovered at Tsing that the Emperor would seek to hide from you. A race of brutal, aggressive killers that—"

"There," the man said, pointing at Jephthah's image in the flatscreen. "Don't you see it?"

"See what?"

"This is an enhanced image. Can't you tell? Look there . . ." He pointed to Jephthah's hair. "And there. Can't you see where the reality stops and the computer enhancement begins? The man claiming to be Jephthah is much younger than he appears, I'm certain of it, and has generated an alter ego for himself." He tapped at the screen to freeze the image. "I doubt that he looks much like this at all."

Adela slapped at the flatscreen, sending it cartwheeling into the tall grass a few meters from the tree. "You're a lie!"

"What do you mean?" he said, truly bewildered by her response.

She jumped up, running her hands over her face and back through her long hair as she turned away from him. "You said you were real, that you only knew what *he* knew! How could you take one look at this and tell so easily that it was all some kind of a 'simulation' if you weren't one yourself? Damn you! Goddamn you to hell!"

He breathed out heavily, the sound so real that she sensed that if she were still sitting next to him she would have felt his familiar breath on her cheek. Had she been closer, would the scent, the warmth have belonged to Javas?

"Adela—"

"Goddamn you," she spat again. "I was almost beginning to trust you. I almost thought you were real!"

The glade was quiet. Nothing but her own breathing—almost sobbing—could be heard. Even the snow sparrows that had noisily flitted across the lake's surface only a few minutes earlier were silent, absent.

"I *am* real," he said, coming to stand before her. He touched her chin, turning her face up to his. "And I know you."

Adela stiffened at his touch at first, but as he played his fingertips across her face and down her neck in the way she remembered from so long ago, she closed her eyes and encircled her arms around his strong shoulders. She opened her eyes and gazed up into his, then pressed her lips warmly against his.

An abrupt beeping came from the comm terminal in the groundcar, but they did not even hear it as they fell to the soft cushion of grass beneath the swaying trees at the lake's edge.

THIRTY-ONE
Visitation Rites

The beeping from the comm terminal had stopped, but it still displayed the number 18 in bright red numerals on a small LED screen in the lower corner.

"We have to get back," Adela said. "A code eighteen is a return-to-base command, part of the system Gareth instituted when he set this place up." She leaned over the side of the car and thumbed the terminal's call button.

"Communications have been disabled. Please see your supervisor for information regarding this temporary situation. Communications have been—"

"We have to get back," she repeated, canceling the call attempt and climbing into the passenger seat. "Something's going on."

He likewise got in, pressing the starter. There was a subtle whine that increased in pitch as the flywheel came up to speed. "I can be Javas," he said abruptly, catching her off-guard. "You can make it possible."

"What are you talking about?" She stared at him, eyes narrowed. "You're already as much like him as anyone could possibly—"

"I can *be* him," he said again. "Give me access to his private files, the years of collected recordings in his sealed personal files at Woodsgate and in the Imperial net. The Gatanni can imprint them on me in such a way that I'll not only have your memories of me, but the sum total of his life, as *he* remembered it."

"His files . . .?" There was a chirping sound from the dashboard, and a green light glowed on the gearshift indicating that the groundcar drive mechanism was up to speed. He smoothly put the vehicle into drive and pulled it in a wide arc around the glade, heading back the way they had come earlier.

"I . . . I can't deal with this right now." She looked away, out the side of the groundcar, not wanting to meet his eyes. "Not now."

South Camp was in what looked like a state of emergency when they pulled the groundcar across the concrete perimeter surrounding the dome. People were running into the dome, those with vehicles leaving them parked haphazardly as they jumped out and sprinted inside. There were no metallic spheres that she could see, but that should not be a surprise in itself: In a situation involving a return-to-base order, the flying orbs—with their speed and agility—would be the first inside.

With the liaison bringing the groundcar to a screeching stop, Adela tightly gripped the top of the windshield and stood, calling over the window to the nearest person within earshot.

"What's happened?"

The woman nearly stumbled as she turned, and she kept moving, walking briskly backward, as she yelled back. "The Emperor himself is here! In orbit!" She turned away and resumed her headlong dash into the dome, not waiting for a further query from Adela.

They shut the car off and left it where it was, and joined the others crowding into the entrance.

"Dr. Montgarde!" A man came toward them, his ID badge orange-striped. He was one of several who were scanning the crowd that was now pushing into the dome through the cargo entrance. He snapped his fingers and five more orange-badges came forward. "Captain Anmoore would like you and the Gatanni to join him in his office. You'll be going up to the *Kiska* as soon as you're all assembled."

"The *Kiska*? Why the *Kiska*? I moved everything I have down here, to the personnel quarters."

He shook his head. "I'm sorry, but I don't have any details on anything. I just need to get the two of you to Captain Anmoore."

She acquiesced, realizing that her question had been a foolish one. Of course the security man would not have been told why; he had only been told to get them, and bring them.

He hustled the two of them through the crowd, pushing and shoving around the edge of the main room to the corridor leading to the office and workroom section. As the security team hurried them into the access hallway leading to Anmoore's private facility, she saw that every security person at South Camp had been lined up in the main work area of the dome. Someone was addressing them from atop the hood of a cargo lifter, and as she looked close she saw that it was Waltz. He ticked off instructions on his fingers as he pointed to one group of people or another, but she couldn't hear what he was saying.

Brendan and his liaison were already here, she saw as they entered the room, as were Gareth and the liaison named Allie. There were more security people here, who stood quietly off to one side of the room. Anmoore had been pacing, but turned as they came in. "Good," he barked to the leader of the security team that had brought them here. There was a coffee urn on a low table in the corner of Anmoore's office, and he went to it, refilling his mug. "Thank you, Cusick. That'll be all; join the others out in the main section, and help out wherever Waltz needs you." As the security men left he indicated a stack of cups on the table, wordlessly offering the two of them coffee.

But between the excitement here—and the events at the glade this afternoon—Adela needed no further stimulation.

"The four of you are going to the *Kiska*," he announced without preamble. "Since most of the personnel who arrived on the ship were reassigned here or to other ships in orbit, it's pretty empty right now and has been deemed the best bet for security purposes. All other passengers aboard the Emperor's ship have already been transferred to the *Kiska,* but the Emperor himself will remain where he is for now. Also, the Gatanni spheres will stay here at South Camp until the Emperor's wishes and plans are made known." He glanced around, his eyes falling first on the two of them, then on Brendan and his Gatanni liaison in turn. "I'm glad there aren't any questions. Let's go."

They filed out of the room, turning down the corridor in a direction that would take them away from the main section and toward, Adela assumed, a private hopper shuttle that Anmoore had arranged for their use.

She felt a hand on her shoulder, and turned to see that Brendan had come up beside her. His face was a visage of concern.

"Rihana Valtane is here," he said simply. "She's on the *Kiska,* and has already asked to see you."

The cabin that had been given to Rihana was similar to the one Adela had used during her voyage, and she was privately pleased to see that the former Princess had not rated any better quarters—or any hastily contrived upgrading of her quarters, for that matter—than anyone else had enjoyed. She took a brief perverse pleasure in wondering just how much the ordinary room must have annoyed the woman.

Their first meeting, at the door to the cabin, had been a cold one. No aide had accompanied her to Tsing, something unusual for the aristocrat, and she had even answered the door herself.

They had exchanged pleasantries, banal talk of appearances and clothing, hairstyles and jewelry, that had lasted but minutes before Adela had discarded all semblance of protocol and confronted her directly on why she had come here with Eric.

"Because I am the only one who can identify him for you, that's why." Rihana leaned back into the sofa, crossing her long legs and resting an arm on the backrest. "Because I delivered your scientist friend from Mercury, along with his sorry alien companion, to the Emperor . . . to your son." She tilted her head, the corners of her mouth turning upward into a pernicious smile. "The one who killed my own son."

"That tells me why you were *permitted* to come," Adela shot back, ignoring the affront against Eric, "and why you aren't languishing in some detention cell, charged with high treason." She sat in the chair facing the sofa, her arms crossed in front of her. "But why are you here? What could you possibly gain by coming here that would profit you?"

"No charges have been lodged against me. I gave this man monetary backing, to be sure; call it an investment, if you will. However, I had nothing to do with his actions." Rihana raised an eyebrow. "But to answer your question: I deal in profit, that is true. But I also deal firmly with those who would stifle my profit." She rose, the fabric of her sapphire-blue gown flowing as liquidly as a waterfall, and leaned against the armrest of the sofa. "He cheated me," she said bluntly. "He used me, and lied to me. And I cannot forgive that. You see, I also deal in revenge when it suits me."

"I do see." Adela nodded. Then: "And just where do I fit into your revenge plans? And my son?"

She shrugged, sending the gown rippling again, and waved a hand to dismiss Adela's remark. "That is all ancient history, occurring so long ago that I do not even wish to recall it."

"Unless it suits you to malign me with it. As you did just now with the remark about Eric."

They stared defiantly at each other, until finally Rihana broke into an amused smile.

"So, your years of sleep have not dulled your wit after all. It is good to see." She went to the portion of the sofa directly across from Adela and sat, leaning forward earnestly, all traces of pompousness and superiority abruptly gone. "I have mellowed in my old age, Adela," she began, and as she spoke, it was as though Rihana Valtane had disappeared, to be replaced by a stranger in her likeness. "I still have my desires and my needs, but things have occurred that have given me a different outlook on who I am. I still want to profit—I suppose that will always be true—but I have been wronged by this man in a way much more personal than by you or your son. Or even Javas." She slammed a fist into the armrest of the sofa. "Yes! I want revenge against this bastard! I do not deny it. But I also want to correct something that I should never have allowed to happen.

"I let my own desires blind me to this man, allowing him to use me in a way that . . ." She took a deep breath, letting it out slowly. "I do not wish ill of the Empire, nor do I wish ill of your son. Even *I* have a conscience, Adela, as surprising as that may be to you; even I have to answer to my own code of honor. I've done my share of cheating and lying and stealing, but never—even when I attempted to subvert the Imperial status to my own ends—did I wish to enslave people in fear."

"And what brought about this change of heart?" Adela asked skeptically. "Surely not your wish to assure yourself a positive footnote in history."

"No. But neither do I want a negative one." She rose, and approached the door to the cabin. "I only wanted you to know my motives. They may be selfish, to the last, but for some reason . . . I wanted you to know that I no longer hold any animosity for you. Do not ask me why."

Adela walked to the doorway, contemplating the expression on Rihana's face. The woman was still striking, even though it was obvious that the benefits of rejuvenation were becoming less effective for her. Her features were still strong—headstrong, even—and there was a fire in her eyes that clearly displayed her strength of will. But there was also a look of . . . what? Regret? Sorrow? She couldn't be sure.

"In that case . . ." Adela offered her hand to Rihana, the woman whose son had tried to kill Eric. Whose son was killed by Eric. "I wish you the best of luck in identifying this madman for us. And I also offer you my thanks."

They looked at each other for several moments; then Adela released her hand and wordlessly pressed the door's opening plate. She turned for the corridor, and did not look back as the door slid closed behind her.

"To Billy and Cathay!" The Emperor of the Hundred Worlds held his glass out over the remains of the sumptuous meal the *Scartaris* chefs had prepared.

"To Billy and Cathay!" They touched glasses, the delicate crystal chiming sharply, and downed the last of the fine wine that Gareth Anmoore had sent, with his compliments.

There were only four of them seated here in the commander's formal dining room. Eric occupied the head of the table, with

Lewis sitting at his right hand, Brendan at his left. Adela sat across from her son.

"I had hoped that Cathay would be here with us," Eric said. "There has never been a time when we have all been together. However, I rejoice in her happiness and welcome a good friend into our family. With luck, we shall all be together very soon."

Brendan looked at his older brother, as if to beg him to begin a discussion of what was to happen. The young commander, in turn, glanced her way, the question on his face the same as on Brendan's.

"I think it is best if we call it a night," Eric proposed before she could say anything. He wiped at his lips with a linen napkin, then pushed himself away from the table. "There will be ample time tomorrow to discuss our plans for the visit to the surface, as well as to set up a partnership of sorts between Mistress Valtane and the security forces here." He paused. "And to meet our new friends staying on the *Kiska.*" His reference was to the Gatanni liaisons.

He stood, signaling that the dinner was at an end. There was a bit of idle chatter as they left, escorting Eric to the room Lewis had ordered prepared for him. The corridors were quiet, vacant, cleared of all personnel by the IPC agents.

"Father," Lewis said when they reached the door, "if you will excuse me there's a bit of business I need to take care of on the bridge."

"Of course."

Lewis shook his father's hand briskly, and with a nod to the others headed down the corridor.

"I know the two of you are going back to the *Kiska,*" Eric said to Brendan. "But could I impose on you to wait for a few minutes while I talk to your grandmother alone?"

"Certainly." Brendan smiled politely, shook his father's hand and turned to go, addressing Adela. "I'll let the shuttle pilot know that you'll be along directly."

"I need to ask you something," Eric said once they were inside the stateroom. "Tell me about this liaison of yours. . . . How much like my father is he?"

Of course he would already know, Adela mused silently. *There is nothing that escapes him.* "He is, genetically speaking, the same man." Hearing her voice, she was shocked at how cold and clinical she sounded as she discussed him. "He is more than a cloned organism, and yet he is so much less. All of 'Javas' that he is comes from me, and from me alone. My memories, my impressions, my understanding of him. He acts precisely as I remember." She bit at her lower lip, and stared at the floor. "But of *course* he acts exactly as I would expect him to; everything he is, is based on what I think of him. And yet . . ." She let her voice trail off, and crossed to a chair near the holoframe in the corner. The blue glow of the holoframe, on standby as it usually was wherever the Emperor went when he was away from the Court, cast soft shadows from the objects in the room. It felt somehow warming, like a clear sky on a summer's day.

"And yet . . .?"

She lifted her head and looked at Eric, who had come to stand next to her.

"He told me that he could *be* Javas. That all it would require would be for him to access Javas' private files, to take the files and have the Gatanni imprint them on him; years of personal recollections and insights, all the recorded thoughts, doubts, and introspection that Javas put into his private journal. He said that with these, he would become Javas."

Eric considered this, then said, "What do you think of this idea, Mother?" He knelt at the side of the chair, his arm resting gently across her shoulders.

"You can't be serious?"

He rose and pulled another chair over, then sat next to her. "This Empire is dead; it has stagnated itself out of existence. We both know that. It needs to change into something else, something stronger that can meet the needs of every one of what used to be the 'Hundred Worlds.' And I am not sure that I am the one to do it."

"How can you say that, Eric?" she demanded. "You have been an excellent leader. What has happened to the Empire, the way it has evolved, is more *my* doing than yours."

"I agree that what it has become during my tenure was unavoidable; nor should anything have been done to try to keep it from becoming what it should naturally be. For me to have attempted to keep it in the form it was . . . surely, that's no better than what Jephthah has attempted." Adela started to say something, but he silenced her with a touch of his hand on her arm. "The people of the Empire need to be encouraged to form a new mutually beneficial association, a commonwealth, but they need as their advocate someone other than me. I am the 'old'; they need someone new. My best role would be to turn the reins over to another who would, with my encouragement and support, take the Hundred Worlds in this new direction." He sighed, shaking his head. "My children have no interest in this. I was hoping that maybe . . ."

Adela took his hand in hers, squeezing gently and looking into his eyes. "This man will never be Javas," she said firmly. "Nor would he ever be accepted as Javas was. If anyone is to do what you wish, it won't be him." She laughed softly, kindly. "Besides, I think you underestimate your children."

THIRTY-TWO
Keeping Secrets

I t is about time," Rihana said testily, as the entrance chime sounded. She still was not used to doing for herself, and even the simple act of answering a door was sufficient to bring her foul mood bubbling to the surface, especially since the security people she was supposed to meet were nearly twenty minutes late. She slapped her hand on the opening plate and immediately turned away and headed for the sofa, calling over her shoulder, "I was told that you would be here at precisely eight o'clock!" She sat, crossing her arms defiantly in front of her, and faced the pair for the first time. "Let's get on with this. . . ." At a loss for words for the first time in recent memory, she could do little but stare at them as the door slid closed behind them.

Both the man and woman wore the standard-issue coveralls she had already grown tired of seeing, and orange-striped badges identifying them both as security. The woman was fair-skinned, pretty, even perky in her short bob haircut, and hardly seemed the type to have made a life for herself in security.

The man, meanwhile, was tall and athletic, with wide shoulders and light brown hair that just covered the tops of his ears. The name on his badge read HANSON. He gave no indication, there was no clue on his face or in his movements, that suggested that he recognized her.

Well, my dear Mr. Rapson, she thought, deciding not to expose him at this time. *I see that we are still into game playing.*

"Since the two of you have seen fit to keep me waiting unnecessarily, may we begin?" She extended her arms to either side of her on the backrest of the sofa, and stared intently into the man's eyes.

"Mistress Valtane," the woman said, smiling pleasantly but professionally. "My name is Cindie Andina, and this is Kal Hanson. We'll be working with you to coordinate whatever information you can give us that may lead to the identification of Jephthah."

"Of course," Rihana replied, still staring at Rapson. "As I told the Emperor himself, I'm very willing to help catch this bastard. Please, be seated."

Andina sat in the upholstered chair facing the sofa, while Rapson got a chair from the dining area. He placed it next to his partner's, saying, "Before we get started, however, there's something you should be aware of." Andina turned to him curiously, the look on her face clearly indicating that she didn't know what he was referring to. He reached casually into the breast pocket of his coveralls and pulled out a small object, which he started to hand to Rihana.

She leaned forward to accept whatever it was, but he suddenly pulled it away and pressed it to Andina's right temple. There was a sharp *pop!* sound and the woman slumped forward, tumbling out of the chair and landing in a heap on the floor. Rihana stared at the woman in disbelief, noting the ugly, round purple-red mark on the side of her head.

"Thanks for not giving me away," he said, ignoring the body on the floor and sitting back nonchalantly in the chair. He slipped whatever weapon he'd just used back into his pocket. "Although I must admit, I'm at a loss to understand why. I was fully prepared to come in here and kill both of you."

"No," she said, "I don't think you would have been that stupid." She recovered her composure quickly from what had just transpired, but the thought lingered, *How do you do that? How do you kill so easily, so remorselessly?*

"So you're not here to identify me, then?"

"If I was, I could already have given them an accurate enough description of you—and your abilities—to have them following you around. But no, I have not done that."

He came over to the sofa and sat next to her. She removed her arm from the back of the sofa behind him, but made no effort to move away. "So, why are you here?"

"I'm here because somehow— Oh, I don't know; maybe it was

the way you deserted me, or the way you deceived me with your 'Krowek' program. But somehow I felt suddenly left out of our bargain. I'm here to remind you that we have a partnership, and to share the benefits of that partnership, just as we agreed."

"In that case," he said quietly, leaning in to kiss her neck, "I guess it's up to me to determine if you're telling me the truth or not." She didn't move, and allowed him the small pleasure. Neither, however, did she respond in kind to his overtures. He sat up straight again, his voice changing to a businesslike tone. "If you're telling me the truth, then I need you to do something for me."

"I'm listening."

"In about an hour, I'm going down to the planet with the other IPC agents to escort the Emperor to the observation deck, an area overlooking one of the native settlements. They've piled on a huge amount of security for this—" His face broke into a sardonic smile, and he added, as if it had just occurred to him, "All because of me, I suppose. Anyway, they've activated every available IPC agent in the system. Those he brought with him, the ones who've been assigned to his sons here without their knowledge, and the four sent along with the astrophysicist as her bodyguards. Oh . . . that's what I am now, by the way."

"A mercenary," she laughed, genuinely amused. "A truly difficult role for you, I'm sure."

"What I need from you," he went on, ignoring the sarcasm, and pointed to Cindie Andina's lifeless body, "is to allow me to keep her here for the next twenty-four hours. There is nothing more scheduled for today for you to do regarding your work with security, so no one else will call on you in an official capacity regarding security matters; and I've manipulated the duty-assignment files so that our friend here won't be missed."

She hesitated, as though thinking over his request. "And just what is it you plan to do down on the planet?"

He raised both eyebrows, and gave a tiny shake of his head. "It's probably better if you don't know. I can give you all the details tomorrow when I come back to get rid of her. Now, can I trust you?"

She reached a hand to him, playing her fingers against his neck. "Haven't you always been able to trust me?"

He took her hand, kissing her wrist gently, then cradled her face in both of his and pulled her toward him. He kissed her on the lips, softly at first, then more passionately. He pulled away slightly, and looked into her eyes. Still cupping her face softly in his hands, he smiled at her again, their lips mere centimeters apart, and nodded.

"I didn't think so," he whispered.

Still smiling, he bent her head sharply back in a single, quick jerk, snapping her neck before she even realized what he was doing.

THIRTY-THREE
Jour Nouveau

I already have twenty Imperial guards at the regular landing site, Father," Lewis said as the hopper shuttle began the pad-down sequence in preparation for landing at South Camp. "And several have already been positioned along the trail—" He interrupted himself with a snort that almost sounded as if he were angry, and frowned deeply as he continued. "I insisted that Captain Anmoore bring a hover platform in the cargo bay. I wish you would take it from the landing site to the observation deck; it's nearly five kilometers!"

"Less than an hour's hike," the Emperor responded, chuckling at his son. "I'm not that old yet. Besides, Anmoore's had everyone going in to the observation deck on foot for a good reason, to keep the chances of being spotted by the natives to a minimum. It's a good operating guideline and I see no reason to alter it for me. We'll hike in."

Lewis looked at him, his eyes narrowed. "You know, Anmoore said that's what your reaction would be. How do you suppose he knew that?"

Eric shrugged. "Good judge of character?" he asked jokingly.

"He said that in the short time he spoke to you, he felt he knew you well enough to anticipate your desires in this matter."

"I was joking before, but the fact is that Anmoore is a very perceptive man; that's why he's a good person to head up a planetary survey like the one here. Dealing with Tsing Four and places like it is one long series of making judgments on one unknown after another, based on available information. I'm just

one more unknown. . . ." The Emperor raised an eyebrow.
". . . just as you were, and yet he anticipated your needs and
reactions, didn't he?"

Lewis didn't answer, but instead settled back into his seat
across the aisle and watched the landing sequence on his viewscreen, trying unsuccessfully to hide his annoyance at his father.
Eric looked around, meanwhile, and caught the twinkle in
Adela's eye, and winked at her in the seat behind him—clearly,
she had heard the exchange.

There were four IPC security agents with them in the passenger
cabin, two sitting in the forwardmost seats and two in the last
row. Another agent, the one in charge, rode with Anmoore and
the copilot up on the flight deck. The liaison "Javas," meanwhile,
was seated across from Adela in the seat just behind his son.

The hopper settled down on the pad, almost at the same instant
as an identical craft carrying Brendan and the other two
Gatanni/human liaisons, as well as four more IPCs. None of the
spheres were with them now, but Ettalira and two others were to
ride to the observation deck with them. He had invited a Sarpan
representative, but Captain Tra'tiss had declined.

The moment they were down, the IPC in front of Lewis turned
and said a few words over the back of his seat. "Captain Anmoore has put the shield dome up over both shuttles, Father,"
Lewis announced once the man had made his report. "We can go
out on the landing pad at any time."

"Well, then; let's not keep them waiting."

They stepped out on the concrete surface of the pad to a roar
of applause and shouting from the hundreds of people gathered
around the perimeter of the dome. The Emperor waved to them,
truly pleased with his reception. These were people, he had
learned, who genuinely believed in what they were doing here;
their loud approval was for the fact that he supported them, even
to the point of coming here to help them prove to the Hundred
Worlds that Jephthah was to be ignored.

You are the people who understand what this tired union needs,
he thought, looking at the faces of those in the crowd and making
eye contact with as many individuals there as he could. *It is not
me who helps you, but rather you who are helping me send this
Empire in the direction it must go.*

At about the same time that Brendan and the others came
around to join them, Eric saw the first of the Gatanni spheres. It
floated from the rear of the crowd, golden and shimmering in the
sunlight, and was followed by another, and then still more until

there was a veritable swarm of liquid copper, gold and silver. They were beautiful. The recordings he had studied since his arrival at Tsing did no justice to the reality of what he saw before him now.

The spheres bobbed along the front of the crowd, settling into positions about a meter off the ground, when a man started walking closer with three of the silver orbs hovering around him. This would be the Allie, the Gatanni/human liaison that had been made for Anmoore. They came straight forward at first, but when the liaison stopped just short of the edge of the shield dome, the spheres arced high above them, as had been arranged, in order to come through a temporary opening that had just formed in the top of the generated safety shield. Two of the spheres went to hover near the liaisons with Brendan; the other floated to a position in front of him. Allie nodded in Anmoore's direction, then returned to the waiting group of spheres at the front of the crowd.

"Your Highness," it said, the voice—his mother's voice—seeming to emanate from a circular, vibrating portion of the liquid metal surface. "It is an honor to meet with you at last."

"And with you, Ettalira." Eric bowed formally, and extended his hand, meeting the tendril that formed at the Emperor's movement. "This is a great day, for both our peoples."

They separated, whereupon he waved to the crowd again and turned back for the hoppers, indicating to Anmoore that it was time for them to get going. The IPC agents conducted them up the short steps of the two spacecraft, with Ettalira riding in the Emperor's vehicle, the other two spheres in Brendan's.

"Thank you for showing me this, Captain," the Emperor said, gazing out over Jour Nouveau. The vista was idyllic, and he wished he could stay here longer. "The work you've done here, the way you've handled a difficult situation, the correct judgments you've made—all speak well of you. My congratulations." He shook his hand vigorously, clapping a hand to the man's shoulder. "And my personal thanks for a job done well."

"Thank you, Sire."

"I hate to leave, but there's much to do before I give my findings to the Hundred Worlds." He released his hand and turned to Adela and his sons, nodding that he was ready to depart.

Brendan and the two liaisons who had accompanied him elected to stay behind at the observation deck, as did the two spheres who had ridden in his hopper. The IPC agent in charge, a man named Hanson, according to his ID badge, assigned several of his people to stay at the deck, while he and the four agents he'd selected would accompany them back down the trail to the shuttles. He wore a headset, and spoke frequently into his collar pickup.

They walked along the trail, the footing and pace easier now that it was in a downhill direction. The air was warm, and the sun broke through the trees in several spots. Several times along the way Eric stopped to examine a tree or other native growth, or to watch an animal as it bounded away at their approach, with Anmoore gladly pointing out what they had learned about the wildlife here. Occasionally, Ettalira would show a similar interest in their surroundings and go zipping off the path to scrutinize one thing or another before coming back to join them. As they traveled, Eric received constant updates from the security team as to their progress, which Lewis passed along sparingly. Lewis knew, as did Adela, that Eric loved the woods, and they spoke to him only on occasion, allowing him to enjoy the serenity of the forest.

At one point, slightly more than halfway to where the hidden shuttles waited, Adela moved ahead in the line of hikers to talk to Anmoore up near the head of the group. Seeing this, and taking advantage of Adela being out of earshot, the liaison who looked so disturbingly like Javas caught up with him on the trail. "May I speak with you a moment, Sire?" he asked tentatively. Ettalira floated up behind him, and extended a tendril that touched him momentarily on the exposed skin of his arm, reading his mood, before withdrawing it back into her lustrous surface.

"I have been anticipating this conversation," Eric replied, regarding them both. "Although I must admit that I haven't been looking forward to it."

"Because of who I am?"

The Emperor laughed. "No, of course not. It's because of who you are *not.*"

"He is not responsible for either," Ettalira put in ashamedly. "Please forgive me, but understand that he never asked to be here. It was a mistake to construct him—in this form—I know that now. He is unlike the other three. They have settled easily into their roles, and have begun the process of developing their own unique personalities, without having a specific persona imprinted on them, just as the natives on this world have done. But he has—"

"I can speak for myself," he interrupted, the power in his voice startling Eric with how closely it matched that of his father. "The others like their roles because they know who they are. They have, from the moment of their creation, been no one but themselves, even though they were incomplete; they correct that every moment of every day that they interact, observe, and become one with their environment. But I . . ."

"But you were given a partial personality that already belonged to someone," the Emperor finished. "No wonder you are confused."

"It is even worse than that," he said, watching the ground below them as they walked. "It is a remembered personality, belonging to someone who saw him through loving eyes, that has been further colored with the passage of time." He looked up from the trail, and gazed around him at the pristine forest.

"I know how much you love the woods," he continued, still regarding their surroundings. "I know how you used to spend hour upon hour hiking the trails around Woodsgate without permission, when you were a child . . . and of how you and Javas were almost murdered in the backwoods. I know all of this because she holds it in her memory." He stopped on the trail for a moment, and swept his arm to indicate the scenery around them. "I even know what it is like to wake up from cryosleep in a beautifully tranquil setting like this one. I know all this because *she* knows it." A pair of the IPCs bristled behind them, suddenly concerned that something was amiss, and he resumed walking. "But I have no memory of it that is my own."

Eric nodded in comprehension. "And you feel that by accessing my father's personal files, you can become whole. Is that it?"

"Yes."

The Emperor said nothing for several minutes as they trudged along the path. At one point Ettalira floated in front of him, trying to read his features, and offered a tentative silver tendril toward him but he waved it away.

"As far as I am concerned, you will never be my father, even if you were to absorb the sum total of everything that he has recorded throughout his life. Even if you were able to absorb everything that made up *him*." Eric looked at this man who so resembled his father, that he felt somehow cruel to turn down his request. "For myself, my answer is no."

"For yourself?"

He raised his head, looking in the direction of the front of the line of hikers, where Adela walked, engaged in heavy discussion with Anmoore. "My mother has a say in this matter. If she wishes it, I will agree."

Eric then turned to Ettalira, saying simply, "You were right: A mistake was made." With that, he picked up his pace, putting himself in front of the two aliens.

THIRTY-FOUR
Flyover

Accor ding to Mr. Hanson, we have a problem along our usual travel route." Anmoore stood next to the hopper they were to take back to South Camp, his arm pointing down the length of a rift valley extending into the distance. Lewis and Adela stood with him; the others were already on board. "All the flight paths are low and unobservable from the surrounding terrain, but we've favored this as our main corridor for coming in and out of the Jour Nouveau area because of the treacherous footing and inhospitable conditions at the bottom—the area's quite remote and sees almost no native foot traffic. However, we placed numerous camouflaged heat scanners along the length of the valley our first trip here to detect small parties of natives that can't be picked up from the orbitals, like the airships and other heat sources can, and check them prior to any flight we make."

He turned away, waving to the security man to get his attention. "Hanson! Come over here, please."

"Captain?"

"Are they still coming along the length of the rift?" Anmoore asked. It seemed to Eric, as he watched the two of them talking, that Anmoore didn't much care for the security agent. "Any luck that they might cross over the edge and into the woods so we can use the primary corridor?"

"It looks pretty doubtful," he replied in a deep, resonant voice. "They seem to be picking out a trail along the very bottom of the rift, traveling lengthwise."

"A hardy bunch." Anmoore sighed in frustration. "All right, then. Get an orbital scan, both visual and heat sources on all the secondary flight corridors. Coordinate with the *Blanca* on the best way to go. That's all."

The man nodded curtly and moved away, talking again into his collar pickup.

It took nearly half an hour to get the departure route set, but they were presently back on the hopper. The camo-shielding momentarily having been lifted, the shuttlecraft rose gracefully away from its companion, and headed directly away from the area on one of the secondary corridors. The seating arrangement in the passenger cabin was the same as it had been on the trip in.

They proceeded smoothly, although the length of the trip back to the southern continent grew increasingly tedious due to the hopper's lower-than-usual forward speed. Owing to the unusual nature of both the secondary travel route and the VIP cargo, Anmoore felt it best to proceed at a more leisurely pace. Eric noted on the viewscreen at his elbow that the day was almost over, and that darkness would be falling at about the same time they were scheduled to reach the northern sea.

The interior lighting had been dimmed, giving the passengers an opportunity to rest from the strenuous activity they had seen in the previous hours. The two IPC agents occupying the front seats were in stand-down, and slept softly before their duty shift came up again. Likewise, both Lewis and Adela napped in their seats. The liaison seated across from his mother was awake, and watched the panorama passing below the hopper on his own viewscreen. He had said almost nothing since they had left; had hardly spoken at all, in fact, since their conversation on the wooded trail earlier that afternoon.

Eric turned in his seat, the movement catching the attention of the two IPCs in the last row. Where the liaison stared idly at the landscape in the viewscreen merely to pass the time or as a diversion from his troubled thoughts, the two men vigilantly observed and scrutinized everything, always looking for some approaching threat. They stared at him a moment, then, apparently satisfied he did not require them, turned back and resumed monitoring their respective viewscreens.

Behind them, floating silently, motionlessly, was the sphere Ettalira. She had not moved for hours, and as he studied her gleaming surface it seemed to him that the luster of her silvery skin was slightly duller. Was she sleeping? Perhaps the spheres had a "standby" mode, enabling them to conserve energy and thereby prolong the length of time before needing to transfer to a new receptacle. The thought intrigued him enough that he used the integrator to access the South Camp database through the hopper's comm system. He allowed the integrator to conduct its own search pattern through the vast amounts of information already amassed on the Gatanni, but could find no mention of it. The liaison "Javas" would certainly know, but Eric promised himself he would ask Adela or Ettalira later rather than engage in a conversation with him. Better, he decided, to leave him alone with his private musings for now.

Eric sat forward again, returning his attention to the view-screen. As the landscape scrolled steadily, almost hypnotically by, he felt his eyes growing heavy and he yawned deeply. The activity of the preceding days beginning to catch up with him, he settled back into the cushioning softness of his seat and stretched tired legs out in front of him, then allowed himself the rarest of luxuries an Emperor could enjoy: Closing his eyes, he let his mind simply drift.

"Father?" The single word startled him, and he blinked, realizing that he had fallen asleep for a short time. Lewis knelt at the side of his seat, and rested a hand on his forearm. Eric looked quickly around as his mind cleared, noting that Adela and the liaison were still asleep; likewise, Ettalira remained floating inertly at the rear of the cabin. The two IPCs at the front were awake and intently watching their screens, as were the two in back. All four ignored him, and seemed more than ordinarily rapt in their attention to what they saw. A glance to his own viewscreen showed that he could not have slept long, as sunset still appeared to be a few hours away, but it also showed that their speed had decreased considerably, and that the hopper was descending to the floor of the valley corridor they had been using as a travel route.

"Why are we stopping?" he asked, keeping his voice low.

"Captain Anmoore has picked up two heat signs just to the south of here, moving north along the same valley we're following now." Adela stirred in her seat and yawned, their whispered conversation rousing her.

Forward view, Eric commanded through the integrator, switching the viewscreen instantly. *Magnify, and orient on the heat sources detected by the piloting scanner.* The image obediently zoomed in.

Airships. There were two of them, riding the gentle air currents straight ahead of the hopper, one vessel slightly higher and behind the other. The general shape and overall dimensions of the two airships were the same as those in the infamous recording and those observed at Jour Nouveau, although the design and coloration of these two differed greatly from what he had seen before. These two, evidently, came from a different city-state than others previously documented.

"What's going on?" Adela rubbed at her face and eyes, but she was fully awake now, and leaned over the back of the Emperor's seat to stare at his viewscreen. "Airships . . .? I thought we chose this route for the express purpose of avoiding native traffic."

Lewis shook his head to dismiss her concern. "They must have been on the surface somewhere outside this valley where the portable scanning units couldn't detect ground traffic, and only recently took to the air and started following the valley northward. They weren't observable until then, either visibly from orbit or by heat scans. We received simultaneous warnings from the *Blanca* and *Scartaris* when they fired up the steam generators and launched. We were already so close to them that the warning from orbit came only a few minutes before we picked them up ourselves."

"Can we avoid them?" Eric watched the screen intently, concerned more for keeping their existence secret from the natives than he was for their safety.

"They're not aware of us," Lewis clarified for both of them. "We're going to land the hopper on the valley floor, put up the camo-shielding and just let them sail on by overhead. Once they're over the horizon behind us, we'll be back on our way."

"Very good, Lewis," Eric said, relaxing. He indicated the liaison with a quick bob of his head. "Better wake him up, too. And Mother, could you explain to Ettalira what's happening?"

She nodded and headed to the rear of the cabin. The ever-nervous IPCs turned jerkily as she passed their seats.

Once Adela had returned to her seat, Lewis informed Anmoore that they were secured, allowing him to power the hopper down in a smooth gliding arc to touch softly in the center of a clearing on the valley floor. Eric checked the viewscreen the moment the soft jarring told him they were down, and saw that the image of the two airships, more angled now that the hopper was on the ground, blurred momentarily when the camo-shielding came up, but the clarity returned almost immediately.

The flight-deck door opened. "We're down and stable, everyone," Anmoore announced as he entered. The IPC leader appeared behind him. "The shielding we're using here is of the same type as at the observation deck. They can't see in, but we can see out." He started for the exit door at the rear of the cabin, adding, "Would anyone care to join me outside to watch them pass over? Take it from me, the sight is impressive."

"Just a moment, sir!" Hanson called out loudly, stopping him. "I think it might be better if we remained inside for safety's sake."

Anmoore turned, the distasteful expression on his face making clear what Eric had thought earlier—this man seemed to loathe the IPC agents as much as Adela.

"Not only is the shielding capable of hiding us," Anmoore replied, "but I've set it the highest level, making it nonpermeable. As long as we stay under it, we'll be as safe on the outside of the hopper as we will be sitting in here." He glared at Hanson. "We won't even get wet if it starts raining," he added pointedly.

"I'm sorry, sir, but as the safety of all aboard is my priority, I must insist." Hanson glanced uneasily around at the passengers, as if counting noses, and it seemed to Eric that he truly was concerned for their well-being.

"Pardon me," he interjected. "Mr. . . . Hanson, is it? I thank you for your concern, and for the way in which you carry out your orders. But I must admit that I would like to observe the native airships myself. I think it would be all right—if Captain Anmoore and Commander Wood agree, of course—to ease back on my mandate for this occasion." He turned to Lewis and addressed him formally. "Commander, are you satisfied with the integrity of the camo-shielding?"

"Yes, Sire."

"And you, Captain?"

"Of course."

"Very well, then," he said.

Hanson nodded reticently. "Sire, if you will permit me to stay aboard the shuttle, I'll monitor the passing airships on the scanners, so that we can have an exact assessment of their movements, as well as receive updates from above."

"An excellent idea, Mr. Hanson."

The man actually bowed, then pointed to one of the agents in the back. The man straightened, and pulled on the headset that was hung around his neck. "Tideki, please accompany them to the outside, and let me know of the slightest indication of trouble from the native flyover." He turned his attention to the other agents. "The rest of you stay inside with me." Hanson nodded respectfully to the Emperor again and returned to the flight deck, where the copilot was still going about his postlanding sequences.

"Excuse me, Your Highness?" the liaison asked as they began moving down the aisle. "I think I'd prefer to remain here as well."

The Emperor nodded his assent; then he and Adela, Anmoore and Lewis—along with Ettalira and their IPC guardian—moved through the rear door onto the lower deck, where Anmoore keyed in the sequence to drop the exit hatch.

This portion of the valley floor was, like most everything Eric had seen on Tsing IV, just as beautiful and peaceful as he could have wanted. There were more shades of green here—trees, shrubbery, lush grasses that flowed beneath the hopper's landing pads like a carpet—than he had ever enjoyed in his beloved backwoods in the Kentucky hills. The air was warm here, warmer than at Jour Nouveau and certainly warmer than the interior of the hopper, and he unbuttoned his jacket for comfort. While Anmoore and Lewis, followed by the shimmering sphere, walked to the front of the hopper to watch for the oncoming airships, Eric lingered in the opening with Adela. The agent identified by Hanson as Tideki had stopped with him, but he ordered the man outside. He reluctantly obeyed, and moved off to follow the others.

"It's going to work, Mother," he said almost cheerfully once they were alone in the hatchway. He took her hand and held it tightly in his. "After all I've seen in only the few days since I've arrived, I'm more convinced than ever that the cooperation going on here among three very distinct races will say more to show the Hundred Worlds that Jephthah's claims are unfounded than anything else we might have done to fight him."

"I hope you're right, Eric." She smiled up at him and tugged at his hand, leading him down the hatchway steps to the valley floor just below them. "It all depends on the next few years, and whether you can keep him bottled up long enough for everyone to begin to accept what we've found here—not only the discoveries, but the real meaning of friendship between our races. I don't think we truly knew that before we came here." She hesitated, an excited chattering from the front of the hopper catching her attention. Anmoore was pointing at a tiny speck on the horizon moving toward them. As she tilted her head, she thought she could hear just the slightest thrumming sound from the south. As they watched, it almost looked like agent Tideki, now standing with Anmoore and Lewis—the shimmering Ettalira between them—was becoming excited as well. "Look," she said, pointing to him. "Even the IPC agent's become enraptured by what's happening here. It wouldn't surprise me a bit if there was actually a smile on his face."

Eric laughed softly, then changed the subject unexpectedly. "What about . . . 'Javas'?"

A pause. "What about him?"

"Do you want him to have my father's personal files?"

She hung her head briefly, letting her breath out slowly in a resigned sigh. "Javas is gone," she said simply, her voice barely a whisper, and stared out across the valley floor at the thick forestation all around them. In the nearest of the trees a bird sang, its song directed at no one and everyone at the same time. She closed her eyes, listening to the crystal-clear sound that brought back an important memory. "He told me so himself, in his own way, in a dream I once had. I just didn't understand what the dream meant until now." She opened her eyes again, and looked up at her son. "No. I don't want him to have the files."

"All right," he responded simply.

"I spoke to Ettalira about him. All that has happened here since we met is a part of him now, and he'll remember everything we've said and done. . . ." Her voice trailed off for a moment as she seemed to meditate on something in particular. "However, she said she can remove the imprinting of my memories of Javas. Without them, he'll be free to develop just as the other three have; he can be his own person."

"Adela!"

They looked up to find Anmoore excitedly motioning for them to come over, his face beaming.

"What do you think of him?" she asked, indicating the survey-ship captain.

"I like him." Eric's answer was immediate, sure.

She didn't respond for a moment. Then: "Let's join them." They walked together—still holding hands—to the front of the hopper.

The six of them, five human and one Gatanni, stared into the sky and watched as the two airships sailed nearer. As they looked on, more details became apparent the closer the ships came. As they had thought from the initial glimpse offered by the view-screen when they were still several kilometers away, the markings and design of these two airships were vastly different from those of the Jour Nouveau craft.

"Wait a minute!" Anmoore reached for his belt, out of habit, expecting his handlink to be there. When he realized it wasn't, he spun about and leaned back, trying to see into the flight-deck canopy, but the angle was too steep from where they stood for him to catch the attention of anyone who might be up there. "We need to get this recorded." He trotted for the hatchway, calling over his shoulder, "I'll be right back."

Tideki touched his earpiece with one hand and pressed the sides of his collar with the thumb and forefinger of the other. "Anmoore is coming up," he said, no longer paying attention to the oncoming airships.

"Why did you do that?" Adela asked.

He shook his head, dismissing the question. "It's just procedure."

She moved a few steps away from Tideki, her expression a mixture of aversion and doubt, and Eric began to get a sense of how disconcerting these agents were to her and Anmoore. And to his sons, for that matter.

"Here they come," Ettalira announced, floating above their heads. The incident already forgotten, Adela turned her attention back to the sky. Tsing was low on the horizon now, the oblique rays reflecting off the two airships in a way that made them gleam almost fluorescently in the air.

They were magnificent. Like the others that had been observed and recorded, these consisted of a main top cylinder, tapered on the ends, with a system of guiding vanes on the tail portion. The gondola slung below was like those from Jour Nouveau in size and shape, but appeared to be made of some solid, light wood rather than the woven material they were used to seeing. Also, where the airships in the recording had been colored for stealth— dull shades of green and brown on top, lighter colors below to help it blend in with its surroundings—the cylinders of these two stood out well against the sky with a pattern of alternating orange and white striping that blended into a deeper shade of burnt orange toward the tail section. As Tsing fell lower on the horizon, the sunset hues it radiated played brilliantly against the airships' coloration. Perhaps these were not, like the others, intended for warfare but for some other purpose—scientific research? Passenger craft? Then again, maybe the city-state from which these airships originated held a different philosophy about coloration for its attack vessels. Eric was glad that Anmoore had remembered to get extensive recordings of this flyover for later study and analysis.

The steady thrumming grew to its loudest as the airships passed directly overhead; then they lost sight of them over the bulk of the hopper looming above them. Just before they disappeared, Eric could see the diminutive natives inside. Everything about them, and about their flying machines for that matter, he had already seen in the recordings. But seeing it like this, with his own eyes!

They circled the hopper, walking around to the rear of the vessel to watch the airships as they proceeded on up the rift valley.

"What did I tell you?" Adela's face glowed, he noticed, as she smiled up at him. "The recordings, even the holographic ones, simply can't convey the wonder of this." He thought a moment of the last time he had seen her for any length of time, back at Woodsgate, and of how troubled she had been then. The loss of Javas while she slept, the disturbing news of what Jephthah had done in her name, Billy's unhappiness—it all seemed to have melted away, and she looked more at ease with herself than he had seen in too long a time. Even the emotional conflict caused by the appearance of the liaison in his father's likeness had served to help resolve many of the issues that had weighed upon her since she had come out of cryosleep.

As they watched the two airships begin to dwindle in the distance, the movement of her hair in the warm breeze caught his attention and he looked at her again. His mother was just as lovely as he had remembered, even lovelier now that the burdens of two centuries had been lifted from her. Not realizing that he was looking at her, she played her fingers alluringly through her hair, pulling it away from her face and tucking it momentarily behind an ear to keep it from blowing into her eyes.

His mother was happy again and, pleased that he was able to have played a part, he felt a warmth flow over him that somehow lifted much of his own regret at what had transpired.

He closed his eyes, listening to the fading sound of the airships, and inhaled deeply of the warm air. The scent of the surrounding greenery, mixed with just a hint of salt and moisture from the sea that lay to the south, came pleasantly to his nose. No wonder the airships traveled this rift valley—the easy, steady wind would make for excellent sailing.

"Are they slowing?" Ettalira asked, still above their heads, the loftier vantage point giving her a better view of the airships.

They all watched the two craft more intently and, yes, it did appear that they were not receding as quickly as they had been.

"Maybe it's just a trick of the distance that—" Adela started to say, but as they continued to watch, the answer became obvious to all of them: The two airships were turning. "Wait—it's all right. From what we've been able to observe, they frequently will follow the valleys for a distance, riding the air currents or simply using them for easy navigation, and then bear off toward their destination."

"But they're making a complete turn," Lewis countered a few moments later, a note of concern in his voice. "I think they're coming back this way."

Eric was about to say something to his son, then again noticed Adela, standing between them, pulling a wisp of hair from her eyes. *Her hair should not be blowing,* he suddenly realized, feeling the breeze playing across his cheeks. *Not if the shield is at its highest setting.*

"The shielding," Lewis said, as though reading his mind. He, too, had noticed the anomaly.

Eric concentrated a moment, accessing the flight deck, but according to what his integrator told him the shield setting had not changed. He took a step forward, but Lewis put his hand on his arm, grasping him firmly.

"Wait a moment." His son confronted the agent, who was speaking through his collar pickup in a voice to low to hear. "What's happening here?" Lewis demanded.

"I'm checking it now, sir."

Lewis nodded, his lips a tight, thin line. "Stay here, everyone." He walked forward slowly, his hand stretched out before him, and stopped a few meters away. Bending down, he grabbed a piece of wood and tossed it away as hard as he could. Tumbling end-over-end, the stick sailed unimpeded in a wide arc to land rustling in trees that should have been far outside the shielding. "It's not there," he said, turning back. "Ettalira, come here a second."

The sphere sailed quickly to him.

"Can you go out about a hundred meters and make a complete circuit of the area, then tell me what you see here?"

"Of course, Commander."

With that she started to arc above his head, but before she had risen even two meters her silver surface shattered explosively, a sharp crackling sound coming to their ears. Lewis crouched at the blast, his hands thrown protectively over his head. The entire area for several meters around him was instantly showered with hundreds of tiny splashing metallic globules that broke apart on impact, leaving the grass sparkling with little dots of silver that reflected the waning sunlight.

"Ettalira!" Adela yelled, immediately moving forward. "Lewis! Are you—?"

"Hold it! Stop!" She froze at Tideki's order, and turned to see the needle gun he pointed at them. "Don't anyone else move. This fires charged flechettes," he warned. Depending on the charge, the flechettes could paralyze or kill. And judging from the effect a single one of them had had on Ettalira, the setting was not low. The agent said nothing more, but motioned with the weapon for Lewis to return to the group.

"What is this?" Eric demanded.

Tideki kept the gun high, but said nothing to them. Instead, he squeezed his collar pickup and asked, "Did you see what happened?" He touched the earpiece with his free hand and nodded, then remained silent.

"The Emperor asked you a question!" Lewis shouted. Although the agent brought the gun to bear on him as he joined the others, he did not answer.

The thrumming of the airships grew louder, and Eric turned slowly to find that they were almost on top of them. They moved sluggishly against the wind, but made steady progress in their direction, and it was clear that one of the pair was coming to a halt altogether. Staying back to what its crew must have thought was a safe distance—based, Eric guessed, on what they knew of their own weaponry—it hovered motionless. The other, meanwhile, came nearer still until it, too, stopped and pointed itself into the wind to hover at a point close enough that they could distinctly see the frightened, but curious, furred faces of the occupants.

"They're coming right in, as I expected." They turned back at the new voice, and saw that Hanson had left the hopper. He walked forward, his hands tucked casually into the pockets of his coveralls, and stood before them. Like Tideki's, his headset was in place over his ear. "Your research here on the planet has been exemplary, Dr. Montgarde. Not only was I able to learn of their aggressive nature through you, but also of their innate intelligence and curiosity. I knew they'd turn around the moment they saw us here."

Hanson was sweating, although whether it was from the seriousness of this confrontation or the warm air, Eric could not tell. He undid the collar and opened the top of the coveralls to allow the breeze to cool him.

"I'm sorry for what has happened. It wasn't really in my plans—at least, not quite this way—but I think this will work for the better." With his collar open, and the electronics of the IPC tone shifter disengaged, his voice was different than it had been moments earlier, and was now even deeper and more resonant. And instantly recognizable.

Eric took a step toward him, but stopped abruptly when Tideki raised his needle gun a few centimeters higher.

"Jephthah," he spat. The single word was a curse.

THIRTY-FIVE
Firefight

The three of them sat cross-legged on the ground. Tideki, his needle gun still leveled in their direction, stood a few meters away. Behind them Jephthah supervised as another of the agents brought out the hover platform and floated it to the ground, while a third agent walked around the hopper with a handheld camera in one hand, calmly recording the two airships and the area around the shuttle. He carried a shield gun cradled across his chest with his other hand. They had no idea where the fourth IPC man was, but assumed he must still be inside holding Anmoore, his copilot and the liaison.

The nearest airship still hovered in place against the gentle wind, the rhythmic thrumming of the steam engine still clearly audible. There remained sufficient daylight for them to see its occupants at the edge of the gondola, looking down.

"I don't know what his plans are," Lewis was saying as he stared back up at the craft. "But it's clear to me now that he maneuvered us into an encounter with them. He coordinated everything with the detailed information they sent from orbit on the whereabouts of any natives here on the surface, and deliberately had us follow a course taking us close to them."

"Without it appearing obvious," Adela put in.

"For all I know, he's known about these two airships for days, long before we asked for the orbital scans. They weren't flying when the information was sent down, so naturally they didn't show up; but he knew they were there. I'm sure of it."

Adela touched Eric's arm. "Any luck?"

"I'm linked to it right now," Eric said. "But it still shows the shielding to be in place, even though we know that to be untrue. The comm system is also working properly, but I have no idea why there hasn't been a response to the emergency hail I'm sending."

"He's done something to it," Lewis stated quietly. "That's clear enough." He stood, slowly and carefully so as not to alarm Tideki as his needle gun traced his movements. "We'd like to talk to him."

The man shook his head. "Sit back down, or I'll shoot you."

His tone was not threatening, but carried an air of certainty that told them he meant what he said.

"You wouldn't—" Adela started to say.

"Yes, he would," Jephthah called out as he walked over, cutting her off. "You three are not to be killed, but the charge the flechettes in his weapon are carrying would put you under in a second. I'd just as soon he didn't—I need you three up and about—but he has my instructions not to hesitate if you don't listen to him."

"What's happening here," Eric demanded.

"You mean, why does your integrator seem to indicate that everything is as it should be?" He smiled, one eyebrow lifted, then squatted down to his level. "I've disabled the direct comm system on the flight deck so you can't access it. Other than the main voice channel on the flight deck—a manual system I've been using to make reports—there is no link to the outside. You're reading nothing but recorded information, just as those monitoring us from orbit and South Camp are."

Eric ignored him for a moment and turned to Adela. "Mother, do the spheres sleep?"

"What?" The out-of-place question surprised her for a second. "Uh, yes. Yes, they do, in a sense. Why?

"Is the information in the main system at South Camp?"

"Yes, but—?"

Eric understood. "I've been cut off for some time now, haven't I?"

There was a call from the agent at the platform, and Jephthah waved for him to wait. "Since we left Jour Nouveau you've been able to access nothing that isn't in the memory of this shuttle. You can utilize almost any system on board if you'd like, but with the comm link disconnected from the rest of the Imperial computer net . . . you're disconnected from it as well."

Eric tried to contact the Imperial net again, and found that it still seemed normal. He concentrated again on one of hopper's other systems, and was gratified to see that the plastiglass of the canopy opaqued at his command in such a manner that they all could clearly see it. Jephthah was telling the truth, for all the good it would do him. He hurriedly tried several of the other hopper systems, testing his limits.

"Enough game playing, Your Highness." Jephthah stood, his knees popping loudly, and spoke to the man on the platform. Although they couldn't make out what he was saying, they could see him gesturing and pointing at the more distant of the two airships. The platform rose and floated northward slowly, but steadily, in the direction of the craft, while the agent with the camera continued to record everything he saw.

Jephthah headed back, bending to the ground to pick up a small solid object, one of several scattered across the area. He turned the gray metal glob over in his hand, then tossed it away.

"Why did you order her killed?" Adela asked angrily.

"Several reasons," Jephthah said as he approached. He didn't look at them where they sat on the ground, but instead followed the movements of the hover platform nearing the far airship. "I couldn't have that silver thing flying around, getting in my way here. Or have it take off into the woods, for that matter, imprinting everything she would have seen on the first sphere she came to."

"You probably wished you could have done it yourself," she said.

"Is that right?" he replied sarcastically. "You've got me all figured out, haven't you? Well, this may shock you, but I hold a great deal less animosity toward both the Sarpan and these . . . new aliens, than you might think."

"You expect me to believe," Eric asked, "that your campaign of hatred against them, the way you've poisoned the minds of everyone who listened to you, was a lie?"

"Please, please." He held up his hands, laughing at them. "I've never considered the Sarpan a threat, any more than I expect these primitives to give us any trouble. But the Empire is changing, Your Highness, and you know it. You saw it coming years ago, just as I did, and knew that the Empire would have to adapt in order to survive." He shrugged, and glanced up to check how far the platform had traveled, then looked down at them again. "I decided to help it change in a manner that would enable me to have the most control over what happened. You know, I suspect that our ideas for what the Empire should become are probably not that far apart, but I like the idea of being able to exert a 'personal touch' in the direction it will ultimately take. There were others who saw the advantage to what I wanted to do, and their financial support was easy to come by—you may know at least one of them, in fact, although I'm afraid my relationship with her has come to an unfortunate end." Jephthah chuckled softly, enjoying the macabre joke before continuing.

"But the Sarpan? They were little more than an easy way to unite people, that's all. With their mysterious ways, repulsive appearance and biological needs, they made the perfect common enemy. And all I had to do was point out how guilty they seemed to be whenever any convenient accident happened near them where humans died without explanation."

"Except when you did it yourself, like on Mercury," Adela said.

"How many other 'convenient accidents' did you cause," Eric asked, "and then blame on them?"

"I created my own opportunities, yes, whenever it was possible; much as I'm doing here. But not nearly so many as you're imagining now." He leaned down to him so close that Eric felt his breath on his face. "Paranoia and fear are marvelous things, aren't they, Sire? With only a few hints from me about what I've done, you've already let your mind convince yourself of all manner of horrors I never even thought of."

He was right, Eric realized. With only a few admissions from this corrupt man, his own mind had conjured up many new suspicions and fears . . . just as the people of the Hundred Worlds had, based on what few facts Jephthah had told them. It was no wonder that the man's efforts had been so effective on the weak-minded.

"I know you think that what you've managed to do at Tsing—the research, the interspecies friendship, the discoveries—will all somehow sidetrack what I've done. But with what I can gather here in the next few minutes, I doubt even that will be able to undermine the spreading sense of apprehension and distrust I've already been able to create for the Sarpan, and now these Gatanni." Jephthah put a hand to the earpiece, gazing skyward, then pointed at the farther of the two airships. "Wait, I think it's time for the show to begin."

He called to the agent with the handheld camera, and motioned him over with a quick wave of his arm. "We have enough on number two," he said, "and the hopper cameras will get anything else we need. Keep your unit trained on number one." Jephthah took the man's weapon, and he trotted to the far side of the hopper, taking up position for his shot.

"The lighting is perfect," Jephthah said, looking up at the sky, now reddening with the final rays of the setting sun. "Bright enough for a good recording, dim enough to make editing all the easier." He whipped an arm out, pointing to the far airship. "Watch, now."

The airship was angled directly toward them, its nose into the steady wind coming up the valley. The platform moved smoothly off to the right of it and took position there. The details of what the agent flying it was doing were not easy to discern at this distance, but they could all see him as he moved around at the controls.

Jephthah folded the collar up to his throat with thumb and forefinger. "Pull back a bit more so you're not in the picture." He paused, waiting for it to move away, then said, "Do it."

The agent on the platform lifted a weapon—even this far away it was evident that it was a shield gun like the one Jephthah was holding—and pointed it toward the main portion of the cylinder.

It was as if an invisible cannonball had been fired at it. The orange-striped fabric of the cylinder punched in at the center, pulling back like a projectile had gored it, and jerked several meters to the side. The entire cylinder collapsed at once, the fabric sagging and limp as shreds of torn material blossomed out above the falling gondola. One of the native passengers tumbled screaming over the side as the basket turned over, and fell instantly to his death.

The gondola hit first, breaking apart and scattering its contents across the valley floor. There had been five passengers, and Eric and the others watched in horror as they were thrown to the ground on impact. The canvas fabric fell atop the crushed and broken gondola just as the gas-fired steam generator ignited, creating an enormous, smoking fireball that mushroomed into a sunset-streaked sky of almost exactly the same color. As the fireball rose upward and dissipated into the sky, what was left on the ground began to burn steadily. The hover platform angled down, landing near the wreckage.

The sound of gunfire—powder projectile weapons—came from the other airship as the natives aboard it realized they were being attacked. But, even as close as they were, their guns lacked the power to do much harm. An occasional *ting!* came from the skin of the hopper as a projectile bounced ineffectually off it.

Jephthah, meanwhile, had walked a few meters away and knelt to the ground, pointing the shield gun he'd taken from the other agent at the remaining airship.

"Dear God," Adela said under her breath at the carnage, and jumped up. "The man is truly mad."

"No!" Lewis, closer to her than the Emperor, lunged at Adela, tackling her just as Tideki fired the needle gun. The flechette missed her, and buried itself into the ground with a gentle spark as it hit. He fired a second time, hitting Lewis squarely in the left shoulder.

Still moving when he was hit, the force of the shot sent Lewis rolling over several times, jerking spasmodically, until he lay still on the ground.

"Lewis!" Both she and Eric were on their feet now, but Tideki was on her in a second, and jammed the gun so hard into her ear that a trickle of blood ran down her neck.

"Don't move!" the agent snarled, both to her and Eric. "The charge isn't strong enough to kill, unless I fire it right into the brain like this." He pressed harder still. She stopped struggling, and he let her back away from him slowly into Eric's outstretched arms. The two of them stared at Lewis where he lay unconscious on the moist grass. Lewis' chest moved, shallow and irregular, but he was plainly still breathing.

My son still lives.

There was a muted sound as Jephthah fired the shield gun, hitting the airship dead center. It, too, collapsed around the propelled force just as the other had. However, this airship was much nearer the ground than the other had been, and the gondola beneath it did not hit with as much force when it fell. There was no fire or explosion, although Eric and Adela could clearly hear the rushing escape of gas as the vessel's tanks ruptured.

Nothing happened for a few moments, but then a gunshot rang out from the piled debris, the mass of fabric, rope and wood that was the downed airship. Obviously, at least one of the passengers had survived the crash.

"Excellent!" Jephthah cried, dropping the shield gun to the ground. "Tideki, go get him."

Jephthah held his hands out before him, and the agent tossed him the needle gun, then touched his belt. A haze shimmered around him for a split second as he activated a skin-shield; then he turned away and headed for the wreckage. There were several more shots fired as Tideki approached the downed airship.

The hover platform returned, and the agent climbed down carrying what looked like two rifles. The weapons were clearly alien in nature, and must have been thrown clear of the first airship when it crashed. He handed them to Jephthah, who slipped the needle gun into a side pocket of the coveralls and examined the workmanship of the native weapons with interest. "It's getting dark. We need some lights out here," he barked to the man, who obediently disappeared into the hopper.

"Look at this," he said, holding one of the weapons out. "It's similar to a revolver, a handgun common on Earth." He looked up curiously at Eric. "Didn't your grandfather collect those? I thought I read that somewhere once. Anyway . . ." He snapped open a hinged rotating cylinder near the trigger mechanism in front of the stock. "It fires self-contained charges consisting of gunpowder that propels a piece of dense metal toward its intended target." He tilted the gun back, pouring the projectiles into the palm of his hand, then slipped them one at a time back into matching holes in the cylinder from which they had come. "They're called bullets."

Could I rush him? Right now? Eric wondered, looking around. The agent with the handheld camera was on the other side of the hopper. Tideki was still at the hulk of the downed airship, although he noted that the gunfire at the wreckage had ceased, meaning he would probably return in moments. The other two, meanwhile, were inside. He started to rise, slowly, quietly.

Jephthah whipped around, leveling the native gun at him, and let a smile spread across his face.

Hide your fear, but show your contempt. The thought came back to him unbidden as he stared up the barrel of the native weapon. McLaren had taught him that so many, many years ago. *Do whatever thing is necessary to survive your enemy's attack,* his old Master had said, *but chief among these things is to let him know the contempt you feel for him.*

"You are mad," Eric said, echoing his mother's words from a few minutes earlier. "Even now my son's forces orbiting above have certainly spotted the explosion. Are you so stupid as to think you can get away with this?"

Jephthah stared at him. "Big words, Your Highness. But seeing the explosion is exactly what I wanted. Your son's people up above will come, to be sure, or will send a ship from South Camp, but it will take hours for them to arrive. I don't need that much time." He lowered the gun, cradling it in his arms.

Floodlights came on from around the perimeter of the hopper, illuminating the area, and the agent Jephthah had sent inside returned.

Not now. Wait for the moment, Eric thought, remembering a day long ago in the Kentucky backwoods when a similar threat had been made on his life. *Wait for when he is vulnerable, or until there is nothing left to lose.*

Tideki came forward noisily, pushing a figure in front of him. The native was dressed as they had seen others, and wore loose-fitting trousers and leather boots, topped with a short-sleeved pullover shirt tucked into his pants. Where the natives near Jour Nouveau were rarely observed without long sleeves and vests or jackets, however, the temperature at this latitude allowed a more comfortable attire. Tideki carried two of the captured rifles, and prodded him forward, trembling and whimpering in terror, with the stock of one of them. The native fell to the ground when the agent gave a last shove upon reaching them. He rose to his knees, his large eyes wide and moist with fear, and babbled uncontrollably in his own tongue.

"Take him over there," Jephthah said to Tideki, pointing to a clear area a few meters away beneath the rear portion of the hopper, then pressed his collar to his throat. "Kantrellis, bring the camera around here." When the agent appeared, Jephthah indicated that he should record what was about to happen. "All right, give him his weapon." The agent dropped one of the guns to the ground, then walked to the cowering native and held out a rifle. He was so frightened that he wouldn't take it at first, but finally accepted it and held it loosely in his shaking hands, not knowing what to do. His eyes scanned the group, falling on each of them in turn.

Eric saw the abject terror in the man's eyes, and fought to keep his rage in check. *Hide your anger!* he remembered. *And wait until you can use it.*

"Make him attack you," Jephthah told him. The agent moved forward and shoved at the little native with both hands. He fell back, still whimpering incoherently. "Hit him again!"

Tideki pulled back his arm and hit the native full force with his fist, sending him recoiling to the ground. He sat up, bringing the weapon to bear on the agent.

"That's it! Crouch as though you're being attacked!"

Tideki did as he was ordered, and the native fired. The bullet impacted harmlessly in the skin-shield, but the force of the blow sent him reeling backward, and he fell to the ground. He got up and approached the native, pulling the gun out of his hands.

"Perfect." Jephthah reached into his pocket and pulled out the needle gun. He thumbed the charge wheel a few notches higher and fired it into the forehead of the native. The little furry man flew backward, jerked twice and lay still. "You can drop the shield now," he said to Tideki, slipping the needle gun back into his pocket. The agent complied.

"I don't believe what's happening here!" Adela started sobbing, and dropped her face into her hands.

"It's not over yet, Doctor," Jephthah said, and pivoted around to Tideki. He pointed the native gun at him and pulled the trigger, catching the man squarely in the chest. As Jephthah brought the rifle smoothly around in a wide arc the agent with the handheld let the camera drop to the ground and looked up, his mouth opening in shock just as the weapon discharged. The last agent outside the hopper had reached for his own gun, but was cut down by a native bullet before he could even level it in Jephthah's direction.

The scene was abruptly quiet, with nothing to be heard other than Jephthah's heavy breathing and Adela's gentle sobs. Directly, even Adela quieted, and the two of them stared at the man as he stood before them, the native rifle now hanging loosely from one hand. He gritted his teeth, his breath still coming noisily through his lips.

"There's one more agent unaccounted for," Eric said, his voice calm, strong. "I'm sure he saw everything. Do you think he's just going to sit up there and wait for you to come shoot him, too?"

"There's no one watching from the hopper," he spat.

Adela stood, pushing Eric's hand away. "Gareth?" She rose and started for the hatchway, a step at a time at first, then broke into a run, ignoring Jephthah as he turned the gun on her. "Gareth!" Jephthah let her go, and turned back to the Emperor.

"She won't find much up there," he said. "The copilot is dead. I killed him first, right after you all came out here. I didn't even need a weapon; I just broke his neck when he wasn't looking. The other agent got a needle up the ear. Anmoore and the Gatanni liaison are down, too."

"You killed them?"

He shrugged. "I don't know, really. I didn't bother to check after I shot them." He lifted the rifle almost casually and pointed it at Lewis where he lay in the grass. "It doesn't much matter, as it's all going to be blamed on the Tsingers anyway."

Eric leapt for him just as his finger tightened on the trigger and managed to deflect the shot, sending the bullet harmlessly away into the darkening sky. They tumbled across the ground, with Jephthah rolling neatly into a crouching position while Eric flopped ungracefully to his stomach; then, seeing the barrel of the gun pointed his way, he whirled quickly to the side, but the bullet caught him in the right side of his chest close to the shoulder, sending him backward to the ground. The Emperor struggled to sit up, clutching at his shoulder with his left hand.

"You stupid fool!" Jephthah vaulted forward and hit him with the butt of the now-empty rifle, sending him to the ground again, and tossed the useless gun aside.

Eric followed his eyes as he spotted another gun lying in the grass a few meters away, and scrambled for it, his fingers just able to close around the barrel.

"Don't!"

He froze.

"Turn around."

Eric did, and saw the needle gun pointed at him.

"Don't try it! I really don't want to shoot you with this—it's just more trouble for me to retrieve the needles—but I will if you don't drop the rifle now."

Eric tossed the gun away and watched it roll under the rear of the hopper where the native had been killed, then collapsed to the ground.

Jephthah came forward to stand over the Emperor's prone form, breathing heavily and wiping at his mouth. "Don't you see you're already dead?" he screamed, saliva sputtering from his lips. "You've been dead for years, just like the Empire!"

Eric rose up on one elbow, and regarded his assailant. *Show your contempt!* McLaren's words rang in his mind. "No, Jephthah," he said, keeping his voice measured and firm. "It's you who have died. The Empire of the Hundred Worlds is only now beginning to live . . . thanks to you."

"How can you—?"

"Turn around, bastard!" Adela appeared behind him, and he spun to face her. She held a shield gun, pointing it at his chest, and ran at him, her face twisted in rage.

He laughed, then, the depraved sound echoing across the rift valley. "Pull the trigger," he said as she advanced, and tossed his empty rifle aside. "Go ahead!" He picked up one of the others the agent piloting the platform had retrieved from the first airship.

She leveled the shield gun at him, but nothing happened.

"Do you think I'd be stupid enough to leave any charged weapons on the hopper and then turn my back on it?" He laughed again, the same arrogant, evil laugh he'd used before. Raising the gun to his shoulder, he aimed carefully along its length and squeezed the trigger.

The bullet hit Adela in the knee, and she crumpled with a cry of pain to the ground a few meters from Eric. Ignoring Jephthah, she dragged herself along the ground toward her son.

Jephthah stepped out of her way as she inched forward.

Satisfied that Adela and the Emperor were no longer a threat, he strode over to where they lay bleeding on the ground in each other's arms.

"You've figured it out by now, haven't you?" he asked, bending menacingly over them. "You know now what your role in all this will be, don't you?"

"Yes," Eric replied, still gripping his shoulder. He felt dizzy, and his fingers were sticky with the blood oozing through them. "You'll edit everything you've gotten, and present it as more proof of alien treachery. 'Here's how our noble Emperor was murdered! Here's how the aliens returned the kindness of Adela de Montgarde!' " He tilted his head back and laughed, loud and long, then regarded Jephthah once more. "This will look like a battle scene when you're through. Our wounds will verify everything once you've killed us."

Adela moaned and he turned to her, fearing that she was going into shock. "Mother," he said softly, but urgently, into her ear. "Are you all right?"

"I . . . I can't feel my leg. And I feel dizzy, like I'm going to pass out."

"Stay awake!" he begged of her, then turned to Jephthah. "What now?"

He walked over and retrieved the handheld camera the agent had dropped when he was shot. He came back, and looked at his wrist. "You were right, earlier. They've certainly picked up the fireball by now and have tried to contact the hopper, only to receive no answer. It'll be hours before another ship gets here, however. In the meantime, I edit what I've collected. Part of it—what the hopper's external cameras would have recorded—gets fed back into the flight-deck files. The rest . . ." He hefted the handheld, holding it out before him. ". . . gets dumped to a microchip along with a duplicate of the hopper files, and hidden on me where no one will think to look for it while they tend to my wounds—Oh, did I mention that I plan to shoot myself after I kill you? Nothing *too* serious, just enough so that when they find me the only one left alive at this 'battle scene' they do whatever they can to save me. A short time later—I don't know, maybe a few days—security agent 'Hanson,' unable to handle the guilt of allowing his Emperor to be killed while in his protection, takes his own life." Jephthah paused, an amused smirk on his face. "They'll find a note leading them to what's left of the body of the real Hanson, whom I'll place in a nice conspicuous spot."

He leveled the gun at Eric's head, pulling the trigger with an audible *click!* He cursed and threw the weapon down angrily, then bent for the other the platform pilot had brought. He checked it, snapping open the chamber, and cursed when he found that it was also empty.

Jephthah looked around and spotted the last of the captured rifles, lying on the ground where Eric had thrown it beneath the rear of the shuttle. He went to get it, and turned back to them as he flipped the chamber open. "Fully loaded," he said, grinning, and raised the stock to his shoulder.

A sudden screech came from the hopper, drawing Jephthah's attention upward. An alarm klaxon erupted from somewhere beneath the craft as it shuddered. Before he could move out of the way, the aft landing pads collapsed up into the belly of the ship, allowing the rear of the hopper to fall crashing to the ground.

Jephthah screamed, his cry of pain cutting through the night air. There was still a small amount of space beneath the rear of the shuttle, but his legs were pinned, certainly crushed by the sheer weight on top of them. He struggled to free his legs, each tug on the lower part of his body causing him to wince loudly, but after several tries it almost looked like he had managed to pull himself forward a few centimeters. A disturbing smile spread across his face as he pulled himself free and grasped the rifle.

"It won't help you!" he cried, crawling slowly, painfully forward. "It just makes my wounds look all the more real." He leveled the gun in Eric's direction and sighted down the length of the weapon.

Wait until he is vulnerable, Eric recited to himself as a bullet plowed into the ground half a meter away. *Or until there is nothing left to lose.* He closed his eyes tightly and concentrated again. Another klaxon sounded. The hopper shuddered.

"No!" Jephthah dropped the weapon and started pulling himself frantically with his arms in an attempt to get out from beneath the hopper, but made it only as far as the edge of the craft when the forward landing pads gave way just as the aft ones had, allowing the full mass of the shuttle to slam down on top of him.

The sound of the hopper crashing to the ground echoed against the valley wall, reverberating the length of the rift for several seconds before finally dying away and leaving the area quiet once more.

Eric struggled to get up, then helped Adela to stand, supporting her with an arm around her waist. Once on his feet, he could see that all that was left of Jephthah was his arm, protruding from beneath the smashed hulk of the craft, grisly and misshapen. The threat gone, he turned immediately to where Lewis lay motionless on the ground, and saw with relief that his son's chest still rose and fell evenly.

"Mother," he asked, moving toward the hatchway. "What's inside the shuttle?"

"The—the copilot and another agent are dead. So is the liaison." She halted, then said, "Gareth is unconscious, I think. I think . . . he's alive. No! He is alive, I know it!"

They made it up through the hatchway and into the lower deck, where he made Adela as comfortable as he could against a bulkhead. He pulled his jacket off, nearly crying out at the pain in his shoulder, and balled it into a cushion behind her.

"Stay here, Mother," he said, playing his hand across her face. "If he said nothing else that was the truth, they must have seen the fireball. They have to be on their way. I'm going up to the flight deck and use the voice channel, let them know what's happened here."

He turned to go, but she stopped him with a tug at his arm. "But what happens after that?" she asked, her voice weak. "What about what happened here?"

Eric smiled, chuckling under his breath as he leaned over and kissed his mother on the forehead. "The shuttle was cut off from all outside links, just like he told us. But I could still access any system on the hopper," he said.

"That's how I collapsed the landing gear." He smiled lovingly at her, gently brushing the hair away from her face with his hand. "And that's how I ordered the hopper cameras to record everything Jephthah said and did."

THIRTY-SIX
New Friends

The Moon glowed directly overhead in the night sky, but underneath the shielding the air was warm and dry. Adela looked up at the brightness of Earth's only natural satellite, and saw reflected in its cold surface the loneliness she had felt for so long.

I'd rather be outside, she thought, *under the starry Australian sky*. But the shielding was a consideration to the others gathered here, she realized, and tried to forget it was there. Still . . . her memories of the night breezes here, cool and moist off the Timor, made her long to be able to leave. To just walk outside, take Eric and Billy and all the others and walk alone on the sand and listen to the cry of the dingo, the calls of the insects and night birds. No dingo would be nearby, she knew, not with this many people assembled here.

Maybe later. Maybe. But she knew better. After the ceremonies here had concluded, Eric would return to Luna with his children. Even though they had been back from Tsing for more than three months, there was still so much to do. And yet . . . *Maybe. Maybe.*

". . . it will not be an easy task," the Emperor was saying from the dais. "But it will be vastly easier, and unimaginably better, to change the Empire of the Hundred Worlds than to maintain it in its present form." A roar broke out from the crowd below, and the Emperor waited for it to subside before continuing.

"For the Empire is dead," he went on, pausing between each sentence. "What it once was, is no longer needed. What it once was, is outdated and obsolete. What it once was . . . is harmful to the needs of the people it pretends to serve in its current structure."

They were in a bowl-shaped portion of the old mining steps on the Kimberley Plateau, at the same place where Billy and Cathay had held the corroboree uniting his people's Song Lines. Eric's Imperial shuttle formed the backdrop for his address, the raised platform from which he spoke centered at the side of the space-craft. His podium was flanked on each side by members of the Imperial Court—academicians from the Imperial Academy of Sciences, Lewis' fleet commanders from the Imperial Forces, and dozens of members of the official retinue of what the Imperial bureaucracy had become.

There were three special sections that had been arranged behind the Emperor. She sat, along with Brendan and Lewis, Billy and Cathay, Templeton Rice—even the House Master, Fleming—in the smallest of these directly behind Eric. To either side of them were the shielded sections reserved for the invited representatives of the Sarpan and Gatanni, about twenty members each. The Sarpan section was climate-controlled so that their representatives would not require E-suits, the misty air inside giving the shielded section the appearance of being a large cube-shaped structure. She knew that Oidar and Tra'tiss would be seated there, but she could not pick out their faces through the haze within it. The Gatanni section, meanwhile, was intended more for security purposes, as they required conditions not much different from humans. Adela looked among the furry faces in the section at her right, finally meeting the eyes of Ettalira, who sat with her husband. She smiled back at Adela, her small nestling sleeping soundly in her arms, and beamed with pride and happiness. There were no spheres to be seen, as biological bodies had been constructed and imprinted long before leaving Tsing. Best of all, this Ettalira was imprinted with memories recorded before the deadly confrontation with Jephthah. She had no first-hand recollection whatever of the events of that night.

And below them, on the valley floor, were thousands of people—standing, sitting on the ground, climbing every rock and ledge to get a better look at the last Emperor of the Hundred Worlds. The sky was only now beginning to lighten with the approaching dawn, but even in the dimness Adela could see the faces, every imaginable shade of black, brown, white, red and yellow all mingling as the Emperor spoke.

And in the distance, ringing the horizon, were hundreds of vehicles of nearly every type, their metal and plastic surfaces glinting in the reflected light from the Moon and stars above.

". . . and a centralized structure is antiquated in a time of faster-than-light travel," he was saying, his words flowing not only over those present here, but to countless unseen others through the tachyon dishes that linked each of the Hundred Worlds. "As I relinquish my throne—a word that I fervently hope will disappear forever—I will help to create a true commonwealth of worlds. With your help, and with the help and cooperation of our friends the Gatanni and the Sarpan . . ." He spread his arms to indicate the sections on either side of him. ". . . we will create a united system of civilizations that will not only dwarf what we once called 'the Hundred Worlds,' but will better it a hundredfold."

He stood tall at a sound that would have drowned out even the loudest thunder. The joyful noise continued for several minutes, not even slowing as he raised a hand to be heard. Finally, the tumult subsided, and he concluded.

"We owe a great debt to many." He turned to his left, regarding the Sarpan. "We owe a debt to you for staying by us even when forces would conspire to make you the object of unfounded hatred. We offer our thanks for the technology you have shared with us, specifically in that which led to a new understanding of shielding. For without that technology, the ability to travel quickly between the stars would never have been realized. Indeed, without that knowledge, we would not be gathered here tonight to watch as the final phase of a project to save our birthworld commences."

He turned, then, and spoke to the Gatanni. "And to you, our newest friends, we owe a debt for the vast knowledge of our galaxy, based on thousands of years of exploration begun long before Sarpan and human had even flown through the skies above their own worlds on artificial wings. And we thank you as well for agreeing to accompany us as we join with the Sarpan to send ships back along the route you took from the galaxy core. Perhaps one day, our three races will stand together on your homeworld, as well as on the surface of a hundred other Gatanni worlds along the way." Eric paused as a roar of approval came from the crowd, and sipped from a glass of water. As the noise continued, he swept a hand at the vista around him, then motioned once more for quiet.

"We owe a debt to the ancient people of this land, the Aborigine, who have shown us that it is possible to hold tightly to the best of the old ways and values, while confronting a new life and a new future. The Aborigine have shown us all how to face up to a new day without giving up the best of an ancient culture. The new Commonwealth, in all its complexity, can learn much from these simple people."

As the roar of the crowd's approval met his ears, he held out his hand to Adela, motioning for her to join him on the dais. An expectant hush fell over the assembled multitude when they saw her next to him, beginning with those nearest the steps and moving in a wave through the farthest reaches of the crowd.

"And we owe the greatest debt of all to someone I love very much. For without her, this world's Sun would soon leave this green planet but a burned cinder, floating in space. Without her dream, and her courage to make it come true, not only would Earth, the birthplace of all humanity, have died . . . but I fear that the Empire would have changed in a way even worse than the mere stagnation we leave behind now.

"People of the Commonwealth of Worlds, people of Earth, our Sarpan and Gatanni friends, I give you Doctor Adela de Montgarde."

Where the noise of the crowd had been thunderous before, it literally shook the very stone now in an outpouring of approval that lasted many minutes. Adela looked at the sea of faces in the growing gray light of dawn, the waving hands, the shouting voices, and could hardly believe that the attention was for her. She felt distinctly uncomfortable with it, and somehow undeserving.

At last the sound died away, and she looked down on them. "I do not want thanks," she said, "for pursuing something I wanted all along. What I did was my dream, as my son has said; but even I could never have predicted what would come of it. But it was your efforts . . ." She swept her arm to include the thousands below her, then looked at the sections on either side. ". . . and yours, our new friends, who believed in my dream, and achieved my dream, and in so doing shared it with me. And *that* is more important to me than any thanks."

The crowd applauded and shouted again, and as they quieted, the first rays of daylight began to color the sky to the east.

"While we have spoken here these last few hours, the final process to refuel the Sun, to link it to the feeder star light-years distant, has been under way." She lowered her head, chuckling in an almost embarrassed manner. "I could show it to you. I could have the Academy technicians project a holograph of what is happening in space right now, and display it over this valley such that its illumination would challenge the very Sun itself. I could do that, but there would be nothing to see. The ships ringing the star would be too small to detect, the singularity that was inserted into the Sun invisible, the thousands upon thousands of people— human and nonhuman—circling the Sun within the orbit of Mercury, unseen in their efforts. And even upon viewing it, you would witness no noticeable change. You have seen simulations, I know, of how the process is unfolding, how the ships are placed, how the singularities work—but simulations are not real, and I will not show that to you either.

"Instead, I will show you this." With that, she turned to the east, gazing at the far horizon, just as the bright star that was the Sun peeked above it. A moving wave of brightness washed over them, then flowed slowly down the sides of the steps as the Sun climbed the sky. "This is not the same star you gazed upon yesterday," she said. "That star was dying, and in its death threatened to take with it all that it had known for the billions of years it shined on the Earth."

The light moved down the far walls as the Sun's angle increased, and began to fall on the part of the crowd on the western side of the valley floor. The crowd was murmuring, covering their eyes with their hands as the light streamed down on them and moved across to those at their sides.

"But this star is new, reborn, and ready to bestow upon us its life-giving warmth for many generations to come."

With that, she left the dais, pleased that no one in that multitude was even looking at her any longer. Their attention, and the sudden burst of joyous approval that came forth as the Sun shone fully into the valley, was directed at the sky.

And that was thanks enough.

"It's not going to be an easy voyage," Eric said. "Even with an experienced survey captain like Anmoore commanding the *Newcome*."

"I know that." Adela looked at him, an eyebrow raised. "But the task you and your children are about to undertake will be no easier."

"Yes, I suppose you're right."

They walked the grounds of the Imperial estate, enjoying a few moments together before she shuttled up to the starship that would take a combined human-Sarpan-Gatanni crew back along the spiral arm to the core. The rest of her family—Brendan, Lewis, Cathay and, now, Billy—all waited patiently near the shuttle, talking among themselves. From here, she could see Gareth Anmoore outlined in the entranceway at the top of the short flight of steps leading into the interior of the spacecraft. Master Fleming's rotund form stood out easily against the others.

There were guards posted here and there around the landing pad, and one at the top of the stairs leading to the enormous oaken doors of the house, but there were far fewer than had ever been necessary before. Above them, the brilliant rays of the early summer Sun streamed down unfettered by defensive shielding.

"Will you return?"

"I don't know," she replied as they walked. "We'll use the network of wormholes that Brendan and Gareth have located and cataloged, and will cover a great distance in less time than could even be imagined just a few years ago." She stopped, shaking her head. "Will I return? Eric, we don't even know if we'll make it all the way there."

"I know that." There was a shout from the direction of the shuttle, and they looked over to see Gareth waving for them to head back. Eric sighed heavily, sadly. "I know the tachyon dish will keep us close, but I will miss you, Mother."

"And I'll miss you, all of you." She looked around at Woodsgate, taking in the trees, the sloping expanse of bluegrass, the gray limestone karst dotting the landscape. "And I'll miss this place most of all."

They walked slowly back to the shuttle, where Adela made her last good-byes to Eric's children, wishing them each luck with their work to set up the Commonwealth. Master Fleming bowed deeply as she neared the shuttle steps, his red cheeks quivering comically at the move.

"I'm gonna miss you, mate," Billy said, his toothy smile beaming. He hugged her tightly, lifting Adela effortlessly off the ground. The two friends looked at each other, then embraced again as Billy whispered in her ear, "I never got a chance to thank you. You talked about dreams, but I don't think you ever realized that you helped me find mine. You know the meaning of the Dreamtime." He smiled broadly again. "I think there may be more Aborigine in you than either of us knows. Good-bye, Adela."

"No worries, Billy."

"Yeah. No worries, mate."

She parted from him and climbed the few steps to the top of the hatchway, looking back at her family before going inside and pressing the closing plate to bring the hatch up. She waved once more as the hatch raised, then turned for the flight deck.

The shuttle was a small one, and since Gareth had no need of a copilot she occupied the empty seat next to him. He had been very quiet this last hour at Woodsgate, staying in the background so as not to intrude on the family nature of the gathering, but he turned to her now, saying, "This is it. Are you sure you still want to go?"

"I'm sure," she replied, smiling at him. "It's time I left the Sun behind and got on with my life."

Gareth returned her smile, then focused his attention on the controls, lifting the tiny craft readily off the landing pad.

Through the canopy Adela took a last look at Woodsgate and the green Kentucky hills as he smoothly arced the craft into a flight pattern that would take it to the *Newcome,* the huge starship waiting in orbit. The craft rose steadily, the horizon falling away below them, and turned to a final heading that allowed a bright shaft of sunlight to stream through the plastiglass of the flight-deck canopy.

Adela felt the warmth on her face and winced at the brilliance of it, the sheer power of the glowing radiance bringing tears to her eyes, but made no effort to shield herself from the light.